Victorian TURNABOUT

TURNABOUT

D. Dolman Heffington

Archway Publishing books may be ordered through booksellers or by contacting:

Archway Publishing
1663 Liberty Drive
Bloomington, IN 47403
www.archwaypublishing.com
1 (888) 242-5904

ISBN: 978-1-4808-3471-2 (sc)
ISBN: 978-1-4808-3472-9 (e)

Library of Congress Control Number: 2016948444

Print information available on the last page.

Archway Publishing rev. date: 09/12/2016

Dedication

I wish to thank four of the people who made this book a reality:
Dr. J.R. Hanson who generously first proofed the manuscript,
Tara Hopfe along with my dear friend Lynn Murphy who
retyped and merged it, and my beloved husband Frank, who
always encouraged me and kept the computers coming.

Chapter 1

The Party August 1865

AT LAST, THE most terrible war in America's history, the Civil War was over! In West Virginia, the Dietrich family of Fox Haven Farm buzzed with excitement to be giving the first party to celebrate the event. Sarah and her cousin Emerald Dietrich had finished dressing in their bedrooms across the upstairs hall from one another. Sarah was slender and regal in a pale green, silk gown with a modest bustle. Her auburn hair was dressed in an intricate twist at the nape of her neck and her large brown eyes danced with excitement. A borrowed pair of marquisate earrings swung from her ears.

When her aunt Lauree appeared in the hallway between their open doors, Sarah smiled graciously and gave a little twirl to show her anticipation of the evening. Lauree turned away and moved to the doorway of her daughter's room. Sarah hoped her appearance was all right, but checked her mirror again. *I wish I knew the problem*, she thought. *No matter what I do...* Well, it was nothing new. Her aunt and uncle had merely tolerated her during the fourteen years she had lived with them. *Tonight, nothing is going to spoil my party. It has been too long coming.* She loved to dance. Picking up her fan and dance card, she joined her aunt in the hall and said, "You look lovely this evening, Aunt."

Petite Lauree wearing a gray lace dress gave Sarah a brief nod. Her daughter, Emerald, preened before the pier glass mirror in her room. Her gown, made from a treasured bolt of rose chiffon, hugged her generous curves and draped into a large, satin- lined, bouffant bustle. Her rosy cheeks matched her dress, her blonde side-curls bounced, diamond and ruby earrings twinkled in her ears.

"How beautiful you are, Emerald! Are you ready to go down, dear? Your father---"

"I *know*, Mama," Emerald replied sharply. "For pity's sake! It takes a lady time to dress for an occasion."

"You're gorgeous, Emma," said Sarah appraising her cousin's figure. "I could certainly use some of your endowment."

Emerald twitched her shoulders. "You should try handkerchiefs in your bodice, Sarah. A girl has to know every trick."

"Tush," reproved Lauree as they moved down the staircase. "Since this is the first affair following the conflict, your father hopes you will make the most of it."

"Never *mind*, Mama. We'll set the stag line on its heels. Wait and see."

Sarah knew the number of single young men from the area was less, due to the carnage of the War. Moreover, some would not be in good health after service, nor have a penny to their names following the purges of farms in the combat areas.

Rupert Dietrich, Lauree's husband, had been in a power mode for days about the party, determined to have every detail managed to his satisfaction. The three women joined him in the entry hall and he gave each of them a critical appraisal. With his portly figure, ruddy cheeks and side-whiskers he was an imposing figure. Often his demeanor struck fear in Sarah, for his word was law and he never let one forget it. He wiped his face with a handkerchief and tucked it into his frockcoat pocket. He glanced about the hall and parlor. Apparently, everything was ready for he gave a satisfied nod.

Music from a three-piece ensemble began to play in the parlor, filling the hallway with the beat of an exciting Gallop. The parlor was clear for the occasion with the chairs arranged around its periphery. The two black household servants, Apennine and Ben, wearing white gloves and black clothes, stood by the front door waiting to relieve visitors of their wraps.

Rupert glanced at Sarah and Emma. "Did you tell them what I said?" Lauree nodded assent and bit her lip.

They took their places in a casual receiving line. The first of their guests, their next farm neighbors, Winston Porter and his parents, arrived. "Good evening," Rupert boomed, offered his hand, and passed the Porters to Lauree.

Emerald bowed low with a throaty "Hello, Winnie," and gave Winston a provocative smile while gripping his hand. His admiring glance colored Emerald's cheeks.

"Evening, Miss Emerald." Winn, he was known to friends, retrieved his hand, bowed, and turned to Sarah. Emerald's smile faded and she snapped her fan.

"We missed you at the church social, Miss Sarah," he said, pressing her gloved hand to his lips.

"How kind, Mr. Porter. I was sorry to be unable to attend."

"Sarah had an attack of vapors," Emma volunteered, tossing her head. Sarah blushed as she greeted the senior Porters.

After most of the guests had arrived, Emerald drew Sarah to the parlor where she was dutifully pressed by three young men to fill her dance card. Next, the men moved competitively to Sarah to register their requests, jostling each other to be first in line. Emma observed the by-play and glared at them. Taken to the dance floor at once, Sarah appeared delighted by the first waltz of the evening.

Spying Winston Porter at the refreshment table, Emma joined him, asking for a cup of punch.

"I do like your dress, Miss Emerald," he said, giving her figure another once-over.

She giggled. "You're quite handsome yourself, Winnie." She watched him over her punch cup, ran her tongue over the rim sensuously, and trusted he knew what she was thinking.

"Thank you. It is wonderful to see our friends together again in you fine home. When I was in the field, I often thought of the socials we attended before the War."

"Are you saying you missed me, Winnie?" she fished, affording him the most engaging tilt of her head.

"You know I did, Emma. The letters from you and Miss Sarah kept me going all the long months I was away."

Why did he have to ruin it mentioning Sarah?

"I very much enjoyed sharing your basket at last month's picnic," he said.

"It was my pleasure." She flashed her eyes. "I'm sure when Ellsworth returns, our social lives will resume fully." Emerald referred to her brother who had not yet returned from the battlefields. She *had* to get Winn alone. "Hmm. As our closest neighbor you've been here many times, Winnie, but have you ever seen our library?" Most farm homes did not have one and she was proud of theirs.

"I can't say I have," he paused, teasing her. "Would you like to show it to me?"

"With pleasure." Emma set her cup on a tray and took his arm to urge him down the hall. "The portrait of my great grandmother hangs over the mantel. The family thinks I resemble her." Inside the library she leaned back against the door and locked it. "There, isn't she lovely?" As if to compare the two, Winnie approached her, took her hand, and slowly turned her into his arms.

"They say she was a passionate woman." She leaned into him and he clasped her in a quick embrace.

"Ohooo." Emma felt his breath on her face and kissed him with unrestrained fervor. She moved one of his hands to her breast and closed her eyes in bliss. His hands told her, he couldn't stop touching her.

His breathing increased heavily and his hands slipped under her bustle to pull her closer. "Easy now, this isn't the barn, Emma." He referred to an earlier encounter they had, shortly after he returned home. "Someone could come in any minute."

"Huh-uh. I locked the door," she managed, writhing under his touch. "We have to—umm. I *want you*, Winnie!" She was not certain *what* she wanted him to *do*, but she needed him to commit himself.

Trembling, he drew away shaking his head. "You're too young to know what you want, Emma. Besides, I have responsibilities."

Her feelings subsided. She had hoped he was about to tear the dress from her body. He moved behind a wing chair to hold onto it, instead of her. She blinked in disappointment and smoothed her dress down, pouting. "I'm seventeen. Luanne Phillips was married at fifteen. In another two years, I'll be an old maid."

"Marriage?" He looked thunder-struck and the freckles on his face stood out. "Oh, *no*. I thought you wanted---I thought you were just flirting."

"Don't you care for me, Winnie?"

She moved to him and pressed her warm, full bosom against his chest. Her scent enveloped him with its heady, rose fragrance.

"Of course I do," he assured her, patting her shoulder. In two strides, he unlocked the door. "Come on young lady. We *need* a libation." As he drew her out the door, he took a deep breath and led her back to the dining room.

Smiling and fanning herself Sarah and her escort joined them at the refreshment table. She thanked the Barnes boy who handed her a cup of punch. Emma gazed at her cousin and, to defuse the interest in her own facial warmth, remarked, "You do look flushed, Sarah, are you feeling well?"

"I'm fine, thank you, Emma. I'm simply breathless from dancing. Isn't the music lovely?"

Emma listened. "I 'spect it's the best we've ever had. I just hope my daddy didn't have to mortgage the farm to pay for it." She laughed. Expecting Winston to ask her to dance, she was irritated when Berthoud Hamm bowed before her, his long hair falling over his thin cheeks and his spectacles slipping down his nose.

"So sorry to miss our dance, Miss Emerald, but I could not find you when our number began." Berthoud required an explanation.

"Do forgive me, Berthoud. I uh, had a small problem. I had to return upstairs for my... shawl." She retrieved the lace piece from a chair and pulled it over her shoulders. She covertly winked at Winston, who pursed his lips.

"Certainly," Berthoud replied pushing his glasses back in place. "Perhaps we can try number seven?"

"Delighted." Emma nodded and entered his name on her dance card.

Winston held out his arm to Sarah. "I believe this is our dance, Miss Sarah." She took his arm and the two went into the parlor, leaving Emma irritated. Nothing was going the way she had planned.

Clifton Barnes, whose blond sideburns gave him a mature, handsome air, smiled, placed his punch cup on the tray, gave a tug to his satin vest and offered his gloved hand to her. Emma did not care if it was a duty dance; she gazed up at Clifton with rapt attention as they began to waltz. That would show Winnie!

Rupert Dietrich moved among his guests with polite conversation, clapping male shoulders and dipping his head to the women guests. He had watched his daughter leave the floor with Porter and noted how long she was absent. Sarah was easy to follow as she moved within his range. His wife Lauree was quietly speaking to the older, seated guests and the two black servants were at their stations. He located Henry Porter having a cigar in the solarium and asked Henry to join him in his study for a brandy. Henry had the weathered leather look of a man who had spent years in the out-of-doors. Shorter than Rupert, he was compact, balding with tufts of gray hair around his ears.

"Here we are," said Rupert, gesturing toward a leather wing chair before a mahogany Empire desk. While Henry looked about the office, Rupert poured their drinks from a crystal decanter on a side table and handed a snifter to his guest.

"Fine party," said Henry, rotating his glass. "Now that the fighting is finally over, it is good to see everyone enjoying himself again."

"Thank you," Rupert replied and raised his glass before taking a drink. "Unfortunately the aftermath of war leaves a great deal to be done."

Henry nodded. "True. However, we're in much better shape than Virginia is, I vow, even though most of our salt wells have played out. There is some expectation coal mining will become our next, major state industry."

Rupert gestured with his glass. "True, but tobacco and cotton should hold their own for us, with Virginia's production down the next few years. It's an ill wind---" He offered Henry a cigar, which was refused, and lit his own. "With taxes and wages for field hands moving up, it takes a firm hand on the reins to make a subsistence farm pay today."

"Indeed," Henry replied. "I'd like to replace stock and equipment we've needed for years, but ready money is still a problem. Have to wait for the tobacco auction. I'm sure it's the same for everyone. Too bad about the Simms family."

The host considered the farmer who had failed financially through the War years. "Yes. It has been touch and go for lots of us. If the militia confiscated their animals and their stores, there was no way... I shouldn't say it, but I was fortunate *we* weren't breeders. How did you manage?"

The neighbor sipped his brandy and licked his lips. "It may have been unpatriotic, but we sent some of our stock into the hills just to maintain a breeding base. I struggled simply to keep enough stock and workers on hand to cover our minimum needs. Do you have a full complement of good hands now?"

"So far, we're all right." Rupert kept a close watch on every plot of his farm, and especially during the War. "We have leased those acres down by the river to some sharecroppers; we're allowing them to build themselves shacks, along the back spread."

Henry nodded. "That's what we've done, too. Things are really worse in the Deep South, I understand, and much of the East Coast is in total ruin." He gave a sad smile. "We consider ourselves fortunate that Winston came back safely." Suddenly his hand with the glass of brandy shook. Stricken, he apparently remembered *their* son had not yet returned home. "Forgive me, Rupert. That was thoughtless. Have you heard anything from Ellsworth?"

Rupert waved the apology aside. "We were fortunate to have him home on leave four months ago. We've written the War Department, to discover if he is in a camp hospital somewhere. We're confident he's still alive." He blew a large cloud of smoke into the air. "Of *course* you're glad to have Winston home. He's a fine young man and a successful farmer. Actually, I wanted to talk to you about him."

"Yes?"

Rupert cleared his throat. "Well, Henry, as you know, I have two, lovely, accomplished young ladies under my roof. I think it high time that Lauree and I arranged their futures." He poured tots of brandy, in each of their glasses. His neighbor sipped his drink and set his glass down on the marble top of an adjacent table. The two men eyed one another for a moment, as old friends.

"You think Winston could be interested in one of your girls?"

"Emerald, yes. Can you think of a better match? Our children have known each other all of their lives and they are fond of one another." Rupert smiled. "If Winston were so inclined, I'm sure Emma would make a competent, loving wife to him." He played his trump card. "The forty acres which run along the length of our adjoining properties will be her dowry." He gestured open-handedly, 'what more could a man desire?'

Henry's eyebrows rose with his nod as he sipped his brandy. "When Ellsworth returns, could that present a problem for you? I mean, would he disapprove of any property arrangement we had made?"

Rupert shook his head. "Worth knows I've long planned the strip of land for Emma's dowry. He'll have plenty to manage with the house and the rest of the farm."

"Naturally," Henry paused. "I can't speak for Winston. He's very much his own man. I'm sure he would have married by now, but for the War. Are you certain Miss Emerald truly cares for my son? There is some difference in their ages, perhaps not too much."

Rupert's eyes flashed, but he kept his demeanor affable and assured Henry, Emma liked Winston very much.

"Then, we shall see what develops," said Henry rising from his chair. "As young as Miss Emerald is, there needn't be any hurry."

"As you say, my friend," replied Rupert with a modest bow. A huge smile conveyed his gratification their talk had borne fruit. Only one small matter he had not mentioned: *Emerald, a determined young woman, might not wait for a lengthy development.*

Chapter 2

Sarah's Evening

ANTON SIMMS BOWED, shook hands and smiled, as he moved past the guests taking their ease beyond the musicians. With intent, he watched Sarah smile sweetly at her partner, when she swept by in a waltz. Anton saw her finish the waltz and thank Winston. Before he could move in her direction, another man claimed her for a quadrille. Good manners dictated a single man did not stand about like a scarecrow. He was there to entertain the ladies. Looking over the field of possible partners, Anton gauged each one: Anna Lee Carpenter was witty, but the poorest dancer in the room. Matilda Barnes chatters like a magpie and makes as much sense. Agnes Parma Forrest is the best of the lot. She is pretty and comfortable. If only she had Sarah's animation. Oh, well. He strolled over to Agnes. Her lace and blue taffeta dress deepened the blue of her eyes. He bowed, pleased to ask for the next dance.

After the number, Agnes eyed him warmly, as he returned her to a loveseat at the edge of the room. She asked, "What, what are you doing now that your parents are planning to sell the farm?" The personal question startled him. "I, I mean you're not occupied with farming now, are you?

"As a matter of fact," he began and sat beside her. "There are countless tag-ends to wrap up regarding the stores, the stock, and the personal property shipment. I've managed to help some of our workers find other positions." Actually, both he *and* his father had done that. "And I've been involved with the sale of our excess furnishings." He had made suggestions, so far his help had been little more than lip service. He was loath to see their farm and the family antiques sold away. He felt guilty that he could not prevent it.

"Forgive me. I had no idea," said Agnes. "I'm sure you've been of inestimable assistance. Do you know where you're going?" She looked at him benignly. "I hope you'll establish residence nearby."

He wasn't about to tell her that his parents were moving in with his uncle in North Carolina, while he was planning to seek employment. Taking up lodgings in a rooming house in Charleston was unconscionable. "It takes time to make a major move." For his parents' sake, he did not want their poor circumstance to be broadcast. He realized he had not been at home to help prevent the sale. "We've several smaller properties under consideration, but---" suddenly, he felt the young woman deserved honesty. "They won't be staying here." Touched by her apparent concern, he said, "You may be certain you will be the first to know my decision." He gently squeezed her fingers and brought her hand to his lips. "May I have this dance, too, Miss Forrest?"

Agnes fingers were warm in his hand. She might think he had feelings for her. She might be right! She glanced about surreptitiously, obviously impressed by his attention. Rising, she preceded him onto the dance area. Her delight must have given wings to her feet, he thought, for she danced even better than before, with her head high and her expressive, gentian eyes glued to his. When the number ended, she asked if he would care for some refreshment. Pleased with the ease of his conquest, he tucked her hand in his arm and drew her toward the dining room. Surprised, he was actually enjoying himself.

In the garden room, Sarah began to feel foolish, strolling about among the potted ferns and palms. She nodded as she passed a seated couple on one of the iron benches. She could hardly appear to examine another hothouse plant, without falling into the shrubbery. Roaming about indefinitely would call attention to her solo status. There was nothing for it, but to go into the buffet alone. Just as she was about to enter the dining room, she was jolted to see Anton and Agnes filling their plates at the buffet. She stopped abruptly, cut to the quick, stepped back from the doorway and turned toward the women's retiring room.

Fortunately, no one else was there. She stripped off her gloves, poured water in the washbowl, dampened a cloth, and held it to her face. Her head hurt and her eyes burned with tears. How could she have been so blind? Agnes Forrest, of all people. Gentle Agnes was without a mean bone in her body, yet, her advanced age of twenty made her an old maid.

Sarah's laces were too tight and her empty stomach demanded food, but the thought of eating now, caused acid to rise in her throat. She blotted her face with the wet cloth, and reached under her gown and bustle to untie her corset laces, in order to take several deep breaths. Retying the strings under her gown required the contortions of an acrobat, and she struggled to secure them. As she thought of

Agnes Forrest, she swore under her breath, using her aunt's favorite explicative, 'Soldiers!'

Chatting and fanning themselves, Beth Lee Carpenter and Marion Brown entered the room and, seeing Sarah's difficulty, Marion offered to retie her ribbons. "It *is* too warm for dancing this September," Sarah said, fanning herself. Pouring the bowl water in the waste pail, she thanked the girl for her help, about to leave the room.

Beth Lee rinsed her hands in the basin and replaced her gloves. "That Anton Simms is certainly giving Agnes Forrest a rush tonight," she said to Marion, dabbing a bit of cornmeal powder on her nose.

Removing one slipper to inspect a hole in her stocking, Marion agreed. "I'd bet a bushel of Federal notes, he has more in mind than dancing." Her knowing tone held a snide implication.

Sarah barely contained her irritation and could not help herself. "Whatever do you mean, Marion?"

Checking her braided crown in the mirror, Marion replied, "We all know his folks didn't survive the war. They're selling what's left of the farm and moving, heaven knows where, leaving Anton without an inheritance, twisting in the wind."

"Really? I don't think he planned to be a farmer," said Sarah in Anton's defense, dismayed to realize, she had never given thought to his financial position.

"Probably not," added Beth Lee. "But he has to do *something*. He can't get by on his looks forever." She and Marion giggled at the notion. "Agnes has a sizeable inheritance, of course."

"Anton may not be affluent, but he has character and good manners. I heard he studied for the bar," Sarah said, trying to sound casual.

"My papa said he didn't finish," Beth Lee replied. "It's rumored he quit school in Philadelphia. I merely mentioned his name once at the breakfast table and my daddy flew into a tizzy. 'Don't you dare cast your bonnie blues in that direction, Beth girl,' he sputtered. 'That poor farmer isn't even allowed in your periphery.' Which took care of that." She dusted her hands together emphatically.

Annoyed, Sarah wanted to speak, but realized she could not defend a man whose interests lay elsewhere, without tipping her hand. Biting her lip, she bowed graciously to the two girls and said, "Thank you again. I trust you'll enjoy the remainder of the evening." With what dignity she could muster, she swept out of the room.

Avoiding the other guests, she clutched her skirts and ran up the hall stairs to her bedroom. Closing the door, she threw herself upon her bed with her hoop flying and her bustle bouncing willy-nilly. The tears fell, and she cried out her frustration, while the unlit room grew darker as evening fell. *Oh, Mama, I wish you were here now.* Since she was a child, she had spoken to her deceased parent, as if she could hear her. *You would have told me about men, and what to expect.* Having lost her mother when she was barely four, she had only a dim memory of her.

Eventually, she sat up, knowing she had duties downstairs. She sponged her face, blew her nose, and groomed her hair before the washstand mirror. She deplored the pink rims of her eyes. Noticing a wrinkle in the taffeta, she smoothed her dress down over her slender hips.

Anton Simms can go to perdition! She was not going to miss the only party of the season because he had made another conquest. Moreover, she did not dare incur the wrath of her uncle by remaining upstairs. Applying a touch of powder to her pink nose, she pinched her cheeks, shook out her petticoats and squared her shoulders. *Anton was not the only bachelor in West Virginia. Besides,* it occurred to her, she *really had not been in love with him.* He had been someone to think about, to tease her imagination, to salve her loneliness. She had simply let the fantasy get out of hand. Now she knew her weakness, she would keep it under control. Lifting her chin in the air, she pulled on her gloves, fixed a smile on her face and majestically floated down the stairs.

Winston Porter stood at the bottom of the steps; his face broke into a delighted smile as he saw her return. He approached her with a hand-sweeping flourish and asked for another dance.

She accepted his arm but, knowing she was not up to the polka in progress, she suggested a turn in the conservatory. As an old friend with whom she was comfortable, she listened attentively to his remarks and kept her eyes on his shoulder during their stroll. The room appeared empty and Winston indicated a bench on the far side of the planted oval.

"My dear Miss Sarah," he began, "I have long wanted to ask about your future plans."

"My plans?"

"Are you going to be presented at the cotillion this year? I mean to say, will you be accepting gentlemen callers afterward?" He reached for one of her hands to press warmly in his own, his cheeks pink and his hazel eyes glowing.

She gave him a rueful smile. "I haven't thought about it, Winn. I finished my eight-year studies at Miss Langdon's Academy last year, but my aunt has never mentioned my 'coming out'. I've simply been a companion to Emma all these years." *Only now, her cousin no longer needed a companion.* "With the War, most of our social customs were curtailed. If the ball takes place, however, I'm sure Emma will be presented."

"Emerald? Yes, of course, but---" He brought her hand to his lips. "Be that as it may, we've known one another for donkey's years. I want to ask your uncle if I may call upon *you,* formally, I mean. That is, if it would meet with your approval."

"Why would you ---" His meaning became clear. "Oh, my dear Winn, I...I don't know what to say. I can't tell you how flattered I am." She again felt the sting of tears behind her lids. She fluttered her fan to cool her eyes. It was touching to have this fine young man say he cared enough to consider a possible future with her. She pressed her handkerchief below her nose to hold back tears.

"There must be something wrong with me, my friend, because, how can I explain?" She gazed beyond his shoulder. "It is like a yearning. I have never told another soul, but I feel as though I have not yet lived, or accomplished anything. I know women are not *supposed* to want anything beyond a home and family, but *I do.* I want to mean something. I don't yet know what." She looked at him, deploring the disappointment on his face. "Do you know that I have not been farther than Charleston since I was four?" She touched his cheek with one gloved hand. "I'm, I'm simply not ready for a mature relationship. Can you accept that?"

"I can try," he replied. "After all, you're young. When the time comes you will travel with your husband and, if he's wise, he'll give you all the leeway possible to develop your interests."

Yet, she wanted more than the banal existence the wife of a farmer would have. She wanted to get up each morning eager to see what the day would bring, not thinking first of a weather report. She longed to travel, to see the rest of the country, to meet interesting, stimulating people. Yet, she didn't want to hurt his pride. Folding her fan she said, "You're a fine young man, Winn. Any girl would be honored to have you court her. However, I am simply not prepared to take that step."

He slowly released her hand. "That isn't a definite 'no' though, is it?" His eyes begged hope.

A tear brimmed over her right eyelid and slowly slid down her cheek. "Nooo, it is not. And thank you." She wiped her cheek and stood up. Before she truly wept again, she had to change the subject. "I'd like that dance now, if you're willing."

"With pleasure." He led her back to the dance floor. She had let him down as gently as possible. Somehow, in her heart she knew, he was not the man with whom she would fall in love.

As they began to waltz, Sarah saw Emerald across the parlor, glaring at them beneath narrowed lids. Oh-oh. She would have some explaining to do. Custom required bachelors dance with the hostesses, but it might not include an innocent stroll among the palms.

On the next turn around the room, Sarah observed Anton Simms bowing before Emerald. He extended a gloved hand and Emma arose, wearing a pussycat smile. To be seen on the arm of the handsomest man in the entire room, Emma appeared to bask in the aura. Sarah hoped it was a duty dance. As they circled the room, Emma caught Sarah's eye. Knowing Anton was one of *her* favorites, she raised an eyebrow, which plainly said, '*Tit for tat, cousin.*'

The Dietrich family stood in the hall bidding their guests goodnight. It had been a fine get-together and Uncle Rupert appeared pleased with the outcome. Her aunt was exhausted, but happily so.

The musicians departed, Apennine and Ben were tidying up the parlor and dining room. Emerald kissed her parents' goodnight while Sarah thanked her aunt and uncle for the evening and turned toward the stairs.

Emerald followed her cousin into her bedroom, closed the door firmly behind her, turned and slapped Sarah across the face with her fan. "Now, miss, tell me exactly what you meant by throwing yourself at Winnie in that wanton fashion?"

Rubbing her cheek Sarah stared at her. "What in the world do you mean?"

"Disappearing for minutes at a time, and dragging him off to the conservatory, when it was time for supper."

"But, I *didn't*, Emma. I went up to my room to refresh myself. When I returned downstairs, Winn asked me to dance, but I wasn't up to a polka and opted for a stroll, instead."

"You know he's practically spoken for and you had *no right*!" Her face flushed with enmity and she choked on her words. Sarah poured Emma a glass of water, unhooked her cousin's dress, released her corset strings, and began to fan her face.

"Sit down, Emma," she urged, but her cousin tossed her head, refusing to be mollified. "You misunderstood what happened. I am ashamed to say, I was simply upset when Anton took Agnes to supper. That is why I did not want to dance. Certainly *not* a polka."

"That's what you *say*," the other replied. "You know as well as I, Winnie's the best catch this side of Charleston. I wouldn't put it past you---"

"Believe me, Emma, I have no designs on him, whatsoever. He is a sweet man, but he's like a brother to me."

"You want him because you know *I* do! How can you repay us this way after all we've done for you?" Emma whined, and drank thirstily.

Sarah flinched and rather than refute the accusations further, calmly removed her earrings and began to unhook her own dress. She turned and spoke patiently, "You're tired, Emma. It has been a long evening. Get some rest, and you'll feel better in the morning."

"You haven't heard the last of this, Sarah! I am warning you! If you so much as touch Winnie's hand again, I'll tell papa!" With that, she opened the door and sailed across the hall to her own room.

Quietly closing the door and removing her dress, Sarah hung it in her armoire. She untied the strings of her bustier, removed her petticoat, put both garments in her dresser and donned her nightgown. She removed her combs, braided her hair, and glanced in the mirror, where she saw the bright pink slash mark across her cheek. Depressed the evening had turned out so badly, she realized, it was time for her to leave Fox Haven. Where would she go, how would she take care of herself? She placed her slippers under the bed and unrolled her stockings. Emerald's remarks resounded in her ears. She had long known about the jealousy, but the extent of enmity regarding her place in the household hurt her deeply. It had never come to a blow before, and it simply would not do. She *had* to leave!

Wryly she thought, perhaps she had been too quick to discourage Winston. Still, she had nothing to bring to a marriage. She did not love Winn. More to the point, he deserved better. The last thing under heaven she wanted was to marry in order to be *cared for*. She washed her face at the washstand and sadly, climbed into bed, murmuring her prayers as always. At their close, she begged: *God in Heaven, please tell me what to do.* Exhausted, she finally fell into a troubled sleep.

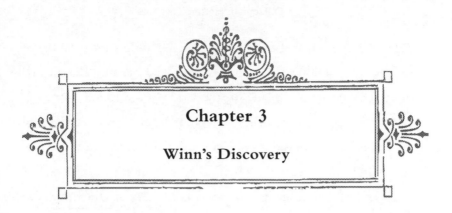

Chapter 3

Winn's Discovery

IN THEIR CARRIAGE on the way home from the party, Winston drove while his parents dozed. He reviewed the evening's incidents. Physically Emma had always attracted him, but not with the passion, he felt for Sarah. He understood, she was restless and not ready for a serious attachment, but he believed he could change her mind.

Winn's father asked him to join him in his office, when he and Mrs. Porter alighted at the front door. Winston drove around to the back of the house and into the barn. An older Negro rubbing the sleep from his eyes greeted Winston and received the reins from him. "Goodnight, Master Porter," said the man tending to the horse.

"Goodnight, Zeb."

Still thinking of Sarah, Winston strolled toward the house, enjoying the moonlit landscape and the sound of crickets in the near shrubbery. What he wouldn't give to take her out on the veranda on such a lovely evening, to share the beauty of their land at night, to take her in his arms and feel her melt with affection for him! Eventually, he would do just that. A confident smile creased his face as he entered the house to join his pa.

Henry Porter sat at the desk in his office looking at the ledger of their farm production and expenses. "Son," he began, "I'm pleased with the changes you've made on the farm. You've done a fine job of resuming management of it, since your release from the Federal Militia. The crop rotation and production changes meet current demands and help us survive, when others have not."

Winn glanced at his father and smiled, knowing his thoughts have been elsewhere. "Sorry, Pa. I was lost in thought."

"Sit down, Winn. What is it?"

Winston sat in a club chair, took a deep breath and said, "I've decided I'm ready to marry, Papa, and I trust you and mama will agree to my choice."

His father smiled. "You know we do. Rupert spoke to me this very evening on just that subject. You may be sure I told him your decision was entirely up to you."

"But how could Rupert know? I only spoke to Sarah about calling upon her this evening."

"*Sarah?*"

"Yes, of course. Who'd you think?" He winced. "*Not Emerald?*"

"That's the young lady we discussed." Nonplussed Henry poured himself a glass of water from a carafe on the desk.

"No! It's *Sarah,* I want, Pa. I thought you'd guessed. I'm fond of Emma, but she's not--" he paused, watching his father's face intently.

His pa studied his hands. "I see. Sarah is a lovely young woman, but you realize she, she is entirely without a dowry."

Winston grimaced and gestured negatively. "But we have enough for the four of us. We live frugally. The farm produces most of our basic needs and should do so, as long as we manage carefully. Tobacco and cotton will always be in demand."

"Those are fine qualities, but not the *only* considerations, Son." Henry stood up and walked around the desk. "You've no idea how hard it was to keep our heads above water during the War. There's going to be more rough times ahead, 'specially with the work force, which may not stay with us, for what we can afford to pay. We were lucky we didn't have slaves, as they did in Virginia. 'Cept for Zeb and your mama's house girl, who landed here when they fled from their owners, ours are all white.

"And then, you know we can never count on the weather. We had a drought back in the 'Forties which cost us some five-years to recover. You were just a tadpole and don't remember, but it was a near disaster."

Winston stood up, his cheeks reddened. "Are you telling me I *can't* pursue the woman of my choice?"

His father put his hand on his shoulder. "No. No, Son. Your mother and I agree, you're to choose the wife you desire, but your only inheritance is the land. We have to be lucky every year to pay taxes and hang onto the farm. We don't have no back up like the Dietrichs. An'---are you forgettin' about children? Any you and your wife have will need care and schooling."

"But you have the bonds, and the Charleston property of grandma's."

His father frowned and ran a hand over his chin. "I've put off telling you 'bout this, 'cause you've had a plenty to deal with here." The lines of his face sank with guilt and he could not meet his son's eyes. "You remember your ma's brother, Jacob?"

Winston frowned. "The gambler?"

"That one," he said with asperity. "Early in the War he used some funds collected for the men in the militia by the Women's Service League."

"He *stole* their money?"

"Sad to say, he bet on horse races. He *said* he 'tended to replace the funds, but he kept losin' 'til something like ten thousand was gone. Your ma grieved so, knowin' he would go to jail and destroy his family, I reluctantly cashed the bonds to pay his debt. It took all of them, since their value was a lot less 'cause of the wartime."

Winston felt the blow in his gut and sat down heavily in the chair. "And grandma's house?"

"We let Jacob live there 'til he could get back on his feet."

Now angry, his face flushed, Winston jumped up. "But he never did! *Right?*"

Henry shook his head. "No. Actually, half of it *was* his, according to the will, but it was left in your ma's name in order to protect his children. He sold the house to cover his new losses. When it come to court, Rose had no choice but to sign the papers and release the deed. Your cousins Joseph and Andrea will have no schooling, 'less we help 'em."

"All this happened while I was gone and you never wrote me about it?" He couldn't believe he'd been completely innocent of his parents' travail. He'd been so busy with the company in his command, he'd completely forgotten his duty at home.

"Oh, Winston! We were scared you wouldn't even make it back from the War. We couldn't add to your burden." Obviously exhausted Henry collapsed in his chair.

Bitter thoughts tumbled through Winston's mind, chasing one-another in galling futility. He was furious at his uncle's manipulation of his parents. Their vulnerability and his absence had cost all of them the security he had counted on for the future. His parents, in their sixties, were worn out, dependent upon him to manage the farm successfully for their very existence.

How naive he had been, thinking he could have Sarah! His anger turned to grief. *Oh, my dear girl! I've lost you!* The painful knowledge brought tears. He blew his nose to prevent their falling.

"Son?" Henry's hand shook as he raised it in supplication.

Deeply hurt, Winn mentally reached for forgiveness and understanding. Finally, he gave a resigned sigh. "It wasn't your fault, Pa. There's a bad one in every family. I'm just sorry I couldn't have been here to---" What? Stand up to his uncle? By God, if he ever had a chance again, he'd make him sorry! He gritted his teeth and gestured helplessly. "Well, it's done. We'll simply have to start over and manage as best we can."

The lines of his pa's face made him ten years older. "I knew you'd understand, Son. I only wish it hadn't been necessary. You'll probably want to forget about marriage for a while."

"Humph," he murmured bitterly. "Yes. Yes, I will, Pa. G' Night." Depressed Winn left the office and slowly went to his room. It was long before he slept, for his thoughts were a tangle of angry regrets and intense disappointment.

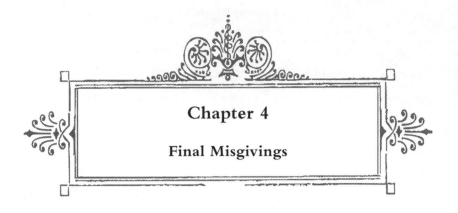

Chapter 4

Final Misgivings

BREAKFAST IN THE Dietrich dining room had the family serving themselves from the sideboard. Lauree was having tea; Rupert was reading his Farmers' Journal. Emma stood at the buffet heaping her plate with sausage and eggs. Sarah entered, greeted her aunt and uncle and asked Emma if she had slept well.

"Fine," Emma said.

Placing eggs and a piece of toast on her plate, Sarah sat at the table. Thinking to fill the awkward silence, she said, "It was a lovely party Uncle Rupert. Everyone enjoyed himself immensely."

"Hum," he murmured and closed his paper. "Did *you* have a good time, Emerald?"

"Yes, Papa, except for one small problem." Sarah recognized the threat of the set-to they had after the party.

"What was that, dear," her aunt asked. Sarah sipped her tea, waiting for the accusations to fly.

"Nothing I couldn't handle," Emma replied with a toss of her head.

"Did anyone indicate an interest in calling on you, in the future?" Rupert asked. "You and the Porter lad were gone for a while."

"You mean Winnie? Of course. He's-- Well, certainly. He plans to call, as soon as he can." Emma tucked into her breakfast.

Rupert slapped his paper. "Well, Miss, I've taken care of it."

"Taken care of what, Papa?"

"I spoke to Henry." A smug expression fixed his face.

Emma's jaw dropped. "About Winnie and me? Really? What did Mr. Porter say?" She was alert with anticipation.

"He was concerned to know if you and Winston truly cared for one another."

Emma waved her hand dismissively and brought her thumb to her lips. "Yes! Yes. And what else?"

"He assured me that Winston would make his own choice where marriage was concerned." He folded his paper and fixed Emma with an intent gaze. "This is a highly serious matter, Emerald. Are you certain he's the man you want to court you? Courting is only a preliminary, of course," he cleared his throat. "But in view of our adjoining properties, it is highly important you be absolutely certain of your feelings. If Winston became enamored and you threw him over, it could make for highly unpleasant relations between such close neighbors."

Emma sneezed into her napkin. No doubt to concoct her reply, Sarah thought. "Oh, yes, Papa," her cousin replied smoothly. "We're quite well suited to one another."

Sarah found the conversation incredible, particularly after Winn's remarks to her in the solarium. Emma looked like the cat that had eaten the pet goldfish, and her parents exchanged satisfactory nods. Poor Winn would not have an option, regardless of his father's assertion. With dismay, Sarah realized what an uproar she would have created had she agreed to Winn's request.

Considering her cousin's accusation of the previous evening, Sarah knew something was required. "As a matter of fact, Winn asked me if there was to be a cotillion this year."

"He *did*?" Emma fairly glowed with the news. "You see, courting is exactly what he has in mind!"

"I'm sure," Sarah murmured. "He's a fine young man, Emma." Looking down at her half-eaten breakfast, she lost her appetite. Asking to be excused, she hurried up to her room with the unbelievable scene she had just witnessed flooding her mind.

Lauree's warm glow of happiness for her daughter, evaporated immediately when she remembered the doctor's warning, following the riding accident Emma had as a four-year-old. Had anyone noticed, she paled at the thought. Doctor Showalter had told her, Emerald's broken pelvis probably meant, when she grew up, she would be unable to carry a child to term. Lauree had never told a soul. For thirteen years, she had feared what her husband and daughter would do, if they discovered her perfidy. Realizing she was wringing her hands in her lap, she released a nervous breath and forced herself under control.

Guiltily, she considered it a redeeming grace the doctor had died during the War. If she never told what she knew, when Emma married, it would be months before it became obvious she could not carry a child, and *she* would be off the hook. She decided now was the time to disclose the back-up plan she had to solve the problem when it occurred. Excusing herself, she left the table and went upstairs.

Unexpectedly, Lauree appeared in Sarah's doorway asking to enter. Surprised, since her aunt rarely spoke to her personally, *or* entered her room, Sarah said, "Please do. I want to thank you for the use of your earrings last night." She handed the pair to her aunt.

Lauree put the jewelry in her reticule. She closed the door, and took the Windsor chair by the window. "I have a highly personal secret, I wish to share with you," she said, kneading a lace handkerchief in her thin hands.

This *was* a first. "Yes, Ma'am?"

"First, I must have your word: you will not disclose this information to another soul."

"Of course."

"It, it's my dear Emerald." She took a deep breath. "Shortly before you came to live with us, she had a serious accident while learning to ride."

"I remember she was in bed when I first arrived and couldn't come out to play."

"Yes. Well, the result of that accident was a broken pelvis. Dr. Showalter told me, Emerald could never expect to carry an infant to term."

Pained, Sarah said, "Oh, poor Emma." Another thought followed immediately. "Obviously, you're worried about her telling Winn before --"

Lauree shut her eyes and shook her head. "No! She doesn't know."

Sarah assumed that was Lauree's problem. "But she *has* to be told."

"No! She *doesn't!* When she marries, and loses a baby, or doesn't conceive at all, it will become apparent, naturally." Her aunt appeared confident.

How blatant! The ramifications of the problem raced through Sarah's head. "What about the nuptials? If you know there won't be a child, in all honesty, aren't you bound to--?"

"Winston's the Porter's only son. It would wound them deeply to know they could not expect an heir from his marriage. I'm certain they would cancel the entire proceedings."

"And *Winn?*" *What about that fine young man, who would never--*

"There is another solution."

"I don't see-- You mean adopt?" Lauree shook her head. "Or, have a child with a Negro?" It was heard of in the Deep South.

"Certainly not!" Lauree asked for a glass of water. Sarah poured one from the pitcher on her washstand. Her aunt's hand shook with emotion. "I'm speaking of a surrogate mother who would give the child to Emerald to rear as her own."

Sarah took the empty glass and placed it on the washstand. "But why would Winn agree to such of measure, simply to spare his parents' disappointment?"

"Because it would be *his* child."

"I see." Such an arrangement was rare now, however. "Then, who would be the actual birth mother?"

Lauree gazed at her and turned one hand over in an obvious gesture.

"*Oh!*" As her knees gave out Sarah abruptly sat down on her bed. Her head turned back and forth with incredible disbelief.

"You are the *logical* person." Lauree's tone was so matter-of-fact, what she said might have been incidental. *What a horrible suggestion!*

"Since our family may not have any other heirs," her aunt continued, "It is important the baby have Dietrich blood. Emerald would be related to the baby, and would undoubtedly share some family characteristics." She made her reasoning bald. "After all, we have cared for you for fourteen years. You should be *more* than willing to do this for us." Her aunt's stare bore into her eyes. "If necessary, we would compensate you financially." Her expression indicated disgust at *that* possibility.

Oh, my God! The obvious complications of such an arrangement over-whelmed Sarah. Lauree suggests financial compensation for something, which is beyond price. Her eyes clinched in pain and she covered her face with her hands. How *could* she go to bed with her *cousin's husband? With Winn.* Let alone, have his child? *Then, give it up?* Live in the same house and watch her baby mothered by Emma?

What about her *reputation?* She would be tarnished! A decent man would never marry her. *Oh, no!* There was more. Emma would not stand to have her near Winn. She would *have* to leave and *never* see her child grow up! *This was insidious!* Stricken to the heart, she could not speak.

"I realize this is something you need to put your mind around." Lauree stood up. "It's possible the situation might never arise. However, you know what would *have* to be done, if it did. This is the only thing I ask in exchange for the years of education and privilege you have enjoyed under our roof." She stood. "Again I warn you, don't dare forget your promise!" She calmly opened the door and closed it firmly behind herself.

The only thing. *Just one, little, life changing, irrevocable* thing! Sarah had received a killing blow. Her small breakfast churned in her stomach. She began to weep uncontrollably and fell across the bed in horrified grief.

At last, she sat up and wiped her face. *There were not enough tears on earth to wash away this despicable threat.* She had to leave the house, had to decide what to do. Throwing on a shawl and a leghorn hat, she hurried downstairs and out to the front garden. Utterly devastated, she fled down the path to the road.

Chapter 5

Just Deserts

THE MORNING DEW glistened on the roses. The air was brisk and filled with the tremolos and the twitters of birds. The sun appearing just over the trees lit the rose garden inducing fragrance. Sarah paused at the hedgerow along the road and looked back at the house. The beauty of the day failed to touch her grief. She would always remember Fox Haven; but she did not love it any more. Her aunt's demand had not only demolished her hope of remaining here, but had made the thought itself, highly repugnant. Indeed, now she was desperate to leave. Charleston was too close to seek employment. Her uncle would find her and bring her back. No. He wouldn't let her leave of her own free will, even if he did not know Emerald's problem. He was a man in control and everyone knew it.

Even if she went farther east, many of the States were still battered and damaged from the recent War. It would take months, perhaps years, to put everything to rights. The local broadsheets would carry a news story about a missing girl, even into Virginia. Insecurity would follow wherever she went. Tutoring was the only occupation she was able to do. However, people who were concerned with restoring their businesses and properties might not be looking for a tutor for a child.

If she had a horse, she could go to the Far West, see the country, and begin a new life. She knew it would not be easy to travel alone, but she could not imagine anything more devastating than remaining where no one loved her and she bore such an enormous debt. Perhaps she could join a wagon train. She understood they formed in some place beyond St. Louis. As far as she knew, St. Louis was over eight hundred miles away! Her savings of about a hundred dollars would not last long, when used for food and shelter. It was all she had to show for the fourteen years she had lived in Fox Haven. She needed transportation. However, what did a horse cost? Just supposing, for the moment she could buy a horse. Where could she go with the little cash she would have left? She would require a saddle and tack, then, she would be penniless. Stopping at a stile, she climbed over onto the road and looked west.

The Far West, where everything is new, where half the country wants to go. It sounded strange, wild and wonderful, an undeveloped paradise. Could a lone woman without any money join a wagon train? She had heard tales of what became of penniless women in the world. Her options grew threadbare from consideration. She was beyond her experience, desperately in need of specific information.

An approaching horse and rider suddenly reminded her, she was alone on the road. Her concern changed to a tingle of pleasure, when she recognized the rider was Anton Simms. He stopped his horse, removed his hat and gave her a nod from the saddle. "And where are you bound on this lovely morning, Miss Sarah?"

Giving him a slight glance, she continued walking. "Morning, Mr. Simms."

Her cool tone must have registered, for he turned around to ride back beside her. "I think I owe you an apology," he began.

She feigned innocence. "Whatever for?"

"I missed our dance last night," he said and grinned, using his charm to the maximum.

She shrugged a shoulder slightly. "Did you? I was so busy with the other guests--- It was a lovely party."

"I wanted to tell you, I have plans." He sounded serious, if tentative, unlike his usual confident self.

"Oh?" Her heart bobbed. Would he be marrying his dinner partner, Agnes Parma? She reined her expression to show mere polite interest and continued walking.

"Yes. I have to leave soon. It seems that the proceeds from the sale of our property won't be enough to set up practice in one of the nearby towns." It was not a marriage to Miss Parma, after all. Unaccountably, she felt relieved and exhaled. She looked up at him, remembering the retiring room gossip: he had not finished law school.

"You intend to practice law?"

He shrugged. "Only if I am able to complete the course and pass the bar."

"In the meantime, what will you do?"

"I don't suppose you have a fortune we could spend together," he asked archly with a twinkle in his eyes.

She made a small, bitter 'phuut' at the idea. "Hardly."

"No. I thought not." He rode along in silence for a bit, as she began to walk again. "Is there any chance you would reply, if I penned you a letter?"

She stopped and searched his eyes for sincerity. A lock of black curls fell on his forehead, as his warm, golden eyes appraised her head to foot. He leaned on his saddle with one gloved hand holding his hat and riding crop. No other word for it, he was gorgeous, the most attractive man in six counties. *Only, totally out of the question. Obviously, neither one of them had a chamber pot to* -- "I would, *if* I received your letter," she said, nearly drowning in his compelling gaze.

"And why wouldn't you?"

"Because--" She tore her gaze from his and turned aside to hide the sudden flood of tears.

He dismounted, took her by the elbow, and drew her over to the shade of a chestnut tree beside the road. He tied his horse to a shrub, tucked a finger under her chin and raised it to look into her eyes. "What is it?"

"Emma is grown. She no longer requires a companion and she expects to marry soon." She would not break her promise to her aunt and did not tell him what was expected of her. Besides, it was such a terribly immoral action, no lady would discuss it with a gentleman. She bit her lower lip willing the tears to go away.

"But you live there," he said. "They are your family. Haven't the Dietrichs adopted you?"

"No. My parents died and we're related, but I've only been here by their charity. I have to make a life of my own."

"You mean to marry?"

She saw disconcertion in his face. They had never had a personal conversation before and she was intrigued. "No, not now. I want to do something else first."

"What? What do you want to do?"

"I don't know." Even to herself she sounded pathetic.

"I would give the world at this moment if I could help you," he said and put his arms around her. "As it is, I own nothing but my horse. I don't even know how I'll make a living. You believe me, I would help, if I could?"

She nodded, staying as she was, feeling safe in the circle of his arms. She relished the fragrance of his pomade, the masculine equine smell, and the warmth of his cheek against her head. It was the closest she had been to a grown man, closer than dancing, since she could remember. It felt wonderful.

"I have to make something of myself. Until I do, I've nothing to offer anyone," he said. She looked up at him. He was a decent fellow after all. He lowered his head and gave her a gentle, chaste kiss. Her first real kiss. It was moist, warm, and a harbinger of what could come. He pressed his cheek against hers holding her close. In her memory, she imprinted the sensations: the sweetness of the kiss, his jaw, his manly scent, his strength.

"Then, goodbye, dear girl. Remember me," he said and released her, his face a mask of reluctance. Still feeling the security of his embrace, unable to speak, Sarah stood in the sun-dappled copse beneath the tree. He mounted his horse, wheeled on the road, tipped his hat to her and trotted away.

Oh, *yes*, she would remember him! He was everything she had hoped he would be. Except now, both of them were leaving, and she'd never see him again. She watched until he rode out of sight at a bend in the road. She reminded herself she did not love him, but the touching scene made her realize how life might have been, had she been able to remain at Fox Haven. The sadness settled in, as before. No closer to solving her dilemma, but unwilling to return to the house, she walked down the road past the farm and entered the woods on an old path she, Emma, and Worth had made as children.

Emerald knew she would be in trouble if her father found out she had no understanding with Winston Porter. She had to see him before everything came out. Winnie would be furious with her, if he were put in the position of having to explain the facts to his parents. Donning her riding habit, she went down to the stable to get her big bay. If she had chosen to, Sarah could have mucked up the whole thing at breakfast. Grudgingly, Emma admitted her cousin had come in handy, for once. Now, she just might have time for one desperate ploy. If she could not pull this off, she mused, she wasn't half the woman she thought she was.

She should not be riding on the road alone, for there could be veteran soldiers going home from either army, refugees, or former slaves passing through the countryside. The roads were still a mess from the armies, heavy armature, and skirmishes, which had taken place during the War, but riding across the fields to the Porter farm was too unseemly to consider. A lady simply did not show up at a neighbor's back door when she went calling. It was bad enough to make a formal call without an invitation. Still, desperate problems called for desperate measures, she thought as she mounted Melchior, the horse Ben had saddled.

It was a fine, sunny morning. Emerald was glad to be out riding on such an exciting mission. Usually exercise did not appeal to her, but she knew she sat a good seat, and hoped Winston would appreciate the vision of her on her handsome bay. She was wearing her new habit because the green waistcoat made her eyes like two pools of jade, she told herself, and tied the green taffeta bow of her bonnet fetchingly below her right ear. She would say she had been for a morning ride in the neighborhood, and couldn't resist stopping. Swinging along the south road at a trot, she enjoyed the cool, shady passage, and slowed the horse to a walk to avoid a dislodged culvert.

Suddenly, without warning, a dirty vagrant rose up from behind a bush and grabbed her reins! Emerald screamed and jerked the horse's head to the side, but the tattered stranger held tight and grabbed her arm to jerk her down from the saddle.

"Now, missy, this horse is exactly what I needs. I'm tired o' walkin' an' you prob'ly has more like it to home."

Lying in a crumpled heap on the road, scared out of her wits, Emerald screamed, and flailed her riding crop at her attacker's hands.

"Stop that, you vixen!" he yelled and grabbed the crop. His blackened teeth and dirty, stringy hair told her exactly what she could expect. "You and me is goin' to have a understanding, right now!" He glanced up and down the road and dragged her over to one side, despite Emma's screams and struggles all the way. He looped the reins over a bush and ripped open the vest and shirtwaist under her jacket. "Now we'll see who's in charge, Ya' little bitch!"

He abruptly threw her riding skirt over her head, held her down with his knees and struggled to release his own clothes. Fortunately, his determination to rape her blinded him to the thick limb, swung like a club, which slammed into his head knocking him down. Sarah helped Emma up from the ground, then quickly mounted the horse and pulled her up behind.

"Oh, my God! Where'd you come from?" Emma asked, breathing heavily and shaking from the escape.

"I've been for a walk," Sarah replied, wheeling the horse, sending him galloping toward home. "Are you all right?"

"No, he hurt my leg," she cried, weeping in frustration. She twisted, trying to examine herself.

"Is it bleeding?"

"I don't think so. Slow down. I have to --" She buttoned her jacket to hide the ripped shirtwaist, and straightened her bonnet. "Don't you *dare* tell papa, Sarah. Do you hear me? You killed that man!" That thought should resonate in her cousin's mind.

Reaching their road, Sarah turned in and slowed the horse to a trot. "I heard you. Neither one of us was supposed to be on the road alone. Where were *you* going?"

"For a ride." A gross understatement. "Who, who *was* that despicable man? He tried to-- I might have been ruined!" Her breathing slowed, and she began to gain control. "You won't snitch on me because you'd be in trouble, too."

At the turn of the road before the house, Sarah drew the horse to a halt, released her knee, and slid off the saddle. "It won't do for us to arrive like this. Here," Sarah handed the reins to her cousin, who slipped down from the back of the horse. Sarah strode down the lane to the house, while Emma casually walked her horse back to the barn.

Chapter 6

Chasin' Daylight

WALKING BRISKLY TOWARD the house, Sarah wondered if Emma really appreciated how close she had come to disaster. When she heard her cousin's scream, she ran through the woods until she located her. Horrified at the scene, she looked about for a weapon, found a short, heavy limb and quietly approached the assailant from the back of a tree. She did not know if the man had a weapon, but there was no time to find out. If he heard her, or dodged at the last minute, both she and Emma could be killed. She took a firm grip on the club and swung it with all her might.

The rest of her life she would remember the sharp crunch as the club struck his head and he hit the ground. They quickly left the scene to get away from the toppled assailant, as fast as possible. The thought she had killed a man, grew in her mind until she was terrified by the time she reached the house.

She had killed a man! If anyone besides Emma knew she had struck the fatal blow, she could be sent to jail. The fear grew as she flew up to her room, shut her door and leaned against it, breathing heavily. What if Emerald --? Oh, no! She would deny she'd been there. Sarah knew her cousin very well. Emma would never admit she had disobeyed her father. Lauree's demand had been a painful impetus for her own walk, but the death of the derelict made it imperative that she leave immediately, before the body was found.

In growing panic, she threw her old carpetbag on the bed and began to fill it. Unable to depart without leaving some explanation, she dashed off a note to thank her aunt and uncle for their care, and placed it on the dresser. She took the ambro-type of her parents, her Bible and her mother's locket and ring. Fortunately, she had a good pair of walking shoes. Where she was going, she would need nothing but the plainest, absolute essentials. She added a worn blanket from the wardrobe. *Let's see...* some sewing sundries; a pair of scissors; bar of soap; some soda for brushing teeth, and packets of powders for headaches. A box of tea she had received for Christmas, and she would *get a bit of sugar and some crackers from the kitchen.* Glancing about the room for the last time, she grabbed her bag and opened the door.

She could hear her cousin in her room changing the torn shirtwaist. She paused considering: what had happened to Emma could easily happen to herself, alone on the road. Only a man could escape unwanted notice traveling, or at least someone who *looked* like a man. Someone who *dressed* as a man? Although, she had never considered such a thing, she suddenly realized, that was the answer.

Holding her breath, she knew exactly where to get the garments she needed: Ellsworth's room. Opening her bag she removed the two dresses, she had packed moments before, and put them back in the wardrobe. Closing her door softly, she slipped down the hall to Worth's room. She located two of his old shirts, sox, a cap, underwear and a belt. *Thank heaven he took after his mother and was similar to her own size!* She shoved two pairs of trousers and a pair of shoes into her bag. She rolled a jacket into a parcel and fastened it with the belt.

Deploring the fact she could not say goodbye to anyone, she hurried quietly down the stairs and the back hallway. The under-maid Apennine was busy at the dry sink washing the pots and pans. The cook, who liked a sit-down after preparing a meal, probably was in the pantry resting, before the one-o'clock lunch service.

"Could I he'p you, Miss Sarah?" The pretty, slender, Mulatto girl with braided hair about her head, wiped her hands on her apron.

"No, no. Thank you, Penne. I just want a snack for later." She wrapped a piece of cheese and a few crackers in a napkin, and tucked the packet in her bag.

She was about to leave, when the girl touched her arm, and asked, "Have y'all heard anything from Master Ellsworth?" She bit her cheek, apparently fearing the reply.

Looking at her Sarah determined she had a serious interest in the answer. "Not yet, Penne." The girl's head drooped and Sarah added, "I'm sure he'll be back one of these days. If he was wounded, he could be recovering in a hospital somewhere. The mail as it is, we might not hear for some time to come."

The maid brightened. "Yes, Miss. That's so. Thank you."

Sarah nodded and walked through the summer kitchen and out the back door. Casually strolling around the house, she decided on a desperate plan. She passed into the orchard and headed toward the fence beyond and the Porter property.

Winn has to sell me a horse, she thought. *It's the only way, I can leave.* She wished she knew what lay beyond the immediate area. Hart's landing was the farthest north she had ever been, which was about twenty miles up the Kanawha River. She had never ventured west.

She thought wryly, Miss Langdon's Academy had not prepared her for the move she was about to make. Classes in household management, manners and social customs included nothing practical to help her make her way alone in the world. Without a horse, she could never travel to the Far West, her goal, because she could never survive alone in a metropolitan city in the East. She felt too insecure even to consider going east. Besides, she had already decided, the War-ravished seaboard states would be an unhealthy climate for a lone woman.

Moving down the rows of fruit trees, she found a couple of windfall apples to tuck in her bag. She went as far as she could before clambering over a log fence and turning into a row of tobacco leading to the Porter home. She was glad to see the row empty of workers, as she was loath to surprise any of the help by showing up in the fields. Passing the barns and reaching the drive, she strove to appear on a casual stroll, and made her way up to the summer porch of the sprawling farmhouse. She saw a young girl there dusting the wicker furniture; she paused at the steps and spoke to the maid. Invited onto the porch, she asked if Mr. Winston were about.

The girl bobbed a curtsy. "Yes, Miss. He is just finishin' lunch."

"Would you please ask him to see Miss Sarah?"

"Yes, Miss." The girl left on the errand.

Sarah wiped her dusty shoes on the backs of her stockings and tucked her bag behind her skirt. She closed her eyes. *Oh, Lord. Please let him help me.* Winston entered the porch, wearing a huge smile. "Miss Sarah, what a surprise! Here, here," he gestured toward a couch.

"Please have a seat. May I offer you something cool to drink? Some lemonade?"

Glancing over her shoulder, Sarah swallowed and wet her lips. "Thank you, Winn. Yes, please." When he turned to call the girl, Sarah pushed her bag behind the end of the couch and sat down.

"I'm so glad you've come to call," he said brightly. "We truly enjoyed the party last night."

"It was lovely, wasn't it?" She blotted her forehead with a handkerchief and breathed deeply to recover from her brisk walk carrying the heavy bag.

"Very much so." His animated expression, suggested he might think she had changed her mind about allowing him to call. Forcing herself to make casual chitchat for several moments, she was relieved when the serving girl returned with the lemonade and a plate of tea sandwiches and placed them on a table. Winn offered the plate to her, so she accepted a glass of juice and took a sandwich.

"I'm afraid I missed lunch," she explained, eating with relish.

"Please, help yourself," he said. He had a puzzled wrinkle between his eyebrows and looked toward the drive. "Did you ride over, or come by buggy?"

Shaking her head, she took another swallow and put her glass down. "No, Winn. I walked." She blotted her lips with a napkin.

His expression changed. "Is something wrong, Sarah?"

"No. Yes!" She licked her lip, and decided he would keep her confidence. "Oh, Winston. I truly need your help. I want to, to buy a horse."

He was baffled. "A horse? Surely your uncle---"

"No. I've never had one of my own and he would not give me one under---"

"Are you sure? I don't understand, Sarah." He rubbed his forehead. She deplored his confusion, but she had no time to answer questions. "You're welcome to use any one of our horses, whenever you wish." He probably thought she'd had some mild disagreement with her uncle.

"It's not that simple, Winn. I have to leave Fox Haven. I can't explain it to you now, but I must have a horse and a saddle." She stood up and clasped her hands in entreaty. "Please, Winn. This is urgent. I need to leave at once. If you could possibly sell me one, how much would it cost?"

He stood up concerned, but he nodded. "I have to go to the office for my ledger and a sale book. I'll be right back."

"Thank you." She tucked two sandwiches in a napkin, slipped them in her bag, and stood by the door waiting his return. Thank heaven he hadn't asked more questions! She did not want to place him in the middle by telling him about the vagrant. It wouldn't be long before the body was found, and everyone in the area questioned. What if Emma concocted a story implicating her? She shook her head to dispel thoughts of the murder, and the equally horrible demand of her aunt. No. She certainly could not tell Winn, why it was necessary for her to leave.

Returning with the ledger in his hands, Winston said, "Our stock of horses is down due to the government's purchase during the War. We wouldn't have any, if we hadn't run a few into the hills, on some remote rental property. A farmer can't work without animals."

She suddenly realized what she was asking and sighed heavily. "I understand, Winn. You need all you have. In another day, or so, I'll find another way---"

"Not at all. We had some colts last spring to help replenish the stock. I want you to have a mature animal." He scanned the pages glancing at the records for each one of their older stock. Finally, he tapped a page with one finger. "Robin will do. He's seven years old, out of Lancelot, a gelding with a good nature, strong, but gentle enough for a lady."

"And tack? A saddle?"

"I've an older English saddle. Not a sidesaddle, I'm afraid. Mama hasn't ridden in years. Will that work for you, temporarily?"

"Oh, yes! I used one as a child. It will be fine." Relief relaxed her shoulders. Since as a 'man' she would have to ride astride, the saddle was perfect. "How much, Winn?" She opened her small pouch purse to remove the money.

Winn reddened and waved his hand negatively. "Nothing. If you need it, I wouldn't think of charging you. You can bring the horse whenever you return."

Hesitating, she said, "It is only fair to tell you, I'm *not* coming back, Winn."

He placed a hand on her shoulder and gazed at her with a longing that touched her deeply. She saw him struggle with the knowledge before he accepted her departure. "Then, he's my gift to you."

Realizing his feelings, Sarah blushed. Her eyes filled with tears and she reached up to kiss his cheek. "Thank you, my very, dear friend."

He took her traveling bag and ushered her down the steps. He found Robin in the stable, located the saddle, and asked Zeb to put it on the horse. Turning to Sarah he asked for a penny, filled out the bill of sale and handed it to her. "You won't say where you're going? Or why?"

She shook her head; a tear coursed down her cheek. "I can't."

"Will I ever see you again?"

Grimly she shook her head. "I'm afraid not."

He put his arms about her and held her close for a minute. "Will you let me know where you are?"

"When I can," she managed. This was goodbye to someone she cared about. "I don't know how to thank---"

"Shush," he said, placing a finger on her lips.

Zeb brought the saddled horse forward and handed the crop and reins to Porter. "Here y'are, Master Winston." He nodded to her, his wrinkled face puzzled.

"Thank you, Zeb. That's all." The black man returned to the back of the stable.

Sarah looked up at the handsome, chestnut gelding and stroked his velvet nose. The horse wrinkled his skin in appreciation and appraised her with large brown eyes. "Hello, Robin," she said. He replied with a low rumble from his chest.

Winn walked the animal to a mounting block, held the stirrup for Sarah to mount and handed her the riding crop. Sitting astride stretched, her skirt and petticoat taut, but she had just enough yardage to keep her legs from showing. He tied her carpetbag and rolled jacket to the back of the saddle. She had worn an old bonnet, gloves and a light shawl secured under her arms and tied in back. Enough wrap for the warm day.

She sensed his sad concern as he walked the horse to the drive. His expression of loss nearly destroyed her determination. She would never see this man again, who had thought to court and marry her. For all she knew, no one else would ever care for her that way.

"Take good care of yourself." His voice graveled. He took a deep breath and gave the horse a firm slap on his croup. Robin trotted down the lane toward the road.

Sarah turned and waved her crop at Winn, as tears streamed down her face. She devoutly hoped she had the courage and grit this move required. *Goodbye, dear friend*, she murmured. The loss left her with a sharp pain in her breast.

It was already afternoon and Sarah knew she would make only twelve miles or so by dark. The tears dried on her cheeks as she turned northwest on the road toward Huntington. She urged Robin into a gallop, looking for a copse of trees to turn into in order to change her clothes. How grateful she was to Winston for giving her the horse! With such a slim budget, she could have been quite insecure before she was able to find work to replenish her capital. She realized what a fine suitor he would have made.

She was bitter at the way the entire scenario had played out. It was fortunate she had told no one Winn had asked to court her, since Emma said *she* expected to marry him and had a prior claim to his attentions. The most galling event was her aunt's demand she bear her cousin's baby; the thought curdled her stomach. The attack on Emma proved the catalyst. *Her* effort to save her cousin had caused the death of an unknown vagrant. Sadly, Sarah realized exactly how convoluted her relationships had become. By leaving, she had at least spared Winn the painful knowledge of how much dirty linen the family had to hide.

Seeing a group of dense foliage, she turned the horse aside and rode between the shrubs and trees to a small clearing, out of sight from the road. Making certain she was alone to adopt the disguise, she dismounted and removed her outer clothing and petticoat. The shirt, which was long in the sleeves, she rolled at the cuffs. She used the belt to secure Worth's trousers snugly about her waist and put on two pairs of hose to make his shoes fit. Retrieving her sewing scissors from her bag, she chewed away at her long hair until she had a short bob that would look masculine under a cap. She longed for a peer glass to check her appearance. Fingering her chopped off tresses sent a wave of regret through her at the loss of her auburn mane. The Bible said a woman's long hair was her glory. She was totally glory-less *now* and she fought another bout of tears. She pushed the cut-off strands of her hair under some leaves. At Fox Haven she could have made jewelry from it. Here, at least the birds would find it to use in their nests. She rolled her bonnet, dress and petticoat into a packet to place in her bag. The time would come when she would need them in the future. A turtledove made his plaintive four-note call in the trees and jigsaw pieces of the sun appeared through the leaves in the west. She had to hurry. Retying the bag to her saddle, she located a tree stump, mounted the horse and coaxed him back onto the road, nervously looking both ways for other people.

She immediately appreciated the convenience of trousers for straddling the horse, for the uneven road was difficult. How in heaven's name could she pass herself off as a man for months to come? There were rumors about women going into the militia dressed as men during the War, often to stay with their husbands. Some were discovered within a few weeks. Others lasted over two years. If they had the courage to masquerade as men to fight in a war, surely she could manage to save herself for a short time to relocate and secure a position.

She tried to think of the feminine gestures, behavior and traditional attitudes she would have to avoid, to appear masculine. If she used a handkerchief, it would be a large one to blow her nose, never to wipe her tears, or blot her mouth. She would have to hold up her head, look people in the eyes and scowl, forget the demure deference proper for a woman. Perhaps she should learn to smoke a pipe, or chew tobacco. Her lips curled and she stuck out her tongue. She heartily disliked the taste of the weed, having secretly dipped snuff with Emma to try it out long ago. Maybe she could simply learn to spit, on occasion, assuming she wasn't too nervous to work up the necessary saliva. She sighed; weary from trying to think of all of the changes she needed to effect. There was more to this transformation than met the ready eye.

A black man and his family of three walking down the road nodded and with one hand on his son's shoulder, he touched his cap to her. She managed a reserved nod thinking how much she wished she had a family of her own. Formerly, she would have smiled and spoken to the boy. She had to think all the time. She had to learn to swagger, take bigger steps, stand about with her hands in her pockets and swear. "Jumping Jehosophat!" she exclaimed, but it did not quite do the job. "Whistling girls and crowing hens always come to no good ends." She puckered up and tried a whistle. She had already come to no good end; she might as well have the game.

Knowing her voice was too melodious, she would have to lower it. Needing a masculine name, she settled on Morgan, her father's middle name, and Kane, her mother's maiden name, certain she wouldn't forget them. Repeating her new name over and again, she increased her speed, 'chasin' daylight'. She remembered the expression from a western pulp magazine she had seen of Ellsworth's, years ago.

Chapter 7

Fox Haven Alarm

AT LUNCH, SARAH was absent. "Lauree," Emma's pa spoke brusquely from the head of the table. "Is Sarah ill or gone off calling in the middle of the day?"

Her mother glanced nervously about. "Not to my knowledge, dear."

"I want you to find her as soon as we've finished. I expect an apology for her absence and make sure she has nothing to eat until evening. This is not the way a lady behaves." He nodded purposefully at Emerald, plainly warning her against any similar behavior.

"Yes, Rupert. Quite right," Lauree said and looked down at her plate.

Emma had a bite of cornbread and saw an opportunity. "She may have gone for a walk, Papa."

"Did she tell you she was leaving the house?"

"No, Sir. But, Sarah has been ... nervy lately." Her tone implied something was emotionally wrong with her cousin.

Rupert's fork clattered on his plate. "Indeed? We will have no airs or vapors in this house. Do you understand, my girl?"

"Oh, yes, Papa." She gave him a practiced smile, as artificial as a Victorian waxed chrysanthemum. "I simply think... Sarah isn't as afraid of the dangers of the roads, as she should be."

Rupert's face reddened. "You know for certain that she has disobeyed me and gone on the roads alone?"

Pretending reluctance, she replied, "Only once or twice, Papa."

He threw his napkin down on his plate and stood up, frowning meanly. "I'll see Sarah the minute she returns. By all that's holy, we'll have this out! And you'd better be telling me the truth, Emerald, or you'll be confined to *your* room, as well." He marched out of the dining room and down the hall toward his office.

Emma twitched her shoulders, gratified to have created a problem for her cousin. *She had that coming. That will teach her to keep her hands off Winnie.* She turned to her lunch with renewed relish.

As soon as she had finished, Emma excused herself and hurried upstairs. She knew it was unlike Sarah to miss a meal, unless she was ill. Making sure she was alone, she entered her cousin's room. Normally tidy, Sarah had left a hatbox on the bed and the wardrobe doors standing open. Her ambro-type and Bible were missing from the dresser; a note addressed to her aunt and uncle stood on the washstand. Emma read the note, replaced it and had second thoughts. If she were to keep the note, they would eventually conclude an ungrateful Sarah had run away. In fact, she *had* done so, but *she* was the only one who knew why her cousin had left. *It was Winnie,* she thought; *because I wanted him, Sarah did, too.*

She slipped the note in the reticule at her waist, quietly closed the door and went across the hall to her own room.

She paced up and down. If she went downstairs and told her parents Sarah had run away, they would immediately set out to find her. Her cousin would not have taken a horse from the stable, knowing how authorities dealt with horse thieves, so she must be on foot. Her father was not about to let Sarah leave the household without his permission. *Oh, yes, he would go after her and bring her back in time for dinner!* Emma picked up her fan and agitatedly circulated the air in front of her face.

The incident in the woods came to her mind. That was another reason she preferred to have her cousin gone. When the man's body was found and everyone questioned, stupid Sarah would tell the truth and implicate *her*. However, if she tidied Sarah's room and kept the note, it might be another day before they knew she had run away. By then, Sarah could have left the area to avoid being brought back home. This would free her of competition, where Winnie was concerned. Nodding with decision, Emerald looked up and down the hall and returned to her cousin's room. Quickly she put away the hatbox and closed the doors of the wardrobe. Pleased with herself, she left the bedroom and pulled the door to behind her.

By late afternoon, when she had been unable to find Sarah, Lauree was beside herself. She checked with the cook about the dinner menu, secured a headache-powder packet and stated she was retiring. On the way to her room, she knocked on Sarah's bedroom door and entered. Everything looked all right. She could not think of another thing to do. Emerald had gone to tea with two of her friends, or she would have questioned *her* again. Of course, *she* will be blamed, if something has happened to the girl. Rupert simply did not understand that she could not keep track of two young girls twenty-four hours a day. Her head was throbbing by the time she reached her room and took her powder.

Changing her outer clothes for a wrapper, she stretched out on the bed with a damp cloth on her forehead. Gazing up at the tester netting, which canopied the four-poster, she reminded herself how fortunate she was to have her parents' home. It was not the same without Ellsworth, especially when Rupert was upset; but when Ellsworth returned, she would feel alive again. Although he would not take her side against his father, he took the brunt of Rupert's attention and gave her peace.

She smiled. *He had been a beautiful baby.* He was the one person in the world she loved unconditionally and beyond reason. *Drat this headache!* If it were not better soon, she would take some laudanum. In fact, there was no reason to bear the pain, when she had help at hand. She sat up, went to her dressing table and located a vial under her handkerchiefs. Taking a swig of the medicine, she hid the bottle and returned to bed. She pulled up a silk patchwork coverlet and eased her head down on a lace pillow. Surely, Sarah would be back by the time she awoke.

Chapter 8

Sarah Meets Louis

THERE WAS A sense of freedom, of being on her own for the first time and flying through the afternoon on horseback. Slowing Robin down to a trot, Sarah spied a copse with a small stream on the right side of the road. After looking about for strangers, she pulled over to refresh herself and her horse. She knew she had pushed him and she wanted to give him a rest. They had made better time than she expected and, according to a sign she had seen on the road, were within two miles of the small village of Hamlin.

She had passed several other riders and wagons along the way, but no one paid her any mind. Reassured regarding her disguise, she began to feel things were going as she had planned. If she had been seen by one of the Dietrich friends or neighbors, she might have been recognized. Fortunately, it was Monday. The farmers and workers went to church on Sundays and to town on Saturdays. For the most part, they would have gone to Charleston, for it was closer to the farm. At any rate, since the War, the roads were in such poor condition, incidental travel on them was curtailed.

She liked her horse. He had a sweet disposition and appeared to have accepted her as his owner. She took hands-full of grass and rubbed him down. He nickered in appreciation while cropping and noisily munching mouths-full of grass. After slaking her thirst, she splashed water on her face and hands, wincing at the blister that had developed from her tight hold on the rein. Thank heaven for the old pair of gloves she had worn! Robin looked up, staring over her shoulder. Before she could turn, a man spoke.

"Please, Suh. Would you have anything to eat?"

Alarmed she whirled about and she recognized Louis Garth, a sharecropper from the Dietrich farm. The clothes on his tall, thin frame were little more than rags, his dark brown hair a rat's nest, but his hands and face were clean.

Surprise spread across his face, he glanced at her male clothing, and took a step closer. "Miss Sarah?" She'd seen him from time to time on the farm, but of course he'd never done more than doff his work hat to her. With a heavy sigh Sarah nodded, thinking the game was over. The stress and effort had all been for naught.

"Yes. It is Louis Garth, isn't it? It seems I've been discovered. Did they send you after me?" Her voice was heavy with disappointment.

"No. *No, M*iss. I, I left the farm. I jest couldn't take my pa's mean ways no more. I lit out Sata'day and I been looking for work all over, today. But what are *you* doin' here, Miss? Why're you dressed like that?"

"It's a long story, Louis. I had to leave Fox Haven, too, for different reasons. Umm…you said you were hungry?"

"Yes'm. I ain't had nothin' to eat since Sata'day."

She turned to her bag and pulled out a sandwich, cheese and crackers. "Here, Louis, sit down." She handed him the sandwich. She broke off a bit of cheese to eat with two crackers. "It isn't much, but I've two late apples I picked up in the orchard. I'll share with you."

He wolfed down the sandwich and leaned over to scoop up water from the stream. *The poor fellow was half starved.* She gave him an apple and scored the other with her sewing scissors for herself.

He smiled and looked better; his lean face was almost handsome. "Thank you, Miss. I guess you 'bout saved my life." He hunkered back on his heels, wrapped his arms around his knees and said, "Yo're a fine lookin' young man."

He was teasing her, she realized; she gave her apple core to Robin and placed the remains of the food in her bag. Garth might be poor and ignorant, but he had a sense of humor. Still concerned about being discovered and returned to Fox Haven, she asked, "Have you seen anyone on the road from the farm?"

"No'm. It was early, when I left. Jest before daylight. If I'd waited any longer, my pa would a' been awake and put me to work." He looked at her anxiously. "D'ya think Squire Dietrich will send the constable after me?"

"How old are you, Louis?"

"Nineteen."

"My uncle has no jurisdiction over you. You and your family are independent farmers sharing your crops with the owner for the use of the land. Besides, you're an adult. You can do what you please."

He stood up, apparently considering what she had just said. "You ain't foolin' about that? My pa always told me I was beholden to the squire. He said they'd beat us like Negra's and put us in jail, if we failed to make a crop or keep their rules."

Clenching her teeth, she had to look away from the poor wretch before she wept. "Uncle Rupert is a hard man, Louis, but he's not legally able to do either of those things. You have brothers and sisters, don't you?"

"Yes, 'um. Two girls an' two boys."

"That's a big family. I think… your father may have told you that to keep you on the farm. I 'spect your pa needed your help to feed them. With the War and money so tight, he might have been afraid of losing your help."

He propped one hand under his chin and nodded. "If I can get some work and send him money, it might he'p more than my stayin' on the farm."

"What other kind of work can you do?" She wanted to help him, but was not sure how.

"I like animals. I can fix a split hoof on a horse, milk a cow, birth colts, lambs and calves. I even know about breedin' animals: pigs, horses, cows, and goats."

"Then you could be an assistant husbandman."

"What's that?"

"A farm manager, an overseer. Did you ever tell my uncle or the overseer about this experience?"

He waved both hands negatively. "No'm, I never spoke to neither one, 'less they asked me a question. Pa told me not to."

Mulling over his words, Sarah asked, "Where'd you come from originally?"

"Kentuck'"

"Do you know anyone back there you could work for?"

Louis laughed. "Law, miss! Ain't nobody in Kentucky got a job today, what with the War an' all. Most of 'em don't even have work for their selves, lessen they work in the mines. An' I swear, much as I've had it with small farming, I won't never work in no mine!"

"I see."

He looked uncomfortable and stood up. "Ah'm sorry to have bothered you, Miss," he said, putting on his hat. "Thank you for the food. But, before I go... you still didn't tell me why you're wearin' men's clothes." A smile played about his mouth.

She wanted to tell him the truth, but felt it best to skirt the issue. "I was a cousin whose parents died. I became Miss Emerald's companion; but she's grown and no longer needs me. It was time for me to leave. Since it's dangerous for a woman to be on the road alone, I thought a disguise would help." She bit her index finger in thought. *If he told them about seeing her---* "When you return to Fox Haven, I would appreciate it *very* much, if you would not mention seeing me."

"Course not, Miss. But, I don't 'tend to go back." He turned around again. "Mayhap I should come along with you to the next village, if you plan to spend the night there."

She had no reason to fear him and said, "That would be kind of you, Louis." She hoped to find simple lodging where she might get some oats for Robin.

"I'll jest git my pack." He helped her mount her horse, and then moved off to retrieve his bundle.

While she waited for his return, she considered his problem. If he had clean clothes, he would stand a better chance of getting employment.

He trotted along beside her and the horse for the next two miles. Smallholdings and farms became more frequent as they neared the village. The sun had set. It was growing dark when she paused beside a public stable at one end of a main road in the hamlet. "Do you think this looks all right?" she asked.

Louis went up to the double doors of the large barn and opened one. After peering inside, he came back and nodded. "Where you goin' to stay, Mis--tuh?"

With a gesture she indicated the stable. "Here. I can't spend money to stay in inns, because I've such a long way to go."

"Well, it looks clean, *Suh*. There's only a couple of other horses. There's a man near the back sitting at an old table by a camp bed. I think you'll be a' right."

She slid down from the horse and he reached out a hand to steady her. "What about you, Louis?"

He grinned. "I'll be fine, uh, Mister."

"Thank you, Louis. Before you go, I want you to take this." She handed him a ten-dollar bill.

He backed up shaking his head. "You hadn't aught to do that."

"Yes, I should. It is not much, but it would buy you a new hat and a shirt, which could help you find work. It will cover a bar of soap, so you can wash your hair, too. There is no use going farther south, if you don't want to stay in cotton. Besides, the War has left too many men looking for jobs. You could ask others, but I've heard…if you head about thirty-five miles north, you'll be in cattle country. You might find work up there." She gave him a tired smile.

His eyes glistened. "I don't know what to say, Suh."

"Good luck, Louis," She waved her crop at him.

"Take care of yourself, an' thank you," he called and set off.

He was a decent young man, and she hoped he would find a better life ahead. Glancing up the main street, she decided it was a nice, small place: red brick buildings, a general store, a few shops and offices lined it. She had come about twenty-seven miles from the farm, she figured, giving Robin a pat on the neck.

She simply could not sleep out-of-doors. The ground was cold and damp; the insects and mosquitoes would find her, even under her shawl. A stable was the answer. She would have to buy what she could afford to eat along the way. That would strain her resources, but she could limit the fare. Thankfully, she had put some clean rags in the bottom of her bag to use at her time of the month. Oh, my gosh, soap! The small bar she had would not cover laundry, too. And, she needed a canteen. Tomorrow, as soon as the general store opened, she would make her purchases.

She entered the stable and arranged for herself and Robin to spend the night for a dollar. For another quarter, the hostler threw in a tin of oats for her horse. She was relieved he didn't question her disguise. He told her where the well was out back and gave her a bucket to fill for Robin. Her back and legs ached, but she managed to slip the saddle from the steed's back and throw it on a rail between the stalls. She put the horse in an empty stall with the oats and some fresh hay. In the yard, she made a rushed job of washing her face and arms, and returned with water for Robin.

Finally, locating some clean straw, she began moving it about until it fit her backside. Then she wrapped her shawl about herself for a cover. Utter exhaustion dulled her senses, so the odor of the barn, the musk and the spikes of straw were barely noticeable. Using her bag for a pillow and gazing up at the dusty beams overhead, she fell asleep mumbling her prayers.

When Sarah awakened in the morning every muscle in her body ached. She was not used to riding a horse day in and out, especially not astride. Still, she had had a good night's sleep, thank heaven! She hauled herself up and brushed the straw from her clothes. "Hello, horse," she said to Robin and took his pail back to the well. She pulled up a bucket of water, splashed some on her face and gargled a mouthful, spewing it onto the dirt. If anyone had observed her from a facing window, he would *surely* think she was a young man. The rest of the bucket-full she took back to the barn. The groom snored loudly in his corner as she passed, and she sat down by Robin to finish her cheese and crackers.

Gazing at the animal, she considered the problem: she had never saddled a horse in her life. The blanket was easy, but the saddle was awkward, and the horse sidestepped causing the saddle to slide off before she could cinch the girth. Robin liked the game. He tossed his head up and down, refused to open his mouth, and eyed her, as if to ask, "What do you want to play next?" She was glad no one was about to see the mess she made of the chore.

Knowing how the girth was supposed to go and making it cinch was something else. After several tries, she realized she had to put the halter on the horse and tie him to a stall rail. By the time the horse was dressed, she was worn out. "We're going to have a talk, Sir," she told him, "as soon as we're on our way."

She secured her bag to the saddle and walked Robin out of the stable. Leading him, she teetered gingerly down the rutted road looking for a mercantile store. The board front had a glass window that displayed clothing and hardware; a sign on the door stated it would open at 8:00 a.m. Looking at her pocket watch she saw it would be another half-hour. Tethering the horse in front of the store, she strolled down the boarded walk, intentionally lengthening her stride, and glancing in an occasional window. She had noticed a bakery earlier, and she wanted something more to eat. It was exactly what she wanted: a bakery, which served tea. The bell rang as she opened the door and a large, ruddy-faced woman wearing a flour-covered apron, wiped her hands behind the counter.

"We don't have any coffee, Suh, but I can give you a can of tea," she said, not waiting to be asked. Coffee had disappeared from the market during the War and it was not yet generally available.

"That's fine, Ma'am," said Sarah, looking in a display case. "And maybe a couple of those crullers?"

"Just sit yourself down, young Suh," the baker said indicating a small gate-leg table in the corner.

Sarah doffed her cap and sat down, neatly tucking her feet under the table. Catching herself, she stretched out one leg casually and threw an arm over the other chair at the table. The proprietor brought the pastry and tea with a bit of milk and sugar. "That'll be twenty cents," she said, holding out a beefy hand.

Fumbling for change from her pocket, Sarah paid the woman and applied herself to the rest of her breakfast. She wrapped the extra cruller and put it away for later. The tea was hot and reviving and she began to take heart. *Come what may*, she thought, *I am going to make this work!*

Wagons rumbled by on the road, and a few early riders passed the window. The town was waking up. Sarah finished her tea, thanked the owner with a wave, and returned to the general store in time to see the proprietor unlock the door and turn the open sign. She had always enjoyed shopping, but this time, she was edgy and in a hurry. She needed to get on the road as soon as possible. Selecting the items, adding a chain for her watch, and some dried apples she went up to the storekeeper. "I'd like these things, Sir. Would you have a map of the area?"

The thin, whiskered fellow took a pencil from behind his ear, wet the tip, and began to total the items. "Uh no. We never had no map. You might try the apothecary down the way." He gestured to his left. Wrapping the items up in heavy paper, he asked for her string bag to hold them.

"Forgot it," she grimaced. "I'll take one of those." She pointed to one hanging on the wall behind the counter.

"Here ya' are." The clerk added the string bag to the bill, and she paid him the total. "Thank you, Suh."

Sarah murmured "Thanks," and went out to tie the bag of goods onto the saddle. Mounting a block beside the horse, she felt self-conscious getting on the animal. Mounting without a block was something else she would have to learn. She could picture herself flying up and *over* the saddle. Self-consciously, she placed one foot in the stirrup, pulled up, and threw her other leg over Robin's back. Laughing with success, she road down the way.

In the square, Sarah found the apothecary. She slid off the saddle and entered the small shop. One wall-displayed cans of snuff, cigars, snuff boxes, bottled compounds and elixirs said to cure every ailment known to man. A table held writing notebooks, pens, ink and pencils. A little, gray-haired woman in a blue dress with lace at the collar looked up from a desk by the door and smiled. "Can I help you?"

"Yes, please," Sarah began, and lowered her voice. "I need a map of the area, if you have one."

The shopkeeper stood and pointed to a large map of North America on the back wall. "There ya' are."

Sarah gazed at the rendering. Dated 1840, it was covered with pinpricks and notes where major battles of the War had been fought. The Mississippi River divided the first third of the country from the rest. Some rows of mountains were indicated in the west. Most of the land beyond the Mississippi was simply marked Texas or Indian Territory. A few railroads lines were shown in the eastern states, but distances were not given, and only a few towns listed. West Virginia, as such, was not depicted. It had only become a state in 1863. Sarah could see the vast reaches involved in her pursuit. Distressed, she began to tremble.

The proprietor approached her. "Are you all right, Suh?"

Swallowing hard, Sarah strove to control herself. "Yes, Ma'am. Thank you. I simply didn't realize how large the country truly is."

"It is big." The woman nodded. "I ain't seen much of it myself."

"No. Hum. I'd like to buy one of those notepads. I need to copy a bit of the map, unless there's a library here where I could find one more up-to-date."

The woman laughed. "A library, is it? In Hamlin? No, Suh, this is the closest thing here." She handed Sarah a lined notebook and a pencil.

Glancing at the map, Sarah quickly began to sketch the West Virginia border, the top of Kentucky, the Ohio River and Indiana. That was the way to go. Handing the pencil back to the storekeeper with "Thanks," she paid for the notebook and a new pencil, and left the shop. With a heavy heart she pulled Robin over to a mounting block and awkwardly mounted. Urging him to a slow trot, she headed up the road and out of town

Chapter 9

Emerald's Ploy

FOLLOWING LUNCH, EMERALD went into the conservatory to do some thinking. After three days, it was obvious to her parents Sarah had disappeared. They had sent the field workers in a three-mile radius of the farm to look for her, without any luck. The searchers brought back the news that an injured tramp found on the roadside, had been taken to the Porter's farm and placed in the barn to recover. Altercation! Emerald swore *the damned vagrant was alive!* He was the man Sarah had bludgeoned, of course, which only *she* knew.

She could not ride over to Porter's to see Winnie as she had planned, for fear of meeting her attacker face to face. It occurred to her that she could write a letter to Winston to disparage the man he sheltered; yet, how could she do so without telling him she knew about the derelict?

It was growing ever more urgent for her to see Winnie, because her father asked her why he had not written, and when he planned to call on her. *When her pa got his teeth into an idea, he worried it until it turned to mush.* If he went over to the Porters' before she had a chance to talk to Winnie, he would know she had lied and placed him in an embarrassing position. Then, hell and damnation would break loose and he would *chew her up and spit her out!*

Rainbow shafts of light darted through the cut-glass windows making her squint as she moved around the room. Her low heels clicked rhythmically on the tiled floor. On second thought, *what if I simply told Winn, Sarah had gone for a ride, a man jumped up in front of her and she had ridden him down? I could say that was the reason she ran away. She obviously would not be back; there was no reason for him to question Ben about the horse she might have taken; he would never know what actually happened. Yes!* Snapping her fingers, she went upstairs to her desk to write the letter.

My Dear Winnie,

Papa tells me that your pa spoke to him about us. Have you all come to an agreement without telling me? From the way you kissed me in the library, I thought you meant it. Now, what am I to think?

I am sure you have heard Sarah has disappeared. No one knows where she has gone, but I alone know why. She told me she had gone for a ride and a vagrant, jumped up in front of her horse, frightening her. She said she rode him down and left him there beside the road. I have not told my parents because we are not permitted to go riding alone, for fear of strangers and returning soldiers on the road.

Will you come to see me, Winnie? I truly need to know that your heart is as entrapped, as my own. Pray,

do not let me endure this agony one minute more. I
cannot rest, until I hear from you.

Your loving, obedient servant,
Emerald

Emerald called for Ben and sent the letter off to Winston, before
she could lose her courage and change her mind. Now she would be
anxious every painful minute until he replied.

Chapter 10

Incident at the Inn

THE AREA SARAH passed through in the southwestern part of West Virginia consisted largely of small subsistence farms devoted to general farming. Most of the hillsides were forested and received sixty to eighty inches of rain annually. That year was especially damp. Loping along on Robin, the rain poured off Sarah's cap brim and trickled down her neck, making her miserable. She had reassessed her goal so many times, she no longer knew what on earth had convinced her West was the place to go. *Lordy!* She must have had other options, but none of them came readily to mind. Her horse began to favor his left front hoof. Not certain what was wrong with him, she slowed down to keep him from further injury.

The rain stopped. However, the clothing, under the shawl she wore was completely soggy. She swore to herself and felt guilty for having done so, because she might have to stay in an inn to dry her clothes and get a good night's rest. There appeared to be a good-sized town ahead. She had begun to worry about finding a blacksmith before dark, when another rider drew up alongside her.

The tall well-dressed man touched his stovepipe hat and spoke, "Good evening, Sir."

Sarah gave him a courteous nod, "Sir."

"I'm sure you're looking for a 'smith," the man said, his crop indicating Robin's leg. "Are you new to these parts?"

She kept her reply brief. "I'm afraid so." From his fine riding apparel, expressive eyebrows, and a small blonde goatee, the man was obviously one of quality.

"It's not far to the smithy in Huntington. I'm going there and will gladly show you the way." He looked at her with polite concern.

Sarah bobbed her head. "Very kind, Sir. Thank you." She had no reason to be apprehensive, but she was reluctant to become acquainted with anyone, until she was more certain of her disguise. What if someone unmasked her? For all she knew, there might be a legal penalty for masquerading as a member of the opposite human race. Something in the stranger's manner made her uncomfortable. Making small talk, the two rode side-by-side for about fifteen minutes and entered the outskirts of the town.

"It's down this way," the man said, turning down a side road. Sarah followed, hardly seeing any alternative. Soon a blacksmith's shop appeared on a corner and the man drew to a stop.

"It's too late. I'm afraid he is closed. Howsomever, there's a decent inn down there, if you plan to spend the night. They'll put up your horse, and you can take him to the smith in the morning."

Swallowing her trepidation, Sarah held out her hand. "Morgan Kane, Sir. Thank you very much."

He covered her hand with both of his and gazed at her warmly. "You're most welcome, Sir. Archibald Greenwald."

Knowing that took care of the exchange, Sarah rode on to the inn and tethered her horse to the hitching post outside. She entered the paneled hallway and found a reception counter at one end. There was a single room available and a meal served in the keep. She asked to have a groom take Robin to the stable for the night and to see he had a good measure of oats. Retrieving her carpetbag from the saddle, she bid her horse goodnight and re-entered the inn.

A house maid took her bag and showed her up to the room, on the floor above. Sarah gave her a coin, and the girl said she would fill her wash jug with hot water. Too hungry and tired to wait to wash up, Sarah went down to have supper.

From the pub at one end of the room issued the cheerful voices of men, amusing themselves with card and dart games and enjoying their pints at the bar. Sarah heard a familiar voice, no doubt the innkeeper's. She took a table near the fireplace and gave her order to the serving girl.

The fire snapped pleasantly exuding warmth a few feet away, and she began to relax at last. There was a middle-aged couple in a corner settle, just finishing their dinner. A bearded older man sat alone at a small table near the doorway, squinting as he read a broadsheet by lantern light. The kitchen maid brought in a bowl of stew, a corndodger, and a half pint of beer, which she placed on the scrubbed pine table for Sarah. For fear of giving away her disguise, she had been leery of asking for tea in the evening. By the time she had consumed the dram and eaten her stew, she was so sleepy she could barely make her way upstairs.

Removing her damp clothes, she hung them on the footboard to dry and placed her soaked shoes near the chimney. It was so pleasant to be enclosed in the friendly, mustard colored walls. The wash water was nicely warm and she gratefully washed every bit of her body and her short hair. She had not become used to the constant odor of horse on her clothes and person. Toweling her hair, she began to feel human. It felt good to have on clean underwear from her bag. She rinsed out her damp hose and long johns in the basin, blotted them in the towel, and hung them on the back of a chair by the chimney. Saying her prayers as she climbed into bed, she blew out the candle, put the chamber stick on a stand, and settled down between old muslin sheets, asleep before she could turn over in the bed.

Sometime later, the desk chair near the door fell over with a clatter arousing her. Startled awake, Sarah sat up, trying to remember where she was, when she saw a tall man silhouetted from a hall lantern standing in the room. She stifled a scream. "Who are you? What do you want?" she asked, as gruffly as she could, pulling the covers about her as if she were cold.

"Hush, Kane," the man rasped, looking over his shoulder. "It's Greenwald. I didn't mean to startle you." His speech slurred as he spoke, telling her he had been drinking. Weaving, he waved his hands. "Shush. I, I only want---"

"Why are you in my room, Sir?" She made her voice as harsh as possible and slipped one hand down the side of the bed, seeking something for a weapon.

"You, you're such an attractive young man. I hoped," he moved two steps closer to the bed. "I mean, I think we may be of the same temperament."

Puzzled, and growing more anxious by the second, Sarah replied stiffly, "I don't know what you're talking about. Leave this room at once." She gestured to the door.

"Now, now, you know what I mean, Sir." The man bowed unsteadily, doffed his hat with a flourish, came close to the bed, and grabbed her arm. His liquor infused breath assaulted her nose. "I bribed the scullery maid to show me your room. I've waited all evening to come to you, after the house was quiet."

Jerking her arm away from him, her panic rose. She could barely make out a smile turned into a leer. "You do prefer gentlemen to ladies, do you not?" he purred.

Alarmed before, she was now scared out of her head! Wrapping herself in the coverlet, she almost fell out of bed on the far side, shaking with indignant fear. She felt behind her with her free hand, found the chamber stick, and hurled it at the intruder with all her might. "Get out! Get out! I've no interest in you, nor any other man!"

The candle missed, but the brass chamber stick struck him hard in one eye. "*Ow*! I was sure--You didn't have to-- My mistake, my mistake!" He backed up holding his cheek, stumbled over the chair on the floor and staggered out the door. She could hear him swearing in the hall, and then falling down the stairs. Other footsteps padded down the passageway. She quickly moved around the bed, dragging the coverlet. Frantically she closed and barred the door, appalled that she had not secured it earlier. Leaning against it with her heart thumping wildly, she had a huge knot of fear in her stomach. Her arms wrapped tightly, she gasped for breath, shaking all over.

She had only heard of such deviant behavior from schoolgirls' naughty whispers; she'd not believed the tales then. It had never occurred to her that she would ever *meet* anyone with those tendencies, let alone be approached by him!

Gradually her breathing slowed and the trembling eased. Righting the fallen chair by the desk, she was grateful it had awakened her. Otherwise, he might have been in bed with her before---Oh, my God!

Still unnerved, she returned to bed, assailed by the odor of wet wool drying by the chimney. The dark, mustard yellow walls of the room were no longer friendly. She shuddered and burrowed deeper in the bedding. She lay awake going over and over the incident in the dark. A weapon. She needed a weapon, if such a thing ever happened again. She repeated her prayers and the familiar habit helped her relax. She spent the remainder of the night keeping guard, until she slipped into deep sleep early in the morning.

Next morning as she dressed, Sarah heard the church bell strike seven in the square. She looked about her room at the inn, picked up her bag, and went downstairs for breakfast. She made herself comfortable at a corner pub table. When she looked up, it was just in time to see a red-faced Archibald Greenwald, with a bandaged black eye, hold his top hat over the side of his face and steal out of the common room. Her breath caught in her throat for a moment, recalling the terrifying scene in her room the night before. It was fortunate things turned out as they had. Now, she was aware and would be prepared. The other possibility was unthinkable.

"Suh, Suh," the scullery maid wiped her table again to get her attention. "Does grits, toast, egg, and a pint suit you?"

"What? Oh, yes." Sarah caught herself before she said 'please.' There were a few other travelers finishing their meals, or collecting their baggage to leave the inn. She overheard part of a conversation between four men at a near table.

"It takes the Assembly too long to make up its' mind," one burly fellow said. "We've barely got statehood and they're not sure whether the separation is gonn'a last."

"True," replied another. "But nobody with any wit would want to return to Virginia now, in its condition. It'll cost the devil to put her back in decent shape."

"And we got our own problems. D' you know it's still legal to take voice votes and secret ballots in some counties?"

A fourth spoke, taking a pull on his pipe. "I s'pose they has to take oral votes, 'cause some folks cain't read or write -- immigrants particularly."

Out of the corner of her eye, Sarah observed the short man with side-whiskers, jerk a nose rag out of his pocket and blow his nose. "By gorah, this is still a wilderness in many respects."

"Well, it won't be wilderness much longer with the railroads throw'n down lines as far as you can see," said the other. "Every Easterner and his horse are headed west these days. Considering the condition of half the seaboard states, I'd emigrate, too. Can you figure what Richmond, Fredericksburg, or Manassas will cost to put to rights?" He shook his head.

"Ayeah," the first man replied. "All that influx is the reason pot hunting ain't worthwhile lately. We're running out of wildlife. If we didn't have the whiskey trade, we'd have to depend on something illegal to make an honest living."

Sarah realized how little she knew about the country. She was gaining knowledge every day, along with the rigors of the journey.

The mention of the railroad lines teased her imagination. If the train tracks were there now, she might have ridden the train to St. Louis. According to the map she'd seen, the distance from West Virginia to St. Louis was daunting.... passing Kentucky, Ohio, and probably several other states. She still did not know how far, for certain, maybe seven hundred more miles. On horseback!

And, that was only the beginning. Afterward, she still had to make it to Independence, which she heard was the jumping-off place for wagon trains started on the Oregon Trail. St. Louis and Independence were across the state from one another, which she remembered from the big map. The Far West was completely beyond her imagination. *Soldiers!* This would take some riding. Up to now, she had only come about fifty miles, according to her reckoning. It could take her a year!

She watched for her breakfast, anxious to eat and be on the way, for she had to have her horse seen to and buy a couple of items before leaving town. When her food was served, she forced herself to eat every bite. She consumed as much as she could, because she did not know when she would have another meal. A village or an inn was not always at hand when she became hungry. With the last bit of toast, she sopped up the remainder of the eggs and grits. Still unused to ale for breakfast, she polished off the rest of the pint and grimaced as it went down.

She left her bag with the innkeeper and looked up and down the road for a general store. She had a little trouble focusing, as the ale made her lightheaded. Halfway down the road she found the store, entered, and quickly selected the necessities she desired. On a table at one side were a few bolts of gingham, calico, and linsey-woolsey. Pausing to look at the fabrics, she reached out to a bolt of blue and white lawn to feel the fine material with one hand. She had not seen new fabric since before the War and, for just a moment, she could see the lovely dress with lace at the neck and cuffs it would make. How beautifully it would flow when she danced!

"Are you looking for shirt material, Suh?" asked a man, who had walked up behind her.

Her daydream bubble burst abruptly. She turned about. The man's green eyeshade and striped apron identified him as the storekeeper. "Ah, yes. I need a shirt, but, my wife isn't fond of sewing."

"We've just received some gentleman's ready-to-wear." He indicated a rack two tables over. "What size, Suh, small?"

Sarah swallowed a blush. "Yes. Humm. Perhaps, the blue stripe."

The clerk found one in a small and held it out to her. "This is good quality cotton. Won't fade or ravel."

The two shirts she had were showing wear at the collars because she wore them day and night. One was always dirty and had to wait until she could find a place to wash it. A fastidious woman, she could not help longing for clean, ironed clothing. "How, how much is it?"

"Four dollars, Suh." The clerked nodded proudly.

Her ready cash was dwindling rapidly and she was afraid to spend the money. "Have you a work shirt for less? I -- have to be out in the fields." She was surprised at her ability to lie for her own protection. Blue was her favorite color, but she had to be sensible.

Returning the shirt to the rack with a frown, the merchant moved to a nearby table and picked up a blue calico work shirt. "Just this work shirt, at two dollars."

Her eyes lit up and she nodded, fingering the coarser, heavily starched material. "That'll do fine." She added the shirt to her other supplies and moved to the hardware counter. There among pewter tableware and ironstone crocks, she found the knives she sought. Feeling the blade of a pocketknife with a horn handle, she decided. That should do it. She would sew a pocket in her nightshirt and keep it with her night and day. When everything was wrapped and tied with string, she paid for her purchases and left the store, pleased to have saved two dollars and reassured regarding her security.

The town was busy with morning traffic: lumbering wagons, carriages, and horseback riders on their separate errands. Mud from last night's rain had not fully dried and the rutted streets made navigation tricky. She passed a one-armed soldier with a cane, whose dirty uniform needed a good brushing and cleaning. Her heart ached for the redheaded young man with sad eyes, whose empty sleeve was pinned up, whose life had been changed forever by the terrible War.

Band music from the square close by lifted her spirits. She watched the small band march around the corner toward the sound of a bell. Excited curiosity impelled her and she followed a crowd of people around the corner to the livery and stage station beyond the main thoroughfare. The crowd had gathered before an arriving wagonload of soldiers, who were waving and shouting from the wagon bed. Jumping and climbing down from the wagon, several of the soldiers found their loved ones among the crowd and fell into their arms. Some limped with canes, or crutches, others had arm-slings. A number needed help getting down. All looked tired and dirty. Those who were not met by someone, shouldered their knapsacks and moved off to their destinations.

Sarah saw the familiar face of one soldier still in the wagon, and her heart leapt with joy. It was her cousin Ellsworth Dietrich! Eagerly she started through the crowd toward him, when a woman in a pink bonnet turned quickly and bumped into her.

"Pardon me, Suh," the woman said. "Ain't it grand? They're home. They're finally home!"

Sarah stopped, ducked her head and murmured, "Yes, grand." She had forgotten her disguise, for the moment, and knew she could not speak to Ellsworth, regardless of her joy. The family *must not* know where she had gone. For another thing, she remembered wryly, she was wearing *his* pants and hound's-tooth jacket. She stepped behind a lamppost to examine Worth's face. He was thin and pale, and must have been ill for some time. Then, he turned on his bench to secure a pair of crutches on brackets against the side of the wagon. A sharp pain pierced her breast as she realized he, too, had been hurt in the War. One tear slipped down her face and she rubbed it off brusquely, as she thought a man would.

She considered Ellsworth the best of the Dietrichs for he had always treated her kindly. He was a gentle man in the shadow of an over-bearing father. Some of her fond memories of Fox Haven, when she and her cousins were young, playing in the woods, picnicking by the river, and learning to dance in the conservatory to tunes from a music box. Playing board games and performing shadow plays on rainy days. *Oh, Worth, I shall miss you more than I shall miss anyone else.* She offered a silent prayer, he would arrive home quickly and once more be safe with his family. *God speed, my dear cousin. God speed.*

As the band played "When Johnny Comes Marching Home" and the crowd began to thin, Sarah turned and walked back to the inn to get her bag and take care of her horse. Robin blew and bobbed a welcome to her. She paid the groom for the livery and for saddling her horse, tied her bundle and mesh bag to the saddle, and walked Robin out to the road. Down the way, she stopped at the blacksmith's to see to her horse's hoof. A large, gray-bearded man, the smith used a curved tool to deftly remove the stone lodged under Robin's shoe, and then brushed some medicine on the bruise. Paying the smith, she thanked him, accepted a boot up and rode around the corner and down the road toward the edge of town.

All morning long in the saddle she thought about the terrible War the country had just endured, grieving at the great loss of young men and the broken families who had survived the devastation. Although disguised as a man, Sarah knew full well, she would have made a poor soldier had she been born a male. Now, without President Lincoln, how would the country ever heal itself? Sadly, she kept on her way, seeing by a battered sign she was about to cross into Kentucky.

Chapter 11

Winston's Letter

SNATCHING THE NOTE, the groom had just delivered from Winston, Emerald hurried to the conservatory to read it.

July Fifteenth 1865

My dear Emerald,

I was stunned to receive your letter. Although I have none but the friendliest thoughts regarding you, I assure you our fathers have decided *nothing* regarding us. Indeed, I have not had time to recover from my military service and have not yet focused on the future. The urgent goal to secure our farm as a continuing enterprise has absorbed me completely. Even when I am not at work, it dominates my thoughts.

You are young and pretty as the loveliest tea rose in our garden. I have tender feelings for you and, when I have time in the weeks to come, I promise to think of you. Let us give these feelings time to flower or to wither, as they may, before we make any hasty decisions.

I am sorry to hear of the disappearance of Miss Sarah, but I know she would have been mortally threatened, before riding down anyone. Had this been the case, beyond doubt, she would have notified your father of the incident. I believe the stranger recovering in our stable can answer that question. I shall put it to him at once.

Your obedient servant and friend,

Winston Porter

Crumbling the letter in her hand, Emerald strode to the windows. Her gaze fell on the rose bushes before the kitchen garden. A tea rose. Picked or left on the bush, all roses wilt in time. Besides, she had not a 'fragile bone' in her body. He had said nothing except he would *think* about her … *if* he had time... *'Tender feelings.' God forbid!* Her feelings were anything *but* tender. Did he not feel the same urgency rushing through his veins, she did? No, he was a typical farmer looking for the right season, good weather and the best way to increase his crop. *God, he was cautious!*

What *would* the horrible man in Winston's barn say happened on the road? He would not admit to the attack on her 'cause he would be jailed. Now, since she had given *her* story to Winnie, she could not dispute the man's version. Once more, she was in the despicable position of having to wait to find out what the attacker told Winston.

Wait for *him* to make up his slower than tobacco-growing mind to call on her and wait to settle her future. Life was one stinking bucket of slop! If Winston thought she was going to wait forever for his decision to saddle a horse, he had another think coming. Her papa was determined to see her wed soon. The War was over and some of the men her age, had come home. She would have an entire county to choose from, if she liked. Mr. Porter had better do more than *think* about her. Or else.

Porter appraised the tramp huddled in a corner of his barn. The man's filthy, shoulder-length hair contrasted to the clean bandage of a faded print material binding his head. The fellow saw him approach and hauled himself up to a sitting position. "Mr. Porter, Suh," the man began, "I thank you for yore hospitality. I wouldn't have made it no way, iffn you hadn't give me roof an' found." He bobbed his head and grimaced as the movement obviously hurt.

"Yes, well, you're welcome. I shall ask Zeb to bring you a bucket of water and some soap so you can clean yourself up. I'll send down an old shirt and some trousers you may have, as well." The man murmured 'thanks' and brightened up.

"Now," said Winston, "I want you to tell me exactly what happened to you and how you came to be injured on the road."

The vagrant's eyes shifted from side to side, before he replied, "Uh, you mean what I was doing on the road? I was lookin' for work. I been through half the state, but there's so much military comin' home---"

Winston gave him a sharp look. "*And?*"

"I, I donno, Suh. I was jest having a nap aside the road when something hit me. I, I don't remember nothing else, but waking up here in yore barn."

Winn knew he was lying, but he could not check his story with Sarah since she was gone. He knew she would never strike an innocent man asleep beside the road, despite the man 's version. Emma had said 'he attacked her'. "Once you're cleaned up and feeling better, my cook will give you some food for the road. You are to leave no later than day-after-tomorrow."

"Thank you, Squire." He ducked his head, then said, "I don' suppose you need a supervisor, or wagon master on the place?"

Noting the man did not offer to do field work or perform menial tasks, Winston shook his head. "We have no openings. You'll find something on the way, especially if you clean yourself up and wash your clothes." Disappointed, the man blew his nose between his fingers, wiped his hand on his pants, and gave a tug to his forelock.

That's that, thought Winn striding forth to mount his horse. *I shall be damned glad to see the last of that lying rascal!* "Zeb," he began, taking the reins from his hostler and lowering his voice, "That man leaves no later than day-after- tomorrow. Make sure he doesn't take anything with him except food and the shirt and trousers I'll send down from the house."

"Yas, Suh!"

Winston rode out of the stable in the sunshine and down to the fields to inspect the harvest of tobacco by his workers. One fleeting thought teased his mind. Emma knew something she was not telling about the incident with the vagrant. He would have to worm it out of her. Perhaps it was time to send word inviting himself to tea.

Penne had been stirring gravy in the big iron stove in the Dietrich kitchen when she blacked out and fell to the floor. The cook threw a cup of water in her face. "Git up from there, gal. What's the matter wif you?"

She pulled herself up and reached for a rag to wipe her face. "Ah dunno. It's so hot in here an' the kitchen jest went round and round."

"Um-hmm." The cook wrapped her hand in her apron and pushed the gravy pan off the hot stove lid. "Have a cup of water an' set down a spell." The cook made sure everything was ready for lunch and in the warming oven, then turned to her, hands on her hips. "An' jist when did it happen? Four, five months ago?"

Placing her cup on the table, Penne looked up. "What you mean?"

"Don't play the innocent with me, gal. You lived in the quarters long enough to know what."

Shaking her head, Penne was puzzled. "Ah don't remember nothin'. Ah been a housemaid since ah was nine. I ain't spent no time in the quarters since."

A look of disgust swept across the cook's lined face. "Then you don't know who the papa is?"

"You mean Squire Dietrich?"

Cook frowned. "Ah never knowed him to do nuffin' like that 'afore, with two young ladies in the house. Fact is, Ah think he has someone in Charleston. Are you *sho'* he bedded you, gal?"

Jolted, she jumped up, "Why you say such a thing? He never touched me!"

Frustrated, Cook slapped her dishcloth on the pine worktable. "Ah'm askin' you who *did*?"

Apennine bit her lower lip and looked aside. "He said… Ah dasn't tell no one. He made me promise."

The older woman sighed with exasperation. "Humph! That sounds familiar. Was he White?"

Penne nodded.

"Louis? That scrawny share-cropper?"

"Who?" She looked at her boss blankly, but an idea formed. "What difference do it make?"

"That's who! One of those no-count White trash! He is the papa, you fool. That's what difference it makes!"

"Papa? You mean …Ah'm in the family way?" The idea struck her with surprise.

"Jis' what you think us been talkin' about?" Cook marched over to the stove and put the pan of gravy back on the hot stove lid.

Penne gasped as the truth sank in. "Ah didn' know. What's I gwin' to do now?"

"Not a cotton-pickin' thing, but have the baby. That share-cropper Louis done lit out las' week, so that's all there is to it." She added kindling to the stove and began to stir the gravy.

"That's all right. I didn't fancy him no-how." Penne thought, *the less she knows*---

"Then why'd you bed him? Don' you know you has to take care o' yourself?"

"Yes'm." She said in disgust. "Ah do *now*. Will they send me away? Have I lost my job?"

The cook scratched her head. "No. No. You be a right fo' a couple more months, if we makes you a loose apron or a smock. When you really starts showin, you may have to stay with one of the croppers for a while. Maybe, Miss Lainey. With two lil'uns an' working in the fields, she needs help. What do you say?"

Penne shut her eyes in relief. "Thank you, Ma'am. It's good wif me, if it's okay with Miss Lainey, I want to keep my job with you."

Mollified, Cook replied, "A right. Git over here and finish this gravy. Ah'll git you a powder to hep' wif the faints."

"Yes'm. Thank you." *Havin' a baby? Ah cain't believe it.* Still shook, she stirred the gravy. The whole idea was almost too much. She purely had a bunch to think about before everything worked out. One thing for sure, she would not leave Fox Haven, no matter what!

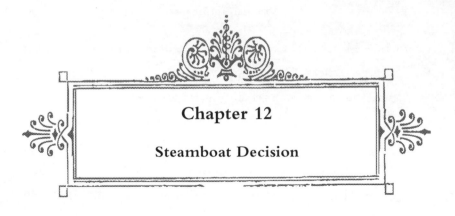

Chapter 12

Steamboat Decision

SARAH AND HER horse loped along the road from Huntington headed west. Seeing Ellsworth had filled her with her first pang of homesickness. It hurt to be unable to welcome him back from the War and to help him recover from his injury. He had always treated her as a sister and she felt closer to him, than to any other member of the Dietrich family. She had written to him and Winn during their service and was grateful both had survived. What Worth would find at home worried her. He was close to his mother. Lauree's possible dependence on laudanum would shock him. (She had only surmised it after seeing Lauree so groggy after her naps.) Moreover, there was Emma's plan to snare Winn, which might play itself out before long.

As the only son, Ellsworth would inherit the Dietrich farm, with the exception of the acres in Emma's dowry. Land to a farmer was the necessity for which he worked. Perhaps the land itself made an alliance with their neighbor necessary. Still, she deplored the possibility of collusion. Winn deserved a more loving and caring wife than Emma might be. Most of all, she knew Worth would be disappointed by *her* absence.

Giving her cap a guilty tug, she knew she was not objective in her feelings for Emerald. Probably, she held Winn in higher regard than she did Emma. *I shall never have an open mind as long as I let bitterness get in the way.* Moreover, the Dietrich problems were no longer hers. It was high time she laid them to rest.

Through the trees, she caught the flashing glimmer of sunlight on water. Excited to see the Great Ohio, she kicked Robin into a gallop. It was wider than she had expected. It cut its way through forested green hills and created a basin along the shore on its way to Kentucky. There was a surprising amount of traffic on the river and the wayside. A skiff, two fishing boats and a hemp barge were making their way downstream. Sea gulls darted back and forth looking for fish. Wagons and riders on horseback moved along the river, perhaps headed for a landing. Robin seemed to be enjoying the change of pace.

She suddenly wished she could go down river on a paddle steamer rather than ride the next five hundred miles on horseback. *Why not?* What if she could board a boat and disembark in the town closest to St. Louis? The map had shown the river followed the Kentucky/ Ohio borders for several hundred miles, but she did not know where it turned south to meet the Mississippi.

There were other considerations. What about poor Robin? She could not sell the horse because he came from Winn; she would need one wherever she stayed. Maybe she could take him on board the boat. At what cost? She had no idea what passage cost, let alone an animal's fare.

Excited by the idea, she followed the road, looking for the next landing where she could get answers to her questions. Up ahead, a wagon slowed. In a clearing, a substantial group of wagons, pedestrians and horses loosely congregated around a dock. Just what she wanted. Nearby to the left, between two hills, she saw a hamlet with several buildings.

A variegated crowd stood in line in front of a small office of peeled pine logs, with a hitching post and watering trough a short way beyond. Two Indians sat by one of the pilings on the dock, begging. Sarah had only seen Indians once or twice before. She believed most of them had been moved to reservations… in a place called Oklahoma Territory.

She approached a middle-aged man wearing a top hat, coat, and striped trousers, who was waiting in the line before the office. Sarah bent to ask, "Excuse me, Sir. Is this line for those seeking passage on the river?"

"Yes, Son," the man replied.

"And, if I may ask, is a boat going down river any time soon?"

"To be sure," the man replied, "The Columbia Belle, a paddle wheeler all the way from Pennsylvania; expected this afternoon, around two."

"Thank you, Sir." Sarah nodded and pulled the bill of her cap. Dismounting, she led Robin to the water trough, then tied him to the hitching post and joined the line.

She listened to the talk of those in line ahead of her. A farmer taking his produce on the next ferry crossing to Ohio was worried about the chance of rain. One young, just-married couple was on their way to Lexington, Kentucky to meet his parents. Cheeks glowing, the freckled bride in a yellow gingham dress, knit shawl and straw bonnet, looked up at her new husband with love and excitement in her face. Two rough-looking bearded men in deerskin breeches, with rifles and canvas packs on their backs joined the line behind Sarah, chaffing at the delay. They were the first frontiersmen she had ever seen. She would have asked them about the West, but feminine reticence held her tongue.

Minutes later, she reached the window of the office and faced a harried clerk, whose pointed chin, tufted gray hair and small round glasses, gave him the appearance of a scholarly heron. "And you, Sir, what do you want?" the clerk asked.

"Some information," she said, pitching her voice low. "How far does the paddle wheeler go? I mean, how close does it come to St. Louis?"

"Lessee." He scratched his head and turned to examine a map. Sarah would have given anything to see that map, but she was not tall enough to look over his shoulder. "Evansville. Yass, that's right."

"Where is that and how far is it, Sir?"

"Indiana. Cain't say e'zackly how fer. Mebbe, four hundred miles, or so. You want to go?"

"How, how much is a ticket?"

"First, or deck passage?"

"There is no second class?" Her disguise might not hold up in the open space on a boat deck.

"Sold out, up river. To Evansville…twenty dollars for deck passage, morning tea and roll and one meal a day." He squinted at her and waved a fly from his head. He was running low on patience.

"And my horse?"

"If they have room, another seven."

"How long does it take?"

"Evansville?" She nodded. "Depends on the weather, delays in loading, unloading and dredging. The river falls this time a' year. More'n likely a week, or there- abouts."

Taking a deep breath, she counted out the money before she could change her mind. She placed her wallet and her ticket safely away in her jacket. As she turned to get her horse, she saw a man in a ragged uniform untying Robin's reins.

"Ho there!" she shouted. "That's *my horse!*" Running to the hitching post she swung her knapsack and pummeled the man with all her strength. He clung to the halter trying to mount the animal, but Robin danced away. Two gentlemen travelers noted her plight and joined the fray. Horse stealing was a serious crime and few would stand idly by to see it happen. The older man applied his cane, while the younger quickly captured Robin's reins, handed them to Sarah, and gave the thief a sound punch on the jaw. Accosted by all three, the thief tore loose and ran for the woods across the road.

Breathing hard, Sarah thanked the men who had come to her aid. The younger man clapped her on the shoulder, nearly knocking her down and told her, she had put up a good fight. "I surely do appreciate your help, Gentlemen," she managed.

"If it hadn't been some po' soldier on his way home," the older man said, "we'd a' chased him down and turned him over to a constable. Jason here could a' out run him by a yard."

"My *dad*, you understand," the young man said with a grin. "We're the Mc Greuders, Suh. Glad to be of help."

"Quite right," she replied to the father. "I wouldn't press charges either, Mr. McGreuder. I'm... Morgan Kane." They shook hands, and Sarah made her grip as firm as possible. Jason was a muscular, handsome-looking fellow, Sarah noted, with shaggy brows, friendly golden eyes, and an engaging smile. *How can I keep from thinking like a woman when I am supposed to be a man?*

"Are you taking the Columbia Belle downstream," Jason asked.

"Indeed I am," she said.

"Let's have a game of cards some evening on the way," he suggested.

Bowing slightly she said, "It would be my pleasure. Gentlemen." She touched her cap, as the Mc Greuders moved away. She was glad to have had their help. Giving Robin a tug on the reins she strode toward the hamlet, she had noticed, a short distance away. It should have a small store.

Considering the trip, she *knew* she could not manage on one meal a day. For a week! She would need dried fruit, tinned crackers and whatever else, she could buy. One thing she had sorely missed on the road was a pillow. And *something* to read. She could not get by one more day without something to read.

Speculating, she smiled. Jason McGreuder is a handsome fellow. *When he said a game of cards, did he mean Patience?* That was the only card game she knew.

She had been right. There was a small store in a casual square before a cluster of houses and barns. Carefully tying Robin's reins to a hitching post, where she could keep an eye on him through the store window, she entered. On display were some yard goods, a few ready-to-wear garments, hunting and fishing gear. The storekeeper stood at a front counter. It was obvious he was able to buy goods locally, for the availability of many food items from the larger market was still limited. Most farmers in West Virginia raised their own chickens, hogs and cows, and depended upon their gardens for vegetables and fruits.

She found a feather pillow and a washcloth she could afford. She gazed longingly at the women's fine linen shifts, then moved to the men's counter and selected a string tie and a dozen large handkerchiefs. She found a bar of oatmeal soap, which she could use for washing herself and her hair. She had a bar of raw soap for her clothes.

Among the foods was a crate of apples. Sarah selected half-a-dozen Winesaps, pleased as punch. A few prunes, some paper-shell pecans, a ball of cheese and a tin of crackers met the rest of her needs, until she saw the candy. Licorice whips, horehound and taffy drew her like a bee to a flower and she paused before the glass containers just long enough for the clerk to ask what she would like.

"Four peppermint sticks and a quarter pound of taffy," she said quickly. It was a sinful indulgence, considering her diminishing funds, but the waxed paper-wrapped pieces should last on the boat. Besides, Robin would love the peppermint sticks.

At the end of the counter was a wire rack containing a few paperback almanacs, Western novels, along with two Charles Dickens books, and a single copy of *Uncle Tom's Cabin* by Harriet Beecher Stowe. The latter was exactly what she had longed to read ever since it was published, before the War. She checked the price and gratefully pressed the book to her breast. Remembering her male persona, she thumped it down on the counter with her other purchases, pulled her string bag out of her pocket and placed it beside her goods.

Full of herself, she paid for her goods and left the store; her sack barely held the acquisitions. She looked forward to her first afternoon on board the paddle wheeler, when she could find a quiet place to settle down, eat an apple, and begin her book. She was taking a riverboat trip! She was happier than she had been since leaving Fox Haven.

Stowing her things on Robin's saddle, she led him over to a mounting block and, with what had become a practiced move, stepped up, fit one foot in a stirrup and threw her leg over the horse to return to the landing. Thinking about the long trip on the boat, she urged Robin into a cantor and exercised him up and down the road for a good half-hour. When she stopped to rest, she walked him about to cool down and crop grass along the roadside. Returning to the water trough near the shipping office, she let the horse drink, and pulled a currycomb from her knapsack to groom him. The chore finished, she removed an apple from her pack and finished it down to the core, which she gave to Robin.

Four long toots of the ship's whistle from the distance galvanized the waiting crowd into a surge at the landing. Riding as close as she could, without endangering anyone, Sarah felt anticipation ripple down her arms and tingle in her stomach. The large, white paddle wheeler chugged its painfully slow way down to the landing with bright flags flying and a calliope smartly playing *Camp Town Races* from an upper deck. Having never seen such a large boat before, Sarah stood up in the stirrups to get a better view, thrilled at the thought of the trip. The two Indians stood up to see the boat, too; their dirty blankets and worn clothes tugged at her heart.

The shipping office clerk wearing a cape of importance pushed his way through the travelers and attached a restraining rope across the dock, while shouting to the travelers to make way for the passengers disembarking. With a creaking of ropes and pulleys, the wide gangplank lowered, and those arriving paraded down the ramp. A few men in beaver top hats, satin waistcoats and polished shoes stepped forth with women in colorful, bustled dresses and silk bonnets. Apparently, they had escaped the violent effects of the past four years, or superficially, they masked them bravely.

Sarah felt a flash of envy at the sight of the fine garments, she might never have. Under the present circumstance, she was unable even to wear homespun. Sighing, she told herself she did not belong in first or second class, monetarily speaking, to say nothing of her criminal background. She shut her mind to the negative thought, refusing to let it dampen her enjoyment. She held her head up and her eyes danced about the scene with curiosity.

The other arriving passengers left the boat and the shipping clerk began to board the waiting travelers. Two rough-looking men, on horseback, rode up to the two Indians standing on the dock and began forcing them to the dock edge, calling insults and laughing. The brave jumped forward to shield his wife from the horses, but the nearest rider forced him off the dock and into the river. His wife fell down and held onto a piling, as the riders' horses pranced nearer.

Appalled at what was happening, Sarah turned Robin, shouted for the crowd to make way and pushed her horse between the Indian woman and the abusive riders. "What in tarnation do you think you're doing?" She yelled at the rider, using Robin to force the bully's horse to move back from the woman.

"Lookie hyer, Pervis! We got us a pissant Injun lover," the rider shouted to his companion. "This 'un needs a bath jes' like the Redskin." With fresh enthusiasm for a new target, both men began to press her and Robin to the edge of the dock, scattering other passengers left and right to avoid being trampled by the horses.

Jason Mc Greuder must have seen her intercept the riders, for he charged through the crowd to grab the rein of the horse nearest to Robin, stopping the rider's advance. "I believe, Suh," he warned sharply, "You forget yourself. You are not about to harm this gentleman." His right hand shoved into a bulge at his hip catching the rider's attention, who jerked the reins backing his horse away from her. Meanwhile, the Indian woman regained her feet and scurried down the dock seeking her husband, who had swum ashore.

Licking her dry lips and swallowing in relief, Sarah bobbed her head and smiled down at Mr. Mc Greuder. "It seems I'm in your debt again, Sir."

"Not at all. That was decent of you, Kane. Dangerous, but admirable. I shall see you aboard, young friend," said Jason, tipping his hat. Her admiration welled as she watched him stride away to rejoin his father.

By the time she was able to board, Sarah had settled down and studied the other deck class passengers she had missed earlier. Some carried their belongings in old baskets, makeshift cloth sacks and worn carpetbags. Their demeanor was anxious and restrained, in contrast to the earlier boarders. She realized some of these travelers were refugees from the War-torn cities of the South and the East, looking for a new start, far away from their former homes. Among them could be poor souls disenfranchised, or forced to leave their homes during the War and the devastation caused by the military purges.

The lack of food and shelter caused by the plunder of food stores, crops and entire farms by military units, had left so many families homeless, those who could afford to move elsewhere were doing so. It hurt to learn many of the soldiers had come close to starving without enough food acquired from the countryside. Some men in the militia had resorted to selling parts of their uniforms to acquire food. On the boat ramp, the crowd contained a few former soldiers in partial uniforms. Several of the women boarding wore widow's weeds and some men had black armbands. Even the accompanying children appeared subdued, hardly managing a playful antic. No wonder these people had not interfered with the abuse of the Indians, she thought; many of them lacked the energy or strength to help.

She was fortunate to have had a life of comfort and freedom from want during the War years. Many of her fellow travelers had not. Whatever her lack of love at Fox Haven, she had not seen the ravages of the conflict and its accompanying devastation on their remote farm. How little she knew about what some of the passengers and members of the militia had endured. She reminded herself, travel was educational; an old Biblical saying from Ecclesiastes came to mind: "He that increaseth knowledge... increaseth sorrow."

Chapter 13

Winston Comes to Court

EMERALD WAS SO excited her hands trembled as she pulled the strings of her corselet. Winnie was coming to see her, when she had almost given up hope. It was high time they got on with courting, before her father began to look for a suitor in some other direction. With Sarah safely out of the way, she felt her competition in the entire county was nil. Besides, Winnie *wanted* her and she knew it. With just a little luck, she would have him wrapped up in lace and orange blossoms before he knew what happened.

She donned the thinnest petticoat she owned, without a hoop, and slipped a voile dress over her head for the slimming effect of the sheer material. Her lace camisole peaked out of the décolletage of her gown, which she opened as low as she dared. She decided, wickedly, to leave the bustle off to increase the diaphanous lines of her dress. Running a green velvet ribbon through her hair, she tied a tiny bow at the nape of her neck and let the ends hang enticingly loose. She worked an enameled gold bracelet over each wrist, decided they were too much, and took them off. Instead, she secured a drop pearl in each ear and approved the effect.

Searching in her glove drawer, she located a tiny pot of cosmetic rouge. If her mother knew she had it, she would skin her alive. She glanced down the hall and pushed her door shut. With her little finger she placed a small red daub on each cheek and her lips, and worked them in to create a warm blush and a berry glow to her lips. Finally, touching her wrists with scent, she whirled out of her room and down the stairs to stride nervously about in the parlor until Winnie arrived.

Lauree joined her and when she saw her, asked, "Emerald, where is your bustle?"

"Oh, Mama, it's too warm to wear one today." She turned away from her mother to prevent her seeing the make-up.

"I suppose that's all right, but it is a formal accessory. You look lovely, dear. I so hope---"

"I *know*!" Nervous exasperation sharpened her voice. "You will let us stroll through the garden alone, won't you, Mama?"

"Emerald! Your father's in Charleston, or he'd---"

"Pish and tush! You can't expect me to get anywhere with you hanging on our every word. Just greet Winnie and leave us alone. After all, we've practically grown up together."

"That's so. You are almost grown now, and you must be circumspect."

"I will! I promise, I will."

A carriage heard in the drive set both of them in motion. As her mother called Penne, Emma seated herself decorously on a loveseat. Winston gave his gloves and top hat to the servant and bowed to her mother who greeted him in the doorway of the room.

Entering the parlor, he made a polite bow. "Afternoon, Miss Emerald. How nice to see you."

"My pleasure, Winnie. Please join me." Emma patted the seat beside her. Winn chose a chair next to her, instead, waited for her mother to sit down, and made himself comfortable.

Her mother cleared her throat and said, "It's warm, but lovely weather we're having, wouldn't you say, Mr. Porter?"

"Indeed." He smiled and crossed his legs, which, Emma observed, were attired in beige linen and showed off his handsome, muscular legs. "We were worried about the drought last month, but with the rain, fall is definitely on the way."

"Are your parents well?"

"Very well, thank you. They're still talking about your delightful party."

She nodded. "I received a lovely note from your mother."

Emma fidgeted in her seat. *We will never get anywhere at this rate.* "Would you care for some iced tea, Winnie?"

"That would be refreshing, thank you."

Emma gave her mother an expectant glare; her parent rose abruptly, excused herself, and went to the kitchen, presumably, to have the tea made.

"My goodness, I thought you were never coming to see me, Winnie," Emma scolded.

"I told you I would, when I could." He smiled pleasantly.

Her lower lip pursed. "What's a young lady to believe whose young man thinks more of work than he does of her?"

"She might think that he has a responsibility to fulfill," he replied, rubbing the bruised knuckles of one hand.

"Um hum. You've been setting fence posts, I see." She fluttered her fan slowly, and she hoped beguilingly. He did not act like a courting man. She had expected flowers, an excuse to sit near her, at least an attempt to hold her hand. Bother! It was up to her.

Her mother returned with Penne carrying a tray of iced tea and wafers. "Here we are. Something cool for a warm afternoon." She indicated a parlor table for the tray, waved Penne out the door, and poured drinks for the three of them. "Winston, lemon? One lump, or two?"

"Lemon please, Mrs. Dietrich, and two lumps." He stood to help with the glasses. He took a glass of tea to Emma and with a bow offered her an iced wafer.

"Thank you, Sir," she said, dropping her fan in her lap. "We could use a butler, if you're looking for a second position."

With a snort of appreciation, he took his glass and resumed his seat. "Very refreshing, Ma'am," he said.

Her ma nodded and sipped her tea. Emma watched Winnie expectantly. When nothing followed, she asked pointedly, "Weren't you finishing a provision order, Mama?" *My mother is a dunce!*

"Oh, no. I--" Lauree paused. "Perhaps I should." She rose and left the room.

"Tell me, dear Emma," Winn began, "Do you miss Sarah? Have any of you heard from her?"

"No. Well, yes, *of course* I miss her," she edited her reply. "Still, we haven't heard a word. We hope she has come to no bad end."

"Indeed, that would be a shame. Your cousin is such a fine person."

"Yes." She examined his face carefully and changed the subject. "How, I mean, how's your tobacco?" *No farmer would want a wife who had no interest in his work.*

"We've begun our harvest." A wave of his hand dismissed the subject of crops and he finished his tea. "I seem to have forgotten what you wrote me about the incident with Sarah on the road."

She rose quickly, took Winston's glass and offered him more tea.

"No more, thank you." He bobbed his handsome red head as she placed his glass on the tray. She turned and moved toward him, she ran one hand playfully down his arm. Apparently not to be distracted, he repeated his question.

Miffed, she replied, "I said she was attacked on the road and used her whip on the vagrant to get away."

"I see."

Annoyed, she forgot exactly what she had written. *Why in heaven's name was he talking about Sarah?* He *was supposed to be courting* her. "Would you like to take a stroll in the grape arbor?" she asked. "It's on the shady side of the house."

"Very well." He stood and offered her his arm.

"Thank you," she said, tucked her hand in his elbow, and pressed it against the side of her breast. "It's so stuffy in the house in the afternoon." They walked down the hall and into the kitchen where Lauree sat at a small table. She gave her mother a warning glare, to belay her joining them, and ushered Winn out the back door.

She was enthralled with the idea of intimacy. Getting Winston alone was enough to set her blood racing. They made small talk about the rose garden and the clusters of purple grapes burgeoning on the vines. Under the leafy, vine-covered arbor, patches of sunlight and shadow played over their faces. He drew her down to a twisted vine bench and wrapped his arms about her waist. As she leaned toward him, breathing faster, she closed her eyes and pursed her lips. She felt his ardor flare as he pulled her against his chest. She parted her lips and thrust her tongue into his mouth, turning the warm kiss into one of passion.

"Oh, darling," he murmured. "You know what that does to me."

They were finally on the same page! She pressed her open mouth hard upon his, inviting his tongue inside to mate with her own. She wanted him to know, at the height of his enthrallment, he was making the only possible decision. She knew by his over-whelming physical response, he would not wait long to make her his own.

Chapter 14

Boarding Columbia Belle

AMONG THE LAST to board the paddle wheeler with Robin, Sarah was directed on the main deck of the boat to the stalls located aft. Robin followed along calmly until the boat shifted in the current and he stumbled to stay upright, whinnying in alarm. Sarah calmed him and got him into a straw-carpeted stall at one end of the row. There were only two other horses in sight. She put up the canvas strip barrier, removed his halter and took off the saddle, which she managed to haul over to a rack in one corner. Making sure he had a bucket of water, she patted his velvet nose and gave him one of the peppermint sticks she had just purchased. Making a humming noise and tossing his head Robin showed his pleasure, crunching loudly on the candy cane.

With her horse settled and her belongings stowed, Sarah ducked under the barrier and looked about the deck. The great paddle wheels at the back of the boat, dripped in the afternoon sunlight, set to take up their task at the captain's order. The smells of the river, wet vegetation, and aquatic life teased her further. As a deck passenger, she guessed she would not be able to explore the boat once it was under weigh, so she located the gangway to the next deck. Up the passage to the next level, she moved casually among strolling passengers awaiting the boat's departure.

The first compartment held the kitchens, where helpers were blackening large iron stoves and preparing food for the evening meal. Two Negro boys carried in wood and foodstuffs to be stored, leaping to obey the shouted orders of a huge cook in charge. Peeking into a second doorway she found the dining room, which held white damask covered tables, and crystal chandeliers. The opulence was delightful. An upright piano against one wall told her the diners would have entertainment. What fun it must be to dine there in formal splendor!

She found the passage to the second class cabins, where the door of one stood open. It was a tiny space with double bunks and the ceiling barely six feet high. Between the bunks, below a porthole was a small desk with a single folding chair. The next section labeled Saloon on the door held a bar and several card tables already filling up with players. Between serving drinks, the bartender with a handlebar mustache and wearing a green apron, diligently swabbed the bar.

In the next open, draped doorway she discovered a charming theater, complete with stage and red velour-covered seats. A row of footlights lit the red drapes fronting the stage, ready for the performance of a melodrama, light opera, or minstrel show. Only once had Rupert taken them to Charleston to see a play, which she remembered with pleasure. She would love to see another. Then she chastised herself. *Silly!* She was lucky even to be aboard, considering--Sarah shook her head to dispel the thought and threaded her way among passengers on the deck. Happy laughter and animated conversation evoked the tenor of holiday spirits, which incited her own, lifting the sad empathy she had felt for her deck passengers.

Taking a deep breath, she ventured up to the first class section where she saw another saloon, the ballroom, and rows of first class cabins. The parade of well-dressed passengers strolling about the deck fascinated her. Cabin boys moved busily in and out of the staterooms delivering portmanteaus, leather hatboxes, and caned valises. Sarah grimaced wryly, thinking of her old carpetbag below, tucked in the straw of Robin's stall.

It was impossible to resist the animated mood of the travelers on the upper decks. Above she could see the pilot's wheelhouse and two of the ship's officers in conversation behind glass windows. Waiters moved among the travelers with trays of drinks. Refusing a glass offered to her, Sarah returned downstairs.

After locating the combination dining and day saloon where the deck passengers would spend their time, she asked a steward about the sleeping accommodations. The short fellow with a pockmarked face simply gestured to the limited area left on the open deck. Stacks of logs lined the boat walls and empty stalls, fuel for the steam engines. Every foot of space on the boat was used. She found the limited gentlemen's and ladies' closets, wondering how in heaven's name she could keep herself clean among men in a five by eight-foot washroom. With a jolt, she noted the commode stall did not even have a door, and she beat an alarmed retreat when two burley fellows entered the water closet. Chagrined, she realized she would have to schedule her visits to the lavatory in the middle of the night.

As for sleeping, she thought she would make a pallet with Robin in his stall. Belatedly it dawned on her; she would have an exceedingly difficult time during her monthly travail. She could hardly wash out her sanitary cloths and hang them up to dry in the men's water closet.

Her only recourse would be to discard them over the side during the night. Thank heaven; she had bought the dozen men's handkerchiefs that afternoon! Washing herself and her clothes would also have to be accomplished at night. Her impersonation was growing more difficult by the second.

Returning to Robin's stall, she doubled her blanket in one corner, put her new pillow on the blanket, and rummaged through her carpetbag for her knitted shawl. Folding it neatly at one end of the pallet, she considered her preparations for the night complete. The steward had said she was responsible for keeping the stall clean, forking the soiled straw overboard and spreading fresh straw every day. She hoped she could exercise Robin, whenever they came to a landing. She remembered seeing grooms leading horses ashore after the arriving passengers had disembarked earlier. Satisfied with her plans, she fished the book and a taffy chew from her carpetbag and wandered across the deck where she found an odd corner with a seat and settled down to enjoy a good read.

The steam whistles gave two loud blasts. At the rail she watched the great steam-driven pistons force the paddle wheels to turn and pull the boat into the mid-stream current. Most of the other passengers enjoyed the drama too, hanging onto the rails, and remarking at being under way. Sarah nodded politely when spoken to. She turned away to get back to her book, but a young lady in a pink crepe-de-chine dress paused in front of her and asked, "Isn't this exciting?"

Sarah bobbed her head in agreement and moved to pass when the girl asked, "Is this your first trip on a paddle wheeler?"

"Well, yes it is."

"I'm Mary Jean Dillon. Glad to make your acquaintance." Sarah gave her a small bow.

"Um, I'm Morgan Kane, at your service." She barely touched the other's hand.

Mary Jean blushed, shook her long, blonde braid, and fluttered a pretty fan. "How far are you going, Mr. Kane?"

"To Evansville." Sarah touched her cap and took another step.

Mary Jean tucked her hand in Sarah's elbow, smiled beguilingly and said, "That must be farther west. I'm going to Louisville, so we'll have lots of time to get acquainted. Shall we take a turn about the deck?"

Before Sarah could muster a reply, a formidable dowager with an angry demeanor bore down upon them and grabbed the girl's arm. "Miss Mary Jean, I've been looking everywhere for you! Your mother is waiting. Come upstairs at once."

The young woman had no alternative. She said crossly, "The stairs are called *ladders*," and gave Sarah a regretful glance, as she was spirited up the steps.

It dawned belatedly on Sarah, the forward young woman, thought *she* was a young man and wanted to form an attachment. *How naïve*; she scolded herself for failing to consider, she might, indeed be attractive to both sexes

A handheld gong sounded to announce the supper sitting. Sarah tucked her book under her arm and joined the crowd entering the dining hall. Long benches scraped noisily on the deck boards as passengers filled them rapidly to sit at wooden plank tables. The pungent odors of cabbage, stewed mutton and onions filled the air. She climbed into an opening on a bench between a man and woman already tucking into their food. Baskets of cut loaves had been passed, and Sarah managed to get the end piece of one. Her utensils consisted of a spoon with no napkin in sight. The stew was not bad, except for the layer of grease on top and a heavy hand on the onion.

Despite a good deal of noisy conversation among the diners, no one bothered her with more than an "Evening, Suh," or a murmured, "How do?" Remembering her recent decision, she did not converse with anyone, attended her bowl of stew, and departed as quickly as possible.

She leaned on the railing watching the paddle wheels do their work and scanned the riverside of trees, small docks, and distant farmhouses as they passed by. One hamlet had a white church spire among the roofs, and she barely heard the distant bell, calling parishioners to the evening service. Piano music drifted down from an upper deck and Sarah was mellow with her first peaceful evening since leaving Fox Haven. It felt so good to be off her horse and making miles on the trip west without her own effort. Unconsciously she rubbed her backside, still sore from riding Robin. A fleeting thought of the scenes she'd experienced before her departure from the farm touched her sadly; it occurred to her, she'd felt restrained and unhappy for a long time. She forced the thought from her mind to appreciate the moment. Rotating her shoulders, the knot of anxiety in the pit of her stomach began to uncurl. She was truly on her way now and hopefully, no one could catch her.

Relief was a pleasant feeling. She had no feeling of guilt because she had bludgeoned a man, who was about to rape her cousin. She had earned her freedom. She was no longer responsible for Emerald's deportment, and she did not have to bear her uncle's sharp tongue or her aunt's indifference. Probably she would never forget the years of hoping her aunt would be affectionate, or at least sympathetic to her needs. What naiveté! Aunt Lauree had shown as much feeling for her as a fence post, had treated her more like a servant than a relative, and studiously avoided a closer relationship throughout Sarah's youth. *I would have loved her*, Sarah thought. *If only*--No, no more regrets. She was finished throwing her affection in the face of the wind.

She turned away from the railing and walked to the other side of the boat. The passengers sat in small, family groups, two young men rolled dice, and the children who were not leaning wearily against a parent, began a half-hearted game of hide and seek. On the other side of the river, the setting sun flashed beams between the leaves of the trees on the shoreline, its glow a golden path across the flowing water. She told herself *it was a symbol* of a propitious future. *Oh, yes.* That was what *had* to lie ahead, not only for herself, but also for all the other homeless refugees on the boat.

Other passengers began to stake out areas of the deck to curl up in family groups to sleep among their few belongings. Sarah sought her own pallet in the corner of the stall, made a nest in the straw beneath her blanket, and spoke to her horse. "You just keep to your side of the stall, big boy. We'll do very well indeed." Robin flicked his ears and looked at her with his large, brown eyes. He made a low rumble in his chest and soon fell asleep standing in the front of the stall. The sound of distant music, the hum of the steam engine, the churn of the pistons, and the splash of the paddle wheels lulled Sarah to sleep.

Chapter 15

Ellsworth's Return

THE SUN WAS setting as the wagon with one last soldier pulled up in the curved drive in front of the farm manor. From the stable, Ben heard the wagon arrive and ran out to help a guest, when he saw Ellsworth. "Master Ellsworth, Suh! Welcome home, Master Ellsworth! Welcome home." The young man of seventeen, in worn livery, tried to assist Ellsworth and his crude crutches. With one leg amputated at the knee, pale and trembling, Worth hopped around on one foot and clutched the wagon for support.

"Here, Suh," said Ben putting an arm around the soldier. "Jest lean on me."

"I'm all right!" Ellsworth exclaimed. "You bring my kit, Ben." He managed to support himself on the crutches, thank the driver, and navigate the front steps. The door burst open, his mother screamed and rushed forth to envelope him, her eyes full of happy tears.

Ellsworth withstood the emotion for a minute, and then gently extricated himself from his mother's arms. "I'm home, Mama. I'm all right." She covered her mouth with her handkerchief and weeping, urged him inside the house. Smiling broadly, Ben carried the knapsack into the house.

Emerald apparently heard the commotion and appeared at the top of the stairs calling, "Mother, what is--" He looked up at her with a faint grin. She screamed, "Worth!" and flew down the stairs to fling herself at him.

"All right! Give a fellow a break." He hopped unsteadily on one leg. Emerald let go of him and stared down at the missing lower limb, her face in shock. Ellsworth bent forward to pick up one crutch, and stumped into the parlor where he sank into a chair and began unbuttoning his uniform jacket.

"Get your father, Emerald," said his mother, wiping her eyes.

Rupert strode into the parlor. "Son? I can't believe --" He stopped abruptly on seeing the crutch leaning against the davenport. Ellsworth shut his eyes at the sight of his pa's pained expression. Then watched him collect himself and move forward with his hand extended. "Welcome home, Son! We're very glad to have you home!"

Ellsworth gritted his teeth, and with determination shook his father's hand. "Thank you, Sir. I'm proud to be back."

Hovering, his mother asked if he would like something to drink. "Tea? Lemonade?"

"Don't be foolish, woman," said his pa. "We need whiskey to celebrate this occasion." He went to the liquor cabinet against the wall in the adjacent dining room, poured the drinks, with port for the women, and brought the glasses and decanter on a silver tray to the parlor.

Emerald's eyes glistened with tears as she stood by his side. She tossed the port down and coughed. His mother sipped hers, sitting across from him with adoring eyes.

He saw Penne peer around the doorway from the hall. "Master Ellsworth! You're home!" She cried, and rushed into the room, her hands waving in the air, when his pa stopped her with an outstretched arm.

"You forget yourself, Apennine!"

She stopped abruptly. "Yes, Suh. Pardon me." Shaking her head happily, she backed out of the room, her face full of smile. He flushed and would have stood, but his pa stood at his shoulder, drink in hand.

"To you, Sir!" said his pa, toasting him with more affection than he remembered seeing before. The liquor burned his throat and tongue bringing a temporary revival, he sorely needed. His father refilled their glasses.

Biting her fingernails, Emerald annoyed him staring at his pinned-up pants leg. Finally, she asked, "Were you in hospital all this time?"

"The past four months," he replied. "I was hit just next to the last month of the war."

"Where were you, Son?" his father asked.

Worth paused, "Andersonville."

His mother gasped and his pa blanched. Newspapers all over the country had printed a description of the Georgian prison. During the sixteen months the stockade was in use, some ten thousand men were held there on bare ground without shelter, clothing, or sanitary facilities. Overcrowding was so prevalent, the Confederates had to enlarge the facility to twenty-six and-a-half acres.

Emerald's hand pressed her mouth. His mother began quietly to weep into her handkerchief. "Where was it located?" Emma managed.

"Southern Georgia. It was hot as---" Seeing their distress, he mitigated his answer. "By the time I got there, most of the prisoners had been moved to avoid Sherman's drive toward Atlanta. I was in no shape to travel, even after the War ended, so they kept me there, 'til I was sent to a hospital."

Frowning, his pa asked, "Is that where you were operated on?"

Ellsworth grimaced as he shifted his leg. "At Andersonville? They had no medical facilities. A third of the prisoners died there, mostly of disease, dysentery and scurvy. My operation was done in a field hospital somewhere." He sighed heavily. "I don't remember." He was so tired, his voice faltered. With a buzzing in his stomach from the liquor, he gazed about the room identifying familiar furnishings. "Where is Sarah?" he asked, suddenly missing his cousin.

"We don't know," his father said, with asperity.

"What do you *mean*?"

Emerald's eyes shifted. "She disappeared."

He looked from one member of his family to the other. "*When? How? Have you looked for her?"

His father replied sharply, "Of *course* we looked for her, but she's been gone two weeks. There was no note of any kind. We believe she was kidnapped… something of the sort."

Ellsworth gripped the arms of his chair. This was not something he could take lightly. "Were her clothes missing?"

His mother shook her head. "Only a few pieces of clothing, an old shawl. Please don't fash yourself, son. If there had been foul play, we would have heard by now."

Ellsworth's agitation grew. "Who saw her last? Emma, could anyone have taken her away? What's been done? 'D you put a notice in the news?" His throat closed making his voice hoarse; he tried to shake the buzz from his head.

"That's enough, Son," his pa warned. "We'll discuss this when you're feeling better. You need to rest now." He glanced toward the hall. "All those stairs--- Fix a bed in the library, Lauree. Call Penne to take care of it, right away."

His mother left to comply. Emerald frowned as he hoisted himself from his chair, grabbed his crutch, and hobbled across the room. She followed him to the library where his mother and Penne were closing shutters, throwing pillows from the couch, and reorganizing the room. He watched Penne as he collapsed in a wing chair, utterly spent. Emerald said she would go to the kitchen for a pitcher of well water. When Penne returned to the library with bed linens, she appeared so flustered; she had difficulty making a bed on the sofa. She glanced anxiously at him before she left for the kitchen to heat water for a bath.

With difficulty, Ellsworth clomped down the hall to the kitchen and began to disrobe. Penne placed a folding screen around the tin tub with soap and towels for his bath, barely catching his gaze. She called Ben from the barn to help him undress, to remove his bandages, and to get him into the tub. Ben pushed the pile of filthy clothes under the screen.

"I'll fetch clean clothes from your room, Master Ellsworth," Penne said. She returned with them shortly. Then busied herself at the stove.

Sitting in the warm tub, Ellsworth began to relax; tears of relief slipped down his face. His hair, fingernails, and feet were filthy and he barely had the energy to scrub them clean. Penne added more hot water to the tub and washed his hair. With tears in her eyes, she saw the horrible scars from his amputation. She met his gaze and her eyes glazed in sorrow. She shook her head in grief. Ben helped him out of the tub and into clean underwear and a robe; he fell into a chair and asked Ben to replace the bandages on his stump.

"Will I bring your tray to the library, Suh, or do you wish to eat in here?" Penne asked, adding a steaming mug to a tray.

"The library, Penne, thank you." The bath and the whiskey had done their work. "I…can't stay awake much longer." He hobbled down the hall to crawl into his sofa bed.

After Ellsworth settled down for the night, Emerald joined her mother in the parlor. "How's he gonn'a manage, Mama?"

"What do you mean, Emerald?"

"How's he gonn'a ride a horse and get around the farm?"

Her mother picked up her tatting and began to work it. "I don't know. Heavens to Betsy! I'm so glad to have him home, nothing else matters. He's the same man he was before. He simply needs to rest up a while."

"Mama, he's *not* the same. He's sick. And even if he was well, he couldn't walk around on uneven ground with crutches."

"They have chairs…with wheels for his problem. They even have artificial limbs." Her ma put the tatting down in her lap and wiped her eyes again. "It's much too soon to think about all of this, Emerald." She blew her nose. "When the time comes ---"

Emma shook her head. "He couldn't use one of those chairs in the dirt, Mama, and I can't imagine him with a wooden leg. I know pa always thought Worth would take over the farm management, when he was ready to take it easy."

"Your father is an excellent farmer, Emerald. Besides, he has an overseer for the crops and the hands."

"Yes, but pa's tired of the paperwork. He said so the other day. I'd be glad to help with the books, but figuring was never my long suit."

"I know," her mother smiled. "We'll simply have to see how Ellsworth gets along. Don't ask him about the farm, until he's much better."

Pacing back and forth on the Oriental carpet, she reached a decision. "I already know the answer, Mama. Even if he could, Worth never wanted to be a farmer."

"What makes you say that?"

Hands on her hips she faced her mother. "Because, it's true. He likes to draw. He always thought he'd study architecture, be a draftsman, or something like that."

"Well I never!"

"So, what I'm saying is: even if he could manage the farm, I think he won't. Especially, now that he's handicapped." She paused in front of her mother. "But *I* want to and *I can!*"

Her mother looked up, *"A young girl run a farm?* I never heard of such a thing. Thank heaven you father is perfectly capable!"

Apennine laid her blue-striped apron on the kitchen counter, glanced at the cook dozing in a chair in the corner, and slipped down the hall to the library. Tentatively, she tapped on the door and entered the room. In the subdued light, she saw Ellsworth reclining on the couch reading a book. "Mm… Master Ellsworth."

He looked up and smiled at her. "I was beginning to fear I'd never get to see you alone." He held out a hand to her.

"Oh, Master Worth, Ah'm so sorry." She knelt beside the couch at his side.

"What's this 'master' business? Moreover, why are *you* sorry? *I'm* the sorry one." He tapped the upper thigh of his amputated limb. "Tell me how you've been, girl? Is everything all right?"

"Very well, Suh, don't you see?" She wiped tears from her cheeks with the back of her hand and reached out to touch his face.

"I've thought of you all these months, Penne; even when I was hurt and in pain, I couldn't think of anything, but getting home and seeing you." He was flirtin' with her again. When he pulled her to him and wrapped his arms about her in an embrace, she recalled everything that had happened five months before.

She glanced at the door. "Ah want to take care of you, iffen they'll let me, to make you well again. Does it hurt all the time?"

He shook his head, his eyes roamed over her face. He pressed his cheek to hers, and she inhaled the sweet scent of him. "I'm getting better now. I'll be up and about in no time."

"Praise be," she murmured. "Ah was afraid you wasn't never comin' back."

"You've put on some weight," he said, running a finger under her chin. "I'm glad. You were too thin before."

She drew back, doubtful. "You don't know? They hasn't told you?"

"Know what?"

"Ah'm having a baby." She held her breath awaiting his response. *If he got mad---*

"You are?"

She nodded, waiting.

He looked her over. "Well, that makes a difference."

"It sure do," she said, thinking of the sick mornings and the expected banishment to the quarters. Her head dropped, certain he was through with her.

"Let me understand. You're with child? Who do you think is the father?"

"*You* are. Because of what we done." She gazed at him solemnly. "Ah ain't never been wif nobody else."

"Who does the family think is the father?"

She chuckled and covered her mouth with her hand. "Cook thinks it was that share-cropper Garth who lit out a couple weeks ago."

"Is that what you told her?"

"No. Ah didn't tell her nothin'. She come up with that excuse, 'cause he left the same time she found out about me."

"Did you know him?"

She laughed. "Ah never even spoke to him. He worked in the north field. Ah only seen him up close once. The doctor took me down to the field to treat his brother's 'mpetigo."

"Forgive me, Penne." A look of wonder filled his face. "I'm getting used to the idea and I think…it's great news! It *does* change the way I feel about you. I mean to take care of you. And I want *you* to take care of *me*."

"They won't let me," she cried. "Specially, after I have the baby."

"Oh, yes they will. You'll see. You're the logical one to take care of me, Penne. I need you. With my leg, I may be able to manage the bookkeeping, but I've an excuse to avoid the farm management. I never liked farming."

The exchange had worn him out, she realized. "You have to rest now, Suh. A' right?" She helped him settle back on the couch and poured him a glass of tea.

"Thank you, dear." He grimaced. "Would you mind tending to my leg? The bandage is so tight, I can't---"

"I be glad to." She carefully unwrapped the wretched stump, removed the blood-soaked binding and dropped it in a wastebasket. She looked up with tears in her eyes. "My poor Master."

"No, no. That helps. Just apply some of the salve from that tin the doctor left. I'll be grateful."

She went to a basin on the marble tabletop, washed her hands with soap, and dried them on a clean towel.

"How did you know to do that?"

"Wash my hands? Ah used to help the doctor when he came to tend the hired hands," she said. "You don't need no more 'fection than you has already."

"You're a jewel, Penne."

She applied the salve with a clean bit of cloth and carefully wrapped the stump with a fresh bandage.

"Oh, that's much better." He gave a relieved sigh. "You do a better bandage than anyone else." She moved to plump his pillow, and he caught her hand bringing it to his lips. There was a light tap on the door and his mother entered the room.

"Apennine! What are you doing?"

She quickly withdrew her hand, her heart in her throat.

"Penne's taking care of me, Mama," said Master Worth. "She just did a first rate job of replacing my bandage. She used to help the doctor with the field hands, and she knows what to do. I won't have anyone else tend me. Do you understand?" He fell back on the pillows, exhausted.

Miss Lauree looked angry, but she sat down in a wing chair with her embroidery. "Take that with you," she said to Penne, pointed to the wastebasket and waved her from the room.

Penne closed the door softly. A delighted expression grew on her face. She almost floated to the kitchen.

Chapter 16

Nightmare on Board

SHE HEARD THE screams, saw her cousin struggling with the mangy vagrant and slammed the club down with all her strength! He hit the ground falling off Emma. Blood gushed from his head. He lay there inert as a bundle of dirty rags. Panic stricken by what she had done, she yanked Emma to her feet, grabbed the reins of the horse, threw herself over the saddle, and pulled her hysterical cousin up behind her.

"Stop screaming, Emma," she cried. "You're all right!" She wheeled the animal, kicked him into a gallop down the road to Fox Haven, holding her cousin on behind her with her free hand.

Sarah bolted upright, her mouth dry with fear. The same dream had haunted her nights since leaving her uncle's farm. God help her, she had never be able to forget that horrible scene. The straw of the stall poked through the blanket, the strong odor of horse manure and the rhythmical sound of the pistons awakened her fully. She had been on the boat headed west for two days.

Dear Lord, she thought, *sleeping with a horse has more drawbacks than I realized! Why did I not aim him in the other direction?* The animal snored softly a few feet away. Standing up, she carefully stepped around the residue and moved out onto the deck. It was a warm, clear night. The ceiling of stars affirmed it was not yet dawn.

She returned to her pallet, located the bar of lye soap, a towel, a dirty shirt and one of Ellsworth's union suits to take to the men's water closet for washing. A dim oil lamp on the wall of the compartment showed the room was empty. She quickly relieved herself, watching the door for a male entrant. That accomplished, she poured water in the small tin basin and washed every body part she could reach without removing her outer garments.

Before she could wash her hair, a small, older man with a beard entered the room and proceeded to relieve himself at the commode. *This is a first*, she thought, kept her back to him and her eyes averted. With her nerves jumping, she poured fresh water in the basin to mask the sounds the man made. She shook the bar of soap in the basin, pressed the clothes down in it and began to wash them.

"You doin' yo' own laundry in the middle of night?" The bald-headed man asked, buttoning his britches, and peering at Sarah through wire-rimmed spectacles.

"Yes, Sir," she replied without meeting his gaze. "I need a clean shirt for a, a meeting later today."

"Well, that do beat all!" He scratched his head. "I'm going on sixty years, and I've yet to wash a piece of linen. You need a woman, boy," he stated and, to Sarah's huge relief, he ambled out the door.

She released a shaky sigh, hastily finished scrubbing and rinsing the garments, and left the closet. Returning to the stall, she hung the wet shirt and towel on the straps across the entrance. Embarrassed to hang the underwear to dry where it could be seen, she hung it on a nail by her saddle on the stall wall. She got a clean shirt out of her carpetbag, dressed, and quietly walked across the deck to wait for the sunrise, gingerly stepping around sleeping passengers. It was too early to tidy up the stall, and the steward was nowhere in sight. She would feed and water Robin as soon as she could.

Goodness, it felt wonderful to be clean! Her head was still itching, but she would wash her hair when it was possible, too. She was glad to have done her washing and relieved to have managed her toilet without a problem. She stretched and yawned, relished the feel of the fresh clothes and the moist river air on her skin. No matter how long the trip took, she would never get used to smelling like a horse. Well, she was living with one, what did she expect? Knowing in time she would resume being a woman, gave her the incentive to endure the present discomforts.

She longed for more than a faint memory of her mother. What would she have thought of her daughter embarking on such an adventure? Much as she wished her alive, it was infinitely better she did not know she had a *murderess* for a daughter. *No mother in the world deserved to endure that grief.* A sharp ache of loss washed through her mind. Wistfully she *hoped* her mother would have understood.

The beginning light of dawn spread across the eastern sky behind the trees on the shore. The boat's churning wake created a rolling blanket of fog over the river and the sound of the paddlewheels drowned out the morning sounds from the shore. One by one, the other travelers began to awake. Sarah crossed the deck to fetch water for Robin. She would finish her chores and go to breakfast. Afterward, she would have the luxury of a whole day to do nothing but enjoy the trip. She had never felt so free in her entire life!

After tea, Sarah decided to write Winn, to tell him what had occurred before her departure and where she was going. She took her pencil and tablet and went into the day room to use a table. *How to begin was the problem.* Several men starting a card game were at one table, a mother with two small children was reading to them from a Bible at another, a woman across from her was tatting a chain of edging.

A baby in a basket fussed, but *his* mother was too busy to tend him, as she tried to control three boys who were wrestling and playing tag among the tables and benches. Under ordinary circumstances, Sarah would have offered to hold the harried mother's baby, or shoo the older children back to the deck to play. Because she felt neither action suitable for a 'young man', she postponed her letter and returned to the deck.

In the corner she had located earlier, she opened her book to read another chapter. She no sooner sat down, than a passenger approached. She looked up to see Jason McGreuder before her, shaking his finger.

"You, Suh, are one difficult fellow to find!"

"Ah… Mr. McGreuder, good morning." She stood and gave him a modest bow.

Jason doffed his hat and said, "It's Jason. Do you know how I found you?" Sarah shook her head. "Your horse." He was pleased with himself. "I knew you'd have to come down here to tend your horse."

"How clever," she replied and, to be honest added, "As a matter of fact, second class was sold out, so I had to take steerage." Jason McGreuder was as handsome and charming as she remembered: his warm, golden eyes glinted with life and his blonde hair glistened in the sunlight. *Oh, my.* She responded to him with a pleasant tingle.

Jason took her arm. "I see. Well, come along, if you will. Join me for some coffee in the saloon above. I'm anxious to discuss your plans and to see what you think of the trip." For the first time she noticed, he had a slight limp. He steered her up the ladder, on the upper deck, and led her to a spacious dayroom. Beckoning to a waiter for menus he said, "I'm sure you've had breakfast, but we men can always enjoy a second one."

Having had only the roll and a cup of weak tea since the night before, Sarah was ravenous. "Coffee? They actually serve coffee? I haven't had a cup since before the War."

"Really? It's time to change that." Jason ordered coffee, a bowl of fruit and sweet muffins. "Now, Mr. Kane ---"

"Morgan, please."

"Yes, Suh. Tell me, is this the first time for you to see Ohio?"

"Indeed, and Kentucky, as well. They are such beau--handsome States, different from our West Virginia hill country. Those fertile fields along the river must be large farms. I've seen some awesome mansions on the properties above the cliffs."

Jason nodded. "The riverboat captains built some of those homes in the early part of the century. There are a number of them on either side of the Cincinnati landing."

"I'd like to visit one sometime." Her enchantment with him grew every second. To pull her eyes away from his, she examined the room. There were olive green, cushioned seats against the wall and small, walnut tables and chairs for card playing, reading, or having a conversation. A row of colored, nautical prints lined the bulkhead. The contrast to her dayroom below was striking. She laughed aloud, surprising Jason.

"Sorry," she said. "I like this lounge. It is like a home away from home. The entire boat fascinates me. You can tell, I've spent my youth on a small farm."

Their repast was served and she had to restrain herself from wolfing down everything in sight. "Oh, this is good," she said, holding her coffee cup in both hands and thoroughly enjoying the taste and fragrance.

"Try these corndodgers," Jason said, offering a plate to her. "I think Columbia Belle has one of the best chefs on the river."

"You've been on this paddle wheeler before?" She munched politely, intrigued to learn more about him.

"Oh, yes. I am working for the transcontinental railroad, the Union Pacific. Since the War, I'm on the road, or the river, most of the time."

"How exciting! Were you in the militia?"

"Yes. The cavalry…Union side. As you know, Kentucky was a border state. If we had been growers, my choice might have been different."

She looked at him knowing he referred to slavery. He was telling her he understood the Southern view. "The fighting must have been horrible." Jason blanched and looked out the window. "You were… wounded?" She suddenly felt she had been too personal. "Forgive me. I don't mean to pry."

"No, no. I was lucky. I only took a bullet in one knee." He changed the subject. "I'm fortunate to have found a position with the railroad upon my discharge. I find it challenging. In fact, I love it."

His modesty and enthusiasm were impressive. "I, I heard they were extending the railroad through southern West Virginia, but I'd no idea it was going to cross the entire country. That's a long way."

"Over three thousand miles."

She shook her head. "Really? What exactly do you do?"

"I'm a front man, in a sense. I check out towns where the stations are to be built, make arrangements for the contractors, labor, lumber, supplies, and so forth."

"What a wonderful position. You must be very capable indeed to handle such a job. Imagine traveling and seeing the country while you work." She was so intrigued, she swallowed and looked down at the bowl of fruit to hide the admiration, she knew must be evident in her eyes. "Umm, where did you go to school?"

"Philadelphia. I'm a lawyer and a purchasing agent." He smiled pleasantly. It was the first time she had met a well-educated man, who was not a farmer. Under the circumstances, it was intensely frustrating to be so attracted to him. "Enough about me," he said, "I'm interested in you and why you're headed West. Tell me ---"

"Did you have one of these peaches? They're at their peak right now." She was peeling the piece of fruit and licking the juice from her fingers to appear as masculine as possible. Seeing Jason's eyes on her she asked, "What?"

"You must come back again," he said. "I'm only sorry I didn't find you sooner."

"Me, too." He could not possibly know *how much*.

What could she tell him? She was not the young man he thought she was; she was a *murderess*. "Let's see…To answer your question, until now Charleston is the largest town I've ever seen." She gave a self-conscious laugh. "I attended a local academy for eight years, but plan to further my education, when I can. As for going west, the desire is an itch, which has to be scratched. I want to see St. Louis, the Rocky Mountains, and maybe even the Pacific Ocean."

"Good for you! But, didn't your parents oppose your leaving home so young?"

"No." She sipped her coffee, and stayed as close to the truth as possible. "I lost my parents before I was four. My aunt and uncle raised me with-- my sister, until I left home."

He finished his coffee and asked, "Is your sister close to your age, too?"

"We're twins." What a bald-faced lie! She had almost mentioned Emerald as a cousin, but caught herself. Personal questions made her uneasy about maintaining her deception.

"Do you look similar? I'd like to meet her sometime." Sarah choked on a bit of fruit, wiped her eyes and took a swallow of water to avoid answering.

Jason clapped her on the back. "All right?" She nodded.

"Where do you disembark?"

"Evansville, Indiana. Have you ever been there?

"A time, or two. It's a thriving manufacturing town and steamboat port. I think you'll find it interesting."

"I hope so. I need to find a position and a place to stay. What about you and your father?"

"My dad's disembarking at Cincinnati on his way to our farm south of there, in Bluegrass Country. I'm going on to St Louis. My office is there."

"Really, you live there? I cannot wait to see it. I kept Robin to manage the distance from Evansville to St. Louis. After I'm working and save up for the trip, of course." She laughed again, placed her napkin on the table and suddenly realized the time. "What am I thinking? Your father must wonder what's keeping you." She stood up, brushed crumbs from her lap, and held out her hand. "Thank you so much, Jason. I enjoyed the conversation *and* the breakfast, thoroughly."

"Perhaps some cards later?" He signed the bill and walked her to the door.

"I'd like that. Thank you." She strode across the deck to return to steerage. She paused at the stair railing, looked back and gave Jason a friendly salute. Lord, he was an intriguing man! Not handsome, compared to Anton Simms, who had been the figure of her daydreams the past year. *No!* Stop. She had no right even to *think* about a man, let alone one who thought she was a *male.* Impersonating a man was one thing, but it did not affect her female heart. She could not help the delicious warm glow just beneath her breast, could she? She licked the last taste of peach from her lip. Oh, my! What a lovely breakfast. It had been an absolutely perfect morning.

Chapter 17

Winston's Proposal

EXPELLING A NERVOUS breath, Winston Porter pulled the doorbell at Fox Haven and was received by Penne. "Winston Porter to see Squire Rupert," he said formally and handed his gloves and top hat to the maid.

"Yas, Sur." She curtsied. "Jes' make yourself to home in the parlor." She placed his hat on the hall table. He gazed about the room to feel comfortable with its familiar furnishings. *I hope to God I know what I am about to do!* He took a seat in a balloon-backed armchair, flexing his fingers. Rupert joined him shortly. Winn stood.

"Ah, Winston, good to see you," Mr. Dietrich said, and shook hands with him. "How's the harvest coming?"

He nodded. "Fine, fine. The tobacco's curing nicely. And yours?"

"We've been short a hand or two, but we've finished picking." Rupert paused a minute. "May I offer you some refreshment, whiskey, or---"

"No, not just yet, Sir." He moistened his lips. "I've come on a particular errand, Mr. Dietrich," he blurted. "I...I've come to ask for Emerald's hand in marriage." The blood rushed to his face. Rupert's eyes

widened, he gestured and they sat down. Winn wondered if the request
came too soon, but Dietrich did not appear surprised.

"Well now, Winston. This requires some consideration." His
mouth turned shrewd and his lips tightened "Did your father tell you
of our discussion?"

"Yes, Sir." *So, why are we hedging about?*

"Hmm." Rupert's chin rose empirically. "First of all, can you
provide for Emerald in the same manner with which she has grown
up?" Winn was nailed by a steely glare.

The current total of his bank account flashed through Winston's
mind. Deploring that reality, his throat tightened. His answer was a
hoarse croak. "Cer-- Certainly, Sir."

"Humph." The squire was enjoying his role of paternal
intimidation. "And you're positive that's what Emerald wants, too?"

There he was on safe ground. "Indeed, I am. Yes, Sir!"

Dietrich leaned forward in his chair; his arms folded; his gaze
hard. "Do you have any question what-so-ever regarding how I would
expect you to treat my daughter in marriage?"

Taken aback, he replied, "Absolutely not!"

"Because if you do, now's the time to spit it out. I assure you that
any problem, any mistreatment would be addressed at once!" He
pointed a finger at him. "Do you understand?"

Winn jumped up. "Sir, I am a gentleman! I would no more abuse
Miss Emerald than..." he searched for a comparison, "than I would
abandon my parents!"

"I thought as much. Your father told you about the dowry?"

Winn swallowed his gorge, but his eyes flashed in anger. "Yes, Sir!"

"And you found it satisfactory?"

"More than fair."

"We've one small problem, now that Ellsworth has returned." Dietrich laced his fingers and rested his chin upon them. "Emerald feels *she* should be the one to manage our farm. What do you think of that?"

Winn was surprised, but on second thought, it was exactly like Emma. "What does *Worth* think of it?"

"He's not yet well enough to discuss business," Rupert said with a dismissive wave of one hand. "I'm sure he'll be able to manage the accounts soon, but the doctor fears outside work may prove too much for him. We just don't know."

Winn sat down. "And you, Sir?"

Rupert looked at his clinched hands, grimaced, and in a lower voice said, "I tell you this in confidence. I am afraid Doctor Anderson said I have developed a heart problem in the past two years. I haven't mentioned it to the family. How-some-ever, Anderson feels I'm not able to manage the property much longer, alone." He muttered an oath.

"I see." The entire picture began to fall into place. Intent on saving Dietrich more embarrassment, he added, "If I could work with Emma, Worth *and* you, Sir, perhaps---"

"Yesss," Rupert nodded. "That's exactly what I wanted to know. I'd never let Fox Haven go out of the family, under *any* circumstance!"

"No, no. Of course *not*." Winn's feelings had ricocheted up, down, and sideways ranging from anxiety to anger during the interview. Now he relaxed confidently. Farming was his life. He knew what to expect.

Rupert stood, smiling. "Then, it's settled. I'll be proud to call you 'Son'." He extended his hand.

Winn rose and shook his future father-in-law's hand, relieved no end. "Thank you, Squire. I promise to take good care of your daughter."

"Just how soon will you have the banns read?"

Winn had not discussed the announcement with Emma. He smothered a smile. "At Emerald's convenience."

Rupert breathed a great sigh. "This calls for a whiskey, my boy!" He went to the dining room sideboard to pour the drinks.

Chapter 18

Kid's Arrival

SARAH HAD GIVEN Robin a thorough workout near the river landing below Cincinnati and let him fill his belly with fresh grass, before returning to the paddle wheeler to resume her journey. It was the first two-hour docking of the three days she had been on board and a relief to get ashore for some exercise. She led Robin up the ramp and around to his stall aft on the main deck. Surprised at the sight of a dirty, young boy fast asleep in the back of Robin's stall, she yelped in consternation. Dropping the reigns, she waded through the straw to the interloper and shook him by the shoulder. "*Who* are you? What are you doing in my stall?"

Aroused, the child threw up both arms to shield himself and shrank away from her. "Don' hit me, please, Sir," he cried and curled in a ball, covering his head with his arms.

Sarah drew back, saying brusquely, "I'm not going to hurt you, but what're you doing here?" His bare feet and filthy clothing labeled him a refugee, or a run-away. "Where did you come from?"

"No one seen me come on," he cried. "I don' know where it was. I was tired an' hungry, n' I had to go somewheres else." He pressed back against the bulkhead, his large blue eyes on her.

"Where are your folks…your family?" Much as her heart went out to the child, she knew he belonged to someone, somewhere.

"I ain't got none. My pa went off to fight and never come back. I don't remember no ma; I never had none." He trembled, apparently still expecting blows.

"What's your name," she asked. "Where do you live?"

His shoulders straightened slightly. "Kid. They calls me Kid. I live on a mountain in the woods."

"What State?"

"State?"

The backwoods accent gave her a clue. "Kentucky?"

"Kentuck'? Sure."

"How old are you? When's your birthday?"

"I don' know. I never had no birfday."

Good lord! He looked about eight years old, but was so thin and undernourished, he could be ten. What was to be done with him? She eyed her knapsack and realized it had been opened. Picking it up, she checked the contents. Food was missing. "So, you're a thief?"

"I…I was hongry." Tears welled and streaked down his face. "I didn' mess wif nuffin' else. Honest. I borr'ied four crackers 'n part of an apple."

Chagrined, she shook her head. A more abject child she had never seen. "Never mind. I wouldn't expect you to starve." She pulled Robin into the stall and removed his saddle. *What was to become of the child?*

"I kin do that." Kid offered. "Is this yore horse?" He leapt up, took the saddle from her, staggered, but lugged it over to the rack on the wall. He wiped his sleeve across his nose and started to rub the horse down with hands-full of straw. Robin looked at the boy and gave a low rumble.

Just when I thought everything was getting better, Sarah mused. The steam whistle shrieked three times, the huge paddle wheels creaked and groaned as the great, steel pistons began their rotating crawl to pull the boat into the current. The boy's mouth flew open and he grabbed the edge of the stall for support, obviously alarmed by the movement and noise.

He must have come aboard at Cincinnati, she reasoned. Apparently, he had never been on a boat before. "It's all right," she told him calmly. "We're under way. Do you want to watch the paddle wheels in action?"

He shook his head. "No, Sir!"

Scared. Something had to be done. She could not simply take him along. For one thing, he needed food and clothes. She barely had enough food and money to last until they docked and she found work. She had to see the steward. "I'll be back," she said. "Wait here for me." However, he released the bulkhead and ducked under the strap to follow her across the deck, seemingly afraid to let her out of his sight.

Finding the steward in a gangway having a smoke, she asked him about the boy's passage. She reluctantly handed over another five dollars of her diminishing finances and returned to the stall, Kid close on her heels. "I've paid for your passage as far as Evansville," she said. "That's all I can offer you."

He stopped abruptly and grabbed her arm, his legs apart to keep his balance as the boat eased into the current. "You did? You paid money for me? They ain't gonna' th'ow me in the river?"

What had she gotten into? "Not now," she said, to keep him on edge. If she were to be responsible for him on the boat, she had to be certain she could manage. A slow grin spread across his face. She could see the possibility of a handsome boy under the grime. She knew what had to be done first. "You can't stay on the boat the way you are," she said, and fished the bar of soap and the towel out of her carpetbag. "I'll show you the water closet, and I want you to go in there, and bathe yourself from head to foot."

"What??" He looked at the soap as if it were a snake.

Just what I was afraid of. Heaving a sigh of resignation, she said, "Come with me," grabbed him by one wrist and drew him around to the lavatory. The W.C. offered only a stall and drain with a bucket overhead on a swivel bracket. Turning on spigots to fill the bucket, she pushed the boy un-ceremoniously into the shower stall, pulled the chain and doused him with water. Yelling and fighting her, Kid tried to escape, but only managed to get her as wet as himself.

A passenger turned from the toilet stall, buttoned his trousers and laughed at the scene. "That's right, Sonny, give 'im thunder! Who wants to be clean?" Highly amused at his own humor he left the closet.

"Shut your eyes!" Sarah yelled. Then, scrubbing the boy's head with the soap, she methodically washed him down, despite his screams and gyrations. She applied a bristle brush to his clothing, sluiced all, and refilled the bucket. *If this is what it is like to be a mother, I'm not ready!* "Now you wash your britches and legs," she said firmly, toweling off her own wet arms. "Or must I do them for you, too?"

"I kin do it," he sputtered and grabbed the soap and brush from her hands. He glared at her, but he did a fair job of scrubbing down the rest of his body and pants.

"Not bad," she told him, and refilled the bucket two more times to rinse the soap from him. "Now," she said, "take off your shirt and wring it out." When he finally quit objecting and removed his shirt, she winced at the red welts across his back. His hands were too small to get the water out of the shirt, so she took it from him and wrung it out. She toweled his hair, surprised to see he was blonde. Then, wrapping the towel about him, she told him to remove his pants.

"No, I *won't!* Yow!" She grabbed his pants to pull them down, but he wouldn't give up, until he realized, there was no way around her. He grabbed the towel when she jerked the pants free.

As she wrung out the garment she saw more welts on his buttocks and legs. *Poor Kid.* Her heart ached to think of what he had endured. At least living at Fox Haven, she had never been physically abused. *I bet you have never even seen a piece of underclothing.* "You'll have to put your pants on wet, and wear the towel until your shirt dries."

She hurried him out and back to the stall. After blotting the boy's shirt in her towel, she hung it on the stall straps and told him to sit down on the pallet. Still glaring at her, he did as told. He squeezed his eyes tight, when she applied a comb to his damp hair to work it into a braid. "You're not a bad looking gentleman," she remarked, and tied the braid with a piece of string.

"I ain't no genta'mun," he replied. "I got no shoes."

She smiled grimly. "None-the-less, we've made a start. Robin here," she indicated the horse, "wouldn't sleep with a dirty boy. And this is *his* stall."

The child glanced at the horse and said, "You're foolin' me," with a knowing glint in his eyes.

Sarah nodded. He was smart, which pleased her greatly. "It won't be long before your shirt dries and we'll go in to supper." Fortunately, her shirt had begun to dry, too. Otherwise, she knew her modest breast could easily give away her gender disguise.

"Food? We're gonna' eat supper?"

How long had it been? "Of course. When the sun sets and the dinner bell is struck. Why don't you stand at the rail, give your clothes a chance to dry?"

He shook his head, apparently unwilling to move to the railing. Instead, he stood at the front of the stall talking to Robin, his face alight with anticipation. "I'm gonna eat supper!" He told the horse. "Ain't that grand?"

Other deck passengers glanced their way as they passed the stall. Two countrywomen murmured to one another and looked at Kid suspiciously. A rowdy group of three children pointed at Kid, laughing at his towel-wrapped shoulders and wet pants. Kid turned his back on them and quietly talked to Robin, stroking his soft, whiskered lips.

Looking at the ragged shirt drying on the stall straps, Sarah pulled one of Worth's shirts out of her carpetbag. "Here," she said to Kid, "Try this on." Of course, the sleeves were too long, and the shoulders drooped, but with her needle and thread, she could improve the fit. Removing the shirt, she made seams across the shoulders and in each sleeve.

"I never saw a man sew before," said Kid, teasing.

Caught me, she thought. "Ah, but you've never been to sea before. All sailors take care of their clothing. Some even knit their own stockings."

"We ain't at sea, 'n you're foolin' me again." He gestured negatively.

"Didn't you ever read Moby Dick?"

When he did not answer, she looked up. He had turned away and was staring across the deck.

Second mistake, she realized. *He can't read.*

The strains of a piano tune floated down from the upper deck.

"Is that a piane?" He asked doing shuffle steps to the music.

"Yes." She shook out the shirt. It would have to do. "Here you are."

He slipped into the shirt and tied the damp towel about his hips. Looking down he stroked the cotton shirt. "Can I borry this?"

"You may keep it."

His eyes glistened and he looked up at Sarah, his face suffused with joy. "I'm beholden to you."

How long had it been since he'd had a change of clothing? She turned her head to hide her own emotion. "No," she said over her shoulder. "Now you'll have one to wear, when you wash the other."

Birds wheeling overhead drew his attention. "Look, pigeons."

"Not exactly," she said, amused. "They're sea gulls."

He laughed. "They don't know this ain't the sea, neither!"

Sarah knew she had done the right thing.

Dinner in the boat's dayroom turned out to be a trial Sarah had not anticipated. Excited, Kid pushed his way into the noisy crowd of passengers, sat at the first table he found and beckoned her to join him. By the time she sat down, he had already grabbed two large hunks of bread, and was wolfing them down, before others had reached the table. Some of the travelers at their table looked daggers at Sarah, and could be seen whispering about the two of them. She calmly put one hand over the boy's and held it still, until the breadbasket had been passed around. Bewildered, he looked up at her and saw the quick, brief shake of her head.

The passage of the stew bowl caused Kid's eyes to glow, as Sarah ladled his portion into his bowl. Picking the bowl up with both hands, the boy noisily drank the contents before she could point out the use of his spoon. Something was happening around them, Sarah felt, but did not comprehend. Kid saw the dark looks, glanced uncertainly at her, and hung his head. "Are you still hungry?" He shook his head.

"Never mind, Kid," Sarah said, patting his shoulder and whispering in his ear. "Here. Have an apple for dessert." She plucked two from a bowl and handed one to him.

"Can I save it?" he asked. "I want to give the core to Robin."

"By all means."

Across the table, a rough-looking character with a leer said, "Ah see you has acquired a little playmate."

When his meaning sank in, Sarah was incensed. "I beg your pardon, Sir! I'm simply giving Christian aid to a homeless waif!" She turned to the boy. "Let's go. I want to show you the rest of our deck." With her head high, she stood and said, "Excuse us." She shepherded the child out of the hall, striding with anger.

"What's a waif?" He asked, hurrying to keep up.

"Merely a child," she said.

"It was one fine dinner, n' I thank you."

"You're very welcome." Of course, Kid's manners needed work, but the behavior of the diners, the whispering and gasps of dismay, infuriated her. These were farmers, refugees, displaced people, and pioneers heading west. Very few of them had her education or background, yet they had drawn terrible conclusions regarding her relationship to Kid, and by implication, were critical of the boy. Obviously, this was another result of her masquerade. Nothing seemed to prepare her for the ramifications of her false identity. The wounds were as painful as those she had endured in her years with the Dietrichs. *Soldiers!* She was not responsible for every ignorant conclusion others might draw. *They could go to perdition!*

She had no choice now and Kid needed help. "To everything there is a season, and a time to every purpose under the sun." The remembered phrase from Ecclesiastes confirmed her purpose, and she mentally forgave her critics. She inhaled deeply of the warm, moist air, and more slowly led the way on their exploratory walk.

The moon had risen beyond the stern and the light spread ribbons of gold in the wake of the boat. Kid looked up and excitedly clutched her sleeve. The great wheels in action, the churning water, and the fragrance of the river vegetation were stimulating, and new enough to keep him close to her. She paused at the steps leading to the upper decks, where they could still hear the strains of music floating down from the theatre.

"It's a wonder, ain't it, Sir?" he asked. "All this happening on the river, jes' like in a fancy house."

She rolled her eyes at the remark, wondering how in heaven's name he knew about--- "Yes, Kid, it is. There is another handsome dining room, sleeping cabins, a bar and a small theater upstairs. Steps are called ladders, passageways are gangways on boats, and walls are bulkheads. We are not allowed to go on the upper decks. The top deck houses the wheelhouse, the first class cabins, and the captain of the boat."

"My!" he said. "I never thought to see nothin' like this."

"Can you go into the water closet by yourself to wash your face and hands before going to bed?" She needed to avoid the W.C. during the busy hours.

He looked up at her and nodded. "Yes, Sir. Would you wait fo' me over by the wall, er did you say, bulkhead?"

Something horrible must have happened to him in a wash room before, she concluded. "I'll be right there."

He entered the lavatory, took care of his needs and returned quickly.

"I never been this clean 'afore," he said with a grin. "It jes' may get sos I like it!" There was no question about his happily settling into the new routine.

Back in the stall with Robin, Kid promised the horse he would give him an apple core in the morning. Sarah checked on water and feed for her horse, then divided her bedding with the boy and made a pallet for him in the opposite corner from her own.

Kid stretched out on the blanket and watched her remove her shoes and jacket to settle down, too. "Ya reckon this is 'bout the most quick way to travel?"

"No," she replied. "A horse can go faster for a given length of time and there are railroads. When train engines get up steam, they can go more than twenty-five miles an hour."

"Is that so?" He shook his head. "I seen a train once, but I never been on one."

"The railroads will cover the country some day in the future. They're building another line in West Virginia now, which will go into Kentucky."

"If that don't beat all," he said, gazing at her in the fading light. "You know, you ain't told me where you're going, or why."

Sarah did not want him to know they would part in Evansville. She planned to make some arrangement for him with the authorities, once they arrived. "I did tell you our passage was paid as far as Evansville. You might say, I'm seeking my fortune."

"Hmm," he said. "Then, that's what I'm doin', too." He snuggled down and looked up at the sky. "They's a whole bushel a stars up there. When we wake up, they'll all be gone."

Tomorrow, she thought, we will have a talk about manners. And, maybe, I can begin his education. "They'll still be out there, but we can't see them. Good night, Kid." Folding her hands, she began her silent prayers.

"Night, Sir'.

Chapter 19

Old Friends Unite

WINN KNEW IT was time he spoke to Ellsworth about combining the management of the two farms, as Rupert had suggested, and he had a second reason for his visit. Because he had been busy with Emerald planning their wedding, he had not seen Worth since his return home a month before. He stood at the paneled door of the Dietrich library, reluctant to enter and see his young friend. *Coward.* In truth, he felt guilty for having returned from the War without visible wounds of his own. He mentally shook himself and knocked on the door.

The servant ushered him into the large room where the drapes were drawn, softening the light for the invalid. Ellsworth was ensconced on a sofa surrounded by pillows, looking wan. He quickly held out his hand. "Winston," he cried, "How good to see you."

Swallowing his shock at the thin, anemic appearance of his friend, Winn strode forth and greeted him heartily. "You old codger! I hear you're king of the roost around here with everyone at cluck and crow! Forgive me for taking so long to welcome you home. How *are* you, Worth?"

"Tolerably good," said Ellsworth, "considering I'm three-quarters the size I used to be." He laughed at his crude description, which allowed Winn to laugh nervously, too.

"Well now, if your brains were in your legs," improvised Winn, "We'd have something serious to worry about."

"True," Ellsworth said. He seemed grateful for a visitor. "Here," he indicated a chair, "do have a seat. I believe you know my nurse, Apennine Thomas?"

Surprised to be introduced to the black girl, Winn covered it well, and dipped his head politely. "Yes, I do." The maid smiled shyly at the introduction, but she managed a modest curtsey.

"Mint juleps, Winn?"

"Indeed, it would be refreshing on such a warm day."

"Apennine, would you be so kind?" With a nod, the girl quietly left the room.

"Now," Worth said, "I believe congratulations are in order. I understand you are to become my brother-in-law."

"Thank you. It will be my honor." Winn smiled. "In fact that's one reason for my visit." His eyes were warm with affection. "I want you to be my best man."

A wave of pain swept across Worth's face. "You know, I'd like that very much, however, it depends upon how soon I'll be on my feet… rather my *foot* again. Ha? Has Emerald set the date?"

"Oh, yes. The first of October. " He considered what could be done. "Have you tried a chair with wheels? Something to use until you've mastered a new limb." Emma had told him Worth was resisting both a chair and a wooden leg.

He shook his head. "That's not for me. Furthermore, I've never heard of a groom pushing his best man down the church aisle in a chair." He barked a false laugh at that idea.

Gazing about the room Winn had another thought. "We could have a small ceremony in here, if Emerald would agree. We've already planned the reception in the parlor."

Ellsworth blanched. "In my *bedroom?*"

Winn could see the problem. "Well, at the library end of the room." He took another tack. "Are you getting out-of-doors?"

"It's been too warm and, as you see, I'm immobile."

A new pair of crutches leaned against the sofa, but Winn recognized an excuse when he heard one. He would have to shake things up a bit. "We'll address the subject later, young man. Meanwhile, get your dress coat brushed and ready. I'll not take 'no' for an answer."

Apennine returned with a tray of cheese, crackers and the drinks. She served Winston, handed him a napkin and took the other to Worth. Then she moved to the end of the library where she began to read a book, which also surprised Winn. Most Negroes could not read.

Both men savored their drinks for a few moments. "Forgive me, Winn, but I have to ask, are you certain you want to marry Emmy? Somehow, I always thought you fancied Sarah."

Winn was aware of the other's scrutiny and, to his chagrin, felt himself blush. "I was…I mean I'm fond of both girls; however, Emerald and I have a very strong attraction to one another."

Ellsworth said, "She's my sister and I love her, but she's far from perfect."

Winston smiled. "Ah, but I'm perfect enough for both of us," and he struck a sophisticated pose. "Have any of you heard from Sarah since she left?"

"No. No, I'm sorry to say. I cannot imagine what happened to her. If I had been here, perhaps I could have, I don't know. I miss her. She was so sweet and considerate of other people. Somehow, coming home was not at all the same, without her."

At the other end of the room Winn saw the maid look up, then return to her book.

"I'm sure," he said with a pang of his own disappointment. He had told no one about Sarah's departure, or of giving her a horse. Perhaps after they heard from her-- He recalled the other reason for his visit. "I also want to ask you about the farms. Your father said you had no problem with his plans for Emerald's dowry."

"That's right." Ellsworth shifted his leg, seemingly restless.

"Very generous, Worth." Winn continued, "Tell me, how long the doctor says it will be before you can manage Fox Haven?"

Ellsworth frowned. "He doesn't know. No one does."

"Emerald believes she could handle the management with your pa, until you are able, if you do the books."

"I know." Worth sounded defeated, even indifferent. "I'm sure she could. Only, to be honest with you, Winn, I never had any interest in farming, even before my...disablement." He shrugged, lifting his eyebrows. "Besides, pa handles everything very well with our overseer. He would like me to take on the bookkeeping, but I'm in no shape to do so, now."

He does not know about his father's heart, Winn realized. "I understand." In a way.

Apennine walked across the carpet, looked down at her charge and said, "Ah'm sorry, Suh. You have to rest now."

Winston arose at once. "Thank you, Apennine. We'll finish discussing these matters later," *and others,* he thought. *He needs fresh air and sunshine.* "I want your advice on how best to combine those acres, Worth. I'll come for you tomorrow morning about ten for a short drive in my carriage."

Ellsworth's eyes darted about, seeking a way to avoid leaving his nest; however, encountering Winn's gaze of polite determination, he nodded.

"Till tomorrow, my friend," said Winn. He made a modest bow and quickly left the room, before Ellsworth could find an excuse.

Chapter 20

Emerald's Wedding

APENNINE LOOKED DOWN admiring her new, black dress and starched white apron as she stood at the parlor doorway to the hall. She nodded to the musicians to begin. The strains of the wedding march from a harp, violin and piano echoed through the room, the entry and the stairwell. Proud and smiling, Miss Emerald, beautiful in a white voile dress with hand-embroidered lilies of the valley, came down the stairs. Penne beamed.

The guests and family standing in the hallway looked up and clapped for the bride. Master Rupert bowed as Miss Emerald reached the floor. He handed her a bouquet of white roses and steph-ano-tis, *a new flower to her,* and offered his arm to take the bride and the immediate families to the library. *I wish I could a' had a wedding,* Penne thought, then scolded herself for such foolishness. She had seen a wedding once in the quarters, but it was nothing like this one. This was society!

Directing the guests back to the parlor, Penne made sure everyone was comfortable to wait for the family ceremony in the library to end. When she checked the serving table to be certain everything was ready for the reception, she overheard a conversation between two of the guests.

"Isn't she a lovely bride?" said Miss Agnes.

Miss Marian agreed. "She's so slender. I wonder what secret she's keeping from us." Penne had seen the young friends before and smiled. Miss Emerald had practically starved to lose weight two months before the wedding.

Miss Agnes chuckled and hid her mouth with her fan. "Be a lady, Marian. Your green eyes are glittering."

"You have to admit, the pickings are getting lean. We must have lost half a dozen eligible bachelors to the War from this county alone."

Thank God one of 'em wasn't Master Worth, thought Penne.

Miss Agnes nodded. "I was hoping to see Anton Simms, but something must have kept him elsewhere. I hope he comes."

"Poor Ellsworth," said Miss Marian. "He's confined to a chair, I hear. I always liked that young man."

That won't do you no good. Penne was pleased as punch.

"Have you heard anything more about what happened to Sarah?" Miss Agnes asked.

"Not a word."

Penne frowned thinking she was the last one at Fox Haven to see Miss Sarah. *God help me, if anyone ever finds out. Miss Emerald would skin me alive.*

The brief ceremony in the library ended, the musicians began something they called the recess-on--al, and the family returned to the parlor, smiling and nodding to the guests, who stood, clapping for the bride and groom. Red in the face, Master Worth entered the parlor in his wheelchair. He had been unable to go to the church. It was the first time, since his return, for him to come among so many people. Penne moved to help him, but Master Winston, smiling, pushed Worth about the room. Miss Lauree, pretty in a gray lace and silk gown, greeted the visitors, but Penne saw, she kept one eye on Master Ellsworth all the time.

Penne began to circle the room serving champagne to the guests. Master Rupert took Mr. and Mrs. Porter into the dining room, where Ben gave them some wine at the sideboard.

Mrs. Porter's eyes followed *her* son, too, as he moved about the room. Penne had overheard that his folks had urged the marriage to get the bride's acreage into their family farm. Penne had wondered about the marriage after hearing, Worth thought the groom had feelings for Miss *Sarah*. All that was forgotten now, seeing him with Miss Emerald. He was such a happy, fine-lookin' fella. 'T was enough thinkin' for a while. She had to watch her serving.

Emerald could not help sashaying a bit, knowing she had secured one of the most eligible bachelors in the county. She watched Winnie carrying out his duties as a host, smiling all the while. They had postponed their honeymoon until after the tobacco auction, but she could not wait for tonight. It had been torture to keep all those strong, intimate urges under control until society was satisfied. She was excited thinking of what the wedding night might include. She would don her new ribbon and lace nightgown, recline on the counterpane in her bedroom, waiting for Winnie. She was peeved that her mama had not told her what would happen. Except, she and her ma had never talked about personal things. Thank heaven, Winnie was a gentleman; he would tell her what she needed to know. Just a few more hours.

The cake? Apennine approached Emerald asking when it was to be cut and served. Emma glanced up to draw Winnie to her side for the customary toasts. He intercepted her nod, pushed Ellsworth's chair to a corner of the large refreshment table, and joined her. The table was gorgeous with an ice sculpture of two doves on a mountain of ice with flowers from their garden. They had kept the ice sculpture covered with tow sacks in the food cellar behind the house. Worth tapped a fork on his goblet and raised it in the first toast to her and Winnie.

After the ceremonies were completed, the bride and groom returned to the library to have their photographs taken. Her heart racing, Emerald could not keep her hands off Winnie; she swept his hair from his forehead, adjusted the boutonnière in his lapel, and clasped one of his hands in her own, while the photographer waited. The short, fussy fellow corrected them, ducked under his camera cloth, reappeared, hands waving, and positioned her head again.

Whispering, Winnie reminded her of the coming evening, causing her to blush, giggle, and duck her head. The photographer's eyes rolled to the ceiling. He once more arranged her dress and this time, he secured her head in an iron clamp. After two more poses, he finally released them.

Walking through the dining room, Emerald appraised the table full of wedding gifts on display. Silver compotes, crystal epergnes, an egg dish with attached spoons, cut glass, covered butter and cheese dishes twinkled from candles glowing on the crystal chandelier above the largess. "Can you believe all of this?" she asked Winn. "We'll have to spend the next three years entertaining to say thanks."

"Such pieces are not back on the market yet. These gifts must be family treasures," he said. "Everyone has been very generous."

"No doubt," Emerald replied, as they returned to the reception underway in the parlor. "More champagne, darling?"

"Yes, sweetheart. I want to make a private toast to my bride." They went to the refreshment table for two glasses of champagne. He whispered the toast in her ear: mentioning her rosebud breast and fulsome thighs, which he planned to ravish later. She was so excited she could barely sip her wine. She felt the blood rush to her face.

At the buffet, her pa's hand shook as he raised his glass and spilled wine on one of the guests. Drat, he has imbibed too much champagne! When his glass dropped to the floor, Emma exhaled in disgust. Bending over to pick up the glass, her pa fell over on the flowered carpet and, as if cut down by an unseen hand, struck his head on the corner of the sideboard. Her mother screamed and rushed to his side, while curious guests formed a ring around him, urging him to rise.

Winston immediately took charge, saw blood gushing from her pa's head, and sent for a doctor. He then lifted her pa to a sitting position, placed a napkin on his head wound and, with the help of Ben, carried her father up the stairs. Her mother called for Penne to bring a wet cloth for her pa, before she hurried upstairs, too.

Stunned by the developing events, Emma watched the guests depart. Worth moved to bid them goodbye at the front door. She told the musicians to stop playing. Penne returned, folded the chairs, and put the parlor back in order. On the refreshment table, the ice sculpture continued to melt in the November heat; remnants of the doves became mere bumps on the sinking mountain. The cake decorated with rosebuds had not been served. *All the careful planning gone for nothing*, Emma stewed, and poured herself another glass of champagne.

Ellsworth's Doctor Price arrived with his black bag and she took him upstairs to her pa's room. In the hallway, Winston caught her hand, telling her not to worry. "But our reception, Winnie. It was ruined," she cried. Her mother stood sobbing into her handkerchief with the senior Porters consoling her.

When the Doctor finished his examination of her pa and saw her mother retired, he proceeded downstairs, followed by the rest. Ellsworth wheeled his chair up to the doctor.

"Sir?"

"He's resting comfortably at the moment. I have sewn up the cut on his temple, but I fear he's had a stroke and may be in a coma for some time. You already know his heart is in a weakened condition. He has to cut back on work, alcohol and cigars. He must take life easy."

Emma glanced meaningfully at Worth and said, "I understand, Doctor. Will he overcome... I mean---"

The doctor sighed. "He's only middle-aged. He should get better. I gave your mother some laudanum, so she could rest." He turned back to Worth. "How have *you* been, son? You look like you've gained a little weight."

"I have. Penne takes good care of me and Winn sees that I exercise every day."

"Good. Fine. I hope you don't find that chair the nuisance you expected."

"No, sir. It's giving me some independence."

"For the time being. We'll measure you for a new limb on my next visit."

Ellsworth winced. "I don't know about that. Would you get the doctor's hat from the closet, Penne?"

"Yes, Suh."

"I've left some pills for your father on his dresser," the doctor told Emerald. "Be sure he takes them three times a day and follows the diet I've given your mother. Doctor Anderson will want to see him tomorrow afternoon. He was away in Charleston today."

Emma sighed heavily. "Thank you, doctor."

The doctor turned to Winnie. "My best wishes to the bride and groom," he said, gave them a courtly bow, retrieved his hat from Penne, and departed.

Emma's new in-laws kissed her and Winnie and left, too. Subdued, she, Winnie, and Worth sat down in the parlor. Penne served each of them another glass of champagne and retired to the kitchen.

"You never told me pa had heart trouble," Emerald began.

"I had no idea," her brother said.

"Try not to worry," Winston said. "We'll see what Dr. Anderson says tomorrow. That is soon enough to be concerned about the rest. Your father is a good manager. I'm sure everything is in order on the farm."

Laying her bouquet on a table, Emerald finished her champagne and wandered casually across the room for another glass. She was peeved that her pa's attack had ruined her reception, until she remembered the evening ahead. Looking over her glass at Winnie, she ran her eyes up and down his figure, letting her imagination have full sway. After all, he was hers now and she could think of him any way she liked, without fearing it was a sin. With a foxy moue, she ran her tongue around her lips and lapped the champagne sensually.

Winston looked at his new brother-in-law. "Would you like to rest for a while, Worth? There's nothing else to be done at the moment, unless there is something you'd have me do."

"Yes, thank you. Let me see if I can maneuver this chariot down the hall to my room. Emma, would you ask Penne to attend me?" He pushed the wheels of the chair to clear the carpet, determined to handle it on his own.

"Of course." She set down her glass, looped the train of her dress, and followed him to the doorway. She would have a snack in the kitchen and a lie-down herself. "I'll be back down in a bit, Winnie," she said. "Make yourself at home."

Ellsworth paused and looked back. "I don't know what we'd have done without you, Winn. I'm deeply grateful."

Winn turned his head. "Nonsense. We're all family now."

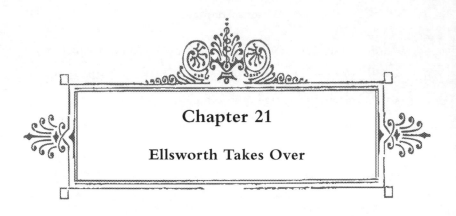

Chapter 21

Ellsworth Takes Over

ELLSWORTH HAD NOT slept well for three nights, worrying about his father. It was necessary to pay the field hands and house servants the first of every month; and he was already a week late. He figured out the necessary bookkeeping method and asked their overseer Pendergast to see him. While checking the books with the lanky, dark fellow in his late thirties, Ellsworth found the man's manner bruising. He made the proper notations in the books, asked about the pay for those who had missed work with illness, listed a new employee, and deleted the names from the personnel of one who had died and one who had quit the job.

"Did you say the woman having a baby wasn't paid until she returned to work?"

"That's right," Pendergast said, smirking. "Your *pa's* policy."

"How does she get by until then?"

The overseer rolled his eyes and shrugged. "That ain't *our* problem."

Thinking of Penne, Worth considered the practice unfair. "We never had slaves here at Fox Haven, but the Negroes and whites who worked for us have always been treated fairly. I know the mothers were housed, fed and cared for, when they had babies."

"In any of the Southern States, Negroes would 'a been slaves and their brats would 'a become *our* property," the man said. "But these bastards, whatever color, are housed *and* fed, so long as they parents is working h'yar. It's years before one turns a hand and pays for its' keep. *Now* the ma *and* pa, if they *is* one," he sneered, "can leave whenever they want."

Ellsworth shifted in his chair. His leg was throbbing despite the fact he had only begun his task. He saw, currently, he could not do much for workers at the bottom of the scale. Tobacco prices were up, but the increased cost of wages absorbed the overage. "We need to keep trained hands. From now on, pay these women a salary for... a month following their delivery, whether they return to work, or not."

Pendergast's fingers folded into fists; his face flushed a deep red. "You're *changing* the policy?"

"Yes." When Worth reached for the accounts book, the overseer swore under his breath. "Pardon?" He pinned the man with his eyes.

"Ah, Ah want to see Master Dietrich." The man challenged.

"I'm sure," Worth replied blandly. "We'd *all* like to see him, up and about. However, for the moment, you're stuck with me. Oh, *and* my sister. Mrs. Porter, will assume her duties assisting you with the management."

"Your *sister?*" Pendergast sputtered, outraged. "Ah've never worked with a woman in my life!"

"I'm sure you'll find she's a hard worker. I want you to teach her what she needs to know about the farm records and personnel. She'll help me manage until my father is capable again." Glancing down at the register, Ellsworth appeared not to notice the increased agitation of the overseer whose grip shredded the brim of the Panama straw hat he held in his hands.

"Let's see. That takes care of personnel," Worth continued, and opened the accounts book. "Do you have the receipts for bills due for supplies?"

"Yes, Suh. Ah takes care of the receipts and payments." Pendergast's stance: feet apart, chest up, and eyes ablaze was an affront. Worth could see the overseer was unwilling to take orders from a young, cripple who was not able to come out to the fields.

"May I see them, please?" Ellsworth held out his hand. "Until my father has returned to health, I'll handle the books and make all of the disbursements." He stared the supervisor down and was given the envelope of receipts. "I also need to see the order forms or requisitions for all supplies *before* they are ordered, or purchased." Then he added, "Oh, and finally, I want you to tender a written complaint to me of any problem with a hand. If you recommend any action for the problem, I need to have that in your report, too. I want a full report *before* any action is taken involving a worker. Do you understand?"

The overseer's mouth flew open and he leaned over the desk aggressively. "Those responsibilities has all been delegated to *me*, Master Ellsworth. Ah cain't turn them over to you and remain in control of the farm."

"*Surely* you have enough to do to manage the workers, plan the daily schedule, check on the progress in the fields, report supply deficiencies and keep me informed, as I have asked," said Worth in a bald tone that brooked no response.

The angry man inhaled and took a step back from the desk. "Master Dietrich knows my performance has been superior. Ah wants to see him, as soon as possible, to clear this matter up."

"Yes, yes. I understand your feelings." Ellsworth smiled benignly. "Change can be very upsetting. However, this is the only way I can familiarize myself with the full responsibilities of the farm, since I cannot be about, yet. We must all pitch in during this emergency. If you find you can't, please let me know. That will be all this morning. Thank you, Pendergast."

The overseer slammed his hat on his head and barreled out the door, striking his shoulder on the frame and swearing; his angry footsteps resonating across the hall to the kitchen.

Taking a deep breath, Worth reached for a handkerchief to wipe his forehead. *There is a bit more to farm bookkeeping than I realized.* He rang the hand bell on the desk for Penne to bring him something cool to drink. *One task done. Still, more to go.*

Chapter 22

Fire on Board

BECAUSE SARAH WAS more attracted to Jason each time she saw him, it was all she could do to keep from taking him into her confidence. She feared he would sense her attraction and be highly repelled, since he thought she was a male. Moreover, if she told him the truth, he would undoubtedly find the fact she had dissembled equally repugnant. Even if he were to forgive her, his resulting behavior might prove another cause for misinterpretation by other passengers. More of a conundrum, than ever. She sat on the pallet in the stall going over the situation. Once they disembarked and went their separate ways, she might never see Jason again. That painful possibility depressed her even more. How...how could she give him up? Ridiculous! She did not *have* him to give.

Kid rushed up breathing quickly from a game of stickball with some of the children. "Hey!" he shouted. "Derrick's ball went over the side. Ain't that a kick? You should a' seen his face, when he watched it bounce away in the river."

"I'm sorry," she said, brushing a fly away from her head.

"Don't fash yo'self," he said, with a wave. "I thought you was going for a stroll with Mr. McGreuder."

She was glad the boy had finally found friends on the boat. "Yes, I had planned to, but...I have a headache, and decided to stay home."

Kid let out a guffaw that she had called a horse stall home. He sobered and asked, "Anything I can do for you?"

"No, no. Thank you. I am somewhat worried about Robin," she improvised. The horse, hearing his name, turned his head in her direction. "That's all right, boy," she said. "I need to get him off this boat for a gallop before he gets weak in the legs."

"Jiminy! Can that happen?" Sarah nodded. Moving to the head of the horse Kid began to stroke him. "Would a rubdown help, do you think?"

"I'm sure, but I wouldn't want to take you from your friends."

"Aw, they'll be around when I'm done." He ducked under the straps to enter the stall and get the currycomb. He began to brush Robin with slow, steady strokes, and the horse rumbled his pleasure, deep in his chest. Kid began to whistle "Camp Town Races" in a reedy tone as he worked his way around the horse.

Sarah was forever surprised at the child's capacities and sensitivity. In her eyes, he had put on weight and lost the sickly pallor she had found alarming when he arrived. He deserved a decent home and she planned to see he had one, when they reached Evansville. The lessons proved he was bright and anxious to learn. He had a future, if she could help him on the way. "That's very nice, Kid. Thank you. Would you like to study a while, or would you rather play?"

He glanced at the children starting a game of tag on deck, and turned back to Sarah. "I don't mind. Where'd we leave off? Huck Finn was just about to leave town?"

"Yes." She reached into her bag for the book she had found in the day room. The two of them settled down in the back of the stall, Kid with a pencil and a pad, and Sarah pointing out the words to help him learn to read. The odd bit of schooling he had had in the past was helpful, or she would have had more difficulty than she bargained for. He wanted to learn, which made the effort challenging and worthwhile. In the few days they had spent at the task, he had learned his A-B-Cs and begun to know a few two and three-letter words.

"You want to write your own name?" she asked, after they had covered another chapter of the book.

"Can I?" His face lit up.

It took so little to make him happy, she thought, as she wrote "K I D" for him to copy.

His tongue between his lips, he frowned with concentration, gripping the pencil to make the letters as she had shown him. "Is that right?"

"Very good. Yes," she smiled. "Perfect."

He continued to draw the letters, sitting back and looking with pride at his accomplishment. "But, that ain't all," he said, "What about my other name?"

She looked at him. "Your Christian name?" He had led her to believe he did not know his last name. "What is it, Kid?"

"If it's the same as my pa's, it's Carter."

She caught her breath hoping she would be able to trace his family, once she knew where he was from in Kentucky. "Here it is," she said, and took the pad from him to write the name.

"That, there's a C," he said, but failed to recognize the other cursive letters, until she printed them. One by one, he copied the letters, working hard to make them just so. When he began to tire, she sent him off to play until supper.

A fine mist filtered the moonlight and wakened Sarah in the late evening. She stirred, threw her shawl over Kid and took two of their shirts and underwear to the W.C. to wash them. Robin nickered sharply as she pulled the clothing from her bag.

"What is it, boy?" She gave the horse a pat on the rump, but he turned, pulling on his halter and blowing noisily. She paused, searched the dimly lit deck for a problem and took a deep breath. Smoke? She smelled smoke! Quickly she wakened Kid. She fumbled for her shoes and jacket.

"Wha's a matter, Sir?" Kid sat up rubbing his eyes.

"Put everything in our bags, Kid, and we'll saddle Robin. I'll be right back! We may have to disembark right away."

"Dis…? You mean… get off?" Awakened fully, he quickly began to comply. She ducked under the canvas stall tape to run across the deck. Peering above, she could see smoke drifting out of the upper deck kitchen and flickers of flame at two of the windows. Somewhere there was a bell, she remembered, as adrenaline flooded her limbs: a ship's bell for landings and departures. Searching the walls and the passageway on the left, she found it and began frantically pulling the chain to awaken the deck passengers. As the sleepy travelers began to sit up and to mill about in confusion, she passed among them telling those she encountered the boat was on fire. *Where is that steward? He should be directing these people.*

The crowd noise increased as they became aware of the danger. Mothers yelled for children, men grabbed their bags and parcels and pushed their companions to the side of the boat. Urging calm, Sarah made her way back to her stall where Kid helped her saddle Robin. They were ready to go.

"It's on fire, ain't it?" Kid asked, his eyes wide with fright.

"Yes. Don't worry. We have time. They need to get the gangplank down. We have to get Robin off, too."

"But, Sir---"

"Not now, Kid. I'll see about the gangplank. You keep Robin calm. He will be too much to handle if he---I'll be right back!" She moved past the stall to the passage, and saw several men working the ropes and pulleys at the opening of the railing. Fortunately, the deck was only a few feet above the water and the fire was on the other side of the boat. The gangplank splashed down with a crash, and the men let out a cheer. Someone had remembered to let down the anchor, too.

Bells began to ring frantically and footsteps pounded on the upper decks, as the passengers above hurried out of their cabins to see what was wrong. Shouts of "Fire!" and women's screams could be heard in the melee taking place all over the boat. "Abandon ship!" stewards cried. "We can't control the fire!"

Passengers from above poured down the steps and the crowd jammed the gangplank, pushing everyone in front of them into the water. Those in the water either clung to the sides of the gangplank, or began to swim to the riverbank some fifty yards away.

Slammed against a bulkhead, Sarah had to force her way back through the tide of humanity jamming the narrow walkway. Gasping from the effort, she rounded the wall and ducked into the stall with Kid and Robin. She wiped her face and put an arm around the boy, who was shaking and breathing hard. "We have to wait, Kid. We can't take a horse into that crowd of people." Reason prevailed. "No. It is best if you dive off the side and swim ashore. I'll meet you there as soon as the crowd thins out and I can mount Robin."

Shaking his head, Kid refused. "Ah'll stay with you, Sir. I *have* to stay with you!"

"But, Kid, I don't know how much time---"

"I'd be better with you, Sir, please!" His hand clutched her jacket tightly and tears rolled down his face. "I can't swim!"

She gritted her teeth deploring her stupidity. Patting his shoulder, she made up her mind. "Don't worry, Kid. We'll both go on Robin, as soon as we can."

"Yes, Sir." He settled down, gripped the reins in one hand, and held onto Sarah with the other.

Watching the pandemonium on deck, Sarah saw a frantic mother trying to herd three frightened children together. "I'll be right back, Kid. You keep Robin calm." She pulled her jacket from the boy's hand and ducked under the tape again. Weaving through the rushing crowd, she approached the woman. "May I help?" she asked.

"They don't understand," the mother cried, trying to keep hold of three children at once. Sarah picked up the smallest, sobbing girl who was hugging a rag doll.

"My husband's disappeared," the woman shrilled, looking about wildly at the crowd.

"Let's make for the side," urged Sarah. "I think he helped to lower the gangplank. Hold on to mother," she told the other boy and girl. "We're going to go swimming."

"Ain't there no boats?" the woman asked, frightened even more.

"I'm not sure." Sarah cried.

"Can you take the baby," the woman asked, holding a child by each hand. Sarah saw no alternative. Carrying the little one and making a path for the mother by weaving through the crowd, she reached the side of the boat.

"I've a boy and a horse to get off, as soon as possible," said Sarah. "If we can get clear in time, I may be able to help you ashore."

"Oh, please, Sir. Help me!" the mother cried and grabbed Sarah's arm. "You have to take Flora Anne," and she bent to kiss the child in Sarah's arms.

"What's your name?" Sarah asked, as the woman pulled away.

"Worthington. Ah'll look for you on shore," she called, pushed away by the rush of passengers. "*Elmira Worthington*." She disappeared in the crowd. Carrying Flora Anne, Sarah struggled back to the stall through the last of the deck throng.

"Who's that?" asked Kid, stroking the neck of the nervous horse.

"Flora Anne Worthington," said Sarah, wiping the howling child's cheeks and patting her back. "She's going with us."

They heard a sudden thump nearby as a carpetbag fell from the upper deck, followed by a man dropping down in back of them. "Good, you're still here," cried Jason McGreuder, brushing his frock coat and appearing pleased with himself.

"Where did you--where are you going?" Sarah asked, startled.

"I thought you might need help with... Robin," he explained, taking a scarf from his neck and wrapping it around the eyes and head of the animal. "I see you've acquired another child." His grin lightened the moment.

"Thank you." Sarah managed a weak smile. "I think we'd better hurry."

"Let's tie the bags onto the saddle with this strap, Kid," Jason said, taking charge of the situation, and handing the boy a leather thong. "Now, you three get on Robin and I'll lead you around the deck." He made a stirrup with his hands to help Sarah mount the horse with the baby. Then he gave a boost to Kid, and led the horse toward the side of the boat. It was none too soon, as burning timbers began falling down on the after-deck.

Some of the passengers still clung to the railings of the boat, either unable to swim, or looking for lost companions. The remaining few moved aside, when they saw the horse coming to the gangplank. Jason removed his coat and handed it to Sarah. "Let us through, please," cried Jason, and they went down the ramp and into the water. When Robin's hooves went into the water, he jerked his head pulling on the halter. However, Jason drew him into the river and gave the lead to Sarah. Jason swam ahead calling to Robin. Holding the baby in one arm with the other wrapped around a trembling Kid, Sarah spoke soothingly to the horse and the children. The distance to the river-bank seemed to grow as Robin fought the pull of the water, but Jason's command in the dark kept them going straight across the current.

On the shore, pitch wands helped the swimmers find their way. Cries of "Help!" floated across the water, and people called to loved ones in terror. Sarah saw Jason grab one sodden fellow, who was sinking, and pull him along, too. He touched bottom, hauled the stranger ashore, and pounded on the man's back, telling him he was all right. The fellow coughed, spewed a mouth-full of river water out on the sand, and looked up to thank his savior. She was about to thank him, too, when Jason removed his wet shoes, handed them to Sarah, and turned back to the river. He pulled a woman and child ashore. Then, he went back for others.

Sarah hugged the children and repeated a silent prayer for their deliverance, as Robin pranced on the sand with water streaming from his mane and tail.

"We made it!" shouted Kid. "Here we are, Mr. McGreuder," he called, seeing their friend return with other passengers from the river. He slid down from the horse to the sand.

"I don't know how to thank you, Jason," said Sarah, handing his shoes and coat to him. He removed his wet stockings and shoved his feet into his shoes.

He shook his wet head and took a deep breath. "We're very lucky. I fear some poor souls didn't make it."

"You're a hero, Jason. I...I must find Mrs. Worthington," she added as the little girl began to cry again. She rocked the child in her arms and peered through the dimly lit crowd on the beach.

"I'll call her name, if you'll stay here," Jason offered and set forth to locate the mother.

"She has two small children with her," Sarah cried, and asked Kid to look through their bag for a dry shawl to wrap about herself and the baby. Kid handed the shawl up to her, then began to rub down Robin with his hands. Noise and confusion filled the air with shouts from fellow passengers looking for companions, and the happy cries of those who found their relatives. Members from the nearby village moved through the crowd dispensing cups of hot cider to the bedraggled passengers and answering questions.

On the river, flames licked the boards of the paddle wheeler and smoke wove eerie patterns in the fog. Light from the fire silhouetted heads of the last swimmers in the river. Small clumps of wet passengers formed and the last of the refugees waded ashore.

After Jason found Elmira and her husband, he returned to Sarah with Mr. Worthington and introduced her to him. She handed the crying child down to her father and brushed off his thanks. Talking to Flora Anne, the man plod across the sand to join his family.

"Now," said Jason, "there's little more we can do here. The nearest village is about a mile down the road. I suggest we get there, as soon as possible to find shelter for the night."

"Thank you, Jason. Where are we?" Exhausted, she slipped down from the horse, landed in Jason's arms, and blushed.

"Lodestone, Indiana," he said.

"I'm sure the swimming must have worn you out." She handed the bridle to him. "You and Kid ride. I'll stretch my legs." The wet wool trousers clung to her legs uncomfortably, but she strode out, determined to play her role. The weary three set forth for Lodestone. Obviously glad to be back on land, Robin danced a bit and tossed his head.

Chapter 23

Management Woes

EMERALD BURST INTO the library where Ellsworth reclined on the couch, with his leg extended, reading a recent Charleston broadsheet. "I'm not doing another thing until you get rid of that obnoxious, over-bearing, bastard!" Waving her hands in the air, she marched up and down the room, growling between gritted teeth, and stopped in front of him.

Dropping the paper, he looked up. "What obnoxious, overbearing bastard?"

"Pendergast! Is there anyone else you want me to toady to?"

"What's he done now?"

"He treats me like a brainless woman."

"Well, you *are* a woman." He smiled.

She ignored his remark. "I didn't spend eight years at Miss Langdon's Academy to be mistreated. He won't let me do anything, but check on the pregnant women on the place, and order his ice tea. How am I supposed to---?"

Ellsworth sat up, easing his leg to the floor. "What about the books, the order lists, the receipts, crop notes, the weekly worksheets?"

"Exactly. I haven't been allowed to see a scrap of paper since I went to work."

"I told him you were to help with those chores, to learn the business of the farm in order to help me manage it." His own ire began to rise and he lifted himself into his wheel chair.

"That isn't all. He caught Reuther Jones picking up windfalls from the ground and beat the livin' daylights out of him! His back looks like two pounds of raw pork. He can't even work this week."

"Now *that* makes me angry! I expressly told him nothing was to be done regarding a personnel problem until I saw a report of it and made my recommendation. Wheel me out to the back door."

She hesitated. "Are you sure? You may not be ready to take on--"

"I'm danged sure!" Entering the kitchen, they found Penne rolling out dough for biscuits. "Penne, would you go fetch Ben? The ground should be hard enough now for him to wheel my chair out to the barn."

Penne glanced at Cook who was turning meat at the stove. He knew the trip could open his wound again, but he had to back up his stand. Penne appraised him with a look, rinsed her hands in the dry sink pan, wiped them on her apron and left.

Looking contrite, Emerald said, "I know you need my help, but I didn't mean to push you to do anything you weren't ready for."

Worth shifted in his chair with discomfort. "I'm ready."

"Would y'all care for some ice tea, Master Ellsworth?" The cook moved toward the tea urn on a marble slab in the window.

"No, thank you, Cook. Maybe later," he said.

Ben arrived, took over the wheelchair, and eased it down the back steps to the brick walk. Ellsworth had Ben stop at the door of the farm manager's office and he stood, wincing from the effort. Opening the door, he held it for Emma and followed her in.

Pendergast, taken by surprise, removed his feet from the desk, set down a beaker of tea and rose. "Why, Master Ellsworth, ya'll didn't have to come down h'year. Ah'd a been happy to come up to the house, if they was a need." He gestured grandly to an ancient Windsor chair, which Emma accepted. The office was filthy and had a wall covered with an old map of the farm, an old whip, a pair of shackles and some broken leg irons.

"Ah, but there *does* seem to be a need. Did you misunderstand me, when I told you Mrs. Porter would be here to help manage the paperwork and learn the operation of the farm?"

"Wall, no. Ah thought you jest wanted to find something to keep her busy. Women don't rightly belong in farm business." The overseer airily dismissed the idea with the wave of a hand.

"On the contrary, I disagree." Worth continued, "*How* was I unclear? I *said*: Mrs. Porter would be here to learn the operation of the farm and to help me assume management during my father's illness."

"But Ah told you, Suh, that weren't necessary. Master Dietrich done give *me* that chore. With yore problem, you've no need to bother yo'self with such boring details. Ah can do it all without help."

Ellsworth put a hand on Emma's shoulder, held his temper with difficulty, and coldly said, "I see. May I see the report on Reuther Jones? I understand there was a problem with theft."

Pendergast looked down and shuffled through some papers on the desk. "Ah cain't locate it at the moment, but Ah'll gladly send it up to you when Ah do." He gave Ellsworth an unctuous smile.

"Tell me, Mr. Pendergast, what exactly was Reuther accused of?"

"Theft, Suh. Stealing apples." The overseer smirked righteously.

"And you've written up a report of the incident for me to decide the discipline?"

"Ah, no. I took care of the matter."

A vein throbbed in Worth's temple, as he asked in a flat tone, "And how *exactly* did you do that?"

"We has to make uh example o' such thangs. Ah whopped him, like always."

"I-told-you *I* would determine any action for a problem, *after* seeing your report."

"This wasn't no matter to bother you with, Suh."

"I *said, I* would determine that, *not* you, Sir. The hands have always been allowed the windfalls."

"Ah had no way of telling if that fruit fell, or was picked from the tree."

"Reuther is a share-cropper. You had no right, *no right* to beat him, nor anyone else! Pendergast, *you are fired!*"

The man's jaw fell open. "You *cain't fire me*! Master Dietrich hired me."

"Until my father resumes his position, I have every right in the world. I will give you the same two weeks' notice we give other workers. I will pay you for those two weeks, but I want you off this farm by five this afternoon. You can pick up your pay at the back door of the house. *Is that understood?*"

The overseer's face suffused a dark red. "You damned right! *You'll be sorry.* Ah cain't *wait* to see the mess a woman *and a cripple* will make running this place alone!" With that, he began emptying the desk of his few belongings; he brandished a pint bottle of his whiskey from a lower drawer.

Ellsworth gestured to the door. Emma rose and swept out of the room before him.

"Ben, would you remove the whip, chains, and shackles from the office wall and put them in the trash to be burned? And ask Mr. Reuther to come up to the house for some salve for his back."

Grinning, Ben bobbed his head. "Yas, Suh!"

Worth glanced at his sister and resumed his wheel chair. "Will that take care of it, Emma?"

She exhaled and gave her brother a look of admiration, then pushed his chair through the barn. " Indeed. I would say *so*! Only, how are we going to ---?"

"We have Winston. He'll help. Once we get that pigsty of an office cleaned up, you'll have a place to work." He looked up at her, proud to have solved a major problem quickly expeditiously.

"May I decorate it to suit myself?" she asked.

"So long as I can eventually use it; mind you, no lace, ribbons, or falderal."

"Wonderful! We'll do a marvelous job, Worth. You wait and see."

"And *hopefully*, have a successful enterprise."

"You make a grand manager, Worth," she said and wheeled him across the hard earth and up the brick walk to the house with Ben hurrying up behind them.

Only one thing marred his complete happiness: *what would his father say when he heard he had fired Pendergast?*

Chapter 24

Safe in Lodestone, Indiana

ARRIVING IN THE small village, the three weary travelers found most of the houses dark. Jason spotted lit torches down the main road and urged Robin in that direction. A small crowd of interested men from a tavern milled about outside of the inn where men on horseback were receiving torches. The mounted men paired and rode off toward the river.

"Be youse from the boat?" one grizzly fellow asked.

"Yes," said Jason. Sarah led the way through the crowd.

"What caused the fire? How many drowned?" another asked.

Jason shook his head. "Not many, I trust. Fortunately, the river was low. They were largely ashore when we left. We don't know what caused the fire."

"What do they need?" asked another rider.

"Hot drinks, coverlets an' transport," replied Sarah. "They're going to need places to stay this night."

"Are there any empty rooms here at the inn?" asked Jason.

"Jest two or three," said one of the men passing out the torches. "Better git yourselves in before the crowd does. Reckon we'll be putting most of them in the livery."

"Thank you." Jason got down from the horse and lent a hand to Kid. At the door of the inn he put a hand on the boy's shoulder. "You take Robin to the barn and arrange for him and me to spend the night there." He took a wet bill from his wallet, handed it to the boy and retrieved Sarah's carpetbag from the saddle.

Kid looked up at her and said, "Ah'll stay in the barn, too, if that's all right, Sir." His eyes pled for permission.

She had to let him be a man. "Thank you, Kid. Have a good night. I'll repay you, Jason." Inside the two-story, sprawling building, they located the innkeeper behind the bar in the pub. The men in the bar realized the two were from the paddle wheeler and crowded around plying them with questions.

Feeling she was not up to another night in a barn, regardless of her masculine role, Sarah moved aside to let Jason make the replies. She arranged for a room. She wanted a sponge bath in the worst way; her legs in the wet pants were shaking with cold. Accepting a lit chamber stick from the innkeeper, she fished in her knit bag for a note to give to Jason.

A man in the bar said, "Nothing so exciting had happened in Lodestone since the end of the War." Before she and Jason left for her room, the men began relating stories of other boat disasters on the river. Several wandered out of the bar to join the group of rescuers outside.

Jason refused her money and accompanied her down the dark passageway to find her room. "Here you are," he said. "If you don't mind, I'd like to wash my hands and face in your basin before going to the barn."

"By all means," said Sarah entering the modest room. It had a narrow bed, washstand and Windsor chair; she placed the chamber stick on the washstand. "I should join you in the barn and give this room to some woman from the boat."

"No," he said. "You've done your share tonight. Get a good night's rest. We'll move on in the morning." He went over to the washstand, removed his coat and string tie, rolled up his sleeves, poured water in the washbowl and performed his ablutions. Sarah tore her eyes away from his muscular forearms and rummaged through her bag on the chair. She got out the quilt and dry clothing, removed her jacket and placed it on the chair back. He looked up, with water in his eyes, groping for a towel. Handing one to him from the towel bar, she sat on the bed to remove her saturated shoes, waiting for him to leave before removing her stockings.

"Ah, that's better," he said putting on his jacket. "I felt like I'd just joined the American Navy. I hope my bag kept some of my clothes dry."

"My trousers reek of the Great Ohio. I trust Kid has found hay for both of you and Robin. Here's a shawl and quilt you may use."

"Thank you, Morgan. We'll be glad of them. I'll keep an eye on Kid."

"Thank you. He's one tired boy tonight."

"Yes." Jason paused. "I've had Kid on my mind ever since I met him. I want to do something for him, later, with your permission, of course."

Sarah's eyelids were heavy, but she rubbed them and asked what he had in mind.

"I'd like to adopt him," he said. "Unless that's what you plan to do."

"Oh?" She gazed at him a moment, glad he felt the same way she did about the boy. "Due to my age, the authorities probably wouldn't let *me* adopt him. In any event, supporting him might be a problem for me. At the moment, I haven't a tinker's dam to my name."

"I know you're fond of the child"

"How could I help? He is a special youngster, bright and willing. I want to keep in touch with him, whatever happens."

"Of course," said Jason. "Let's see what we can work out, once you're settled. I had best go before every last blade of straw is taken. I'll check on your horse, too."

"Thank you, Jason. I shall look for you in the common room for breakfast. About half past six?"

"Perfect. Goodnight." With a modest bow, he left.

After barring the door with the wooden slide, Sarah stripped off her wet pants, hose and pantaloons, rinsed the damp garments in the basin and poured the used water in the waste pail. Wringing the clothes as best she could, she blotted them in a towel and hung them up to dry on the wall clothes hooks. Then, washing herself and replacing her underwear, she fell into bed exhausted from the night's escapade. She said her prayers, aching for sleep, but Jason's intention for Kid played itself over in her mind. In the few days they had been together, she had come to care for Kid. Jason was a fine young man; if anyone could take care of the child, it was surely he. Still, the thought of letting Kid go surprised her with its pain, despite the fact she could not hope to support him and herself. At any time, she could be found and arrested for the murder. She could not even offer him secur---Sleep claimed her at last.

Next morning the three of them shared a breakfast of gruel, biscuits and ale amid the cacophony from other diners who were discussing the sinking of the boat and the travelers' dilemma. A few passengers were among them, and some had tragic losses. Many had lost their savings as well as their passage, and they planned to see the boat's captain regarding return on their tickets. Jason told Sarah he had left their names and his father's address for the three of them, with the purser from the boat, in hopes that they might eventually receive some restitution.

It was sad to hear three people had lost their lives, one a member of the crew. Several passengers had lost farm implements, guns, household goods and the clothes they had for setting out to homestead in the West. Others felt lucky to retrieve the livestock that swam ashore the same side of the river and were subsequently identified and tethered. The boat had taken down crates of building tools and housing supplies carried by merchants to sell to settlers in the West. A prayer meeting was scheduled later in the day for those who had lost family members.

"We'll do whatever you say about the meeting, Morgan," said Jason, "but I feel you may prefer to get on your way on the first stagecoach. We can tie Robin on behind, and he'll get the kinks out of his legs from being on board so long."

Sarah glanced at Kid who was dipping his biscuit in his ale and thoroughly relishing breakfast. She plucked a tiny piece of straw from his hair and turned to Jason. "When does the coach arrive? How much are the tickets?"

"It's already here and will be departing for Evansville at eight-of-the-clock. The passage is reasonable, only five dollars each. Two for Kid, if he rides up top with the driver."

"Can I? I'd like that," said Kid. Sarah mentally calculated the amount of money she had left and agreed. She could not possibly stay here and find work in such a small village.

"Are we really going in a coach?" Kid asked. "I've only been on a boat an' a wagon, before."

Nodding, Jason stood and paid for their food, *again* refusing reimbursement. He asked her to meet him in front of the inn, when she was ready to leave, and he left to attend to their tickets for the trip. She gazed after him in consternation, determined she would pay him later. She had Kid come with her to wash up and to change his shirt and pants. He was still not entirely used to being tidy. In the room, he turned his back to her while dressing. *He is growing up*, she thought.

Once outside of the inn, the boy ran excitedly around the coach drawn up in front. He was thrilled with the idea of riding on top with the driver. "Can I go up now?"

"When the driver is ready," Jason said.

"You'll be up there some time," cautioned Sarah. "You'd better take care of any physical needs you might have, and make sure Robin's fed and watered."

"I already did. Should I get him now, Sir?"

Jason checked his pocket watch and looked at Sarah.

"Yes," she said. "We'll leave soon."

"Yes, Sir." The boy dashed off.

A middle-aged man and wife, and a pretty girl joined them with their bags. The older couple nodded affably, but the girl appeared shy, and edged away from the others. Sarah glanced at Jason who winked at her, indicating his appreciation of the young girl. Playing her part, Sarah smirked, knowingly, but her thoughts were far from playful. Naturally, Jason was attracted to the girl. He was a healthy man without a wife; but it was a pin pricking her own fantasy bubble. She took a deep breath and turned her attention to Robin, who Kid brought forward.

"Well, old boy, did you have a nice night?" she asked, patting the horse, which lipped her hand.

"Let's tether him behind the coach, Son," said Jason, and the two of them took care of the horse.

The coach driver returned, stowed the baggage, and opened the door for the passengers to get into the coach. Jason assisted the young woman into the coach and moved to the other side to take a seat. The older couple seated themselves across from them. Sarah climbed in by herself, feeling the burden of her masquerade and an unfamiliar pang of jealousy from the attention Jason was giving the girl. The driver called Kid to the top, and Sarah watched him climb up.

With a crack of his whip and a shouted command, the driver started the team. Kid yelled "Hyeah!" Sarah was pleased; the child was having fun. Jason politely introduced himself to the girl, Miss Trudy Adams, and readily chatted away. In her corner, Sarah's heart sank as she faced reality. She had no more right to Jason's attention than she did to Kid's affection. She ached for the trip to be over, so she could get on with her life as a woman. Considering Jason's manly interest, he was completely lost to her. By the time he knew *she* was a woman, some other woman, if not Miss Adams, would have him in tow.

The woman across from Sarah leaned over. "Are you well, Sir?"

Chagrined, Sarah realized her depression had shown in her face. "I'm fine, Ma'am, thank you. Just a ghost from the past," she explained. *Jealousy*, she deplored. *I am jealous of the attentions of someone who does not even know I am a woman!*

The passenger's wife chuckled and waved a gloved hand. "You're too young to have ghosts, Sir." Jason looked over at her, puzzled, and then continued trying to engage Miss Adams in conversation. Sarah strove to ignore his remarks. She deeply regretted not telling him of her masquerade. If she had known they would be traveling together all the way to Evansville, she would have given up the male clothing and ... and what? Placed herself in his care, whether he liked it, or not? No, no! She didn't want him to take care of her. Somehow, she planned to make the change when they separated, after he departed for St. Louis. Confusing him with her perfidy left her completely up in the air. Feeling a twinge behind her eyelids, she fought the urge to weep. *Soldiers!* What a mess she had made of things!

To give her credit, Miss Adams barely replied to Jason, although she gave Sarah a smile. She said, she was just out of school and going to visit an aunt, but her tacky clothing seemed inappropriate for her age. Sarah forcefully directed her attention to the older couple who were on their way to St. Louis to visit their first grandchild. She answered their questions about the fire of the previous evening.

They rocked along for some time. Sarah opened her novel and tried to smooth down the wrinkled pages from the river damp. The constant movement of the coach made her dizzy and unable to follow the printed word. She put the book away. The landscape out of the coach windows indicated they had left the coastline. Jason gave up on Mistress Adams, put his head back, and went to sleep. No doubt, the straw bed of the night before had not been too comfortable. His gentle snore pleased her.

Eventually, the man across from Sarah sought to engage her in a discussion of national politics, of which she was ignorant. With relief she realized, the coach was beginning to slow down at a way station for lunch and rest.

Alighting from the vehicle, she found young Kid bubbling with excitement, relating the driver's tales of Indians and robbers who had attacked the coach on other trips. The driver winked at her, to say they were fiction and shot a stream of tobacco juice between an opening in his teeth at a hound, which had rushed up barking at the passengers. Sarah strode back to Robin, untied his tether, and took him over to a water trough. With a twinge she had observed Jason aid Miss Adams to alight from the coach and accompany her into the log way station. Sarah lingered by her horse, chiding herself. When Kid claimed he was starving, she turned the horse loose to graze near the building, and led their way inside.

After lunch, the other two women repaired to the outhouse in the back and washed their hands at a graniteware basin on a wooden bench. Sarah waited, before making her own trip to the back, then whistled for Robin who trotted up promptly, munching on a large sheaf of grass. Miss Adams approached Sarah.

"I don't suppose you'd consider selling him," the girl asked and reached out to stroke Robin's long, chestnut neck.

"No," said Sarah. "He's on loan, in a manner of speaking. I want to return him to his owner."

"Where is *he*?" She was less shy, than Sarah had first thought, and perhaps two years younger than she was.

She almost answered, 'West Virginia,' but caught herself. "East of here."

The girl's eyes filled with tears. "I need to get away before they find me."

"Get away from whom?"

Miss Adams wiped her cheeks with the back of her hand. "I cain't tell you."

Sarah said, "I see." She did not, of course. "We've come at least twenty miles from Lodestone. Doesn't that help?"

The young girl shook her head glancing over one shoulder. "Not for Jake Percival. He's got partners from Cincinnati to Louisville. He'd drag me back quick as that," and she snapped her gloved fingers.

"Not your father, then?"

"Hell fire, I hope to God not!"

Sarah did not know the problem, but suggested, "Let's ask Mr. McGreuder."

Abruptly, Trudy turned to her. "No, no! He's a gentleman. He'd never understand."

It struck Sarah that *she* was supposed to be one, too. "And *I'm* not?"

Trudy's face turned pink with agitation. "I don't mean that. It's just you're more---" she glanced back at the men by the coach, "You're a woman."

Sarah felt herself blush, squeezed the bridge of her nose, and said, "Well, you're right. But please, don't give me away."

Trudy placed a hand on Sarah's elbow. "You have your reason, pretending to be a man, but don't fret. I won't tell nobody."

"How did you uncover my disguise?"

"I 'spect you ain't never been 'down the line'… as the soldiers call it." Sarah shrugged her shoulders. Trudy added, "To a madam's parlor?"

Sarah's eyes widened, amazed at the question, she covered her mouth in embarrassment and cleared her throat to hide it. "You're right. I haven't."

"Well, my pa got killed early in the War, when I was thirteen. My step-ma said she couldn't feed me no more, unless I --"

Sarah shut her eyes for what was coming, "Unless you --?"

Trudy bit her cheek and gestured with open hands. "Changed my name and went on the street."

Hardly knowing what to say, Sarah inanely asked, "What *was* your name?"

Trudy wrinkled her pretty nose, "Gertrude."

"But, your step-mother ---*Why*? Why would she do that?"

"I 'spect she didn't have no choice. She had the twins, who was six, an' no work. It wasn't long before Perse the Worse found me, an' agreed to split my earnin's with her, if she'd give me up."

"How long ago?"

"Three years. It took me all this long to save up my tips to leave. Ya see, they don't give you nothin' but food and keep and they collect the money before …." She nodded. "You know."

Wondering if she did, Sarah exhaled. "Would Evansville be far enough away, do you think?"

"Maybe. I don't even know where it *is*. It depends on whether they come after me. I'm skeered I'll run out of where-with-all, before I kin find work." She hastily added, "Decent work, mind you." The petite, sad figure with great, brown eyes, wearing a blue sateen dress touched Sarah's heart. Trudy stared down the road, they had just covered, apparently to make sure no one was following. Sarah realized, uncomfortably, just how far from reality her speculations about the girl had been.

Kid ran up and said, "It's time to go." He took Robin's rein and walked him over to the coach.

Sarah patted Trudy on the arm. "Try not to worry. I'll see what I can do when we reach our destination."

"Thank you," the girl replied. "Somehow, I jest knew you'd help me."

The two of them walked over to the coach where Jason stood by the open door to assist Trudy. Sarah clambered up and settled into her corner. *I seem to have some strange affinity for people in trouble,* she thought. She only hoped to God, she would not be weighed and found wanting.

Chapter 25

Awakening

SORTING LINENS IN the upstairs hall closet, Lauree heard Rupert roar from their bedroom and hurried in, pleased to know he was awake again. "Good morning, Rupert. I'm so glad you're--" She leaned over to kiss him and smooth the covers on the bed.

"Why in blazes didn't you wake me?" He gestured to the daylight in the windows, threw the crocheted coverlet aside, sat up abruptly, clasped his head and fell over on one side. He gave a throaty growl, glared at Lauree and exploded, "What have you *given* me?"

"Nothing, except the elixir left by Doctor Anderson. You remember, Rupert, we discussed it before." The hand with her handkerchief pressed her mouth.

"Elixir? What for?"

"Your heart, dearest. You had a stroke; when you fell, you hit your head on the buffet."

"That quack wouldn't know a stroke from dyspepsia! Where are my trousers?"

She glanced at the wardrobe and backed out of the room, unwilling to give him clothes against the doctor's orders.

"Where in tarnation are you going?" he bellowed. "Get that girl up here to help me dress. Hear me? Right now!" Her last glimpse was of his furious red face as he struggled to right himself in the bed.

Worth. She rushed down the hall and the stairs.

"Ellsworth…" He looked up from the books on his father's desk, saw his mother's face and stood up. "Your father's awake again. You have to go up."

"Of course." Worth struggled around the desk with his new wooden leg. Lauree followed him, knowing mounting the stairs was a trial for him. They had been hoping Rupert would awaken fully. So far, he'd had only brief, groggy awakenings. *This* morning, Lauree could not handle him without help.

Entering the bedroom, they found Rupert twisted, face down and swearing into his pillow. "Here, Papa. I'm glad to see you're feeling better." Ellsworth helped his father sit up in the bed.

"Where the devil have you been, Boy? Don't you know we have a farm to run?"

"Yes Sir. Believe me, I do," Ellsworth said dryly. "With Emerald's help, I've been tending to business ever since you became ill." He appeared calm, but he shot her a look of alarm.

"I got to get out there to see things. Help me dress," Rupert commanded, but he began slipping to one side, unable to accomplish his goal. "That crank doctor has given me something to muddle my brain. I'm so weak, I can't sit up."

"That's all right, Pa. Everything is being taken care of. You have to rest and get well before coming back to work."

"But, what about---" Rupert could not complete the sentence.

"Everything is fine. The last of the tobacco is curing in the sheds and we've let ten acres in the south quadrant lie fallow, as you planned. We've only lost two hands, but the rest of the workers seem happy and productive now." Her son's tone was business-like and encouraging.

"Humph. Ne'r mind how '*happy*' they are. They'd cost us farm and home, if they had their way." Lauree sat in her wing chair by a window.

"Unfortunately, we have to compete with everyone else to hold experienced help these days," her son continued. "Try not to fret, Father. Everyone on the farm misses you and asks about your health."

"Humph!" Rupert obviously expected no less. "You had better see everythin' continues as--"

"Of course. You'll be pleased to know your new son-in-law has been most helpful, too. With the three of us on the job, you need not worry about a thing."

"Ssson-in-law?"

She exchanged another look with Ellsworth.

"Emerald's marri...d?"

Worth smiled. "Very much so. I need to have the dowry deeds signed and released to Winston. If they are in the safe, I don't know the combination."

Rupert looked at him a long moment, then turned his head toward her. "'S-true? Emerald and Winston are mareed?"

"Oh, yes, dearest. Don't you remember? You had your attack at the reception." He shook his head. "Emerald was the most beautiful bride ever. You gave her away handsomely in your new frock coat." She enjoyed, remembering.

With the last of his bluster expended, Winston's voice weakened. "How long'st been?"

Wincing, Ellsworth replied, "Four weeks, Pa."

Rupert clutched his face with his hands. "A month…my God!" He gave a great sigh and moaned.

"Can I get anything for you, Sir?"

"Water."

"Of course." Worth poured the drink from the cut glass carafe on the bedside table and held the glass for him.

Rupert looked at his son and rubbed his mouth with a shaky, weathered hand. "I 'member now, *you've* been ill."

"I'm much better."

Lauree knew he still looked white around the gills.

"Yes. I gave my word, to… Henry 'bout the dowry. My birthday. Safe com'ination."

Worth nodded. "Thank you. I'll take care of the deed at once."

Lauree moved to the bedside and took her husband's hand. "Is there anything else, dear? Would you like a little soup, some custard?"

He shook his head, closed his eyes and slid down in the bed, going to sleep.

Ellsworth said, "Whew," in relief and nodded to her. They left the room to return downstairs. "I've longed for his improvement, but to be honest, I've dreaded each encounter. Do you think he's really better?"

Lauree shook her head. "I'm afraid not. Doctor Anderson says there is some damage to his brain and his heart is worn out. He said, even if he was truly alert, we couldn't expect a full recovery." She blinked to hold back tears. "I must tell Emerald."

"I'm so sorry, Mama," Worth replied, breathing heavily as he maneuvered down the stairs, one step at a time. "I know this is hard for you."

"Actually," she said giving him a faint smile and wiping a tear from her cheek, "I'm at peace in a strange way. I haven't had one of my headaches for weeks and I'm---" She could not say she was no longer afraid of his father. "Knowing he needs me, for the first time in years, I feel wanted." She looked up at her son. "Is that selfish?"

He paused in the hallway and gently kissed her on her temple. "No, Mama. You deserve every bit of happiness you can have. There are all kinds of adjustments in life." He tapped his wooden leg with his cane. "Our job is to make the most of today. God willing, whatever comes cannot be worse than what we've had." It was the closest he'd ever come to saying that he knew she'd been unhappy for years; and it was the first time to her, that he appeared to have accepted the loss of his lower limb.

"You're a good son, Ellsworth. I'm truly proud of you." She gave him a sweet smile.

Chapter 26

Ellsworth Sets His Goal

EMERALD ENTERED THE house and slowly walked down the hall to her father's office. The love and security she had found with Winston had given her what she needed to mature. Because of her father's illness, she had assumed responsibilities she'd never had before. It pleased her to help Winston and Ellsworth manage the farm. She felt significant, knowing the family depended upon her, as they did on her brother.

She stopped in the doorway observing Worth, with wrinkled brow, seated at pa's desk in an apparent struggle with the farm books. *He's doing well, with Winnie's encouragement and exercise, he's learning to manage his disability.*

He looked up and said, "Oh, good morning, Emma. Do come in. I've good news for you."

"Splendid. What is it?"

"First of all, I got the safe combination from pa, and I have the dowry deeds ready to sign. I'll ask Cook to prepare dinner for all of us to celebrate the transfer of titles. How about tomorrow night?" She knew he was proud of himself for carrying out his father's promise.

"That's wonderful, Worth! Winn will be so pleased. Since pa awoke and spoke to you again, he must be much better."

The lines of his face sobered, while he pushed the papers on the desk aside. "Dr. Anderson says, 'no.' Although his speech is still affected, the stoke could have been more severe. But his poor heart is simply too weak for him to recover fully. Mama and I haven't informed him of his condition, but when he realizes he can't get up---"

Emerald moaned sadly. "Is there nothing that can be done?"

He shook his head. "Anderson said the time might come when an operation will help weakened arteries, but there's nothing now."

One tear brimmed over her lid and ran down her cheek. After a moment she asked, "How is mama taking it?"

"She appears accepting. I have the feeling she's known for years, something of this sort would eventually occur, and she is...resigned. Speaking of mama, the most wonderful change, she's no longer afraid of everything. We had a good talk."

"Really? That relieves my mind. Is she upstairs? I'll go see her."

"I think she's in the grape arbor working on some needlepoint. I'm sure she'll be glad of company. However, there is something else---Oh, never mind. I'll tell all of you about it tomorrow night."

"Fine. Worth, what are you planning to do about an overseer? Have you interviewed anyone yet?"

"No, I want to discuss some ideas, with both you and Winston. Is he available to come over this afternoon?"

"He'll be over to make the rounds. We'll have plenty of time. The senior Porters are in Charleston visiting Jacob's son and daughter, so we'll only have a light supper."

"How are the cousins?"

"Andrea and Joseph are doing well. We have them in classes in the Witherspoon Academy, where they are both applying themselves. Winn hopes to send Joseph to agricultural school when he finishes his eighth year. They are good children, despite having an inveterate, gambler father and no mother."

"What's happened to him?"

"He's gone again. Probably gambling somewhere, on a riverboat. I wish he was out of their lives forever."

"Winston told me before you were married, he felt a responsibility for his uncle's children. He told pa, that was why he couldn't build a house for you at once."

"I know. But the Porters are pleasant and easy to live with. Considering the work here, I wouldn't have time to oversee a large house anyway." She shrugged.

Her brother looked up at her. "I'm proud of you, Emma. You've really taken hold of the job. I don't know what I'd do without you."

Emerald blushed, pleased with his praise. "You've done the major work, Worth. I think we're quite a team."

"Sit down, won't you? We could cut a road between our two properties and save all that jumping fences and riding through the orchard and tobacco field." Both of them laughed; that was what she'd been doing ever since the wedding. "For that matter, this is such a large house; you and Winston could live here, too, if you so desired."

"That's something to think about," she said. "Winnie might like the idea, but he'd consider his folks first."

He stretched his fingers and took a deep breath. "I've been meaning to speak to you about another matter: Apennine. You should know I am fond, no, I *love* her. I want to---"

She covered her ears with her hands. "You mustn't talk to me about that! Ladies never discuss these things." She was shocked he would even broach the subject.

He stood up. "Well, I *am telling* you! I know I can't marry her---"

"Certainly not! It's against the law for Negroes to marry!" The words alone were *unthinkable.*

"That law will change now. For one thing, papa would never permit it and mama would feel compromised. In all likelihood, we'd all be shunned in our own church." He shook his head and stretched out a hand to her. "But I want you to understand this: Penne is partly responsible for getting me back on my feet and...she's carrying *my* child." She gasped at the news. A dozen thought bees buzzed in her head.

"Moreover, I can't have her continue as an under-maid in our household. She's young, but I, I want to make her our housekeeper, if mama agrees. You see I intend to recognize the child as my own." He released a nervous sigh, apparently glad to have his plans out in the open.

Emma felt faint. She bit her lips to keep from making the wrong reply. "I heard that share cropper who ran away was her--the father."

"In the Biblical term, she never knew him or anyone else, except me."

She had believed her brother would eventually marry and make Fox Haven home for his family. If she understood him now, he had no such plan at all. Curiosity prompted her to ask, "Will she be your... uh, concubine in residence?"

"No! She will be my wife in every way, but in my name. If this doesn't work---" He gave her a warning stare.

The implications of his plan began to surface. "Worth, how can I treat a Negro as a sister? Winston and I expect to have children, too, and with a darkie as a family member---Lordy, I can't begin to feature!" She paused scrutinizing his face. "You said, 'If this doesn't work--"

"We'll go away." He waved his hands. "Out West, make a new life for ourselves. Out there, I've heard, neither society nor laws dictate *who* one can marry." He scrubbed his hair with his fingers, an old habit.

He was serious! "Worth, how can you even *think* such a thing, with pa sick and the farm---"

He rubbed the back of his neck, obviously in stress. "I *know*. But I have a responsibility to Penne, too. I can't evade that."

"Oh God, Worth!" He *had* to see reason. She leaned forward, imploring. "Send her away. Support her in Charleston. *Anything* else! You can't just give up on a suitable marriage, Worth. Please?"

Her brother looked down at his injured leg, grimaced and met her gaze. "Emma, I can't make a home, start a business, or even manage this farm without your help and Winn's. Let's face it. My health will never fully return any more than my leg will. I *need* Apennine, if I am to do what is necessary here. Try to understand, Sis', I love her for her generous spirit, her kindness, *and* her intelligence. With our help, she'll make a fine wife and mother. I'll try to fill papa's shoes, but I can't do it without the support of you all."

Emerald pressed her upper lip to keep tears from falling. "I'm sorry, Worth. The shock was just unexpected." She studied him for a long moment. When she could find no wrinkle of indecision in his countenance, she decided. "I understand. We'll have to see what mama says. No matter what, she would never want to see *her* papa's farm sold. From where I sit, I doubt she has much choice. We couldn't manage to keep the farm without you."

"You know I wouldn't leave the folks in these circumstances. And I won't give up Penne, either. It might have been different, if Sarah hadn't disappeared."

Emma caught a guiltily breath. "*Sarah?* Why do you say that?"

"She grew up with us. I thought I loved her, when I first entered the militia. I knew we were cousins, but she wrote me at school and when I was away in the War." He looked out of the window and sighed deeply. He was about to admit something she never knew before. "However, after combat, when I came home on leave, I was too-- I was changed, bitter and angry. I believed I was not man enough for Sarah. I'm ashamed to admit, I didn't even have the courage to approach papa on the subject. Worse, selfishly, I had no future intentions for Penne, either.

"When I lost part of my leg and finally came home, Sarah was gone. Well, everything is different now. Sarah may be lost to us forever, but Penne is here for me. And we need one another." His face lined with the strain of making the admission, but there was no question of his determination.

For the first time Emerald realized what she had done by lying to the family about her cousin. In the past few weeks, she had gradually understood, her jealousy of Sarah had caused her willfully to dissemble regarding her cousin's disappearance. Had she told the truth at the time, they might have found Sarah and brought her back. Now, she couldn't bear to admit she'd lied, knowing how disgusted both Worth and Winn would be with her. No. That was a risk she could not take.

She pushed the guilt away and stood up to leave. "I'll go see how mama's doing." She paused in the doorway and turned back. "Perhaps it would be best if you tell her everything *after* dinner tomorrow night. Winn and I will be here to buffer the blow.

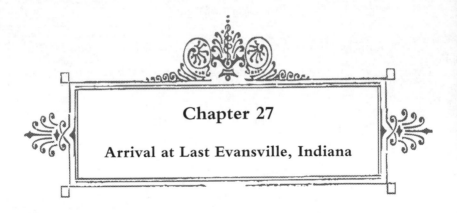

Chapter 27

Arrival at Last Evansville, Indiana

As THE COACH slowed for the station in Evansville, Sarah's anxiety grew. She could not locate rooms as a 'man' and then turn into a woman. What if Jason lingered to see them settled? She liked him so much; the thought of telling him the truth was a gnawing pain in her heart. Moreover, there was Kid. She must tell *him* she was a woman. He might hate her for the deception, or even run away.

Jason had offered to help her and Trudy find a room when they arrived. If he thought it strange that she and Trudy Adams had become friends, he had not commented. Since making friends with her and Kid, Trudy appeared much more at ease. Disembarking from the coach, Jason helped the coachman with the luggage and went into the station house to ask about available rooms to let.

Kid thanked the coachman, untied Robin and led the horse to the water trough beside the station. After Robin had quenched his thirst, Kid tied him to an iron hitching post and bounded up to Sarah, to ask what was next.

She was glad to see the boy had taken care of the horse. Highly uncertain, she stood by the station house waiting for Jason's emergence to hear his plans. She could not resolve her concerns until she knew his.

Jason came out of the station with a tag for the luggage he had checked. "I must take a barge leaving tonight for Cairo. Due to the fire, I'm late on my schedule. I'll find a carriage at the livery on the main street to take me to the dock. Here is my office address. I'll write you." He handed her the card and a list of rooms for rent. "The agent in the station has assured me, you'll have no trouble finding a place. There are numerous vacancies in this part of town."

Torn between relief and regret at saying goodbye, she forced a smile and held out a ten-dollar bill for his payment of their coach fares. "It has been my pleasure, Jason. We hope to see you again soon."

He waved away the proffered money, clasped her hand instead, and gave it a hearty shake. "It's been an honor to make your acquaintance, Morgan. I'll write you regarding Kid." He said to the boy, "You behave yourself, young man. I should be back in about three months. Good luck to you all." His affection for them was evident. He tipped his hat to Trudy and said, "Miss Adams." Then, he picked up his bag and strode off down the street.

Bereft, Sarah watched him until he turned the corner. She knew how much she had come to care for and depend upon him. Somehow, when he returned, she would have to admit her deception. It would not matter; he could not possibly relate to a murderess.

"Can we go now, Sir?" Kid asked.

That was that. "We need to find a boarding house." Looking at the list of rooms, Sarah saw there were three they could try in one block.

Hopefully, there would be signs with street names. "Kid, you may ride
Robin. You'll have to come back for our bags when we find rooms."

"Uh, yeah. I've only rode a mule before. D'you think he'll know?"

She smiled. "I'm sure he won't. Besides, you've taken good care
of him and he likes you."

"He does?" Kid untied the horse, adjusted the stirrups, led him to
a mounting block, and jackknifed up on the animal. He held the reins
with his elbows out, proud to be on the horse. Sarah hoped his hands
were not too small to handle both reins.

"You make a fine jockey," said Trudy.

"Oh, law! You mean a rider in races? That'd be a grand job." He
bent over the neck of the horse and pulled his feet back, as he must
have seen in a broadsheet, amusing both young women.

"Uh, Kid," Sarah began, "I've something to tell you." She put her
hand on his arm. "This isn't easy. I'm not what you think I am. There
were circumstances---"

He looked down at her and smiled. "I know."

"I *mean*... I'm not a young man!" He laughed. "What?"

"I know'd for a long time."

"How? I mean---"

"I saw the clothes in your bag, whenever you asked me to get
something. I know'd there was a reason for dressing like that, and it
weren't none of my business. Besides, when you give me a bath that
first day, your shirtwaist was soaked." He grinned broadly.

She blushed. "Thank you, Kid. That's a huge relief. Sometime, I'll
tell you all about it. Will you look out for Miss Adams a few minutes? I
want to get my bag and change my clothes out back in the outhouse."

"Never mind, Morgan," said Trudy. "I'll fetch it for you." The girl took the luggage tag and entered the station house.

The young stationmaster looked up from his counter and gave Trudy a full, flattering appraisal. "What can I do for you, Miss?"

She knew that look and she squared her shoulders. "The old, carpet bag with flowers that Mr. McGreuder just left here."

He selected the bag from a storage shelf, but kept it in his hand. "Since you've just arrived in town, may I say, I think you'll like it here? Do you have time for a cup of tea?"

That was the worse line she had ever heard. "No, I don't. Are you gonna give me that bag, or not?"

"Of course, Miss. I simply want to introduce myself. I'm Judd Corday." He put the bag on the counter and extended his hand.

Mayhap she had misjudged him. He had brown, curly hair that fell over his forehead and, without his cap, almost covered one of his green eyes. *He was several inches taller than her and had a lop-sided grin.* "Sorry. I am just tired from the long trip. I'm Trudy Adams." She barely shook his hand, took the bag and went to the door. She opened it, gave him a small wave and went out to give the bag to Sarah, thinking, *he was a nice fellow.*

"You don't seem surprised," Kid said, as they watched Sarah walk around the building to the back.

"You mean that she's a female?" He nodded. "Well, I'm a woman, too. I know'd right away."

"She must a' had her reasons."

"That's right. For one, ladies can't go anywheres alone on the roads these days."

Kid thought a moment. "But you did."

"Well, I ain't, I mean…I had to leave town in a hurry."

He looked at her carefully and she felt herself redden. He gave Robin a good pat. "Yes'm." He changed the subject. "It's gettin' on to dinner time. You recon we'll get something' to eat soon?"

After all, he was a growing boy. "I'm sure. As soon as---" Trudy stopped at the sight of Sarah in a brown, calico dress and bonnet returning from the back of the building. "If you don't look nice!" she said. "I don't see how you fooled anyone all those weeks."

"I'll say!" Kid agreed.

Sarah gave them a charming curtsey. "I'm Miss Sarah Dietrich." She shook out her skirt. "It's terribly wrinkled. I didn't bother changing my shoes. These have to do until we find rooms." She attached her bag to the saddle.

Trudy and Sarah started down the road with Kid on the horse alongside them. He kept staring at Sarah in women's clothes. "Watch where you're going," Trudy told him, trying to keep up with Sarah's long stride. She paused to adjust her slipper. "Sorry," she said. "These shoes wasn't made for dirt paths." Sarah slowed.

The road had not yet been cobbled, or bricked, and probably not named, Trudy thought. However, there was a weathered sign on the corner, which she could just make out. "This is First Street! Are there any vacancies on First?" she asked Sarah. She pointed to some houses in the distance. "The houses on that hill yonder must be rich folk." They had spires, columns and brick walls.

"There are three," Sarah said. A block down they found one of the addresses on the list. There was a Rooms to Let sign in a downstairs window. Sarah asked her and Kid to wait on the path, while she knocked on the door. A skinny woman, with graying hair shoved into a messy bun, came to the door wiping her hands on a dirty, brown apron. Even down on the path Trudy could smell cabbage cooking from the open doorway.

"What do you want?" The woman asked, suspiciously.

"I, we want to know about the rooms," replied Sarah.

"They's jes' two."

"How much are you asking?"

"Five dollars a week and two meals a day." The woman looked beyond Sarah and added, "I don't take no children, or animals."

"I see. Thank you." Sarah walked down the steps and shook her head. "It wasn't clean. There'll be something better. We've time before dark." Trudy told her not to worry and they continued down the way.

The next house with a sign was a few houses beyond. A smiling woman answered the door, with a child on one hip, and three little ones running about the hall. Though she looked tired, the woman kindly told the young'uns to play elsewhere. However, a small boy raced out the door and ran full tilt into Trudy.

"Jeremy! I'm sorry," the woman said.

The boy, about five looked up at her. "Sorry, Miss," he said, and hurried back into the house. Trudy spoke to her, but the woman had only one room.

Farther on, they saw a sign in the bow window of a nice, brick house with lace curtains. The small, older woman who came to the door had a sweet face and a white ruffle at the neck of her black dress. She said her husband had recently died and she wanted some folks to live in the house. She asked what they needed, mentioned the barn in the back where the horse could stay, introduced herself and showed them the three rooms on the second floor.

The rooms were light and clean, five dollars each a week, with two meals a day. There was a parlor, Mrs. Perkins, the landlady said for use in the evenings. Trudy and Sarah were thrilled to see, there was a washroom and water closet on the sleeping floor. The landlady said she had a cook and housekeeper, too. It was more than they wanted to pay, but they expected to find work, before they ran out of money. And, they could move right in! Kid went back to the coach station for the rest of their bags, while she and Sarah went to the kitchen for kettles of hot water to fill the tin tub upstairs. They could not believe their luck. Imagine, hot baths, too!

Sarah was pleased. The evening meal was good, plain food, decently served in the dining room. Kid made a hit with the owner of the house by remarking, it was the first room of his own he had ever had. If his manners or his odd wardrobe surprised the landlady, she was too kind to say so. "Is Robin taken care of, Kid?" Sarah asked.

"Yes'm. He likes the other horse out there, too."

"How can you tell?" Mrs. Perkins asked with a smile.

"Well, they kinda spoke to each other. I gave 'em both some oats and water, iffen that's all right, ma'am."

"Thank you very much," she replied. "Lightning's getting on, but he still likes to pull the carriage. Just tell the cook she won't have to bother with him tonight."

"Yes'm. An' tomorrow, if you like, I'll clean the stable."

Mrs. Perkins was even more pleased. Sarah mentioned she would be looking for a teaching position in the morning. The woman suggested she speak to the headmaster of the local academy, down the road. Meanwhile, Trudy had become quiet and introspective at the table. Sarah knew Trudy was also concerned with finding a job. Sarah told her they would make their plans for the next day, later.

After supper, Sarah had to get her clothes in shape for the marrow and, borrowing a wrapper from Trudy, went to the kitchen to press her only blouse and skirt. On returning upstairs, she found her friend sitting on her bed in a dejected heap. "What's wrong, Trudy?"

The young girl shook her head. "Nothing. I like our rooms and the food is good."

"Kid thinks he's in heaven. We were fortunate to find Mrs. P." She yawned. "What with laundry and job hunting, tomorrow will be a busy day."

Trudy ducked her head, but not before a tear glistened on her cheek. "I don't know what kind of work I can do."

Sarah sat down beside her. "What would you like to do?"

"I donno. I ain't trained for nothing decent." She glanced meaningfully at Sarah and shrugged. "I kinda like to work with children. I took care of my stepmother's kids, back to home."

"You might find day work in an orphanage, or a nursery."

"You think they has some here?"

"I'm sure. Don't worry about it tonight. We'll look into it tomorrow."

"Thanks, Mor...Sarah."

"Have a good night, Trudy." She turned back the counterpane and blew out the lamp. Down the hall, Sarah made sure Kid had bathed himself before going to bed.

"I did. I found the drain for the wash water an' poured it down the sink. D'ya ever see anything so up-to-date before?"

"No, I haven't. I understand Mr. Perkins was a pipe man and he figured out what to do with the used water. The W. C. is a big improvement over the outdoor privy. We'll see about some new clothes for you, as soon as I can. Until then, I might be able to make over Ellsworth's things."

"Was he the one you borrowed 'em from? I don't need nothin' more right now, Miss Sarah."

She was pleased he used her name for the first time; she gave him a pat on the shoulder, glad to be female again. "I'll tell you about Worth some time. I cannot wait to wash your clothes and get some stockings on you. The pair of shoes I've been wearing might fit you eventually, too."

"I was skeared o' that." He gave a false moan and curled up on the counterpane.

Laughing, she said, "You'll get cold on top of the covers, Kid."

"Ah never had no sheets before and this bed is lots more soft, too." He slipped off his shirt and, when she pulled the covers back, snuggled down between the sheets.

Sarah folded the spread to the bottom of the bed and smoothed the quilt. She was grateful to have Kid with her, even if it were only for a little while. "Sweet dreams," she said, and extinguished his candle.

Back in her own room, she went to bed. After her prayers, she fell asleep at once. 'Sufficient unto the day....'

Chapter 28

The New Overseer

PENNE QUIETLY PLACED a cup of coffee on the desk by Ellsworth's elbow and turned to leave, when he grabbed her and pulled her down on his lap. Her face shown with pleasure, but she said, "Honey, your mamma won't 'preciate this, if she happens by."

"Then, she has to get used to it," Worth murmured, his face in the folds of her head cloth at the base of her neck. "How's that youngster doing?" he asked, rubbing a hand over the swelling at her waist.

"He's just fine," she pressed her cheek against his own. "Now that I don't have the heaves in the morning, he is one happy fella'."

"You think it's a boy?" She nodded. "How do you know?"

"Cook says cause of the way I'm carrying. And he's up 'bout half the night, twistin' and bendin' like he's hoein' cotton." She laughed outright.

"He sounds healthy. Are you drinking milk and eating enough for two, as I told you?" He turned her head to look into her eyes.

"Yes, Sir. Every chance I get." She got up, smoothing the wrinkles from her apron.

"When is my mother seeing you today?" He wanted her training to progress.

"We already spent an hour goin' over the household keys and covering the lock for each one. She'll see me again before supper." She paused, her head tilted to one side. "They's, I mean *there's* a whole lot to learn about takin' care of a house. An' Miss Emerald, she's giving me schooling an hour each day, too. Kin you believe: Ah's, no. *I'm* learnin' to write!"

He nodded, his eyes bright with tears, pleased that his mother and sister were doing what they could for Penne. "Very good. I'm proud of you, Penne. You'll not only make a fine chatelaine, but a good mother."

"Thank you, *Sir*," she smiled sweetly, and then paused by the door. "What's a chata---?"

"A keeper of the keys and the lady of the manor."

"Me? All o' that?" Her eyes were brown orbs of wonder.

"And…" he nodded slowly, "my wife." His eyes conveyed his love.

"Ah." She clasped her hands to her breast and returned his gaze. "Then," she sighed heavily "I'd best get along. There's a whole passel to learn, before I can manage all of *that*." She kissed her fingers with a wave as she left.

Ellsworth sipped his coffee thinking of the changes being made. He hoped to God he was man enough to see them through, successfully. He had drawn up plans for the alterations he wanted to make to the house. He decided it would be best if he and Penne used the library for their quarters, with a bedroom at one end, and a lesser room for dressing, bathing, and the nursery. The three of them housed upstairs with his parents was out of the question. He felt certain his ma would agree with the plan. If his father was well and still in charge, *none* of this would be possible, or necessary… except for Penne.

Finishing his coffee, he checked his watch. He had an appointment with Anton Simms. Taking a notebook and pencil, he grabbed a cane and limped down the hall to the parlor.

The doorknocker sounded and Ellsworth was pleased to see Apennine hurry down the hallway to the door to admit Simms. She took his hat and ushered him into the parlor. Ellsworth greeted his guest and asked him to sit down.

"I haven't been here since the party," Anton said. "You've grown up, since I last saw you, Ellsworth. You're looking fit."

"Thank you. I'm much improved."

"And how is your father? I was sorry to hear he became ill at Emerald's wedding. I was in Charleston and unable to attend the reception."

Worth nodded. "So I understood. Papa is better, thank you, but he won't be able to resume management of the farm. I've assumed that responsibility. As a matter of fact, that's why I wanted to see you."

"Oh?" Anton said.

Ellsworth took a breath, and began. "Have you decided on your next move, since the sale of your farm?"

Simms shook his head. "My parents moved to North Carolina to live with my uncle." He paused, reached for a leather holder of cheroots in his pocket and asked if he might smoke.

"By all means," Ellsworth replied rejecting one himself.

"To be honest," Anton said, bending his handsome, curly head to one side and blowing a smoke ring in the air, "I'm not sure what a single gentleman farmer does under these circumstances."

"Without a farm?"

"Just so."

"Have you considered returning to law school?"

"Yes, but it would take several years to pass the bar, and more to establish myself. I'm already twenty-three, you know, and to put it bluntly...I've no income."

Worth made a note on his pad. "Did you help manage your father's farm?"

"Only before the War." He raised one eyebrow looking chagrined. "My father seemed so capable I let him convince me it was more important for me to attend school. When I should have been helping at home, I was taking classes in Charlestown and blithely enjoying a bachelor's social life. By the time I woke up to the affect the War was having on small farms, our property was in jeopardy. It was my fault, 'Worth. I haven't even the excuse that I was away in the militia. I'm color blind, you see."

"Sometimes it takes an anvil falling on our heads to make us grow up."

"You're kind to say us." He tapped his cigar on the rim of a pot metal ashtray on an adjacent table. His eyes fell on Ellsworth's cane leaning on his chair and looking up he said, "I can't begin to imagine what you've gone through these past three years, my friend."

Worth waved the remark aside with a sardonic expression. "As I implied, we mature quickly during a catastrophe. We do what we must to survive. I certainly never expected to lose my leg, and I never intended to take on farm management, but here I am. In the course of the latter, I quickly discovered some of the pitfalls of responsibility.

I'm forced to do what I can to keep us afloat during this...what are they calling it, Reconstruction Period?"

"I hadn't heard that term, but that's what it is, throughout the country. Pitfalls?"

"Yes. I'm fortunate to have Emerald and my brother-in-law Winston to help cover the transition. However, I recently discovered that our overseer was mistreating our workers; he was quite incapable of adapting to my program. In fact, the man even refused to help me grasp the methods of record- keeping necessary to run the farm. I've had to fire him."

"That was a *big* step." Anton carefully doused his cigar and gave his full attention to Ellsworth.

"Which brings me to the reason, I contacted you. Is there any way you would consider assuming that position?" Ellsworth folded his hands and watched Anton, awaiting his reply.

Obviously surprised, Anton said, "To be honest, I've had no luck in finding work. But you, you're offering your overseer's position *to me*?"

Worth nodded. "If you think you would like it, if you feel you could work with the three of us and our employees, *and* if our housing arrangement would suit you."

"I don't know what to say. I never thought---." His eyes roamed the room while he considered the offer. "I believe I could handle the job, with your help, but---"

Encouraged, Ellsworth asked, "But?"

"I've never *heard* of a gentleman overseer, Ellsworth. Although I grew up on the farm, my management experience is modest." He stood up and nervously paced up and down the Aubusson carpet.

His sincerity encouraged Ellsworth. "I'm sure there are a great many gentlemen without employment since the War. You tell me, what's the use of having knowledge and experience, if you can't put them to work?"

"I don't know." Anton resumed his seat and leaned forward. "Do you think your people would accept me in that role? I have only my horse and my two hands."

"I don't see why not." Worth scratched one ear. "They put up with a contemptible supervisor before, and not one of them came to me with a complaint. I think they would welcome anyone who gave them fair treatment and support. Those are the other two requirements I have for this position."

"To be sure." Anton paused and pursed his lips. "Tell me, have you given any thought to educating the people working for you? I mean the Blacks, as well as the Whites."

"No." He sighed. That was something *else*. "I've had my hands so full learning farm management, that I haven't fully considered the abilities of our workforce."

Anton nodded. "I understand."

Worth knew that Anton needed the position and sensed he could contribute to their operation.

"I only asked because I became interested in education in law school. I'm convinced it is the one thing that can improve our entire society."

"I'm sure you're right." Worth wove his fingers together, thinking. "I see no reason why we couldn't start a small program, once we've met the current short-falls of income and established production stability."

"That's good." Anton nodded. "I know you grow less cotton, than we did, but you have tobacco. I'd have to learn about growing tobacco."

Ellsworth continued. "We didn't have slaves before the War, but we had several Negroes on the place who worked more or less for their room and keep. They're on salary now, too. We've hired some free people in the last few months. We still have more Whites and sharecroppers. There could be a problem keeping peace between the two races, but so far it hasn't developed." He used his cane and drew a small circle on the carpet. "I wouldn't want any favoritism. I feel the best way to have a successful enterprise is to discover each worker's ability, encourage its development and use it for our good and his own. In addition to farming goals, I want to relieve any physical difficulties our workers have, improve the equipment, outbuildings, wells, and other facilities on the place."

"I know with the War new equipment was hard to get. That's one of the things we miscalculated on our farm. Although my father had only a few slaves, when they became free, they exercised their initiative and left to work elsewhere. I think we would have managed better, if I'd been at home to help and we'd been more far-sighted."

Ellsworth nodded. "Having some share-croppers probably made our transition easier. At the moment we're holding our own where help is concerned."

"And keeping them in this economy will be a challenge." Anton bit his lip and gazed at his friend. "I do have a problem. I've no place to live."

Ellsworth appreciated his candor. "I can't work with anyone who is not completely honest. Those pre-War days when the overseer was the big boss are definitely over. I need someone who is determined to help us maintain a successful enterprise. If that person is you, we can offer you two rooms to live here in the house with us, take your meals here, and see your friends here as part of your salary. The quarters occupied by our former overseer are not suitable for someone like you. The starting salary we are prepared to pay is a hundred a month with room and board. Depending upon the weather, crop prices and performance, within six months we should be able to increase the wages. What do you think?"

"I'm overwhelmed!" He stood and strode over to Worth with his hand out-stretched. "I'd be honored to work for you, Sir! Thank you, very much!"

"Good. I'll draw up the contract this afternoon." He stood and took Anton's arm. "I think this calls for a mint julep. What do you say?"

"Pleased to join you, Sir," Anton said, and ducked his head graciously. As they moved into the dining room, he added, "*I* have a question to put to you. How shall I say? What have you heard from Miss Sarah?"

Ellsworth was surprised by the question. He told Anton no one knew anything about Sarah's disappearance, which had occurred before he returned home.

Anton's expression changed. "That's strange. I saw her, you know?" Ellsworth shook his head. "Two days after the party. She was walking on the east road down by the woods. I rode up to bid her farewell. She was truly sad because she had to leave Fox Haven."

Ellsworth paused making their drinks. "What do you mean, she *had* to leave?"

"She said, because Emerald was practically grown, she was no longer needed as a companion. Now that I think of it, something more was bothering her. She wept when she bid me goodbye."

"But this was her *home*." Worth stirred the drinks and handed a silver beaker to Anton.

"I thought so, too. In fact, I assumed your parents had adopted her."

None of this made sense to Worth. It hadn't occurred to him that Sarah might have left of her own volition. "That means she's alive! If she *chose to leave*, she may *not* have been a victim of foul play."

Anton looked at him in dismay. "Is that what you all thought? That she'd been kidnapped, or worse?"

"Yes. That's what I understood from my father."

Anton drank deeply and shook his head. "*I* don't think so. I'm glad I mentioned the encounter." Both men sipped their cold drinks, each lost in his thoughts.

"I'll look into the entire story thoroughly," said Worth. "So much has taken place since my return, I haven't explored the facts of Sarah's disappearance. I am very fond of her. I can't thank you enough for the information, Anton. You see? You've already helped me." He smiled warmly and raised his beaker in a salute. "When would you like to move in and begin your employment?"

"Would this week-end be too soon? The new owners are almost ready to move into our house."

"No. No, indeed. I am very glad to have you as a member of our operation."

"Thank you, Ellsworth. I'll be here early Saturday morning, ready to work." The men shook hands, both obviously happy with their decisions.

"Come along. I want you to meet Penne." He paused in the hallway. "By the way, she is our housekeeper." He watched Simms's eyes intently. "And, I should add, for all practical purposes, she is to be accepted and treated as my wife."

Anton's eyebrows rose and he swallowed. "Whatever you say, Sir." And he bobbed his head in acceptance.

Chapter 29

Seeking Work

KID HAD BEEN up before the chickens, watering and feeding the horses in the Perkins' barn. He entered the kitchen through the back door and sniffed the fragrance of warm biscuits on the counter and sausage popping in a skillet. The buxom cook, Sophie, whose blonde, braided hair covered her ears, thanked him for taking care of the horses and gave him a biscuit to stave off hunger until breakfast. Munching away, he still could not believe his luck. No one was beating on him, he had a warm place to stay and the food was good. Miss Sarah had promised him new clothes. It was only the shoes he was *not* sure he wanted. He made up his mind, he would do everything necessary to keep his life just the way it was. "Thank ya, Ma'am," he said to the cook. "I'm goin' to see what I can do about them bushes in front"

"You'll find clippers in the barn," Sophia said, turning the meat. "There's also a basket, and some work gloves that might fit you out there." He left for the barn.

After breakfast, Sarah peered at herself in the front hall mirror. She was relieved to look like a woman again. She tucked her short hair under her bonnet, knowing it would grow fast. She smoothed her blouse over her bosom, observing that she had grown during the past few weeks. Despite the limited fare on the boat, her skirt band was tighter, too. Suddenly she realized she had missed her birthday; she was nineteen… almost an old maid!

No question about it, she needed clothes. Trudy had kindly offered to share her wardrobe, but their sizes differed and the colorful style of Trudy's wardrobe, did not suit Sarah. However, she had borrowed a challis, fitted jacket, to make herself presentable for interviews this morning. Her worn shawl was ready for the ragbag. Putting on the jacket and adjusting the shawl, she heaved a sigh of dissatisfaction with her appearance, opened the front door and set forth to beard the lion… who-so-ever he might be.

Trudy came downstairs slowly, reluctant to leave the house. She had asked Mrs. Perkins about the main part of town, where shops were located. Not that she knew anything about working in a shop, but she *had to start somewheres*. She had removed all but one white ostrich feather from her hat and put on her plainest dress with a small bustle to modify her appearance. Pausing before the mirror in the hallway, her face looked pale without paint for the first time in four years. She bit her lips and pinched her cheeks to give them color, and murmured: "Damnation!" With trepidation, she went out the front door.

Locating the academy nearby, Sarah climbed the steps and entered the new red brick building, nervously licking her dry lips. Down a dark hallway she walked, peering into two classrooms until she found the office. Speaking to the secretary at a desk, she sat down on a bench, to await the professor's convenience. Shortly, she was ushered into the schoolmaster's office.

Professor Guttman was a red-faced, chubby fellow whose bushy side-whiskers contrasted to his pink, bald, head. When she introduced herself, he rose and came around his desk to offer his hand. He held her hand so long smothered in his hot ones, Sarah became uneasy. Chattering away, he finally released her and indicated a ladder-back chair in front of his desk. Somewhat taken aback by the personal questions he asked: her age, birthplace, faith, family connections, and time in town, she supplied only minimal information. Although reluctant to use her own name, fearing she was sought for killing the vagrant, she needed the reference.

"Well now, Miss Dietrich," he said, leaning back in his chair, hands folded over his considerable, vested paunch, "Let's see what you know. Can you teach arithmetic, as well as grammar?"

Sarah swallowed. "I believe so."

"History?"

"Of Ohio, or the United States?"

"This is Indiana. The United States."

"Yes, Sir." She knew she could keep ahead of youngsters in any text.

"Hum." He rocked forward, slamming the legs of his captain's chair on the floor. "Are you prepared to teach the lower, or upper level?"

"Lower, I think."

"The first four years. Then, we won't have to worry about history or calculus."

Sarah exhaled, gratefully. "No, Sir."

"You attended school, where?" She hoped that he would not write Miss Langdon's Academy for a reference, but she had to give the name and address of the school.

"I must think on this," he said writing a note on a paper pad. "At the moment we have no opening. However, I have considered dividing the first form, which has thirty students, into two classes. Give me your address. I'll let you know if the school board agrees with that decision."

"Mrs. Perkins's home, Sir, number Five, First. Just down the block. If I may ask, would the board be meeting any time soon?"

"The end of the month, to be sure."

"I see." Concerned, she twisted the strings of her purse in her hands. She had only enough money to last two weeks. "I will have to take another position, if I can find one."

He looked at her sharply. "Very well, I shall see what I can do. You'll be hearing from me." He arose and held out his hand. "Thank you."

The interview over, she stood to shake his hand and leave. Again, he smothered her hand even squeezing her fingers. Just before she jerked her hand back, he let go, with a lecherous gleam in his eyes and a smug smile. Back on the walk, Sarah was relieved to be out of the building. However, she was also anxious. She did not like the schoolmaster and nothing was definite. She needed to find work at once. She walked until her slippers felt thin. Although she located another elementary school, they had no openings, either. On Main Street, when she decided to have a cup of tea, she saw Trudy trudging toward her. Her exhaustion was evident, and she appeared without success.

"Hello, friend," Sarah said. "Let's have a cup of tea and get off our feet." She took Trudy's arm and entered a corner confectionary.

Trudy collapsed in a chair at a table. Her eyes filled with tears and she ducked her head to search for a handkerchief. "This is just our first day, Trudy," said Sarah. "There's much more of the town to cover."

"I swear I've been from one end to the other." Trudy choked and swallowed hard. "Nobody wants me 'thout references, and I didn't even finish the sixth level."

Sarah reached across the small table and covered Trudy's hands with her own. "They want you. They simply don't know it yet. Have you found notices for *help wanted* anywhere?"

Wiping her tears Trudy said, "In the grocer's down the street there's some posted for child care, but I don't have no place to keep children."

"Maybe they'd want you to care for them in their own home."

"You think?"

Pondering the problem, Sarah went up to the counter for two teas and a cruller and returned with them to their table. "Why don't we follow up on one of those, to see what is expected?" She broke the cruller in two.

"Today?" Trudy sipped her tea. "My feet won't take me any fu'ther. Besides, I don't know where the folks on the notices is located."

"We'll get the addresses on the way back to Mrs. P.'s. This is all I can manage today, too."

Back at the boarding house, they found Kid hauling a large basket of clippings and leaves across the front lawn. "Hey," he called and lowered the basket. "D'ja have any luck?" Sarah exchanged a wry glance with Trudy and both shook their heads.

"Not yet," Sarah replied. "Looks like you've been busy."

"I have. They's lots to do around this place. I got these here leaves raked up, an' tomorrow, I'll do the beds."

"The bushes look better, Kid," said Trudy. "You've found work before us."

"I have. Miz Perkins says, as long as I work around the place, I don't have to pay no rent!"

"Really, Kid?" That was the best news Sarah had heard all day.

"No lie! An' I like it, too. I'm my own boss. Ain't that swell?"

"Indeed it is," she said, patting him on the shoulder. "You're a good worker."

Ducking his head at the praise, he added, "The cook give me an apple and a piece of meatloaf on a biscuit, for mid-day. Well, I got to finish up in the barn now." He picked up the basket and went around a corner of the house.

"I don't know how to tell him, he has to enroll in school," said Sarah, as they entered the house.

Chapter 30

Truth to Tell

ELLSWORTH AWKWARDLY PACED the hallway in front of his office stamping heavily on his right foot. He found it painful and uncomfortable to use the wooden leg. What Anton had told him about Sarah's distress, had upset him and indicated he was not privy to what had taken place regarding her disappearance. He crossed the hall to the kitchen, poked his head in the doorway and beckoned Penne to follow him to the office, where he asked her to sit down. "What do you know about Sarah's departure?"

Penne's gaze faltered. "Miss Emerald done, I mean, I was tol' not to tell."

"Emerald? Not to tell *what*?"

"That I knew Miss Sarah wasn't kidnapped."

"How did you know that?"

"Miss Emerald said she ran away." She bit her lip.

He raised a placating hand. "There is no reason for you to be anxious, Penne. I simply must know everything I can about Sarah's disappearance."

She relaxed visibly. "I haven't told no one else, but I saw her leave."

"You knew she left? You *saw* her?"

"Yes, Suh. She come, came to the kitchen carrying her bag."

"What kind of a bag?"

"Her travelin' bag."

"Did she say anything?"

"Yes. She said she wanted some cheese and crackers for a snack later; I got them for her. I asked her if they'd heard anything about you. She told me no, but you might be in a hospital somewhere."

"And that was all?"

"Yes, Suh."

"Did you clean or dust her room later?"

"I did."

"Was anything missing clothes, personal things?"

"Well, the good book, her pichers, and the clothes she was wearing."

"Her Bible, or Testament?" Penne nodded. "You mean the pictures of her parents?"

"I think so."

He digested that information. "Thank you, Penne. That's all."

"I'm sorry I didn't tell you before, Worth. So much has happened"

"No, I understand. I'll see you at supper."

She stood, gave him a concerned glance, and returned to the kitchen.

Now, who's next? Emerald. She should be in the barn.

Grabbing his cane, he limped across the hall, nodded to Penne, and went out the back door. Watching his step on the uneven brick walk, he finally reached the barn and the overseer's office. From the doorway, he saw the room had been painted a soft green with white trim, the board floors stained, and the furniture replaced. Emerald looked up as he entered.

"Welcome, Worth. I'm so glad you've come to see me. Come in and sit down."

"I see you've done the place over. It's quite an improvement."

"Glad you like it. What can I do for you?"

"I know you'll be relieved to hear, I've just hired Anton."

"Thank heaven! I've reached the place where I might plant cotton in a tobacco field, or ask a hand to go to town who can't read."

Ellsworth chuckled. "He'll start on Saturday. I promised you would help him settle in. He's going to live in our house for the present, which will save on salary." He twisted in the chair to relieve his leg. "Now that's done, I've a question to put to you… about Sarah."

With the change of subject, her expression froze, and she took a deep breath. "Yeees?"

"What did you tell me about the day she disappeared?"

Emma searched her memory. "You mean that she might have been kidnapped?"

"Yes."

"That's what we all assumed."

"Why? What made you think that?"

"Well, she didn't say goodbye to any of us. And--"

"The last time you saw her was at breakfast?" He would know if she lied.

"Noo. I saw her in the woods."

He frowned. "What were you doing in the woods?"

"I…uh, was taking a ride on the road."

"Alone? That was dangerous. I'm sure pa-- And Sarah?"

"I think she was simply out for a stroll."

"And you met?"

"Well, yes." She looked at her fingers, rubbing them together. He sensed it was to relieve tension. "I rode back to the house and she walked down the drive."

She was leaving something out. "Didn't you have a conversation? What was said?"

"You know, pleasantries? That sort of--"She dropped her eyes, moved a few papers on the desk and picked up a pen.

He caught the tremble of her hand. "I know something else happened, Emma. Tell me what it was. I have been in the dark far too long. I want to know the whole truth, once and for all." He leaned on the desk commanding her attention. He hated cornering her, but he had to know everything.

"To be honest, it was just an incident. A vagrant jumped up from the side of the road, grabbed my reins, and pulled me off of Melchior."

"My God!" The potential danger shook him. "Did he--What happened?"

"He threw the reins around a bush and dragged me into the shrub. I fought him with my crop, screamed and kicked, but he ripped my jacket open and secured my arms. I twisted and turned, but he pulled my riding skirt and knickers down to -- when he was hit over the head by a heavy club and fell to the ground.

"It was Sarah who heard my screams. She crept up behind him, and struck him on the head with all her might!" Emerald breathed heavily. "She helped me up, mounted Melchior and pulled me up behind her. We galloped for home."

"Heaven be praised! She saved your life, to say nothing of your virtue. '*Incident*'? My God, it was a calamity! Why didn't papa tell me about this?"

Guilt colored her face and she bit her lip before further admission. "I never told him. He would have skinned me alive if he'd known I was on the road alone."

"But, what about Sarah? Did she disappear the same day?"

"Yes. Before lunch."

"What reason would she have had to leave?"

Emma bit her thumbnail. "She might have thought...she killed that man."

Worth shook his head. "Did *you* think so?"

"I, I didn't know."

"Have you told Winston about this attack?"

Her gaze fell to the desk and she rotated the pen between her thumb and forefinger. "Sort of. More or less."

Undoubtedly, his sister had not been totally honest with Winn, either. "Did they ever find the body?"

"You mean the vagrant's?"

"*Of course.*" His irritation grew.

"No. He, he..." Ellsworth's eyes bore into her own. "Someone found him in the woods a day later and took him to Winnie's farm to recover."

"Then, Sarah didn't know he had survived before she left?"

"Probably not." She stretched a hand toward him. "I'm sorry, Worth. At the time, I wasn't forthright. I believed it was better if the folks didn't know what happened. I hate to admit it now, but I thought Sarah had set her bonnet for Winnie. So, I let papa and mama think she was kidnapped." She put her elbows on the desk and her face on her hands. "I may have made some poor decisions." Tears seeped through her fingers.

He clenched his fists, thinking his sister was an utter *fool*. "That's a *gross* understatement! I am extremely glad to know she is alive; but her trail is now too cold to follow. I *have* to find her. There are wrongs to be righted. Above all, she deserves to know that she's a heroine, not a murderess."

"That's probably true, Worth. Only, I don't know where she could have gone on foot. She didn't take one of our horses." Emma took a handkerchief from her sleeve to blow her nose.

"No. But I intend to find out where she went, if it's the last thing I do on this planet!" He stood up, and left the office reviewing everything Emerald had said. It hurt to realize how intensely unhappy his cousin must have been to run away. Depressed, he walked doggedly back to the house. Emerald would be afraid that he would talk to Winn about the incident; for two pence, he would! It would serve her right. Still, he was not a vindictive person, simply one who had been intentionally misled. At least now, he had part of the story; somewhere, there was more.

Chapter 31

The Girls' Success

MRS. PERKINS SMILED pleasantly at the three newcomers at her breakfast table. "I'm glad to see you young people are neat and tidy, my housekeeper, Sophia, tells me. I appreciate that."

Sarah said, "Thank you, Ma'am. We don't want to be any bother."

"I've already told this young man, he is so helpful, I'd like him to take care of the yards, the horses and the barn." She glanced at Kid and passed the toast around the table. "Tell me, where have you come from? You said something about a boat."

Trudy and Kid looked at Sarah. "We met on the paddle wheeler and a way-station, when the boat caught fire."

"Then you're not related?" The three shook their heads. The landlady set her teacup down with a clink. "You were on the boat when it caught fire?"

"Yes,'m," said Kid. "That was scary! We barely got off before it sunk. Mr. uh, Miss Sarah saved me an' the baby, or we wouldn't a' made it."

Mrs. P., as the girls had begun to call her, was intrigued. "My goodness! We have a heroine in our midst! Did you say, a baby?"

Sarah replied, "It was nothing. One of the other passengers had three small children and, since we had a horse to make it ashore, she asked me take her youngest."

"Where did the boat go down?"

"Between Cincinnati and Lodestone," Sarah said. "We took a coach from there."

"Well," the landlady replied. "You've all had quite an adventure. Are you girls looking for work again today?"

"Yes, Ma'am," both replied.

"And as soon as I find a position," said Sarah, "I'll look into school for Kid."

Kid's mouth fell open and he dropped his spoon on his plate. "School? What for? I got me a job."

"I know, Kid, but you need as much schooling as possible. You're too bright to remain uneducated." When he started to protest again, she added, "You can do your work after school. Besides, I promised Mr. McGreuder I'd see you in school before he returned."

Kid looked down at his bowl of porridge and murmured, "Yes,'m."

"Mr. McGreuder? A relative of Kid's?" asked 'Mrs. P.

"No. He's just a good friend," said Trudy. Sarah gave her an appreciative glance and applied herself to her breakfast.

"Did you meet the headmaster at the Academy, yesterday?"

"Yes, Ma'am." Sarah wiped her mouth with her napkin.

"Professor Guttman, I believe?"

"Yes, Ma'am."

"Wha'd you think of him?" Her lips pursed and her eyes twinkled.

"He seemed to know his uh… profession." Her voice was bald.

Mrs. Perkins glanced at Sarah and pushed her chair back from the table. "I'm sure he'll hire you. Just don't let him bully you."

"I beg your pardon?"

"He has something of a reputation."

"As a principal?"

"As a lady's man. An aggressive one."

"Really?"

"So I've heard. Excuse me." She stood and left the room.

Sarah looked at Trudy. Her eyebrows rose in confirmation.

Kid pushed his chair from the table. "You won't have to fret, since he has no openings."

"Thank you, Kid. Excuse yourself, please."

"Yes'm. 'Scuse me," he said, and left, apparently returning to the stable.

"Well," said Trudy. "Little pitchers---"

"Yes. Apparently, I had something of a narrow escape." She giggled and finished her cup of coffee.

First, the young women went to the grocer's on the main street to look at the advertisements for help. Trudy wrote down the addresses of two families requiring nursemaids and Sarah took one of a family desiring a tutor. Thus armed, they set off in separate directions.

Sarah's search took her up the hill three blocks away, where it appeared some of the more affluent townspeople lived. The homes had front lawns, trees, and young shrubbery on large lots. She was growing more anxious by the hour to find a position promptly. While she had only been looking two days, the responsibility for Kid weighed heavily on her mind. She feared her education might not garner enough pay to provide for both of them. Unquestionably, Jason McGreuder would care for him, if he knew she was unable to do so. Still, his work was on the road, and he was a *single* man. The thought of being separated from Kid had become painful to contemplate.

She found the address she sought was for a handsome, brick mansion with Corinthian columns. Impressed, she admired the large, brass figurehead mounted on the paneled front door. She pulled the doorbell at one side. A young servant, in an immaculate apron over a black dress, answered the door.

"Yes, Miss?"

"I'm Sarah Dietrich," she said. "I wish to inquire about the position of tutor."

The servant looked her over briefly, asked her in to wait in the entry and disappeared up a winding staircase at the end of the hall. Sarah admired the black and white tile floor, an Oriental carpet, and cut glass wall sconces twinkling beside a mirror on her right. Shortly, an attractive, blonde woman in her mid-thirties, wearing a blue silk, afternoon dress, descended the stairs.

"I'm Evangeline Grayson." She asked Sarah to follow her into the parlor on the left. She proceeded to interview her and, after taking notes on Sarah's background, appeared satisfied with her responses. "Our daughter, Megan, is twelve years old. She had Infantile Paralysis, as an infant, and is confined to a wheel chair. She is quick of mind and needs special instruction. We want her to be educated at home."

Sarah nodded. "Do you require all subjects be taught?"

"No. Megan receives music lessons, privately. We are interested in the basics for her level, with an emphasis on art, history and subjects that will open up the world to her. Captain Grayson and I feel girls often have such restricted training, they are unable to manage when life presents them with challenges." That struck a note in Sarah's memory. "Megan's disability makes it important she receive a versatile education to develop her mind and to provide her with the best possible future. Would you feel competent to undertake her instruction?"

"I should like to meet Megan, before I answer," said Sarah. If the child were spoiled, slow, or unwilling to learn, Sarah felt she might not have the training to meet her needs.

"Of course," said Mrs. Grayson. She rose, went to the wall and gripped a bell pull to summon the servant. "Mary, please bring in Megan."

"You have a lovely home," said Sarah, admiring the soft green, brocade drapes, the maroon Oriental carpet, and crystal chandelier. Two matching Empire couches flanked the marble fireplace at one end of the room; a wing chair, beside a Pembroke table, wore a sewing bag on one of its arms.

"Thank you. We enjoy it. My husband was a ship's captain on the Mississippi. He joined the Western Gunboat Flotilla on the USS Lexington during the War. He was wounded in one of the battles on the river and is now recuperating." Mrs. Grayson's eyes reflected a shadow of the concern she must have borne during the War.

"I trust he will be well soon."

"Thank you. We believe so. Ah, here you are, darling," Mrs. Grayson said, as her daughter wheeled herself into the room. "Megan this is Miss Sarah Dietrich, a teacher, who would like to talk to you about classes."

The child murmured, "How do you do?" She held out a pale hand to Sarah, who gently clasped the small, limp member. Sarah felt the girl's large brown eyes take in her worn dress and crushed bonnet, as she slowly wheeled around her in a silent inspection.

Taking a breath, Sarah said, "I understand you play the piano forte, Megan. I do as well. Do you have a favorite composer?"

"No. I like whatever I can play." Her eyes were cool.

"How long have you studied?"

The child glanced at her mother. "Three years?" Mrs. Grayson nodded.

"Do you like art?"

"What kind?"

"Charcoal drawing, water color."

"Drawing."

"If I could show you some artists' tricks to save you time and preserve your work, would you like that?"

"Maybe."

Sarah noticed a hole in the seam of her right glove and covered it with her left hand. She tried again. "Have you ever been on a paddle wheeler?"

"You mean a boat, like papa's?" Sarah nodded. "No. I have seen 'em on the river, once, or twice."

"I could show you how to draw the one I came down the Ohio on, if you'd like. We'd have to do some arithmetic in order to get the proportions right. Would that interest you?"

"Maybe, if I could board one sometime."

"That is a possibility. We would need to get permission from your parents and the captain of the boat, and acquire timetables for arrivals and departures of the vessels. That would require the writing of letters, and perhaps some persuasion."

"Could I, Mama? I mean could I really go on a boat? I'll draw a picture for you, if I can." Her face lit up at the prospect and she clutched the arms of her chair.

Mrs. Grayson's eyes flashed her approval at Sarah and she replied, "I don't see why not. That is…you *may*, if Miss Dietrich becomes your teacher."

"You will, won't you?" the child begged.

Mrs. Grayson lifted both hands in concession. "It looks like you've been hired, *if* the position is satisfactory with you," she told Sarah. "Say good afternoon to Miss Dietrich, Megan. We have things to discuss."

"I could have fun in class for once. I hope you agree, Miss Dietrich," said Megan. "Goodbye." With a friendly wave, she wheeled herself across the rug and out the doorway, as Sarah nodded goodbye.

"Do you think you would like to work with Megan?"

"She's a darling and anxious to learn," replied Sarah. "How many hours a day do you have in mind?"

"Five, I think, with breaks for recess and lunch. Of course, lunch would be provided here. We are willing to pay one dollar an hour as a starting salary to be increased semi-annually, if you work out. We would like a month's trial period, if that is also agreeable, Miss Dietrich. What do you say?"

Sarah saw she would have enough to support herself and Kid and save some, too. Still, she wondered about the Captain. Women seldom made financial decisions in Victorian households. "Won't Captain Grayson want to meet me, too?"

Evangeline Grayson strode over to the mantel and gave a short shake of her head. "Not right now. He's leaving this to me."

"Then, I'm happy to accept! I would like to begin tomorrow, if that is satisfactory. Nine o'clock?" Mrs. Grayson nodded and offered her hand to her new employee.

Trudy could not reach their rooming house fast enough to tell Sarah, she had found a job. She had been hired as a nursemaid, down the road in the second house they had applied to for rooms. The poor woman, Mrs. Johnston, was so grateful to see her on the doorstep, she asked her to go to work at once. After Trudy removed her jacket, the woman handed the baby girl to her. At the end of the day, she had played with, read to, fed, bathed and dressed the four children for bed before she left for home.

Wearily she trudged up the steps and, hearing Sarah in the bath, collapsed on her bed incredibly tired. She fell asleep before she could convey her news and slept soundly for an hour.

When everyone convened for dinner that evening, the girls shared the news of their success at finding work. Mrs. Perkins was delighted for them and served some blackberry wine to celebrate.

"This is especially good news for you, Kid," said Sarah, happily. "We'll enroll you in school in two weeks!" By then, she would have earned the money to buy him some clothes.

"I knew they had to be bad news, too." The boy pretended to pout, but he was so happy for the girls, he joined them in laughter.

Chapter 32

Sarah's Rewards

SARAH REVELED IN teaching Megan Grayson. Living in a town for the first time since she could remember pleased her no end. Enjoying the ambiance of her new surroundings, she began to relax and to feel safer than she had since leaving Fox Haven. It was good to be a young woman again. She was amused when she caught herself walking, sitting or speaking in a masculine manner. The masquerade had left its mark; sometimes she slipped into a reverie seeing both male and female aspects of any subject or discussion. It was strange.

Thinking about the riverboat trip reminded her of Jason. She daydreamed about him and missed his candor and intelligent conversation. Moreover, she realized she had tender feelings for him and longed for his presence. He would never know how much she cared for him, or that he might be the only man she would ever… love? She needed to be sure. Hoping he would return soon, she fretted about the problem of her resumed identity.

Meanwhile, she had promises to keep where Kid was concerned. One evening after dinner, she took out the clothes worn on her trip and appraised them for revamping to fit the boy. The shirt he was wearing was nearly threadbare, and he had to have shoes before it became much colder. She could cut down two pairs of trousers and Ellsworth's work shirt. She went downstairs to ask Mrs. P. for the name of a shoemaker who might rework a pair of her shoes for him.

"Oh, child, I have all of Mr. Perkins clothes that could be cut down to fit Kid. I apologize for not thinking of them sooner. I'll have my seamstress take on that job for you." When Sarah began to protest, Mrs. P. said, "I owe Kid much more for the work he is doing with our horse and the yards. I believe you'll find it easier and more reasonable to have new shoes made to order."

Sarah was overwhelmed. If she only had to buy shoes for Kid, she would soon have enough to revamp her own wardrobe. "My dear lady, you are too kind. I know that child has never had a suit of clothes, let alone fitted shirts or under clothing. I can manage new shoes for him under these circumstances. He has never worn a pair in his life, so I want them to fit well. How can I ever thank you?"

"Now let's see. I have always liked diamonds and rubies, if you have any of those to spare. No? Then we'll just have to put you on a tab."

Sarah smiled. "No, truly, if I can do anything for you, please let me know."

Mrs. P. had a thought. "As a matter of fact, there is something. Since I shall be in mourning for more than a year, I need some things sorted for the Ladies Aid Society. If you could help me with them some Saturday morning, I would be most grateful."

"I'd be more than happy to do so. And thank you again."

"Pshaw! 'Tweren't nothing." Mrs. P resumed her knitting and Sarah returned upstairs to begin handwork on a shirt.

After helping Mrs. P. the following Saturday morning, she took Kid over to the main street to find the shoemaker. Getting the boy to stand still, while his last was determined, was a chore in itself. "Kid, if you don't stop jiggling about, these shoes are going to be the wrong size entirely."

"What are those iron things, Mister?" he asked the shoemaker, pointing to the standing iron forms.

"They be what I work the shoes on, lad. I can make any size shoe, once I take a drawing of the buyer's foot."

"I kinda like the smell in here. Is it hide?" Kid asked.

"Yes, indeed, also dyes, wax, and thread," the shoemaker replied.

"So you make a shape?"

"Pattern."

"Pattern. Draw it on a piece of hide--"

"Leather that's tanned and dyed hide."

"Cut it out o' the leather--"

"Yes, and put it over the iron last to sew it up," the man finished.

"Ain't that a job?" Kid shook his head in admiration.

"It's a craft, lad," the man replied, "and a gratifying one, too. Ya see, leather feels so soft in my hands, that my fingers itch to cut it, sew it and finish a pair of shoes with trim and buttons."

"I swan! It's fine to see something you done with your own hands, ain't it?"

The shoemaker gave Sarah an appreciative glance. "You understand mighty well. It gives me -- satisfaction. Yes, sir. I like my work." He picked up his paper drawing. "That's all, Son. You can jump down." He turned to a wall of shelves where pieces of leather were stacked. "What color do you want, ma'am?"

"We get to pick the color?" Kid asked

Sarah eyed the shoemaker. "Uh, no. Not this time. You'll have to wear these shoes every day and they have to go with your entire wardrobe."

"My what?"

"All of your clothes."

"Well, that's no never mind. I don't got but these. I'd like to have me some red shoes." The child looked through the stacks of leather for the color.

"For the present, we'll have to go with black or brown," said Sarah.

Kid paused in his perusal of the rolls of leather. He looked disappointed, but seemed to understand. "Yes'm. Could we have brown, then?"

"Here's a nice Cordovan color, young man. It has some red in it." The man pulled forth a fine piece of leather in a reddish-brown color.

Kid then ran his hand over the piece and leaned over to smell it. "That's grand. Don't cha' think, Miss?"

She nodded. "I do."

The shoemaker showed them drawings of several styles, and they chose one suitable for every day. "Two weeks, Ma'am."

"How much, Sir?"

"Four dollars."

She heaved a sigh of relief and confirmed the order. Her own selection took less time, for she knew her size. They left the shop and went to the dry goods store for stockings and underwear.

He looked at a pair of BVDs. "You mean I wear these to school?"

"Under your shirts and britches."

"Thanks be! I was scared I'd have to wear 'em outright."

She chuckled. "And this is a night shirt to wear to bed."

She was pleased to see how delighted he was with the first underwear he had ever owned. Then, she found a ready-made shirtwaist she could afford. That would help her get by until she could replenish her own wardrobe. It had been such fun shopping with the boy. She had thoroughly enjoyed the experience. Afterward they went to the confectioner's for hot cider and cinnamon buns.

Two weeks later, Kid was fully dressed for the first time in his young life. Sarah was delighted with the transformation. He awkwardly tried out his new shoes, as if he were walking on marbles. She was glad to see Ellsworth's altered pants were trim and fit. Even the made-over shirt pleased the boy.

"Now, for the jacket." She slipped the jacket on his arms and shoulders, and exclaimed, "Well, if you don't look smart!"

"Can I look in Mrs. Perkins's mirror downstairs?"

He clomped down the stairs in his new shoes, and then turned in front of the peer glass, admiring the way he looked. "Ain't I grand?"

Sarah was amused by his pride and incredibly pleased that he finally had proper clothes. "Indeed you are."

"I'm a gentleman for sure. I'm not a kid no more. If you want to, you can call me by my name, Clay. I don't know how to thank you, Miss," he said and his blue eyes swam with happiness.

"You're welcome …Clay." Her throat tightened to learn his Christian name at last. "Let's go thank Mrs. Perkins, too. She's having more shirts and pants made for you."

"More? I can't imagine it. Yes'm." He took one last glance in the mirror and they went into the parlor.

"Now you're ready for the public," the older woman said, nodding her approval

"The who?"

"School, of course." She gave him a tin of wax to preserve his new shoes and a clothes brush to use on his pants and jacket. "You may keep these, Kid."

He brushed a thread from his jacket sleeve and thanked her. "It's a real nice'n," he said, stroking the smooth wooden back of the brush.

He looked up at Sarah. "School?" She nodded. "Pshaw! I thought I needed clothes so's I could get a full-time job."

Sarah met his gaze and gently said, "School first. Besides, you have work to do here after school. You're already earning your room by working for Mrs. Perkins. You won't need another job, until you finish your education." She hoped she would be able to manage his board and necessities until that time.

"How long does that take?"

"We'll see. You want all of the education you can get before you're grown, so you'll be independent and able to do the kind of work you enjoy."

He wrinkled his forehead, running the clothes brush across his hand. "I won't have to go too long then, cause I'll be grow'd next year."

She smothered a smile. "We'll see. Tomorrow, when I come home from work, I'd like you to be dressed and ready to enroll in school."

He sighed resignedly. "Yes'm."

Sarah exchanged looks with Mrs. Perkins, and the women watched the boy leave the room to go upstairs.

"Thank you for giving him the clothes brush," said Sarah. "He had nothing but a marble and a toothbrush to call his own.

"Not at all. He's a deserving boy and so lucky to have you."

Sarah blushed. "Thank you. If he'd been difficult, I couldn't have managed, but, he's smart and appreciative. There are scars on his back and legs from the mistreatment he suffered before we met. He has never told me who beat or half-starved him. Between the two abuses, it is a wonder he survived. He just remembered his given name is Clay."

Mrs. Perkins gave a disgusted cluck of her tongue. "No one will mistreat him here, thank heaven! He's safe in your care, I'm bound."

Sarah said good night. On her way upstairs, she hoped Mrs. P. was right. If the constabulary ever learned the truth about the vagrant and her past, it would cost her freedom and Kid's, no, *Clay's* security. Despite her distance from West Virginia, she was leery of becoming too comfortable. She longed to know how everything was back there, but she was afraid to write to Winston, as she had planned. It could make him an innocent accessory to murder. She shook her head at the bitter thought.

Chapter 33

The Investigation

SATURDAY MORNING ELLSWORTH welcomed Anton into the Fox Haven household. He had not realized how much Anton needed the job, but the fellow's enthusiasm, his quickness in moving into his rooms upstairs, and joining him in the office, suggested he was motivated. They spent the morning going over the responsibilities of the position and the record keeping required of Anton as the overseer. Until Worth saw how Anton applied himself, he thought it best to turn over the financial aspects of the position, gradually.

His mother seemed to brighten at the mid-day meal with two young men at her table. She contributed to their discussion, laughed and smiled, as she had not done for some time.

"I've always admired your home, Mrs. Dietrich," said Anton. "Can you tell me something of its history?"

"Yes indeed, Mr. Simms," replied his mother. "It was built by my grandfather in the early part of the century as a home for his bride. An architect from Philadelphia executed the plans and the furniture was brought down the Kanawha by keelboat. The diamond dust mirror in the entry was a gift to my grandmother for their first anniversary."

"Please call me Anton, Ma'am. I appreciate the information. This is a showplace in the entire county. I'm happy to be in your home."

Her eyes shown with pleasure. "Thank you, Anton. I hope you found your rooms satisfactory."

"Indeed! They more than meet my needs. Please don't worry about any riotous living while I am under your roof. Any of my visitors will be seen, at your convenience, in the parlor or the solarium." He bent his head to her.

"I had no concern, whatsoever, Anton." She appeared completely won by his charm.

Following lunch, Worth took Anton's offered arm and they went to the barn to see the office Anton would share with Emerald. She and Winston arrived shortly to show him about the farm and to introduce the other workers.

Leaving Anton in their hands, Ellsworth stumped back to the house for a word with his mother. He had postponed research on Sarah's disappearance due to the press of work, but he was anxious to get on with it. He found his mother working some embroidery in the parlor. He took a seat and rested his hands on his cane.

"Mama," he began, "Thank you for making Anton comfortable. I am certain he will be an asset. I couldn't be overseer *and* do the books, and Emerald has her hands full." She nodded. "Also, I greatly appreciate your help with Penne. She's happy with the decisions we've made."

His mother looked up from her sewing. "They were *your* decisions, Ellsworth, but I understand why you made them. Apennine learns quickly. I only hope she retains it. I was surprised to discover she could read -- it seems your cousin taught her. That was against the law, you know, until after the War."

The tone of her remark reminded him: prejudice could not be erased overnight. It had to be worked out with determination and education. He stood and limped nervously about the room. "How's papa today?"

She sighed. "About the same. I declare, when he's awake he's railing at me to help him up, and when he's asleep, I'm so relieved, I feel guilty."

"I know, Mama. This has been a trial for you." She waved her hand. "Penne is coming along with your training and she'll prove even more helpful in the future. I hope you know how much I---"

"I do. Not to worry. It won't be long before-- We should start with the changes you want to make in the library, don't you think?"

"Yes. With Anton here, I shall have time to draw the plans. Fortunately, having most of the materials we need on the place will save expenses. I trust this won't be too much activity for you, or pa. I wouldn't know how to manage, without the alterations."

"No. You're doing the best you can." She sighed. "Your father would have a conniption, if he even suspected *half* of our arrangements. To begin with he'd never cotton to Emerald's being out there in the barn."

"She's had the office repainted and made it quite habitable. You'll have to go see it."

"Me? Why, I haven't been down to the barn since I quit riding, years ago."

"Which reminds me--" He braced his cane and placed his hands on the back of his chair. "I want to ask you about Sarah."

His mother focused on her embroidery. "Yes?"

"Tell me. Can you think of any reason she might have left of her own accord?"

She caught her breath. "I don't think…that is, we thought she was purloined."

"I don't think so. Did anyone tell her she was not needed here any longer? Did papa?"

She looked down and pricked her finger with her needle. "Ohhh." She put the finger in her mouth, but her eyes darted about. He knew she had kept information from him.

"Mama?"

"I, I can't tell you, Ellsworth," she said, wrapping her handkerchief about her finger.

"Pray, why not?"

"Because, it probably had nothing to do with her departure, and it would hurt other people, if it was told. As far as I know, Sarah simply disappeared."

"Good God, the plot thickens! For one thing, Emerald tells me, Sarah left after an unfortunate mishap in the woods. Anton saw her the same morning and she told *him* she *had* to leave, because she was no longer needed as a companion."

"Well, *that's* true. She wasn't." She glanced up and frowned. "What mishap?"

"Emma will tell you about that, if she chooses. Suffice to say, Sarah may have left thinking she had injured someone. I *want* to know: what did you, or papa, say to her that could have caused her to leave?"

"Your father didn't say anything to her. He didn't even see her after breakfast."

"But *you* did?"

She flinched, compressed her lips and shook her head. "Ellsworth, I won't tell you!"

He could not force his mother to answer him, but the circumstances were suddenly more complicated than he had suspected. *Poor Sarah. Was I the only one in the entire household who loved her?* She may have had several reasons for leaving. *What I need to know, is how she managed it, and where she went.*

He reached for his cane. "I'm going up to see papa. If he's awake, he may be able to answer my questions."

His mother rose quickly. "Please, Worth. Don't bother your father! He becomes angry, if you even *mention* Sarah's name. He felt she was an ungrateful, prideful girl. She…she always outshone Emma, making it awkward all the way around. Some of the local bachelors seemed to prefer her to your sister. No! Don't even *mention* her! He'd become agitated. He may even have another attack. *Please?*"

Ellsworth finally, saw the animosity Sarah had endured growing up in their home. It occurred to him that he never saw his parents hug her, or give her a kiss, even when she was a child. He'd held her hand when they ran through the fields together, put his arm around her watching the fireworks at the church on the Fourth of July, and she was the first girl he'd ever kissed -- before he went away to school. He pitied his mama, that she had not loved his cousin. It was her loss, for Sarah would have returned her love as long as she lived.

"Very well, Mama," he said, though frustrated, and left the room.

Back in the office, he pondered the problem. Looking to find Sarah's birth certificate and something about her family, he opened the safe and shuffled through the deeds, stock records, and other papers for the manila envelope with her name on it. Settling into the desk chair, he opened it.

Sarah had been born a year earlier than he believed. There was an opened letter to her from her father.

The Fourth of March 1851

My darling Sarah

It pains me to tell you the loss of your mother from childbirth, when your brother was stillborn, has caused me such grief, I have never recovered.

If anything happens to me, I know your Uncle Rupert will care for you and raise you as his own. The deed to our home and property has been put in his name, in order to insure a future and a fine marriage for you, when you are grown. The emerald and diamond ring, ruby earrings, bracelet and necklace, of your mother's, are of fine quality and will give you something of hers to treasure, or to use as needed when you become a young woman.

My sweet girl, I hope you understand why I left you. Please believe both your mother and I loved you very much. Yet, since the death of your dear mother, I have suffered periods of memory loss. My grief is so great; I can no longer distinguish fantasy from reality. I am ashamed to admit, I may pose a threat to your very life. With all my heart, I make this decision for your safety, well-being and future happiness.

I commend you to my brother and to God,

Your loving Father

Indeed, if Worth remembered correctly, *his uncle had taken his own life soon thereafter.* Sarah probably never knew what happened to her parents, or even that she had a baby brother. He stared at the letter for a long time, while all sorts of ramifications presented themselves. Although the letter had been opened, he suspected Sarah had neither seen it, nor known its contents. Moreover, the only jewelry he had ever seen her wear, was her mother's small locket and a plain wedding band.

First, there was the matter of the deed to her property. Ellsworth sorted through the envelope, until he found a bill of sale for the house and one hundred and twenty acres; it was for forty thousand dollars! His father had signed the bill, and must have saved, or invested the money for Sarah. Looking carefully through the papers again, he found there were no stocks or bond certificates and no record of any bank account or investment made in her name.

Checking the date on the bill of sale, Worth looked through his father's record books to see where the money from his uncle's house had gone. In the accounts of fourteen years before, he found a deposit for the exact amount of the sale listed in his father's bank ledger as a transfer, from the solicitor in Philadelphia to Rupert's bank. It was described, in Rupert's hand, as the payment of a loan. *What loan? Why the false listing of the source?*

Worth felt a sharp pain in his chest; his father was not an honorable man! How could he have treated his own flesh and blood with such callous indifference? More than that, with criminal betrayal? What about the jewelry mentioned in the letter? Searching the vault again, he found only a strand of his mother's pearls on the shelf. Nothing more. A growing, bitter anger suffused him. His poor cousin had not known she had an inheritance. Had his father intended to tell her about it, when she was ready to marry?

Clutching the letter in one hand and his cane in the other, he stalked back down the hall to confront his mother. She looked up at his entrance, saw his face and seemed to shrink in her chair. Shaking the letter in his hand, he thrust it in front of her. She did not read it, as she apparently recognized the letter.

"What happened to the monies from the sale of Sarah's home, Mama?" His voice was cold as death.

"I...I don't know," she attempted.

"That's a lie, Mama!"

"Your father applied it to her education and keep."

"Forty thousand dollars?" He spat the words.

"Perhaps, not *that* much." He saw her search for an excuse. "Times were hard, Ellsworth. The house needed repairs, and there were three of you to edu--"

He shook his head. "He *never intended* to give her *any* of her *own* money."

"I, I'm sure he planned to, when she married, probably." The embroidery frame trembled in her hands. His father could have removed those papers, before he found them, but he never expected *him* to have access to the safe.

"Sarah might have stayed here, if she'd known she wasn't a pauper. What happened to her jewelry?"

Her eyes fell. "We, we had to have new farm machinery just before the War and---"

"What else?"

She whispered. "We gave, uh, we let Emerald wear the earrings and necklace to the party. The rest went toward the wedding."

"Then, you still have the earrings and necklace, for safe keeping?"

Again, she looked away. "Not exactly."

Learning his mother had been partner to the fraud, was even more disillusioning than his father's betrayal. He strode to her and lifted her chin, none too gently, forcing her to look up at him. Tears slipped down her cheeks. Her fingers writhed in her linen work. "*Where are they*, Mama?"

"Emerald has them. Don't ask for them, *please,* Ellsworth. She thinks we bought them for her engagement." She wept openly.

Ellsworth swore under his breath. "*Perfidy! My own parents!*" He grit his teeth in disgust. The distaste sent a shudder through his entire body. "Now, you would make *me* party to your theft? No! No! What you, papa, and Emerald have done must be rectified. *You* will have to tell Emma where the jewelry came from and ask for its return."

His mother moaned, "Noooo. *Please*, Ellsworth, don't make me do that!" She extended a hand in supplication.

"I suppose that would be *too much* to ask." His sarcasm hit her on purpose, and he stared at her without compassion for the first time in his life. "No. Dealing with Emerald, after I retrieve the jewelry, will be your reward. *I'll* return it to Sarah, as soon as I can. Somewhere, we have to find the money to repay her, too." He stomped across the floor and turned at the entrance to say, "It will be *years,* before we will be solvent again!" He left his mother sobbing broken-heartedly.

Chapter 34

School for Clay

PUTTING ON HER bonnet, Sarah paused in the doorway of Kid's room. Seeing his drooped shoulders and the angry way he slapped his new book strap over and again on his quilt, she tried a ploy. "It's time we called you by your Christian name, don't you think, Clay?"

"Why not? Everything else has changed," he said in a hurt tone.

Moving his feet in circles, Clay looked at his new shoes. He seemed proud to be fully dressed... except for going to school. She was enrolling him today and she sensed he was scared.

That was so unlike him, she sat down on the bed beside him. "What do you mean, Clay?"

"I won't have time to exercise the horses any more, or trim the bushes, or eat lunch in the kitchen. You said I was doin' a good job, 'n I like workin' for Mrs. Perkins."

She slipped an arm around his shoulders. "I told you could keep your job, but you'll learn wonderful things about the world at school, and you'll make new friends. Give it a chance, Clay. You have a fine mind, and it would be a great loss if you didn't develop it." She stood up and held out her hand. "Let's go see what that new school building is like inside."

He heaved a sigh, gave her his hand and followed her downstairs and out the front door. At first, the boy walked tentatively in his new shoes. Sarah's lips twisted in amusement. He stumbled a bit getting used to the soles, and then he tried running a few yards to see if they still worked. "What do you think?" she asked.

"They're okay. I don't get rocks between my toes."

"Right. And they'll keep your feet from squishing in manure, too." He grinned at her and trotted ahead. At the steps in front of the red brick building, he paused and glanced up in case she has changed her mind.

"Here we are, Clay." She preceded him up the steps into the school; he dragged his new heels, but followed. The two schoolrooms on either side of the hall were noisy with children reciting the alphabet in one and reading aloud in the other. The smells of oiled sawdust, chalk powder, and green wood assailed them. A boy in shabby clothes hugged one wall, head down as he passed them, returning to his classroom. Sarah ushered Clay into the office and, as the secretary's chair was empty, knocked on the schoolmaster's door.

"Yes?" Guttman called. "Come."

She opened the door part way and said, "It is Sarah Dietrich, Professor. I've brought my ward to be enrolled."

The principal quickly left his seat and came around the desk. "Hello, Miss Dietrich. I was afraid we'd seen the last of you." He folded her hand against his flowered vest. "We have a position for you." He beamed.

"I'm sorry. I've already found another," she said, withdrawing her hand and pushing Clay forward in one move. "Professor Guttman, this is Clay Carter."

Guttman's jowls shook with peeve. "I'm sorry to hear that." He turned back to the desk for a slate and pencil and handed them to Clay. "Sit there, boy." He pointed to the bench in the outer office. "Write your name, age, and your numbers one to ten on this slate. I'll collect it shortly." He drew Sarah into his office and shut the door.

Remembering the professor's penchant for women, Sarah moved behind a wooden chair, and watched him resume his seat.

"What kind of background does that boy have? Has he ever been to school?"

She sat down and appraised the schoolmaster, whose chin had moved an inch higher than necessary. "Very little, I'm afraid. He's an orphan, under the protection of Mr. Jason McGreuder, who plans to adopt him."

"Humph. First form, no doubt," he said, drawing a conclusion without even speaking to the child.

Sarah's fingers itched with distaste, but she made a point of appearing calm. "Probably for the initial term," she said. "However, I believe you'll find he's a fast learner and a hard worker."

"They're all lazy scamps, given any opportunity at all. But I have ways to turn them into students."

Her lips compressed. "You mean punishment?"

"By all means, if it's needed."

She stood, holding up one hand. "No. I'll have none of that!" She gripped the front of his desk earnestly. "If you have any problem what-so-ever with Clay, I am to be informed. He is not to be physically punished, by you or anyone else. Do you understand?"

He rose and moved around his desk. "Now, Miss Dietrich, you know a school cannot operate successfully without discipline." He spoke down to her and shook a fat finger in her face.

"Discipline is one thing, Professor Guttman, if it teaches a child to control himself, punishment is another. Through no fault of his own, this child has already had enough mistreatment to last him a lifetime." She met him eye for eye. He rested his fat rump on the edge of his desk. She moved away.

"I see." He grabbed her hand and wheedled, "Tell me how much you're making in your new position. I'll offer you twice the salary." He pulled her toward him, bodily forcing her against his knees. Sarah shrieked and swung at him with her string bag. Clay opened the door abruptly. In two strides he pulled her aside, cried "No!" and shoved the principal away with both hands.

"You need to be taught some manners, boy," Guttman said, huffily, brushing the front of his coat. "I'm the master here! What did you do with my slate?"

Clay gestured to the outer office where the slate lay broken on the floor. "It's in there. I can't write my new name." He stayed between Sarah and the principal until she moved to the door.

"Eight o'clock sharp on Monday," the red-faced Guttman said. "And *you,*" he pointed to her, "can forget that job offer."

Breathing quickly, she hustled Clay down the hall, fury in her every step. "Thank you, Clay," she managed and took his hand. "That man is a womanizer. I hope I'm never within ten feet of him again!"

He stumbled to keep up with her as she flew out the door and down the steps. "What's a woman--?"

"No gentleman!"

Delighted he did not have to stay for the day, Clay released her hand, did a cartwheel, slipped on a rock as he landed and sat down hard, laughing. "New shoes," he said, jumped up and skipped awkwardly down the path toward their home.

Chapter 35

Jason's West

IN ST. LOUIS, Jason's new assignment covered the railroad right-of-way from St. Louis to Santa Fe, New Mexico; it had him walking on clouds. The government had offered the railroad companies a bonus for the one who made it to Promontory Point, Utah first. The Central Pacific forged its way eastward from California, while the Union Pacific worked its way west through the Rocky Mountains, from Omaha. Jason began to see, one railroad bridging the country would not be enough to handle the passengers and goods, California and the West would demand. A southern line known as the Missouri Pacific was also planned. Jason saw the railroads as alive, challenging, and compulsive drives to knit the disparate United States into one country.

The terrible War Between the States was finally over; it was time the country's dream of Manifest Destiny be realized. Jason believed the government would now turn its energies to the growth and transportation necessary for taming the West. Perhaps his distance from Washington, D.C. kept him from the political and fiscal realities of the administration as a whole, but it was common knowledge single-minded people could accomplish much, given the opportunity.

He had read about the Indian wars in Kansas and southern Colorado; he had heard tales of the deceitful relationships between the 'white eyes' and the Native American Indians; but he believed expansion of the country would solve the problem for all Americans. The Indians would receive the necessary help to live side-by-side with pioneers and absorb the best of their society to improve their own. He did not consider himself naïve…simply hopeful.

Jason had grown up in an era of developing transportation systems, when passenger travel progressed from carriages to stagecoaches. Now, pioneers and entrepreneurs of all sorts were climbing aboard trains, as fast as the tracks were laid and the first, rough passenger cars could be built. He knew many displaced persons from the War-torn Eastern seaboard and the devastated South would seek new lives in the undeveloped West. Unquestionably, immigrants pouring into the country from Europe and the Orient would join them. The possibilities were unlimited for those with the courage and determination to make the effort in the untamed country. He was proud to be a spoke in that great wheel of progress.

The advent of the steam engine on boats and trains caused a reluctant government to reassess the new form of rail transportation. It offered a land grant subsidy to the rail companies of six alternate sections for every mile of track they laid. A section, 640 acres, could be sold as the rail companies wished. This ignited a huge advertising campaign by the railroads to lure immigrants out West, to purchase the adjacent lands, and increase commerce along the tracks. The potential for business from one side of the country to the other fired Jason's imagination.

He propped his feet on his desk in the Union Pacific office gazing at a new map of the country. The eastern third was heavily populated

following the War. The Louisiana Purchase made up another third
where, so far, only six states had been admitted to the Union. Of the
final third, only Texas and California had an established government
and statehood. Beyond a few settlements in California, Plains Indians
and a mere sprinkle of settlers and farmers inhabited the Far West.

Remembering Morgan and his young ward, Jason was certain he
could convince them to share in the great adventure. Morgan could
easily find a job with the railroad. He was concerned, he had heard
nothing from his young friend in the three months since their parting.
He hoped no mishap or illness had prevented Morgan's response. Since
letters from his father had arrived, he knew his P.O. Box number was
correct. He decided to telegraph Morgan in care of the stage station
in Evansville. If he received no answer from the wire, he would resort
to his second plan: to find them in person upon his return.

He had left no question that he intended to adopt Kid. He was in a
better position to do more for the boy than Morgan, and he hoped the
young man was agreeable to the adoption. Because Kid was so young, he
could accompany him on his trips west, until his job no longer required
traveling. He would school the boy on the road to prepare him for
further education later. He thought it was a highly practical plan and a
grand opportunity for the boy to learn about his country and its goals.
Jason was not entirely selfless; he knew Kid would be great company
for him on his lone treks across the prairie. He had no concern about
the Indian problem, because he felt the Army was taking care of it. All
things considered, what more could a young boy ask?

Motivated to put his plan into motion, he dropped his feet to the
floor and purposefully went downstairs to the train station Telegraph
Office.

Chapter 36

The Bearer of News

AFTER CHECKING THE contents of her tea tray, Lauree sat down to wait for Melissa Langdon. Emerald's former teacher had sent her a note asking to visit that afternoon. Lauree could not imagine *why* she was coming, but the recent lack of Dietrich social life made any visitor an occasion. She picked up her sewing of a bib for Apennine's baby. Her son and daughter's baby clothing remained in the attic, because she could not stand the thought of seeing them on a *pica-ninny*. Thinking about it she missed a stitch of the crocheted edge she was working.

The brass knocker struck at the front door and the housekeeper answered it. Apennine greeted Miss Langdon, took her bonnet and gloves and placed them on the hall table. Putting her sewing in a basket by her chair, Lauree went to the archway to greet the thin, gray-gowned principal and to usher her into the parlor.

"Do make yourself comfortable. It's good to see you again." Lauree resumed her own chair. "How is your dear mother?" Melissa's mother had suffered a stroke the year before and Melissa was her provider.

The guest settled into her chair and sighed. "The same. Although she can't speak, she is no problem to tend, due to her sweet nature.

Everyone has asked about Squire Dietrich since the wedding. How is he?"

"He is awake mornings and fussing to be up; however, he's much too weak. Doctor Anderson says his heart would not stand the activity. I'm afraid we've had to accept his diagnosis."

Melissa pushed her glasses up on her nose and 'tsked'. "But how in the world are you managing the farm? In view of poor Ellsworth's--"

Lauree preened. "As a matter of fact, we're doing quite well. Worth's health has improved and he has tackled the farm books with enthusiasm. He has hired an overseer and has Emerald and Winston working with him." She picked up the teapot and poured Melissa a cup.

"That's remarkable. One lump, please, with milk." She looked at the tray, as the tip of her tongue peeked over her lower lip. "Are those lemon curd tarts?"

"Yes. Cook is known for her pastries. " She passed the teacup, napkin, and dish.

Melissa helped herself. "Humm. Delicious." They sipped their tea and smiled at one another. "Tell me, is dear Emerald enjoying married life?"

"Indeed. It suits her exceedingly well. As I said, she is helping with the farm management and personnel. I think occupation is what she's always needed."

Nodding, Miss Langdon agreed. "I'm not surprised. She has all that pent-up energy."

At some loss for another subject, Lauree ventured, "How is the academy attendance this fall?"

"Some better, now the War is over. Our local families are gradually resuming their former life styles, despite the general lack of ready cash. We have a new instructor for domestic science who is working out nicely. I am thinking of expanding our curriculum, perhaps to include more physical activity and art classes. Of course, I've missed your girls this year." She finished her tart and blotted her lips. "Have you heard from Sarah lately?"

Startled, Lauree nearly dropped her cup of tea. "Why, no! We only recently learned that she may have left of her own accord and *not* been kidnapped, as we had assumed for several months."

Melissa leaned forward with animation. "Then, I have news for you!" She fished a letter out of her quilted bag and waved it in the air. "I received this letter, a few days ago, from a Professor Guttman of Evansville, Indiana."

Lauree observed that Melissa reveled in the news and drew out her moment of suspense as long as possible. "*And?*"

"He wrote asking for a reference for Sarah, who had applied to teach in his school." She beamed with satisfaction.

"Evansville, Indiana? That must be a long way off," Lauree said, while a dozen negative epithets for Sarah, flew about in her head.

"Yes! Some three hundred miles, I should think."

"Really? How strange." Lauree set down her cup and saucer, to prevent their rattling in her shaking hand. Jealously, she wondered how her niece could have gone so far away alone and without funds. "No doubt the school master will be greatly disappointed in your reply."

Melissa's expression fell. "Whatever do you mean?"

Lauree could not restrain her enmity. "I'm sure Sarah would make a poor teacher, at best," she replied smugly.

Miss Langdon firmly set her own cup and saucer on the tray. "Forgive me, Mrs. Dietrich, but I disagree. To be candid, I found your niece to be one of the most intelligent and well-mannered young ladies, I have ever been privileged to teach."

Taken aback, Lauree said dryly, "Really?"

"To be sure. I would have asked her to join our small faculty, had the War not severely affected our budget. Sarah is a young woman of outstanding character. I gave her an excellent recommendation."

Lauree struggled with the accolades for a child she had heartily disliked, all the years Sarah had been under her roof. Furious, she fought for the necessary physical control, to handle the social situation. Eyes flashing, she stood up, implying the visit was over.

Melissa ground gall in the wound. "Knowing Sarah, I'm certain you will hear from her, as soon as she is settled. In the meantime, I'll leave the professor's address, so you can contact her." Melissa placed the envelope on the tea tray and followed Lauree to the entry.

Not bothering to call Apennine, Lauree gave the teacher her bonnet and gloves and opened the door. Miss Langdon quickly replaced her gloves and donned her bonnet, tying the strings with testy emphasis. Lauree managed a cold, "Thank you and good day." Then shut the door, behind her guest, just short of a slam.

The sound of the door closing resonated down the hall. Ellsworth joined his mother in the parlor. "Did you have a nice tea, Mama? She didn't stay very long."

Lauree assumed a bland smile. "Oh, yes. Miss Langdon had another appointment." She picked up her sewing.

"How strange that she called, after all of these months," he said. "Did she want something? I thought the academy might be in financial straits."

"No. No. Nothing like that. It was purely a social call." She focused intently on the crochet.

He apparently spied the tarts on the tea tray and went over to get one.

Suddenly remembering the letter, Lauree stood up and moved to divert him, saying, "Have you finished ordering materials for the new addition?"

"Just about. I wanted to be sure the plans met Penne's needs, too." He licked his fingers, saw the envelope, and picked it up, before she could. "It looks like Miss Langdon left her letter here."

"Oh, yes. I'll see that she gets it back." Hastily, she whipped it out of his hands, and stuffed it in her pocket.

He looked at her. "Where was it from?" he asked curiously.

"Ah...some place in Indiana, I think." She gathered her sewing and quickly stepped toward the hall.

"Mama?" He stopped her in the archway.

Guiltily, she slipped her hand in her pocket and replied over her shoulder. "Yes?"

"Did Melissa leave the letter on purpose?" His hand at her elbow detained her.

"Yes, she did. The letter referred to a former student." Again, she tried to leave.

"May I see it, please?"

She turned to him pleading, "Ellsworth, it won't do any good."

"*Give me the letter*, Mama."

"Oh, all right," she cried. With frustrated tears in her eyes, she thrust the envelope at him. "Will we never be shut of that ungrateful girl?"

He scanned the letter and his expression changed. "What great news! We know where Sarah is! I can write her in care of the schoolmaster and begin to repay our debt!" His excitement diminished as he turned to his mother in disbelief. "You weren't going *to tell* me? You *know* I've worried about Sarah for months." Disgust shook his voice. "I *don't* understand you." She crushed her sewing to her breast and rushed upstairs to her room

Chapter 37

Trudy's Young Man

TRUDY SLIPPED QUIETLY down the stairs of the Johnston household, where she was employed, to avoid wakening one of her charges. At the entry, she removed her shawl from the coat rack, took her crocheted bag and left the house. She was glad it was Saturday night, as she did not work Sundays. It was just dusk, and the lamp lighter had not yet lit the streetlamp at the end of the path, but she wanted a short walk, to work out the knots between her shoulders. She loved her job, but six days with four young ones wore her out. One thing she sorely missed was talkin' to another adult besides Mrs. Johnston. Not *just* another adult, but a man.

She had not forgotten the handsome coach-station manager she had seen when they first arrived in town. The memory, tucked in the back of her head, had teased her, despite the fact she had only seen him once. Wryly she admitted, she did not know a damn thing about him, but she had not even seen another male, since their arrival. Not surprised, she found herself across the road from the stage station.

A coach and horses stood waiting in the yard, as four passengers left the station house and climbed aboard. The man loading bags on

271

top of the coach looked around as the light from the open doorway hit his face. Sure enough, it was him! Corday, she thought, was his name. He jumped down, shut the coach door, spoke to the driver and waved him off. He was about to re-enter the station, when he saw her cross the yard and approach.

"Can I help you, Miss?" he asked, walking over to her. "Why it's… you gave me your name…ah, Miss Adams?" He had broad shoulders, a dimpled chin, warm eyes and was only a few inches taller than her. From beneath a billed cap, his blond hair tumbled over his forehead and his face wore a happy grin.

She was greatly pleased that he recognized her. "Trudy Adams, Mr. Corday?"

"That's right. You remembered, too." He took her elbow and drew her into the station. "How are you? Did ya find a good place to stay? Where have you been? I've looked everywhere up and down Main Street for you."

His enthusiasm at seeing her again, put her at ease. "You have? We're only a little ways up the road with the Widow Perkins."

"All this time…" He shook his head. "Just up the road. But what are you doin' here? You ain't leavin' again, are ya?'

"No, no." He was better looking than she remembered. She managed to answer his questions. "We like our place. I was just out for a stroll. Have you been busy?"

"You betcha. We have at least four coaches a day and a dozen or so covered wagons." He indicated a row of chairs. "I'm running on. Take a seat. I just put on some water for tea. Will you join me?"

She glanced about the station, saw they were alone, and knew Sarah would not approve. "I, uh, please don't go to no trouble."

"It's no bother. I'm finished for the day. That coach was late, or I'd a' been gone by now. As I said, I've tried to locate you and the man you was traveling with. I received a telegram for a Morgan Kane. Wasn't that the fellow's name?"

She gasped with surprise. "Ah…yes." No one she knew had ever received a telegram. Alarmed, she moved over to the counter, while he located the wire underneath.

"Here," he said. "First one we ever got. Is he a relative?"

She could not explain that Sarah was not a man. "No, just a friend. Thank you."

He leaned on the counter; his eyes seemed to enfold her in the light from an oil lamp hanging from the beam overhead. Self-consciously, she touched the curls that had escaped her combs and framed her face. Her mouth suddenly went dry as she met his gaze. "Is the tea ready?" She asked nervously and put the telegram in her bag.

He turned to the stove and lifted the iron kettle to pour hot water over a cotton bag. "You take sugar?"

"Iffen you have it." While the tea steeped, he kept his eyes on her. He served her placing a chipped, blue and white sugar bowl and a nickel spoon on the counter. "Thank you." He propped his elbows on the counter to drink his tea, and stare at her over the cup rim. She sipped, feeling funny tingles in her breast from his attention. Nervously, she turned to stroll about the station, making sure to keep him in sight. He had the start of a mustache and, she imagined of all things, he would look great on a horse! She did not know what to say. Talkin' to a customer in a bawdyhouse was one thing; polite talk with a decent man was something else. Weren't it?

"Where'd you come from?" he asked, cradling his cup in both hands.

"At first? Uh, Louisville." She had to watch what she said.

"Ya don' have much of a accent."

"Well, I guess not." She wanted to forget where she was from.

"Your folks back there?"

"No, not any more. My pa died in the War."

"I'm sorry." He sounded like he meant it. "Is that why you left Kentucky?"

"More or less." God! If'n he only knew! "I wanted to... see another part of the country."

"You're quite a traveler."

She returned her empty cup to the counter. "Hardly that." She needed another subject. "I don't know nothin' about you, Mr. Corday."

"My given name's Judd. There ain't much to tell. I grew up on a farm in the north part of the state. My older brother is the farmer in the family, but I wanted--"He shrugged one shoulder, "something else. I wasn't about to work in a coal mine, neither. After normal school, I left home to seek my fortune...and here's where I landed."

"And did ya' find your fortune?" She teased.

He raised his eyebrows at her and narrowed his eyes. "I may have done just that."

Afraid she had misunderstood him, she quickly replied, "I 'spect your folks miss you."

"Some. They have my younger brother and sister to home, as well as Hiram. They understand me purty well."

She tightened her shawl. "I'd best get going. I thank you for the tea."

"If you'll wait by the door, I'll bank the stove, and turn down the lamps. You dasn't walk home alone." He set the cups on a washstand in back and quickly completed his chores. Ushering her out the door, he padlocked it.

The moon was on the rise, bathing the pathway before them in a silver light. Trudy had never felt so happy. She tucked her hand in his arm and he snugged her close to his side. She quit worrying about what to say. She was so happy; she could have danced in the road! As laughter bubbled up in her breast, she forced herself to take lady-like steps. It was *such* a short walk home. She bent her head toward him enthralled. He described his work, the opportunities of the field, and what he hoped to become. Judd. Judd Corday. She loved his name. He was the most perfect man she had ever met!

Sarah looked up, as Trudy paused at her bedroom door with an envelope in hand. Her friend said, "I hope this ain't bad news." Alarmed, she felt her hand tremble when she realized it was a telegram.

Reading it quickly, she exhaled. "No! It's only Jason requesting our address." Thank heaven! It could have been from Fox Haven about the derelict. Trudy seemed distracted as she simply smiled relief and went to her room.

Sarah read the wire again. MORGAN: (the wire said) REQUIRE ADDRESS STOP REPLY: ST. LOUIS GRAND HOTEL TO RELIEVE CONCERN STOP SEE YOU SOON STOP Jason

She had been so consumed with her finances, her new job and Kid, she had pushed everything else aside. Now, her problems rushed back in full swoop: the painful, loveless years in her uncle's house, the need to leave, and the constant fear of discovery for the murder, which she had borne the past three months. Although she was preoccupied during the day, fear still tortured her in nightmares at night.

He said 'soon', and she was back to query one. She still had no idea how to tell Jason that Morgan Kane did not exist. Various fanciful ideas bounced about her mind. What if she replied to Jason as Morgan's sister? She could tell him, Morgan was traveling, for some personal reason to find work. She rubbed her temple where a tiny ache had begun to throb. Jason was no fool. That solution sounded like complete fiction. The thought of lying to him again was despicable. As hard as she had fought it, she remembered every minute of each encounter with him on the trip. Moreover, she respected him. *Soldiers!* She had no business fantasizing about Jason, or anyone else. The whole problem was one, enormous mess. The tiny pain spread, threatening to turn into a full-blown headache.

Getting up, she went down the hall to ask Trudy's opinion, but she paused at her doorway, unwilling to disclose her shady past to her friend. It could make Trudy something called a conspirator. *No,* an accessory. While Trudy knew of her masquerade and change of person, she had never told her why *she* left West Virginia. Quietly, she returned to her room.

Sarah washed the blouse she had been wearing to work every day and, as she ironed it, realized how thin the sleeves had become at the wrists and elbows. Most of her earnings so far had gone toward their keep, shoes and clothing for Kid. She had kept the new blouse she had bought for good. Worried, she went downstairs to the parlor to play the piano. She could forget herself, while playing and music soothed her mind; however, Mrs. Perkins was sitting in her rocker doing some hand sewing. Sarah took another chair to be polite.

"How is your teaching going, Miss Sarah?" the older woman asked.

"Quite well, I believe. Megan is bright and eager to learn. We are working on letters to a river boat pilot regarding a planned tour."

"She's Captain Grayson's daughter?"

"Yes. A lovely child." Which reminded Sarah, she needed another shirtwaist for work, and she blurted out, "Is your dressmaker very expensive?"

"I don't think so. What do you want done?"

"I need another shirtwaist, or two…depending on the cost of material and labor. With winter on the way, I'll have to have another skirt and a heavy coat."

Mrs. Perkins lay her sewing aside. "Forgive me, my dear, I've been meaning to tell you: I have bolts of material, which I can't use."

Sarah shook her head, embarrassed. "Oh, no. I didn't mean--"

"Of course not. But you really would be helping me. You see, I need the space in the hall closet for storage. I won't wear anything, but black and gray for the next two years. I bought that yard goods before Herbert got sick. Go see what's in the cupboard."

Sarah returned with the goods and put them on the loveseat. Fingering the material of one bolt, she said, "This is lovely and expensive, I'm sure. I could make two blouses from this lawn. The royal blue faille would be beautiful as a suit. How much do you want for them?"

Mrs. Perkins waved her hand. "Pshaw! I wouldn't think of selling them. There is some serge in the back of the cupboard, too. I had planned a coat, but the maroon is too bright for me."

"But I couldn't --"

"I won't beg you to take the goods, but I'll have to give it to the Ladies Aid Society, if you don't. They're having another sale in two weeks. I've so many pairs of shoes and things of Herbert's to collect, I can't manage to pack another thing."

"Then I accept, with great appreciation, only if you let me pack the boxes going to the Society for you. Kid will put them in the buggy and we can take them to the mission hall on Saturday." Her eyes returned to the material, as she began mentally to revamp her wardrobe and that of Trudy's. She could even afford to hire the tailor, now. Her eyes filled with tears of appreciation as she bundled up the goods. She kissed her landlady on the cheek, and said, "Thank you, so very much."

Stowing the material in the bottom drawer of her dresser Sarah went down the hall to see Trudy. She found her friend waltzing about the room, humming to herself.

"You're happy tonight," Sarah said. "Did you work late? We missed you at supper."

Trudy's hand flew to her mouth. "I forgot all about supper."

"I don't remember; did you say where you got the telegram?"

Trudy blushed, but could not help grinning. "At the coach station."

"Ah ha! The plot thickens." Sarah teased.

Trudy clapped her hands. "Well, now, I went for a stroll after work…and ran into Mr. Corday in the coach yard."

"Who?"

"Judd Corday, the station manager."

"Um hum." Sarah rolled her eyes.

"Honest to God, Sarah, he is the nicest man I ever met. He wouldn't let me walk home alone in the dark." Happily, she did another twirl about the room. "He's taking me to tea tomorrow afternoon." Her expression glowed.

"That's wonderful. You deserve an outing."

"Yes, I do." Her face suddenly fell. "Mayhap he wouldn't 'a asked me out, if he knew, I'm damaged goods." Abrupt tears filled her eyes and she dropped down on the bed.

"Don't say that, Trudy! What happened to you at thirteen was not your fault. You have as much right to happiness, as anyone else." She went over and put her arm around her friend. "We have to forget the past and live our lives as best we can. Surely, that's all the good Lord expects of us." She gave Trudy a pat on the back. "You're a fine young lady and a dear friend." She paused and gave her a concerned look. "I wouldn't want you to be hurt, 'though, if this friendship didn't work out, one way or another."

"Oh, I won't." Trudy brightened and brushed her tears away. "But this is the first time I ever had a male friend. I don' know how to act. What if I say the wrong thing, or make a dumb mistake?"

"You won't. Is this fellow kind? You know, is he polite?"

"Yeah. It's just me. I've had the wrong kind a going's on with men, in the past, 'n' I don't know 'zackly what I should do, or not do." She gestured open-handedly.

"You'll do fine. Now, what are you going to wear?" Sarah began to pull clothes from the wardrobe for her to consider. "How about this peach silk with your brown jacket?"

Trudy examined the dress critically and plucked the large silk flowers from the bustle. "I could sorta hide the low neck with some lace. Ya think?"

Sarah nodded. "That would be perfect. And suppose... we put the flowers on your bonnet?"

Her friend tried them there and exclaimed, "They look just right." She was again a positive, young girl. "Oooh, I forgot to ask. Since McGreuder 'tends to come back soon, how in blazes are you goin' to explain to him, Morgan has become a girl?"

Sarah raised both open hands. "A miracle?" Both girls fell on the bed in mirth.

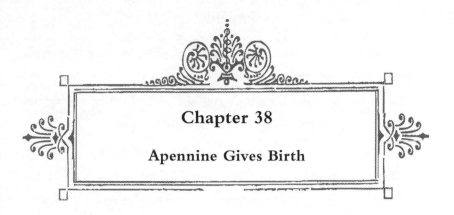

Chapter 38

Apennine Gives Birth

APENNINE STOOD IN the library, which had become a parlor and bedroom for Ellsworth and herself. It was difficult to imagine having a parlor of her own. Tall shutters divided the room and Ms. Dietrich had the couch and chairs covered in a heavy material in a jade color, which she liked. She did not know exactly why her lady did it, when the velvet stuff underneath had been in perfect condition. Walking into their sleeping room and seeing the big four-poster bed loaded with white pillows and a feather comforter, she could hardly wait to jump into it with Worth. They were going to move into their quarters, as soon as the dressing room was painted and the doorway to the kitchen was cut. *We're gonna have a tin tub in here for baths!* She still did not believe it. They would bring the hot water right through the doorway from the kitchen.

A carpenter measuring the trim bobbed his head to her. It surprised her since she was just a housekeeper and colored at that. They had made a new outside door for Worth, so he could go straight to the barnyard without bothering the rest of the house. Their chil'ren could use it, too, instead of running through the house. They would be private and cozy with a nice place for their young'uns to grow up. My, my!

The baby moved in her womb, and she rubbed her hand over her stomach. "You *know* I'm thinking about you, don't you?" She felt a strong kick and laughed at the direct answer to her question. Turning back down the hallway, she went to the kitchen to get a cup of tea. Her back was hurting, but she wanted to see if Cook needed her before supper.

The cook looked up from the stove wiping her shining face with a cloth. Her new helper, a sharecropper's daughter named Naomi, was busy washing pots at the dry sink. "You looks kinda poorly, girl," said Cook to Apennine. "Would ya like to set a spell in the arbor where it's cooler?" The cook had been good to her even with her new job in the household. She said she liked to see the coloreds better theirselves.

"No'm. Ah jes' need to--" She groaned deeply and looked up at the cook. Sudden tears flooded her eyes.

"Um hmm, tha's what Ah feared. Come on, gal, we's gwain down to my cabin. Naomi, never mind them pots. Don' you let nothin 'burn, or you'll be back in that cotton field with yore pa." The cook took Penne's arm to urge her out the door.

"All the way down there? I cain't make it."

"You has to. White folks don't like to hear them birthin' noises."

Penne nearly fell as she pulled her arm out of the cook's hands. "No. I'm going to my own bed." Holding on to the wall, she moved down the hall, back to the library and her new bedroom.

Hastily, the cook rummaged in a chest of drawers for old sheets and towels, grabbed wrapping paper, soap and basin, and followed Apennine. Quietly she shut the library doors, admiring the fine, parlor on her way to the bedroom. *That gal's done herself proud*, she thought. *Who'd a knowd?* She shooed the carpenter out the side door, stripped the bed of the new pillows and sheets, spread wrapping paper on the mattress and whipped the worn sheet on top. Then she helped Penne out of her dress, leaving her in a shift, just before the girl's water broke. "You was right. Ya' couldn't a made it to my cabin."

"You sure the baby's coming?" Penne asked.

"Ah's positive. Now, git up on the bed and wait for the next pain."

Penne groaned and tears washed her face. Another pain gripped her back. Crying out, she fell over on the bed.

"Don't you go carryin' on, gal. Birthin' takes time, jes' like dyin'." She folded the clean linen from the bed.

Writhing Penne cried, "I want Master Worth!"

"*No you don't*," the cook said, wiping up the floor. "He's in the field an' won't 'preciate bein' called. You has a way to go. We won't 'sturb him til it's time."

Penne gave a high-pitched scream of agony. The cook shuffled into the new dressing room, found a small scrap of trim board and gave it to her patient; then she pleated a piece of rag which she tied in a loop from the bedpost.

"You bite down on this when the next one comes, and pull on to this here post-rope. Ah'm gwan' to the kitchen for a knife to put under the bed." Penne put the piece of wood in her mouth as told. Leaving the library, Cook surprised Miz. Dietrich in the hallway.

"What's going on in there?" the woman asked, sharply.

Feeling guilty for being caught in the front part of the house, Cook bobbed her head and said, "Ah's sorry, Miz. Dietrich. Miss Penne is havin' her time."

Fear froze the missus face. "You mean the baby's coming?"

"Yes'm. It sho is."

Miz. Lauree's hand flew to her mouth. "Do you need help? Is there a mid-wife on the place?"

"No'm. Ah kin manage, but..." she glanced toward the kitchen, "Ah cain't serve supper, too."

Miz. Dietrich winced. "Never mind. I'll supervise Naomi. She has to learn some time."

"Yes'm. 'Scuse me. Ah'd best git back."

"That's right. You take care of her," the mistress said. "If you need anything--well, *someone* will respond." Another scream from the library caused her to flinch and she hurried to the kitchen.

Ellsworth came through the back door from the fields, worn out from walking too much and too far. His mother gave him a drink of water and he saw she was wearing an apron. "Thanks, Mama. What's going on? Where's Cook?"

Before she could answer, a long scream came from the library. His mother drew back as though struck. Puzzled, he dropped into his wheel chair and pushed himself to the hall. A noise at the top of the stairs caught his attention.

There stood his father in his nightshirt holding on to the newel post. "What in tarnation is that caterwauling?" his pa bellowed hoarsely, swaying alarmingly above the stairs

"Hold on, Pa. I'll see."

"Where's your mother? This ish no way to conduc' a household!" Before Ellsworth could reply, his father lost his balance, took a header down the stairs, and rolled all the way to the landing.

"Mother!" Worth yelled, struggled out of his chair and up the steps one at a time. His mama rushed from the kitchen and screamed at the sight of his pa lying on the landing in a crumpled heap.

"Merciful God!" she cried, flying up the steps.

Ellsworth reached him and tried to straighten his legs. Feeling his father's wrist for a pulse, he moaned, and helped his mother sit on a step beside him.

"Oh, my dear. I'm sorry I didn't hear you call," his mother crooned, stroking his father's cheek, and brushing hair from his eyes. Apparently seeing his face, she cried, "No, no, Rupert! Call someone, Worth. He can't be--"

"I'm sorry, Mama. He fell from the top step." His temples pulsed and his eyes filled with tears.

The cook, leaving the library with a pan of soiled cloths, stopped in the hallway alarmed by the scene on the stairs. "Can Ah help? Is *Master Rupert--*?"

Ellsworth stood up and nodded. "He's gone, Cook. Would you call Miss Emerald, Ben, and Mr. Simms from the barn? We need help."

"Yas, Suh." She hurried to the kitchen.

After the men placed Rupert on a table in the solarium, and the doctor was sent for, Ellsworth explained to Emerald and Anton what had occurred. They sat in the parlor talking softly to one another. Then, he remembered seeing the stained cloths in Cook's basin and the reason he had headed to the library.

"Mama," he stood, offering her his arm. "We have someone to see."

His mother wiped her eyes, tucked her handkerchief in her sleeve, and followed him into the library. Penne looked up anxiously when they entered the bedroom. She was a shiny, brown pile of leaves among the white pillows of the bed. Beside her, a bundled, tan-faced baby sucked one tiny thumb.

"How are you?" He leaned over to kiss Penne's brow.

"Fine, jes' sleepy." She bent her head toward the baby. "Cook says she has all her parts."

Worth picked up the baby and held her for his ma to see. "She?" Penne nodded with a tired smile. "Your first grandchild, Mama. Isn't she pretty?" Sudden pleasure warmed his chest. "Penne, you've done us proud."

His ma looked at the baby, bit her lip, swallowed and nodded to Penne.

"I'm sorry 'bout the noise," Penne said. "Ah hope I didn't 'sturb nobody."

His mother covered her mouth and swept from the room. Penne gave him a questioning look. He cuddled the infant next to his neck and said, "My father fell down the stairs, Penne. I'm afraid… it was his time. We'll be preoccupied with his funeral for the rest of the week."

Penne bit her lip, and a tear slipped down her cheek. "I'm so sorry, Worth. Don't worry about us none. I'll be up to help in the morning."

"Thank you, dear. I'm so glad you're all right. I'll be back after dinner." He nuzzled the baby's cheek, gave her a kiss, then tucked her back in her mother's arm. "She's darling. I will see Cook takes good care of you. Get all the rest you need, sweetheart." He kissed her gently twice and left the room.

One leaves and another comes, he thought. He had lost a father and become one himself. *A papa.* He slowly wrapped his mind around the fact on his way back to the parlor.

Chapter 39

Fox Haven Peace

IN THE HALLWAY, Ellsworth held the bundled baby in his lap and rocked his wheel chair back and forth. The effort to be on his wooden leg and in the fields sapped his energy, so he still resorted to the chair indoors. "Well, if you don't beat all," he said. One, tiny, tan hand grabbed his finger. Apennine leaned over his shoulder smiling. She had told him she was grateful to have the baby born and to be settled in their new quarters.

"Don't she look like you?" she asked.

"It's early to tell, but the light skin doesn't hurt. Look at her smile."

"Um hum, but Cook say it's jes' gas."

"Cook *also* said she was going to be a boy. I don't put much credence in her knowledge of anatomy."

She laughed. "Anatomy?'

He nodded. "The human body. Here. You take her." He handed the baby to Penne. "I need to check on the construction."

"Worth…." She paused. "Miss Emerald gave me the purtiest pink dress with pantalets for her. 'N your mama had the family crib brought down from the attic. I's…*I'm* so grateful."

"So am I." He hoped the gestures meant she was winning them over.

"We have everything we need. Bountiful, you might say, except…" He heard her reluctance. She looked down at the baby. "I need to know when we're gonn'a name her. I can't go on callin' her 'chitlin', forever."

He knew it was time to settle the child's identity, but he had been dragging his foot. Possibly it was his mother's attitude, or Anton's cynical silence. Naming in the Christian tradition was important. "We'll discuss it tonight."

"You hear that, 'chitlin'? We're gonna name you tonight." Humming softly she walked back to their quarters.

Ellsworth watched her go, knowing she had pinned him down. He admired her returning, slender figure, and he loved the privacy of their new rooms. Penne took care of him and the baby, as if she had done it always. For a young girl, she looked so…womanly sitting in an old rocker in their bedroom nursing the baby. It touched his heart. When the two of them snuggled up in their big bed, they slept like puppies, until the baby cried for her twelve and four-o'clock feedings.

There was a peace in his heart, he had never expected to know after the horrors of the War. He would never have two legs again or fully regain his stamina, but he was happy. He had also accepted the financial responsibility for his mother, for Emma's inheritance, for the farm and for the debt owed to Sarah. He was proud to be the one who would meet all of those challenges.

In her unadorned, black silk dress, Lauree came up the hallway, nodded to Penne at the library door, then smiled at her son. Her face was still pale from the grief of the previous few weeks. She carried the last of the season's roses in a basket. She would place them in a crystal vase in the parlor.

"How are you, Mama?" he asked.

"Fair to middling, Son." She stopped by his chair. "And you?"

"Well, Ma'am. In spite of everything, life goes on." He waved a hand of acceptance. "I need your help with something I've put off: the baby's name. Do you have strong feelings about what we call her?" He knew she would not want a family name used, but being a father was new territory for him.

Lauree shut her eyes and sighed. "We can't have a christening."

"No. No, I think not." He waited.

"Would you like Harriet, or Josie? Maybe Penne would like to use her mother's name."

"I'll see. She was a slave, though." That kind of name was not what he wanted for his baby…daughter. "Thank you. We'll decide tonight." Lauree nodded and went into the parlor.

Ellsworth wheeled himself over to the front door, took his cane, and walked out onto the porch. On the west side of the house workers were busy painting the porch railings and trim on the door and the windows of the new extension. They had already removed the balance of building materials from the site. Supervising the work, Anton turned toward Worth.

"Good morning, Sir." Simms pointed to the steps and siding. "How does it look?"

"Fine, Anton. Just perfect. You've accomplished the job speedily. Apennine didn't give us a second to spare." Ellsworth chuckled and looked to his friend for some mention of his new baby girl.

"Glad you like it. The men have finished the interior, too, so you have your own dressing room, now, and a door to the kitchen. The exterior door will have its hardware installed by tomorrow."

It peeved Worth that the overseer ignored his relationship with Penne. Anton was polite at meals, thanking her for service; otherwise, she was invisible to him. *'Rome wasn't built ...'et cetera.* "I'm glad you thought of the door, Anton. The access will save steps and traipsing through the house. Are there any materials left that can be used on the out buildings?"

"As a matter of fact, yes. We've begun repairs on the barn and two cabins of Cook and the Garth family. Now that the tobacco is in the sheds, we are down to turning the leaves and clearing up the corn and cotton fields. We've hands to spare for the repairs needed."

"Fine. As soon as a brief period of mourning is over, we will have the harvest supper. My father usually planned that for a Sunday after the apples were picked, but we'll take a half-day on a Saturday, instead."

"That's a good idea." Anton paused a moment. "If you don't mind, could I bring a guest to the supper: Miss Agnes Forrest?"

"It's high time you resumed your social life, old man. Emerald, Mother, *and* Apennine would be pleased to see Miss Forrest again."

Anton smiled faintly and looked away. "Your field hands work hard. We have listed major repairs and replacements needed and revamped the tool shop to sharpen and recondition equipment. Miss Emerald has filed copies of all contracts, revised requisition and sale forms, and up-dated the personnel files. As you noted earlier, with tobacco prices up and your crop's quality, it should do very well at the tobacco auction."

"That's encouraging. I *knew* you could manage the job. See you at dinner."

"Thank you, Sir."

Chapter 40

Clay in Trouble

SARAH ENTERED THE house, removed her bonnet, hung it on the coat rack and climbed the stairs. It had been a long week and she was ready for a nap before supper. She was pleased with the way her young pupil was progressing and she believed the child was happy under her tutelage. However, her own hours had increased, in order to cover the day-trips she had included in the curriculum. Megan's lack of playmates worried Sarah. She planned to take Kid, no, *Clay* she reminded herself, over to meet Megan some Saturday, to see if the children would enjoy one another's company.

Reaching her bedroom, she removed her shirtwaist and washed her face and arms in the washbowl. Slipping on a wrapper, she gathered the week's soiled clothing, and took it to the washroom to soak before washing. Passing Clay's bedroom, she noticed that his books and his school clothes were not on the bed. Surely, he would not go to the barn in his good clothes. He was so proud of his new shoes, he would never wear them to--He must be late from school.

Replacing her wrapper with an old shirt and a skirt, she went downstairs to find Mrs. Perkins. The landlady said she hadn't seen

Clay, but thought he must be in the barn. The tall-case clock in the hallway struck six as Sarah went out the kitchen door to the barn.

There on a bale of hay, neatly folded, was his jacket. His new shoes sat atop his schoolbooks. "Clay?" she called, but the only reply was a 'whuffle' from the Perkins' carriage horse. Neither Clay nor Robin was in sight. She stepped out into the alley, looked both ways, saw no one and returned to the house. Since she had just ridden the horse home from work, Clay had no reason to exercise him, especially not in his good pants. Barefoot perhaps, but….

On her way through the kitchen, she asked Sophia if she had seen the boy; the cook said, 'Just when he came through on his way to the barn.' Putting on a jacket from the hall tree, Sarah went out the front door and looked up and down the street. The street-lamp lighter was just making his rounds, but he had not seen Clay, either. Back in the house, Sarah told Mrs. Perkins the child and the horse was missing.

"Surely he's simply having a run before dinner," the landlady replied. "You know, Clay wouldn't miss dinner, if his life depended on it."

"He wouldn't, but---" she looked at the older woman. "I had better see if I can find him. Please don't hold dinner for us."

"There's only Trudy." Now concerned, Mrs. Perkins went back to the kitchen.

Hurrying down the path, Sarah had no idea where Clay might have gone. She turned right toward Main Street. The windows of the houses she passed glowed yellow, lit by oil lamps. The last blush of the sunset's pink stained the western sky. Something has happened to him, she felt. It was not like him to leave, even to exercise Robin, without telling her. He could not have been gone long. She had only been home half an hour.

Trudy could not stop herself from going back to the stage station. Judd had been gobs of fun the few times they had been together, and her attraction to him had grown with every visit. She tried to keep in mind what Sarah had said about not getting too fond of him, but her feelings were over-whelming. His curly hair made her fingers itch to run her hands through it. She had already imagined his muscular arms wrapped around her, and his sweet breath on her neck. Maybe soon he'd tell her how he felt about her. If those things were not enough, his sunny, sure personality drew her as a child to cookies.

Way she saw it, there was only one hitch to their friendship lasting: her past. It *was* friendship, she had in mind, wasn't it? She had a right, 'cause she hadn't had a choice for three, miserable years. She stopped in the middle of the road across from the station. How could she go on lying to Judd about her family, her birthplace, and her job as a shady lady? If she meant anything to him, he might not care about her past, although Sarah would say, he needed more time to really get to know her.

A man entered the station throwing a wedge of lamplight from the briefly open doorway. She was undecided, hesitant to carry out her plan, yet unwilling to go home. With lies, she knew their friendship was doomed. Sarah might be disappointed in her for letting her heart rule her head, 'cause her feelings were already beyond control. It was all up to Judd, now.

What would she have to lose? *If it wasn't gonn'a work no ways, a make-believe romance wasn't fair to him.* She liked him. That was all there was to it. She crossed the road and the coach yard, braced herself and entered the station.

A man at the counter talking to Judd turned around and surprised Trudy no end. It was Mr. Mc Greuder! He doffed his hat and gave her a nice bow. "Miss Trudy, how glad I am to see you! Do you like it here? Have you found a good place to stay?" He waved one hand, dismissively. "Sorry to bombard you with questions. I have been deeply concerned about all of you. I was just inquiring about Morgan Kane. Do you know where he resides?"

Trudy glanced at Judd, while frantically composing what to say about Sarah. Come hell or high water, she would not betray her friend. "I... believe I know someone who might could tell us," she managed to say.

"Good. Very good. Is that person nearby?"

Trudy's mouth was suddenly dry. She licked her lips and swallowed. "Yes, Sir. Just down the road." Judd frowned at both of them. Jason, who turned to pick up his gloves, missed her dismay.

"Do you have business to conduct here, or could you show me the residence? I have a room at the inn for tonight, so I am free, if you are, to renew our acquaintance. I wouldn't want to affect your plans, but you can appreciate my anxiety." He grasped her hand with enthusiasm.

She glanced at Judd and said, "Nothing that can't wait," she hoped, as she nodded goodbye. Judd raised a hand, probably wantin' to say something, but she took Jason's offered arm and they left the station. Half-way listening to Jason's conversation regarding his recent work plans in St. Louis, and answering his inquiry regarding her own life since he last saw her, she guided him down the path to their rooming house. Her anxiety increased the closer they got to home, as she weighed the possible outcome of Jason's sudden arrival. There was no way to warn Sarah, or to prevent the painful blow she was about to give her.

Sarah had searched two blocks of Main Street and not seen Robin tethered to a hitching post anywhere. She would have gone down to the port, but the distance was out of the question. Fear knotted her stomach. As she turned back to her own road, she murmured a prayer. Seeing the coach station on her right, she decided it was the last place she would look before returning home.

"Oh, Mr. Corday," she began. "I'm Trudy's friend, Sarah Dietrich."

He bobbed his head. "Glad to meet ya. Quite a coincidence…"

"Yes," she interrupted, distractedly. "I'm looking for a young boy of ten. His name is Clay. He's my ward and he has disappeared. Has a boy been here this evening, by any chance?"

"As a matter of fact, a child inquired about passage to St. Louis, a few minutes ago. I told him we hadn't a coach 'til morning. He wanted to know the cost, 'n said maybe he could work his way. He seemed, I don't know--"

"That had to be Clay! He may have returned to the house. Did you notice where he went when he left?"

Judd thought a moment. "Miss Dietrich, let's look out back. He might 'a hunkered down in our stable."

She followed him out the back door to the station's small barn, and was relieved to find Robin tethered, alongside of four coach horses, munching away in a stall. The horse nickered when he saw Sarah. She gave him a pat and looked for Clay. The boy stood up, backed into a dark corner, wiping tears from his face with a dirty hand. "Oh, Clay," she cried, and crushed him in a relieved hug. "What's the matter, Son? What happened to…?"

Clay yelled, pulled away from her, sobbing in obvious pain. "He beat the b'Jesus out a me, an' I didn't do nothin'!"

Sarah and Judd exchanged glances. "Who beat you?"

"Ol'man Guttman!"

His sobs nearly broke her heart. Sarah asked him to turn around and gasped at the sight of blood oozing through his shirt. Carefully she peeled the shirt up his back. "Oh, my Lord!" She fell to her knees in the straw at the sight, afraid even to touch him. The child's back was bloody, raw meat. Her tears spilled over, and she pulled a handkerchief from her sleeve to wipe the boy's face gently, then her own.

"I ain't goin' back there no more. I don't care if I'm dumb as a post. Miss Sarah, I can't take it no more!"

"I am so sorry, Clay. I had no idea." Wiping her eyes, she asked, "How long? When did he begin to mistreat you?"

"A couple weeks after school begun, 'n most ever' day."

Her eyes closed in pain, she gritted her teeth, and moaned. "And you never told me… I promise you, Clay, you will never have to see that devil again!"

Judd had gone into the station and returned with liniment and a wet cloth. "Here you are, Miss, for his face. Would you like some of this turpentine for his back?"

"Thank you, Judd." She stood up brushing the straw from her skirt. "Clay, this is Mr. Corday. Here," she wiped the boy's face and hands with the cloth. "Until he's had a bath, I'm afraid to put anything on his back. I want a doctor to see him, first.

"You're coming home with me, aren't you, Son?" She could not legally force him to come, if he chose not to.

For a moment, he looked as if he might say 'no'. "It ain't your fault, but it wouldn't 'a happened, if you hadn't made me go to school."

"I'm sorry, Clay. It was the right thing to do, but the wrong place to do it." She would have her own guilt to resolve later. At the moment, medical help and reassurance were more important. "Again, I promise, you'll never have to go back there."

He looked at the horse. "I wasn't keeping Robin. I was going to leave him here to be sent back to you." He cleared his throat. "They won't hang me for horse stealing, will they?"

Amused, in spite of the situation, she shook her head. "No, Clay. You're not a horse thief."

He heaved a shaky sigh. "Then, I'll come back with you. But..."

"No more Professor Guttman. Here, you ride Robin. I'll walk."

Judd gave the boy a boost up, received his murmured 'thanks' and said to Sarah. "I've closed up the station. It's dark. If you don't mind, I'll walk you home."

"Thank you, Mr. Corday. What do I owe you for the hay Robin ate?" He waved his hand negatively and they set forth.

"By the way--" he began, but she did not hear him. Her attention was on the boy, who bent over the horse in the road beside the path.

She could not believe how close she'd come to losing him. Every time she thought of Guttman, she wanted to use strong language. What a perverted bigot, picking on a child who could not defend himself! She was glad of Mr. Corday's company, for it had become quite dark. Probably he wanted to see Trudy, as well. She was anxious to get Clay in a warm bath, hoping he could then go to sleep. She gave a silent prayer for having found him; relieved they were almost home

Chapter 41

Jason's Return

SARAH WENT WITH Clay to stable Robin, leaving Judd Corday waiting on the stoop. She felt remiss for she had let the boy down. She needed to stay as close as possible to him. They returned and the three entered the house. Mrs. Perkins met them at the door to say Sarah had a guest waiting in the parlor.

To Clay the older woman exclaimed, "Law, child! Where have you been?" Before he could answer, she took him by the arm. "We'll go to the kitchen to give you a clean-up before dinner."

Trudy came out of the parlor. "Oh, Kid! We've been in a stew. Are you alright?"

"Yes, Miss," said Clay. He ducked his head, ashamed to look at the concerned faces of the two women. He went along with Mrs. Perkins. With unconcealed pleasure, Trudy greeted Judd, took his arm, and drew him into the dining room. Quietly she closed the pair of pocket doors leading to the hall.

Her heart in her breast, Sarah removed her bonnet and shawl and hung them on the hall-tree. She was certain the Pinkertons had found her and the jig was up. She was not ready for this, especially when Clay needed her. Steeling herself, she entered the parlor. Jason rose from a chair sending a shock of relief and surprise racing through her breast. Her heart trip-hammered and her breath quickened, as she bowed low to hide her face. She offered her hand to him saying, "How do you do, Mr. ---"

Stunned, Jason took Sarah's hand. "Jason McGreuder, Miss. But, you must be..."

"Sarah Dietrich, Sir. How do you do? Morgan spoke of you, often."

"You're Morgan's sister! The likeness is uncanny." He turned her so the lamplight struck her face.

"How perceptive." She reluctantly withdrew her hand from his.

"But your last name...?"

"Ah, yes." She had rehearsed this scene in her mind so often, the lies spilled forth as she gave it her imaginative best. "When you met him, for personal reasons, Morgan was traveling incognito." She managed a disarming smile. It worked. Jason urged her to sit down. With his usual energy, he began to pace up and down the room. She remembered he was as active as ever.

"There's so much I want to ask Morgan. When do you expect him to return?"

She was ready for that, too. "As a matter of fact, I don't."

"Really? Why not? Where has he gone?"

"I don't know. He's...looking for work." She gave a casual shrug. "He's most unpredictable."

He stared at her and gave a shake of his head. "Forgive me, I found him entirely reliable."

She folded her hands. "How kind. Our papa would have been pleased to hear it."

"And you? You're making your home here now?"

Too close for comfort. "For the present."

"When did you arrive?"

"Shortly after Morgan. I heard about the paddleboat burning and was anxious---"

Mrs. Perkins returned to the entry with Clay. Sarah stood, to tend the boy. "If you will excuse me, Mr. McGreuder."

Seeing the child in the entry Jason cried, "There you are, Kid!" He strode to the boy and clapped him on the shoulder. Clay flinched and cried out.

"What is it, boy? Have you hurt your--" As the child turned to hide fresh tears, Jason saw the blood spots seeping through the clean shirt, the cook had put on him in the kitchen.

"Wait, son," he said and gently pulled up the boy's shirt from his back.

"What in tarnation?" Jason thundered! "How did this happen? *Who* abused you like this?"

"I, I can't talk now," Clay said, weeping from pain and embarrassment. Sarah told him to go on upstairs.

She turned to Jason. "Against my explicit orders, he's been beaten almost every day since he started to school. I'll *never* send him back there."

"Morgan must be told. He won't stand for this *one minute*! Was this a schoolmaster?" She nodded. "The man's a monster! Where is this school?"

"Just down the road." She gestured and turned to the stairs. Despite her reluctance to leave Jason, her duty lay above.

"Please stay, Miss. There's so much we need to discuss. I had an understanding with your brother---"

"I'm sorry, Jason." She slipped using his given name. "I must get Clay to bed and see about a doctor. In the morning, if you'll return, I'll try to answer your questions."

"By all means. I understand. I'm glad to have met you, Miss Dietrich. Until tomorrow." He asked Mrs. Perkins, for her doctor's address, and said he would ask him to come to see the boy. He bowed, put on his hat, and departed.

"I've never seen anything like it," Mrs. P. told Sarah, grimacing. "I'll bring up a tray for you both. God bless the child. I hope he'll be better in the morning. I will pray for him."

Thanking her, Sarah followed Clay up the stairs, her mind in turmoil with him and the arrival of Jason. Oh, my. He was as handsome and irresistible as she remembered. However, she could never belong to him! Utterly exhausted, she felt a pain leave her breast and run up to her head. Her tears fell before her as she reached the top of the stairs. She had agonized over Jason's return for more than three months. Now he was here, she remembered his strength of character and his passion for right. Bitterly, she realized how very much her masquerade and criminal past would shock him.

In the dining room, Trudy sat at the table with Judd. "Thank you," she said, her eyes roved warmly over Judd's rugged face and broad shoulders. "It was kind of you to see Sarah and Clay home."

"Nothin' to it," Judd said, and reached for one of her hands. "It's been some sort of evening. Wouldn't cha' say?"

"Whew!" She could not wait to hear what Sarah had told Jason. "I do, indeed."

He moved closer to place one arm along the back of her chair. "I thought mebbe that fellow in the parlor was your, uh, intended, or something like. He's a dandy, in a nice sorta' way."

"Mr. McGreuder?" She rolled her eyes. "No. No. Not likely."

He smiled his relief. "That's good. I mean, I wouldn't want to step on anyone's toes, ya' know."

She cocked her head. "You mean because of me?" She *hoped* she understood him.

"That's right." His arm slipped down from the chair back to her shoulders. "I bet soon as the rest of the bachelors in town see you, I'm gonna' have to fight my way through the crowd."

She laughed at the exaggeration, then sobered remembering why she had gone to the coach station, earlier in the evening. "Do you want anything to eat? I'm sure there's something from supper, if---"

"Nope. Not a thing. I'm happy as a toad in a mud puddle right now." His eyes smiled with affection.

She swallowed hard, determined to tell him the truth. "Judd, uh, I wasn't exactly on the level with you, when I told you about my past." A shudder of anxiety ran down her back.

His eyes questioned.

"It was true, my pa died in the War; but my stepmother signed a paper for me to work in a house---"

"As a nursemaid?"

She looked down at her hand in his warm one. "Not exactly. It wasn't *that* kind of house. It was more like a... a whore house." She expelled a nervous breath.

His face sobered and he released her hand. "As what? A servant? You couldn't a' been more than thirteen."

"That's right," she had to work her tongue around a huge knot in her throat. "It started out that way, 'til I learned the business. You know... how to please the customers." She watched him, biting her lower lip, holding her breath.

He removed his arm from her shoulder. "Why didn't you leave? When *did* you leave?"

"Jus' before I come out here. I saved every penny I could, to get away, for three years. They wouldn't never let me go. I sneaked out early one morning, three months ago. They're looking for me, even now. There's a real mean bugger in charge a' the place. If he found me, he'd come all the way here, beat the devil out of me and drag me back."

Judd rubbed his eyes, as if he could blot out what she 'd told him. It was a whole bunch to swallow at once. He didn't meet her gaze. He stood up and turned his back. Her hope fell down a well. She suddenly knew what the Bible thumpers meant by *the wages of sin*. This was *it*. And, she *had* to pay.

One tear slipped over an eyelid. "That's what I come to tell you, when Mr. McGreuder showed up." She stood up, clenching her fingers. A small moan escaped her throat and her fingers spread in supplication. "I didn't want no misunderstanding or lies between us. I know I'm what cha' call *soiled goods*." It was finally out in the open, and she ached with the pain of telling. Her tears fell in earnest.

He snatched his cap from the sideboard saying, "I'll, I'm going now, Miss. You, you take care." Hurriedly opening one of the wooden doors, which slammed in its pocket, he strode to the front door and let himself out.

The sound of the closing door echoed in the entryway. Helplessly, Trudy stared after him. Her sobs turned to grief. Covering her mouth with one hand, she ran up the stairs to her room, and threw herself on her bed in utter despair. *There won't never be no one. No one who'll know what I been and love me!* She smothered her face in her pillow to muffle a heart-broken wail.

Chapter 42

The Dietrichs' Sunset

ELLSWORTH HAD ONE more thing to do before he could settle his father's estate. He had to square things with Sarah. Although he had not yet heard from her, he hoped he was on the right track and would hear soon. He deplored the necessity for another talk with Emerald. She was not to blame for having Sarah's jewelry; but she was responsible for pretending her cousin had been kidnapped, and for telling lies regarding the reason for her disappearance. He reread the letter from Sarah's father relating what had happened to him. There was no question, *his* father had appropriated her inheritance, sold part of her jewelry, and given the rest to his sister. *No*, he decided. He had no choice.

Grabbing his cane, he went from his office to the barn. Emerald was working with the personnel ledger. Looking up she smiled.

"Emerald," he began, "We have to correct a serious mistake which has been made by our parents." He eased himself into the old Windsor chair and leaned forward resting his hands on his cane.

"Whatever do you mean, Worth?"

"Do you remember the earrings mama gave you to wear for the party you had six months ago?"

She frowned. "Of course. They are rubies, mama said, for my birthday."

"Well, they weren't hers to give."

"But they match the necklace they gave me for my engagement."

"I see. Unfortunately, that was not theirs to give you, *either.*"

"Don't be silly, Ellsworth. They wouldn't have given---"

"The jewelry belonged to Sarah. It was left to her by her father as part of her dowry."

"I don't believe you! Papa would never have--"

"I'm afraid he did. In fact, there's *more*," he said bitterly. "He also sold a diamond bracelet and ring of Sarah's. Even worse, he hypothecated her inheritance, from the sale of her parents' home, and used it... as if it were his own."

Furious, Emerald flew up from her desk and strode to the window, where she turned to face him. "I don't know why you're saying these things, when papa's barely cold in his grave. He would horsewhip you, if he were here to defend himself!"

He struck his cane firmly on the board floor. "Emmy! I have *the records*, the bank statements, the bill of sale, *and* the letter Uncle Dan wrote to Sarah before he killed himself. It's in the safe in the office. Our cousin was deprived of her inheritance by our parents. It's all there in ink, on paper."

She grimaced and glared at him. "Even if you have the proof, what do you expect *me* to do about it?"

"Return the jewelry you have, for one thing." His tone was flat and bitter cold.

"Why you---What kind of a brother *are* you? Sarah doesn't know about the inheritance, let alone the necklace. There's no reason to inform her when she's run away. I'm not about to--"

"Yes, Emerald, you *are*!" He stood up. "It's going to take us *years* to repay the monies we owe her, but the jewelry can be returned as soon as I receive her address. I can't live with myself, unless these wrongs are righted. You owe her your *life*! The very fact you covered up her heroism and were instrumental in her disappearance, further constitutes a moral obligation, a debt of honor you *have* to pay!"

She shut her eyes, took a deep breath, and fisted her hands. "If all of that's true, Worth, I suppose, I have no choice. But, I'll *never forgive* you for airing this dirty linen!"

"Emerald, this *will be* done. I am papa's estate representative. I am determined to do it as honestly and as rapidly as possible, for the sake of the entire family. Bring me the jewelry in the morning, and we will say no more about it.

"I'm sorry I had to disillusion you regarding our parents, but it couldn't be helped. Apparently, both of us were naïve regarding the financial status of our family. In any event, we could not have influenced papa's decisions when we were young. He was in charge. Now, it's different. It is *up* to you and me to put things back to rights, honestly, and quickly. I'll see you tomorrow." He gave her a firm nod and left the office.

She brushed one tear from her cheek and returned to her desk a contrite, unhappy young woman grinding one depressing thought: *Sarah*. It is *always Sarah!* I'm *glad* she's gone, *and* I hope to God this is the last of her, *forever!*

The next morning Emerald whipped into Ellsworth's office and dropped the velour jewelry box on his desk. "I wanted to tell you something, but it isn't important now." She turned to leave.

"Why don't you tell me, anyway?" His tone was ameliorating. He arose and politely held out one hand. He loathed having difficulty with his sister. As siblings, they had always been close; even when they quarreled, they had quickly made up.

She turned back in the doorway with a tentative smile, spread her skirts and took a seat. "Anton, Winston and I have been working on a surprise for you. It is a plan to start a school for the children of our workers and the tenants. It was Anton's idea weeks ago, but I've been so busy, I've only recently found time to see what could be done."

"That's splendid! Ever since Anton mentioned it to me, I have mulled over the need. What do you think we can do?" He leaned over the desk interested to hear the plan, despite his concerns

"First, we haven't many horses, so the barn is half empty. If we clear a place near the southeast corner, it would work for a schoolroom, until we have a building for use. A potbelly stove in one of the stalls could provide the heat we would need. We can cram cornhusks, or straw between the two-by-fours, also. Adding two or three windows would give us more light and air. Anton says the men doing the carpentry, could also make a few simple tables and benches for us." Her enthusiasm lit her face.

"What about a teacher?" He knew the answer, but wanted her to tell him.

She blushed and twitched a shoulder. "Well, I'd do part of it. You know...the basics of reading, writing, and arithmetic. Winston could ve instruction in agriculture methods, and the care of livestock. We would include upkeep of the property, the use of tools and even some carpentry. He says the basics of sanitation and home medical care demand attention. If we are successful, they could be taught in the future." Out of breath, she eyed him hopefully. "What do you think?"

"Obviously the three of you have done a lot of work." He picked up a pencil to make notes on a writing pad. "What about supplies? And other costs?"

"Supplies will be pretty simple, to begin with. Slates, pencils and some books. We have some old ones in our attic, and I could ask Miss Langdon for those she doesn't use any more. Winston and I won't be paid, especially if he can include some of his people, too. I'd teach three days a week and he'd teach the older boys, two."

"You mean *five whole days*? That would cut into our work force and cost--"

"Not that much." She shook her head. "We'd only hold class three hours in the mornings on week days. The younger ones don't work much anyhow, and with some education, the older boys would prove more valuable as skilled workers."

"Do you know how many children and work hours we're talking about?"

"I'm working on that. There's at least a dozen small ones and only five or six older ones here."

"That's six hours a week for each, times six...thirty-six hours for the older boys alone! What if the ones from our crew don't want to lose their pay for those hours?"

She pursed her lips and examined her fingernails. "Well, poor as they are, they wouldn't go to class, if they lost their wages. We could credit the croppers for their hours at harvest time."

He gazed at her and slowly shook his head. "You expect me to credit, or pay them *and* educate them, too?"

She raised her chin. "Winston plans to."

His eyes rose to the ceiling and then narrowed on her. "You have it all figured out, don't you?"

"We didn't want to overlook anything. Worth, we think the increased value of each worker will more than make up for the cost." She continued, "I never thought I could be a teacher, until I saw how little these people know. Hardly any of 'em can read simple directions, or a schedule. Some of the older tenants have trouble with any sort of record keeping, and can't even go into town alone to purchase supplies. Mama might help the girls with needlework or cooking. We think this would work. Can we give it a try? Worth, please?"

He knew the idea was good, so long as those they educated did not up and leave them. He needed a total of the expected costs, before he could decide the plan's feasibility. He seriously doubted his mother would want to be involved. She was already having difficulty with his changes.

"I'll talk to Anton and Winston today. I need to look at the entire picture. You have done a good job, Emmy. I will let you know. Meanwhile, I want to thank you for the excellent work you've done on our forms and records. Anton told me how much you've accomplished." She was turning into a valuable partner.

Gratified, Emerald swept out of the room.

Worth sat down feeling everything was finally back on an even keel. Maybe he *would make* a decent farm manager, after all. Thankfully, he considered his evolving relationship with Penne and Josie, too. Thank God! When one door closes…

Chapter 43

Sarah Undone

SARAH ENTERED THE dining room from habit more than hunger. She had barely slept the night before. Clay had slept lightly, moaning every time he moved. She had kept a cool cloth on his head wishing she could do more. She greeted Mrs. Perkins and thanked her for sending the doctor to treat the boy.

The landlady asked, "What did the doctor say? The cook let him in before I was up."

Sarah shook her head. "Clay's going to have a few rough days. The doctor applied some salve to the cuts and gave him paregoric to help him sleep. Hopefully, he won't get an infection while the cuts are healing."

"Poor mite. How could a schoolmaster treat a child harshly? You don't look so good either, Miss. Lack of sleep?"

Sarah took a deep breath. "Afraid so. I didn't want him to roll over onto his back."

The older woman nodded sympathetically. "You're finding out what it's like to be a mother."

"So that's it." Sarah rolled her eyes. "I thought I was *dying*."

"As I remember, motherhood was *exactly* like that. Would you eat some hot cereal?"

"No, thank you. I'll just have tea and toast."

With a smile Mrs. P. asked, "Wouldn't you rather have coffee? The cook found some yesterday at the grocer's."

"Oh, good. I could really use some this morning."

A knock at the front door called the landlady to answer. Sarah looked up as Jason entered the room. She felt a familiar warmth in her breast. His tie was askew and his jacket unbuttoned, which were surprising for the usually tidy fellow. She exchanged questioning expressions with the older woman.

"Good morning!" he announced heartily.

Mrs. Perkins gestured to a chair and took the coffee pot to the kitchen for a refill.

Wearing a smug grin Jason seated himself. "It's wonderful to see you so early in the day, Miss Dietrich."

Still puzzled, she replied, "You seem full of yourself this morning, Mr. McGreuder. Has something happened to---?"

"I'd say *some*thing."

"Such as?"

"I made a satisfactory call on a bas--*No*, a *devil* named *Guttman*."

"Really?"

"You bet your bottom dollar!"

Mrs. Perkins returned with hot coffee and muffins.

"Did he attack you?"

He pretended offence. "He was hardly in a position to do that."

"*You* attacked *him*?"

"I simply punched the weasel in the nose two or three times, picked him up, and dropped him among the books and papers behind his desk."

"You *did*? Was he hurt?"

"I certainly hope so. Not as much as poor Kid, however." He picked up a napkin and placed it in his lap. "Th*e professor* will need his nose packed and one arm put in plaster. Otherwise---"

Sarah could not keep from laughing. Mrs. Perkins clapped appreciatively, poured Jason's coffee and offered him a hot muffin.

"Did you have any conversation?" Sarah asked.

Casually he sugared and stirred his coffee and picked up the muffin. "It was more of a soliloquy. I told him, if I ever heard he had even *touched* another child, I would personally break every *other* bone in his worthless body!" He was indeed pleased with himself. "Humm, good," he referred to the muffin, nodding to Mrs. Perkins. "I've some hickory sticks that I took from Guttman's office for your fireplace, Mrs. P."

Mrs. Perkins patted his shoulder. "Good for you!"

"Clay will be happy to hear about his comeuppance, Ja...er Mr. McGreuder. Normally, I wouldn't relate such an act of violence to a child, but---" Sarah smiled wickedly.

"Considering what was done to *him.*"

"Exactly."

He sipped his coffee and bent his head in obvious appraisal of her. Flustered, she carefully buttered a muffin. Excusing herself, Mrs. Perkins left the room.

"You're calling him Clay now?"

"Yes. He *remembered.* His given name was Clay Carter."

"That's amazing. How is our boy this morning?"

She told him of the doctor's expectation for the child's recovery.

"Three days?" She nodded.

"That will give us more time to get acquainted, wouldn't you say?" Apparently he was pleased with the delay.

Sarah blushed, then a sudden wave of reality swept her mind.

Observing the change in her expression, he asked, "Are you all right?"

She pressed her eyes knowing tears were just behind the sting. "I'm sorry. I didn't get much sleep last night."

"Up with Clay?" She nodded grimly. "Forgive me. I'm sure you'd like to rest this morning."

"I knew you'd understand."

"Would you enjoy a drive this afternoon? We could have dinner at the hotel."

It would hurt to spend more time with him before saying goodbye, but the temptation was too great. It would be the sweetest pain she could endure. "I'd like that very much. Perhaps, about four?"

He asked, "Earlier?"

"Well, of course. I'm simply reluctant to… take up so much of your time." She could *not* discipline herself to limit seeing him.

"Are you serious?" He *wanted* to spend time with her; her breast swelled with a delicious warmth. "Will two o'clock give you enough rest?"

She savored his words. Figuratively, she would have tucked him in her apron pocket had she been wearing one. *To blazes with decorum, fears, et al.* "I shall be ready." She finished her coffee and walked to the door with him.

He took her hand and brought it to his lips. "Adieu, dear friend. Two o'clock it is."

Had she not been exhausted, she would have skipped up the stairs. Listening to her heart, she turned her back on common sense. She'd dreamed of him every day for three months. Now, she deserved some real time, didn't she? She determined to have it!

Leaving the house Jason stopped at the sight of Judd seated on one of the steps. "What? Oh, sorry, Mr. Corday, right? I nearly bowled you over."

Judd sighed heavily. "No matter. I couldn't feel no worse than I do."

Jason leaned on the wrought iron railing to consider the younger man. "Did you come to see Miss Trudy? I believe she's at work, now."

"No. I wanted to see how the boy was doing. That bastard 'most killed him."

Agreeing, Jason joined Judd on the steps and told him about the doctor's visit. "Is that why you're so blue?"

"Well, that's enough, but no." He looked at Jason, soulfully.

"Work, health, or love life?"

"That covers it." Judd agreed. "I've lost interest in my job, I feel like I've been run over by a coach, and my love life is in the outhouse." Lines scored his young face and his eyes swam with disgust.

"That sounds serious," said Jason. It must have something to do with Trudy. "Has Miss Trudy---?"

"It ain't *her* fault. Did you, I mean do you know about her past?"

Jason rubbed his chin. "Maybe. But not expressly."

"I must be stupid or something, 'cause I never guessed. Anyways, last night she…she told me about her life and, yellow as a cur, I ran in the other direction."

"You had a right to---"

"No, I *didn't*," Judd declared. "She weren't to blame. She was nothing but a defenseless kid of thirteen. She's only sixteen, now."

Jason rubbed his chin. Largely he *had* guessed the truth about the young woman, months before. "Right. Tell me, does this knowledge frighten, or disillusion you?"

Judd compressed his lips in thought and then shook his head. "Neither. Not anymore. She's doing her level best to make a better life for herself."

Jason nodded. "That speaks of character."

"Yes, and it ain't easy. She is takin' care of a passel of young 'uns for a woman, when she never had a childhood of her own."

Jason surmised, "She's a hard worker."

"And you'd think I'd a' had the brains to figure that out, before stomping off like a pinch-nosed Puritan, last night." In self-disgust he punched the air with a doubled-up fist.

If Judd needed legal advice, Jason had no problem. Advice to the lovelorn was another matter. However, he liked Judd and he decided to make a suggestion. "Maybe you could see her after work tonight and ask her forgiveness."

"She wouldn't even *look* at me after that. An' I don't blame her."

Jason put his gloves on and said, "She might. I believe she would understand it took time for you to… appreciate her honesty in telling you about herself. Perhaps she'd like to know, nothing that happened before you met her would *ever* affect you again."

The stress eased in Judd's face as the thought took hold. "It won't, ya' know. That's 'zactly how I feel. You think she might forgive me, if I try?"

Jason stood. "That's the ticket!" Then, he offered him a ride back to the coach station.

After dropping Judd off, Jason had several things to do before his two-o'clock appointment. He urged his rented horse and buggy around the corner to Main Street and the courthouse. He wanted no impediment to taking Clay with him, as soon as the boy was well.

While the horse trotted along, lawyer that he was, Jason reviewed the arguments he had posed regarding his adoption of the child. In the future, if a lady he chose to marry considered a ready-made family less than an asset, (he snapped his gloved fingers), he'd forget her. Any woman who did not like children would not suit him anyway. He had affection for Clay and desired to protect him and educate him to the best of his ability.

Although, when he first met Sarah's brother, Morgan had been jobless, he had said he hoped to move to St. Louis. However, Miss Dietrich was a different person. She had a position and was able to care for Clay. Moreover, she might not want to give up the boy. In fact, she could *refuse* to let him go. He had no idea where to locate Morgan to firm up his position. Dad burn it!

Um-hum. *A few* sticky details needed to be managed to complete his plans. This afternoon, he would see where he stood. Come what may, he would not leave without Clay. Meanwhile, he would look into the legal application. He drew up before the courthouse, dismounted and tethered the horse to a hitching post. Confidently he strode up the stone walk and into the building.

Sarah put the final touches on the rolled bun of her hair, glad to see it had nearly grown out. Humming a little tune, she pinned on a hat she had borrowed from Trudy. She was thrilled to be spending the afternoon with Jason. She went down the hall to see Clay. He was awake and he looked up at her.

"Hey there," she said. "You're looking better. How do you feel?"

He wiggled up in the bed, wincing with the effort. "I'm doin' better. Cook fixed me lunch with bread pudding and she's gonna' look after the horses for me today. I 'tend to get up purty soon."

"I'm glad you feel up to it. A little while might be good for you, just don't get over-tired. We want your back to heal."

He frowned running his hands over the sheet. "I got something to tell you." He looked down. "I've decided, I ain't goin' to St. Louie."

Good grief! With a pang of conscience she realized, she had *not* asked him if he *wanted* to go with Jason. Knowing she could not take care of him indefinitely, she had assumed, when Jason returned, Clay would leave with him. Appalled, she had never discussed it with him. "I… thought you wanted to go to St. Louis with Mr. McGreuder. Even last night you tried to go there on you own."

"I didn't know no other place to go." He licked his lips. "Only now, since I don't have to go back to that school, I've changed my mind."

Sarah sat down on the edge of the bed. "You like Mr. McGreuder, don't you?"

"Some."

"And you're interested in railroading and would like to explore the West, wouldn't you?"

"Yes."

"Then, why don't you want to go?"

He pressed his lips together, and finally said, "'Cause of you, an' Robin and everyone else. Except for the school, I never had it so good. I hated to leave t'other night, but I was skeered I'd *have* to go back there, whether I liked it, or not."

"I see." She was touched and patted his knee. "I wish *I* could offer you the kind of life Mr. McGreuder can. He would take care of you and give you the education you deserve. It is a marvelous opportunity. He wants to be your father, something I could *never* be. You can't begin to appreciate what he wants to do for you."

"I don't need no pa, an'...I *won't* leave you! You can't make me." He bent over with his head in her lap and began to cry.

Fighting tears herself, she pushed his hair back and gave him a handkerchief. "My dear Clay, I won't force you to do anything, however, it's only fair to talk to Jason, since he's come all this way to see you. When you feel up to it, I promise, we will discuss how you feel before any final decision is made. All right?"

He cleared his throat, blew his nose, and gingerly leaned back against the pillows.

"Please don't worry. You need to rest and get well. Will you do that for me?" He nodded again. "I have a catalogue you might like to read while you're lying here. It has toys, horse tackle, and all kinds of interesting things in it. Shall I bring it to you?"

"Yes'm. I'll look at it." She went to her room for another handkerchief and the catalogue and returned to him.

He cleared his throat and said, "Thanks." She leaned over and gave him a kiss on the cheek. His eyes warmed with affection.

"I'll see you this evening."

Still deeply touched by the scene, she headed downstairs. She'd had no idea Clay did not want to leave, or that he had become fond of her. She paused on the landing. Love for the youngster filled her heart. How could she get him to go with Jason? If he refused to leave, when the Pinkerton's found her, the separation would be even more traumatic. What would happen to him, then? Mrs. P. could not take care of him. She needed someone to ask for advice. She thought longingly of her mother again, believing she could have helped her.

Chapter 44

Formal Date

JASON MADE QUITE the picture of a young dandy driving her about town to see the environs she had not covered since her arrival. Of course he'd spruced himself up since morning, and now he politely tipped his hat to ladies crossing the street, remarked with interest upon the houses and shops, and smiled at her while driving the buggy with casual efficiency. She sensed there was a great deal more to learn about her friend, beyond what she had gained from their earlier experiences. He had charm, humor and strength. She already knew he was a kind, gentle man; she liked the way he took charge and solved problems, too.

"Have you been down to the wharf yet, Miss Dietrich?"

"No, I haven't. I should very much like to see it, if we could. One of these days, I plan to take my student down there."

"It's nothing like St. Louis. The Ohio isn't the Mississippi, but with the coal-mining here and steamboat building nearby, Evansville has become a very busy, industrial center. You'll see, there's plenty of activity on the waterfront," he said, urging the horse toward the river.

As they drew near the port they saw paddle wheelers wooding up and stevedores unloading everything from whiskey to hemp from barges and flatboats on their way down river. Two boats were boarding, or discharging travelers. A polyglot of walking humanity made its way along the quay: painted ladies, boatmen, military men in haphazard uniforms, frontiersmen and beggars.

Carriages with sightseers and passengers, as well as wagons loaded with lumber, tools, and building supplies crowded the roadway. The tempo and noise excited Sarah and she was unwilling to miss any part of the scene. Oh, how she wished she were one of the travelers! She envied those caught up in the fascinating, frenetic surge of people taking part in the commerce of the port, or leaving for new, unknown destinations. She knew she must be fiddle-footed, because her previous trip had not exhausted her love for travel.

"I thought you'd enjoy this," Jason said, maneuvering the buggy in and out of the traffic on the quay. "This is where Morgan and the rest of us would have docked, had our boat not burned on the way."

"That's right," she said. "Cincinnati didn't seem this large. This is a far cry from our quiet part of town. I'd almost forgotten how much went on in a busy port." Observing the activity and sensing the emotional climate of the crowds of people on the dock was like reliving her own trip down the river.

Turning the buggy around at the end of the quay, they started back. Leaving the port, Jason found a shade tree to stop under, to give their horse a rest, and to broach the subject on his mind. "Now, Miss Dietrich, suppose you tell me about yourself. Morgan said that you attended an academy near the farm where you grew up."

She told him what she could about her past without divulging her secrets.

"I think you were very brave to travel all this way to join your brother."

Blushing at her deception, she improvised, "A friend came part of the way with me."

"I wondered," he said. "Now that Morgan is gone, have you anyone to look out for you, or to represent you, if need be? Have you a banker or lawyer, for example?"

How strange of him to ask, as though her legal status might be insecure. Which of course it was, but he did not know that. Unfortunately, she hadn't thought in that vein at all. "It's kind of you to ask, Mr. McGreuder. Hopefully, I can take care of Clay and myself. We have work and, as you've seen, have a nice place to stay. That means a great deal to us."

"Please call me Jason." He reached into his pocket and pulled out a bag of butterscotch candies to share with her. They sat there comfortably enjoying the hard candy and one another's company. "I'll bet you were always your own person, even as a child."

She could not be that objective about herself and demurred. "I don't know; but, tell me about you. Do you dress formally at work?"

He laughed. "Only when calling on young ladies, or handling legal business in court. At work, I've an open shirt, a suede jacket, and riding pants. I am on and off horses and end-o-track workers' trains, all the time. There's hardly room for a cane or top hat."

That gave her another side of him to think about. "How old were you when you learned to ride?"

"About three, I think. I loved riding, but I never planned to train horses. As an only child, I didn't want to affect my parents' plans for me, so I hid my dream of seeing the West for years. Fortunately, by the time I was sixteen, my father had retired, and I was able to leave home for school with a clear conscience."

"You certainly haven't disappointed him. Does he know about Clay?"

"As a matter of fact, yes."

"What did he say?"

"He said to bring him home, as soon as I could, so he can teach him to ride. He thinks Clay would also enjoy the steeple chasing and horse racing, we have in Kentucky."

"Indeed he would." *A whole different way of life.* "Your father's a kind gentleman." But, it struck her she had almost given herself away with that remark.

"Thank you. I wouldn't want the boy to miss any part of the life, I've known." Jason brushed the hair off his forehead. "Did Morgan tell you what I hope to do for Clay?"

"Yes. Yes, he did. He felt you could offer Clay a better life, than we could, for a number of reasons." She saw sincerity in his eyes. "You're more mature than Morgan. He really is not ready to become a father." She wanted him to know how much she appreciated his qualities. "Your character and your experience comprise the sort of man any child would admire and respect. At present, I can care for Clay financially," she glanced down the street speculating about her own future. "But, I won't be able to do so indefinitely. He is a fine boy. He deserves… a father, an education, and a secure future."

Jason smiled his appreciation and turned his top hat around in his hands. "That's quite a reference, my friend. Thank you." He gave her a discerning glance.

She had to change the subject. "Please tell me more about St. Louis. It sounds fascinating."

They spent another pleasant hour becoming acquainted, before driving to the hotel for their supper. By then, she found her affection for him over-whelming. Entering the large brick hotel for the first time, Sarah was impressed. The high ceilings held glowing oil lamps hung with winking, crystal prisms, flowered carpets softened the wood floors, and the polished walnut reception desk, with two clerks, commanded one lobby wall. There was a bar, according to the sign on etched glass doors, from which the sounds of laughter and male voices issued. A dining room to the right held tables set with damask, silverware and candlesticks.

"Lovely...." she exclaimed, as Jason seated her and beckoned the waiter to their table. It was still early, but several tables already had other diners. In one corner of the room, a pianist entertained the guests with lively tunes. "This is a rare treat, Jason. Thank you," she said and handed the menu back to the waiter. "Mr. McGreuder will order for me." Jason nodded, pleased.

They had a delicious dinner of catfish, corn pudding, green beans, apple pan dowdy and coffee. Sarah enjoyed Jason's confident, mature manner. She basked in his deference and was fascinated watching his warm eyes, his sensuous lips, and his expansive gestures. His conversation and was so colorful, she could readily see the pictures he painted. She appreciated his enthusiasm for his work and the development of the West, and she asked him questions to learn all she could about his life.

Casually, he reached across the table for one of her hands and held it, gently rubbing his thumb back and forth over her wrist. "I want to call you, Sarah," he said, pleasing her enormously to hear her name on his lips.

"Then you must," she replied, heady with the gaze he focused on her. If the approach was planned in order to acquire Clay, she no longer cared. She was so completely happy in Jason's presence; it was all she could do to keep from telling him. Yet, he had only just met her as a young woman and couldn't possibly feel the same as she. Even if he did, their feelings had no place to go. She reluctantly released the fantasy and gently withdrew her hand.

"I don't want to spoil such a lovely evening, but I must tell you, there is a problem with your plans, Jason. You will have to make a concerted effort to convince Clay to leave with you. I fear we both forgot to ask how he felt about the move. This afternoon, he insisted he did not want to leave. I won't force him to do so. I promised."

"By gosh, I'd no idea. You are right. I didn't discuss it with the boy. Of course, I will talk to him. He is still too young to appreciate what we have planned for him. Let me say, I've no doubt he would receive the best of care from you and Morgan," he said kindly. "On the other hand, I hope having a father and an exciting future would prove equally attractive to him."

"As you said, he *is* young. You'll have to gauge his feelings when you see him, tomorrow." Even if she had another talk with Clay, she doubted she would be able to change his mind.

"Yes. Shall we go?" When she nodded, he signaled the waiter. While he paid the bill she replaced her gloves, secured her bag and stood up.

Once more in the buggy, she told him how very much she had enjoyed the afternoon. Noting her subdued manner, it suddenly occurred to him to ask her to come with them to St. Louis. *There are plenty of schools there. She could teach there as well as here.* "I've been an utter dolt. There is absolutely no reason why you should not come with us. I am certain you could find a position there without any problem. I have no doubt it would help Clay to make the change, as well. Morgan already knows I want him to come to St. Louis. So, there! Wouldn't that be better?"

The offer touched her, despite the fact that it was made for Clay's benefit. If only the solution were as simple as that. Her spirits sank to a new low.

"There would be no question of propriety on the trip, either, with Clay as our chaperone. Would you like that, my friend?"

She looked away, fearing she would weep any minute. "I'm sorry, Jason. It's quite impossible."

"Come now. What is the stumbling block?" He had been sure she wanted to go. "My intentions are strictly honorable. If Morgan were here, he would vouch for me."

She could not prevent the tears that began to run down her cheeks, but she hoped he did not see them in the dusk, with his attention on driving the buggy. "I'd find you a nice place to stay close to my own, so you and Clay could see one another, as often as you liked. He could even stay with you, if I had to leave town without him."

She covered her face with her hands as the longing to do just so, wrenched her heart. "Please, Jason, no more. I appreciate your offer, but I *can't*." She wiped her eyes and tried to stem her tears.

He drew up in front of her boarding house. "Now, dear, I didn't mean to upset you. I am certain when you think it over tonight, you will decide to come with us. I know you don't want to be separated from Clay." He jumped down to help her out of the buggy.

She shook her head. "Nothing you can say will change my mind! I *cannot come!*" She whirled about, ran up the steps and rushed into the house, slamming the door behind her.

The puzzled young man climbed into the buggy, wondering what he had said, or done, to cause her reaction. *Tomorrow,* he thought. *Tomorrow,* he *would find the underlying cause. For now,* he was certain; *taking both* of them with him was the right answer.

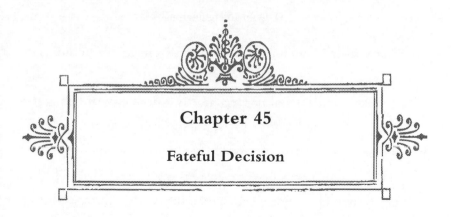

Chapter 45

Fateful Decision

SARAH STARED AT the breakfast table with no appetite. Again, she had barely slept, thinking of her lost future with Clay and Jason. Should she have told Jason about her past? How could he change what had been done, or mitigate the expected punishment? Every day meant less time before she was traced here and arrested for the murder of the vagrant.

Noticing her preoccupation, Mrs. P. asked, "Did you have a nice time, Sarah?"

Sarah nodded with a faint smile. "Sorry. Um, would you pass the biscuits please?" She selected one from the basket and mechanically began to butter it. "We had a lovely afternoon and evening. Jason took me down to the harbor. The activity was exciting."

"Did you like the hotel? I haven't been there since my husband took me for our last anniversary."

"Oh, yes. It was splendid. The dinner was delicious, but not a patch on one of Sophia's. I loved the atmosphere, the crystal chandeliers, and piano music."

"Did...I mean, are you better acquainted with Mr. McGreuder now?"

Sarah sighed. "Very much so. I only wish, oh, you know, I did not have to let Clay go. He's feeling much better today."

Mrs. Perkins set down her teacup. "Is it decided that he's going with Mr. McGreuder? I don't know what we shall do without him. It will cost me more than room and board for a grounds keeper and, without a groom, I will have to give up my horse." She looked at Sarah. "Pshaw! That's not what's bothering me. I will miss him. It has been fun to have a youngster in the house again." She placed her napkin in a ring by her plate.

"Yes, well, it's all up to Clay. Jason is going to speak to him this afternoon. It will be best for him eventually. I can't offer him what Jason can, no matter how hard I try." Sarah made herself take a bite of biscuit. It was sawdust in her mouth and she quickly took a swallow of coffee to wash it down.

"There is nothing you can do to---"

"No."

A knock at the front door sent the land-lady to answer it. Jason's voice carried across the entry. "Looks like I've become a regular boarder, Mrs. Perkins."

"You're more than welcome, Mr. McGreuder. You will find Sarah in the dining room. I'm just on my way to the kitchen."

"Indeed. Thank you." He greeted Sarah and poured himself a cup of coffee at the sideboard.

Sarah said hello, but could not help the affection that invaded her eyes, or the slight tremor of her hand at the sight of the young man.

"Well," he said taking a seat beside her. "Has Kid, I mean *Clay* changed his mind about going with me?"

"As far as I know, he's still torn about leaving."

Jason set his cup down. "I understand. I want to see him, but what about you, my friend? Have you given any more thought to my invitation?" He reached for one of her hands.

She had thought of little else, but she said, "No," sending a pain of incredible regret to her head. "I can't possibly come with you. Please, Jason. Don't make this worse than it already is." She withdrew her hand to clinch it in her lap, hoping to convince him without giving him the shameful reason for her decision. He would *never* have asked a murderess to join him.

"Worse because you'd *like* to come, or worse because you don't *want* to?" He smiled, apparently aware of her interest from the beginning.

She stood up to move away from him. It was one of the more difficult moments of her life. All she wanted was to throw herself into his arms. "Because," she shut her eyes and turned away, unable to face him and lie, "I don't *want* to come with you."

Merely glancing at him, she saw his expression change to one of complete dismay. He stared at her, shook his head and finally sighed heavily, as he stood up. "Please forgive me, Miss Sarah. I fear I have misunderstood. I mean to say, I'm sorry if I've put you under duress. We would have enjoyed your company." He gazed at her intently. "I'll return later this afternoon to talk to Clay. If you'll have him ready, I won't take up any more of your time." He gave her a formal bow and left the room. She heard the front door close firmly, shutting down her romantic fantasy, too.

Her throat tightened as she fought tears. She flexed her fingers to relieve her stress, walked through the entry and up the stairs. By the time she reached her room, her tears were blinding. She knew she would not force Clay to leave with Jason. Finally, she came to the inevitable decision. With the heaviest of hearts, she retrieved her carpetbag from under the bed and began to pack her few belongings. Clinching her teeth with determination, she located the old tablet she had used on her trip, penciled a brief note to Mrs. Perkins, and enclosed it with twenty dollars to leave on the pillow of her bed. It was most of her money and the only goodbye she had time to make. She washed the tears from her face in her basin and picked up her bag and string purse.

Going into Clay's room she found him dozing. With a terribly, painful longing, she gently kissed his forehead and went back down the stairs. Her eyes swam as she donned her plain bonnet and shawl and left the house.

Jason decided not to see Clay that afternoon. He thought to give Sarah more time to think about his offer before he saw the boy. He was quite unable to concentrate on paperwork he'd brought with him from St. Louis and spent most of the day pacing his room in the hotel. The two meals in the dining room had been tasteless and lackluster. He missed companionship for the first time in all the years he had been alone.

Early the following morning, he took Mrs. P.'s front steps two at a time and rattled the doorknocker impatiently.

"What is it, Mr. McGreuder?" The landlady stepped back as Jason removed his hat and entered the house.

"I have to see Miss Sarah immediately," he said, removing his gloves and dropping them with his hat on the hall table. "Something isn't right here." He strode distractedly across the parquet entry.

"Pardon?" Mrs. Perkins replied. "I'm afraid, she isn't down yet. Make yourself at home in the dining room." Noting his agitation, she added, "I'll go see if---" She went up the stairs.

Waiting for her, he walked up and down the hall. He could not have been that mistaken about Sarah's attraction to him. There had to be something else preventing her from leaving with them. Mrs. P. returned with a note and a confused expression.

She handed the note to him saying, "She's gone. This is unbelievable."

My dear friend, (the note said,)

    I am sorry to leave so quickly, but I have no choice. If I remain, I will bring disaster to everyone and cast a blemish on your excellent home and services. Clay will not go with Jason, if I am here, which is the best possible course for him. My heart felt thanks for your kindness. Please give my love to everyone.

In all sincerity,
Sara

Jason shook his head. "What on earth? Could my offer have upset her to this extent?"

"Yesterday, you asked her to marry you?" A smile creased the landlady's face.

"No. I asked her to go to St. Louis with us. I said they needed teachers there and I was sure she'd find---"

’m re

"Well, no wonder." She frowned in disgust.

"What do you mean?"

"Miss Sarah is a moral, young lady. She would not go away with a single man. What were you thinking?"

He shook a hand negatively. "Oh, *nothing* like *that*. I assured her my intentions were strictly honorable."

"Um hum. But you asked her in order to get Clay to go with you?"

"At first, it's what I *thought*. I knew she did not want to give up the boy; but you see, last night I realized I had a much more, personal reason in mind. Sarah is a beautiful, intelligent woman. It may be premature, but I have fallen in love with her. I came here this morning to ask her to marry me."

Mrs. Perkins sighed. "You may be too late."

Jason thought a moment. "It can't be. This is not such a large town. I will find her. I wish Morgan were here. He might know what was wrong."

"He's her only family?"

"In a way. Let's see, where to start?"

Trudy came down the stairs and paused upon seeing Jason striding about. "What's happened?"

He turned to her. "Sarah left."

"Left? You mean---Sarah wouldn't go away without saying goodbye."

The landlady handed her the note. Trudy shook her head, mystified.

"You might check the carriage house," Mrs. Perkins offered.

"That's right," said Trudy. "She wouldn't leave without Robin."

They found Robin ensconced in the barn. He bobbed his head, obviously happy to have visitors.

"Then there's the coach station," said Trudy, on the way back to the house.

Jason gave her a knowing look causing her to blush. "You're right. Judd knows the town better than we do and might prove helpful."

Trudy nodded. "I'm sorry I can't go with you. I got'ta go to work."

"That's all right," said Jason, "I'll start at the station. My buggy is out front. I'll drop you off on my way." They told Mrs. Perkins where they were going and departed in the rig.

Over an hour later, Jason was even more anxious. Judd had not seen Sarah. The train station was several miles north and Jason felt she could not have made it up there without transportation. He even went down to the wharf where he found only one paddle wheeler had been scheduled to depart, since Sarah disappeared, and she was not listed on the manifest. As the fruitless minutes passed, Jason became increasingly agitated. He checked the hotel where he was staying, but had no luck there, either. He knew the longer he spent looking, the less chance he would have of finding her. Pulling over to the side of the road, he stopped, realizing what a mistake he had made earlier, asking her to go to St. Louis with him. She was the girl of his dreams and he would never find anyone to compare with her. Utterly dejected, he slapped the reigns to return to the house, just in case she had come back.

At the boarding house, Mrs. P. opened the door, shaking her head. "I'll be back shortly," he said. "I'm going to the Constable's office." It was a last resort, but he had run out of ideas. Maybe the law could help him find her.

The wooden frame building took up one corner of a block on Main Street. Jason found the constable, a wizened man in his late fifties, sitting at his desk, chewing a wad of tobacco, and going through a stack of papers. "Good morning, sir."

"Morning. Yeah?"

"I'm looking for a young lady."

"I would, too, if I was your age," the man laughed at his own joke and spat a stream of tobacco juice into a brass cuspidor five feet away.

"I'm serious, Sir. If you're the constable, I need your help to find her."

The official put down the papers in his hand and evaluated Jason. "This woman is lost?"

"Well, no, although I don't know where she is."

The constable picked up a pencil and tablet. "Sounds lost to me. What's her name and age?"

"Miss Sarah Dietrich. She's nineteen."

"Why didn't you say so?" The officer stood up giving him a suspicious stare. "I got her in a holding cell in the back, since yesterday. Are you an accomplice?"

"A what? My God, no! What are the charges? What is she doing here?"

"Murder! That's what. I'm going through these notices to find out if there is a record of it." He indicated the papers on the desk.

Jason felt his stomach turn over. He did not believe the constable, although he knew *something* had caused Sarah to leave, and he *had* read the note. Taking a leather case from his jacket, he removed a business card and handed it to the officer. "I'm an attorney. I need to see my client, Miss Dietrich."

The officer scratched his cheek. "And you swear you didn't have nothing to do with the crime?"

"What crime?"

"The one she confessed to yesterday."

"Why'd you arrest her, if you had no record of a crime?"

The constable frowned. Jason guessed he was unsure of the law in such cases. "I *didn't*. I mean, she marched in here yesterday and gave herself up. Said, she was tired of waiting for the Pinkertons to find her."

"The Pinkertons?" Determined to see everything had been done to protect Sarah's rights, he asked, "Have you telegraphed their agency in Chicago?"

The man replied grudgingly, "I never sent one of those things. I don't even know how they work."

"The telegraph is a simple, fast method of communication. You send a message, or a question electrically by a telegrapher, and you receive an answer in a matter of minutes. There is a telegraph station in the post office, or the nearest train depot. I suggest you get one of your deputies to handle that for you. In the meantime, I must see Miss Dietrich."

The constable looked at Jason's card and gave him a cunning smirk. "All right, McGreuder. Come on back to the cell. I'll lock you in while you talk to the prisoner."

Desperate for information, Jason followed the man down the short hall to a cell where Sarah was detained.

Chapter 46

Apologies

SARAH CRIED, "JASON! What are you doing here?" She had planned to avoid seeing him again. The gated cell door was opened and shut, and he was locked inside with her. The constable went back to his office.

"I believe I'm the one to ask *you* that question," he said, reaching for her.

She made an evasive turn in the small area. "How did you find me?"

"It was my last resort. I looked over the entire town. Dear Sarah, don't you think it's time you told me what has been bothering you and why you are here?"

There was nowhere else to run. She threw her hands up in defeat. "Apparently I have no choice." She sat down on the cell bunk and gestured to an old, oak captain's chair for him. A man who wanted to find her this much, deserved to know her rejection and her incarceration were not capricious. "Jason, I'd rather do anything in the world than tell you this, because you'll never feel the same way about me again."

"The constable said you turned yourself in rather than be arrested by the Pinkertons."

It took all of her remaining courage to disenchant him. "That's right-- I killed a man back in West Virginia. It doesn't matter why." She swallowed, slowly shaking her head.

Jason absorbed the news and leaned forward in his chair. "It might not matter to you, but it *certainly* does to me. I want to hear the entire story."

She moistened her lips and told him about the day when she learned she was no longer needed as Emerald's companion. Her *aunt's demand, she bear a child for her cousin, was too awful to relate.* She described what had taken place in the woods, when Emma was attacked.

As she completed her tale, Jason's expression changed, and he sprang to his feet, pulling her up, too. "You're *not guilty!*" he exclaimed. "It was self-defense. You've *nothing* to worry about."

"Self---? What do you mean? He wasn't threatening *me*."

"That's true, but no court in the nation would convict you for saving your cousin's life *and* virtue."

"But I'm in jail!"

His smile widened. "A mere technicality. I'll take care of it right away. When you gave yourself up, did you explain why you hit the derelict?"

Her heartbeat slowed. The mental agony of four, long months held at bay. "No. He didn't give me time." A faint hope crossed her mind. "You're certain I'm not to blame?"

Jason nodded and held up one hand.

"All this time I've lived in constant fear, for no *reason?*"

"I'm sorry, dear heart, but it would seem so. Now, *I* have something to confess to you. In the first place, I wanted you to join Clay and me to make the parting unnecessary for both you and the boy. Now, it's different. For some reason, I feel as if I have known you a long time. Sweet Sarah, my feelings for you have grown so rapidly, I cannot believe them. Beyond a doubt, I simply want to spend the rest of my life with you." He took her in his arms, but she began to weep. "Tell me what's wrong, Sarah. We will fix it. I promise you."

She pulled away and wiped the tears from her face as feelings of mixed relief and guilt filled her mind. She had to tell him of her of her deception. "You may not forgive me for this, but... when I said Morgan would not return, I wasn't exactly honest with you."

He gestured with open hands. "I'm glad to hear that. I truly like the young man. With all that has happened, I want to see him as soon as possible. *Why* did you tell me otherwise?"

She grimaced and took a deep breath. "Because... you won't see *him* again, there isn't any *him*. Only me. *I'm* Morgan, or I *was*." He looked incredulous. "After the loss of my position and killing the man in the woods, I had to leave the area immediately. As a gentle woman, I couldn't travel alone, so I settled on a masquerade. There were more compelling reasons, too awful to relate, why I had to leave Fox Haven. I borrowed my cousin's clothes and assumed a masculine role. Once I had met you as a man, I could not shed the masculine role until I'd gone far enough to resettle. You can't possibly forgive me."

Jason fell into his chair again. "That was *you*, all of those days on the boat?" She nodded. He stared at her shaking his head. "No wonder I felt I'd known you for months. I thought you were identical to Morgan when first we met. I never guessed. Oh, my!" He struck his head with his palm. "It is *I* who owe *you* an apology. When I think of the way I treated you: letting you walk after the fire, while I rode Robin, washing up in *your* room at the inn; not even helping you into or out of the coach on the road."

"Well, the latter *did* bother me," she smiled. "But, you were incredibly generous with your notes and food when I was hungry and you helped save us from the fire. How could I not appreciate an honorable gentleman, who wanted to adopt an orphan?

"Before we met, I had several alarming incidents on the road; I'm certain your companionship kept me from having more. I am especially grateful you taught that horrid Guttman a lesson. And now, I am, so glad you studied law. You have solved my greatest concern. How can I ever thank you?"

He tucked his fist under his chin, as if in deep thought, and gestured with one finger. "You could *marry* me."

Delighted laughter bubbled up her throat. Her dearest wish could come true. She took his hands and drew him up. "What a marvelous idea! Yes. *Yes*, dear Jason, I would be *honored* to be your wife."

He let out a war-whoop, picked her up, and whirled her about. "Thank heaven!" He kissed her with the fervor of a man in love. "I'll make you happy, dearest. I promise with all my heart. But first,"--- he kissed her again. Then he began to shout for their jailer.

Mrs. Perkins, hearing their voices and laughter as they entered the house, appeared in the hallway delighted to see Jason had found Sarah. "Are congratulations in order *now*, Mr. McGreuder?" The delighted young man confirmed they were, and kissed her on the cheek. She asked, "What happened, Sarah?"

"Jason found me in jail and proposed," Sarah over-simplified. "I'll tell you all about it later. I am truly sorry to have worried you. We have someone to see upstairs, Jason." The two of them holding hands, hurried up the staircase.

Judd could not wait another minute to see Trudy. He sent off the last coach of the day, hurried into the station, washed his face and hands, and closed up the building for the night. Shouldering his leather jacket and pulling his felt cap on his head, he strode down the street to Mrs. Johnston's house, hoping Trudy had not yet left.

If she refused to talk to him, it would kill him. Maybe he did not deserve forgiveness, after throwing her confession in her face and bolting like a scared jackass. Somehow, he had to make her see he was sorry. He really cared for her and had to know how she felt about him. Even if they never became more than friends, he was unwilling to forego that possibility. If only she was able to forgive and forget his behavior.

He pulled the bell at the Johnston's house, hoping she would answer the door. Trudy opened the door with her bonnet in hand and pailed, asking what he wanted. He removed his cap. "I have to speak to you, Miss Trudy. Are you through working for the day?"

"I was just leaving," she said. "I must tell Mrs. Johnston who was at the door." She was gone over a minute. She returned, closing the door behind her.

From her expression, he knew she was still angry. "Can I walk along with you? Please?"

"I don't know why you'd want to do that, Mr. Corday." Her tone chilled him.

"Because I owe you an apology."

Marching down the path, she shook her head. "You don't owe me nothin'."

"Yes, I *do*. You were honest enough to tell me about your past, an' I wasn't man enough to…hear it." He tried to take her elbow, but she jerked her arm away.

"I know exactly what you thought," she said. "You made yourself perfectly clear."

"It was the surprise. Right then, my image of you was pure fantasy. I mean, it had nothing to do with a young girl who had no one to take care of her; or one who had to make her own way in life, or starve to death."

She glanced his way. "I'm sorry I was such a disappointment. I didn't *want* to tell you." The sadness in her voice cut to his heart.

"No, *I* disappointed *you*. You were… courageous. I am *glad* you told me. It was the only way we could become real friends. If you'll forgive me, I'll never bring it up again."

She paused and looked into his eyes. "I forgive you, Judd."

Without another thought, he grabbed her for a relieved hug. "Oh, thank you, Trudy! From now on, anytime you want to talk about your life, I'll listen. I promise, I won't make no more judgments. Is that a deal?" They stood there on the path, in the fading light, finding one another, all over again.

He felt her nod and begin to cry. "Oh, honey. Don't do that. I am a stupid oaf! How could I hurt such a sweet girl as you?" Pulling a bandana from his pocket, he gently blotted her tears. Her beautiful, moist, brown eyes began to smile. With tenderness, he drew her closer and gave her their first kiss, then another, and…

Chapter 47

The Denouement

THE BRIEF WEDDING ceremony took place in Mrs. Perkin's parlor that evening. Sarah wore a white dress, which had started out as a nightgown, now covered with a lace curtain served her purpose. A Battenberg runner pinned in her hair, framed her happy face and fell to her shoulders. Their delighted friends, Trudy and Judd, were witnesses for them. Clay, whose back was much improved, proudly gave her away. Mrs. Perkins and Sophia completed the small gathering and generously provided a cake and punch for refreshments.

Judd made a toast to the couple, and then turned to Trudy to whisper, "I'm glad it was Miss Sarah he wanted, and not you."

Trudy archly replied, "Oh? What if it *had* been me?"

He wiped his mouth. "Well, I reckon I'd of had me some sort of a dilemma. Me and McGreuder would a had us a set-to."

Trudy's eyes danced with amusement as she tucked her hand in his elbow.

"Mrs. McGreuder," began Jason.

"That's *me*!" Sarah exclaimed.

Clay asked, "What do *I* call you now?"

She put a hand on the boy's arm. "Sarah is just fine, Clay. Thank you for giving me away."

"Is that what I done?" He gazed up at her, one hand-full of coconut cake and the other clutching a cup of punch.

Sarah laughed and reached over to erase the purple punch ring on his upper lip. "Are you packed to leave tomorrow morning?"

His mouth full of cake, he nodded.

"Good. I'll be spending the night in the hotel with Jason," she said shyly, and glanced at Jason with the thought of the evening spilling into her eyes. "We'll be by to pick you up in the morning."

He swallowed the bite of cake. "Yes,'um. I'll be ready."

She and Jason thanked the minister and their friends for the ceremony and went to the door amidst congratulations and best wishes. Trudy hugged her and was given the veil and small bouquet. "You'll be next," Sarah whispered to her. She wrapped her shoulders with a new shawl from Mrs. Perkins, gave her travel bag to Jason and hurried down the steps. Beaming, Jason helped her into the waiting buggy, joined her, touched his whip to the horse, and smartly drove away.

In the morning, following breakfast, Jason took Sarah by the Graysons' to tell Megan goodbye and resign her teaching position. Mrs. Grayson gave her a small silver bowl for a wedding gift. She was sorry to see her leave and Megan wept. Mrs. Grayson promised she and the captain would take Megan down to the wharf to see a paddle wheeler. Back at the boarding house, Sarah flew up the stairs to gather her belongings and make sure Clay had packed everything.

"I liked the wedding," Clay said, excitedly.

"Me, too. It was simply perfect. You're sure you want to go with us?"

His eyes enlarged. "You wasn't thinking of leavin' me *behind*?"

She laughed. "No chance. You are part of our family."

"Truth? Me too! Let's go." He gathered up their bundles. Sarah tied her bonnet in place and they hurried down stairs.

"We've a last detail to take care of," said Jason, in the hallway. "Would the two of you sign these papers?" He pointed out a quill pen, ink and two sheets of paper on the hall table. Sarah read the adoption papers aloud and they both agreed to the terms. She showed Clay where to sign and helped him add Carter to his name. Jason secured the papers in his pocket and held out his hand. "Hello, Son," he said to Clay.

"We're a family?" Clay asked.

Sarah nodded and looked at Jason with stars in her eyes. "In every way."

"What's my name now?" He looked from one to the other.

"Whatever you like," said Jason. "Clay Carter as before, or Clay Carter McGreuder, if you prefer."

A look of wonder swept his face. "All of that? I'm a big wig! Clay Carter McGreuder. I'm a *somebody!* Thank you, Mr., I mean, just Pa. Is that okay?"

Jason's eyes glazed with tears. "That's absolutely okay, Son." He blew his nose and turned to her. "It's time we said goodbye."

Mrs. Perkins and Sophia hugged the young couple. Eager to help with the satchels, Clay thanked the older women and shyly hugged them, too.

"You need to bring Robin around to the front," Jason reminded him. Clay set off to take care of the horse. It was hard for Sarah to leave, but she managed with grace and the promise of letters to follow.

Jason thanked Mrs. Perkins heartily, and helped Sarah into the buggy. The two women waved goodbye from the stoop.

The new family set off with Robin tied to the buggy. They headed north to New Harmony, Indiana to board the train for St. Louis. Clay would have ridden Robin, but Sarah guessed, he was loath to be separated from them, by even a few feet. He looked at first one and then the other; a happy smile on his face. He shoved a hand in his coat pocket. "Oh," he said, pulling out his marble and an envelope. "I forgot about this. I got it the last time ol'…uh Mister Guttman called me into the office. It's for you, Miss Sarah."

She saw the Dietrichs' return address and eagerly opened the envelope. In it was a postal money order for two hundred dollars. "My goodness!" she exclaimed, and then began to read Ellsworth's letter. "Stop. Stop the buggy, Jason!" A happy, new husband, he quickly pulled over to the side of the road.

"I'm *not* a murderess!" she exclaimed. "The man survived. Not only *that*, I am not a pauper! My father left me our house when he died. I am to receive the payments for it from Ellsworth, every month, as soon as I send him an address." She grinned in wonder. "He writes… he is married to, well, to his sweetheart, and they have a baby! My cousin Emerald married Winston and is helping Worth run the farm. Oh, my uncle died, poor man. I'm sorry for my aunt."

"And all along I thought you didn't have a family," said Jason. "You'll have to tell us about each one, so I can get them all straight."

"I will," she said. "There's *more*. Worth is going to send me my mother's earrings and necklace, as soon as he hears from me. I do not ever remember seeing them, but he says they are diamonds and rubies. Can you imagine that?"

"We're happy for you, dearest. Apparently everything has worked out for you after all."

She tucked the letter and check in her bag. "After all, indeed. Absolutely everything! I am the most fortunate girl in the entire world." She hugged Jason with one arm and Clay very carefully with the other.

"Did you really kill a man?" Clay asked.

"No, darling. Thank heaven!" She nodded to Jason to start up again.

Clay cried, Here we come! Hyah!"

About the Author

WITH DEGREES IN English, from Northwestern University and The University of Northern Colorado, D. taught college courses, edited a small-town's newspaper and a military magazine. Her checkered career includes airline positions, merchandising and real estate sales and design. An inveterate traveler she lived abroad six years. She owns and manages Antique Legacy with Adam, her son, in Colorado Springs.

On the Other Hand, is her guide for collectors and inheritors of personal property. Victorian Turnabout, her post-Civil-War novel, depicts four romances of courageous women who fight Victorian social mores to achieve their hearts' desires.

Printed in the United States
By Bookmasters